THE SHADOW
OF
OLYMPUS

Book One of the Lowellsville Chronicles

THE SHADOW
OF
OLYMPUS

Book One of the Lowellsville Chronicles

"Be bold, always be bold," Frederick the Great. King of Prussia.

A Novel by E.M. Smith

authorHOUSE®

AuthorHouse™
1663 Liberty Drive
Bloomington, IN 47403
www.authorhouse.com
Phone: 1-800-839-8640

First published by AuthorHouse   09/01/2011

ISBN: 978-1-4567-9665-5 (sc)
ISBN: 978-1-4567-9664-8 (ebk)

Printed in the United States of America

Dedicated to the memory of my brother, David, who loved Robert Heinlein's stories as much as I did; and to the future pioneers who will make Lowellsville a reality.
Emmett M. Smith

Prologue

A Friday in June, 2048

The President of the United States of North America, Theodore Reynolds Kerrigan, stood looking through a window of the oval office at a deceptively calm looking , early summer day.

His thoughts were only partly on the White House's lawn and the new, electrified fence at the far edge of it. The rest of his mind was thinking about events in far away eastern Asia and on the news that his expected visitor would be bringing from there soon.

The intercom unit on his desk beeped briefly behind him and as he turned around the voice of his appointment secretary came from the device: "Mr. President, Mr. Warner is here."

"All right, Marjory, send him in, please" Mr. Kerrigan replied. A few seconds later a door at the far side of the office opened and Vernon Darnell Warner, the Vice President of the U.S.N.A. entered the room. There was a worried expression on his usually jovial looking face.

As he closed the door, the president greeted him. "Hello, Vern how was your trip?"

"Not at all encouraging, I'm afraid, Ted" the vice president replied as the two men approached each other and shook hands in front of the big desk. Ted thought his friend and political ally looked tired and discouraged.

"Have a seat" Ted invited, as he motioned toward an expensive, antique arm chair in front of the president's mahogany work place. His visitor complied and Ted went to his comfortable, executive's office chair.

"Okay, Vern, give me the bad news" said the president grimly.

"I talked with the mainland Chinese leader for about an hour and a half" Vernon began.

"He was polite enough, but I was unable to convince him that neither we nor the Tai Wanese spy agency had anything to do with that outbreak of a fatal illness aboard their now abandoned, Red Comet Space Station. He is also still convinced that we have been under reporting our robotic, lunar mining activities to the United Nations' Lunar Mining Commission in order to reduce the amount of money that we pay into the Third World Development Fund."

The president muttered an obscenity, then he spoke more clearly. "So, I suppose he wasn't cooperative about restraining North Korea's provocative actions toward the South, either."

"I'm afraid not, Ted" his guest replied, "—and he still insisted that the Tai Wanese people's decision in a recent referendum that their government should declare a state of permanent, separate nationhood had no validity. He compared that to the formation of the Confederate States of America in 1861."

"Did he say what he intended to do about it?" asked the president.

"No, he just said that, like Lincoln, he would not tolerate having 'a house divided against itself.' I warned him that our mutual defense agreement with the government of Tai Wan remained in effect. After that he said that we had nothing else of any importance to discuss. So, after a short consultation with our ambassador aboard Air Force Two, I told the pilot to head for home."

"What did the ambassador say about <u>his</u> situation?" asked the president.

"He said he wanted to be 'called home for consultations',—<u>with his family</u> "the vice President replied.

"Then I'd better grant his request, Vern" Ted concluded, "—<u>and</u> I'll warn our military people in the far east to <u>prepare for trouble</u>."

"I think those would be <u>wise precautions</u>, Ted" said Vernon. "This new Chinese leader is not as reasonable as his predecessor."

"If there is a war—even a short one—it will really be difficult for us to finance, Vern. As you know, we're still searching for ways to pay for our past conflicts."

"If it becomes a nuclear exchange, Ted, money will become the least of our problems.

Now, if you don't mind, I'd like to go home and catch up on my sleep."

"All right" said the president, as both men pushed back their chairs and stood up. "I appreciate your efforts to patch up our relations with the Chinese. I'm sure you did everything that was possible." The two men shook hands again, then they walked to the exit door that led to the corridor. As Vernon departed, Ted closed the door behind him, then he went to his desk and telephoned the secretary of defense . . .

Cast of Characters (in order of appearance):

Theodore Reynolds Kerrigan — President of the U.S.N.A. He was elected to his first term in 2044 and is campaigning for reelection in 2048 when these chronicles begin.

Vernon Darnell Warner — Vice President of the U.S.N.A. and a long time friend of President Kerrigan. He is experienced in foreign policy and is often used by the president as a diplomatic trouble shooter.

Michael Edwards — Lowellsville's Chief Geologist and Sophia Collins' lover at the start of these chronicles. Later the Assistant Administrator of the U.S.N.A.'s Mars colony.

Sophia Sandra Collins — Lowellsville's Chief Biologist and Life Support Technician. She is also the colony's most beautiful woman and handsome Michael Edwards' lover.

William Schaefer — Lowellsville's Chief Hydrologist and manager of the William's Bluff Water Drilling Project.

Robert Harris — Lowellsville's Assistant Hydrologist and a talented amateur mechanic. He is the handsome, younger brother of Roger Harris.

Barbara Waverly	William Schaefer's secretary, radio operator and lover.
Janet Hudson	A communications technician and frequently Lowellsville's first shift radio operator. Doctor Hudson's devoted spouse and occasional medical aide.
Bryan Mulroney	The tallest human colonist on Mars. Pipe fitter, plumber and occasional well driller. He sometimes assists Bill Schaefer.
Erik Schonbaum	Lowellsville's Chief electrician. He was born in Germany and is Karl Richter's first cousin. Erik is also a skillful pianist.
Vekrin	An overly zealous, Kotterbrocki security robot. He is also the first alien to be encountered by citizens of Lowellsville!
Fredrick Snyder	He is a skilled machinist and an occasional well driller. Fred is also a friend of the tall Texan, Bryan Mulroney.
Daniel Morris	Lowellsville's Chief Administrator and a part-time robotics technician. Daniel is also Patricia Franklin's lover.
Louisa Monique d'Alsace	Lowellsville's Assistant Biologist and later its Life Support Technician. Sophia S. Collins' best female friend.
Penelope Carter	Famous writer and roving television reporter. Sophia's beautiful, red headed friend from past college days.
Marvin Showalter	Penelope's professional cameraman, friend and admirer.
Sheila Graham	Senior Radio and Radar Technician of the interplanetary liner *Wernher von Braun*.
César Guerero	Lowelllsville's Senior Radar Technician.
Peter Gordon	The space liner's Second Officer and Hydroponics/ Wastewater Technician. An admirer of Penelope Carter.
Juan Hernandez	Captain of the *Wernher von Braun* and one of its designers. He was born in

Argentina and is now an employee of the Interplanetary Transport Service.

Anne Jordan — First Officer of the *Wernher von Braun* and its Robotics Technician. An Avid and skillful player of card games.

Mieko Kurosawa — A passenger aboard the space liner and eventually Lowellsville's first professional chemist.

Pastor Joseph Boswell — Lowellsville's Chief Botanist and Hydroponics Technician. Also a Baptist Preacher and the first human cleric on Mars.

Karl Johannes Richter — Erik Schonbaum's first cousin who is also an electrician. The two men were born in Germany (within the European Union), but they emigrated to the U.S.N.A. They became contractors to NASA on Earth before they were accepted for job assignments in Mars Base One (later renamed Lowellsville). They later added well drilling to their list of skills and are indispensable members of the colony.

Joe Standing Bear — A Cherokee Indian who is Lowellsville's Senior Lighting Technician. He will work at almost any height and sometimes helps Erik and Karl as an electrician. An admirer of Helga Svensen, the colony's glazier.

Patricia Franklin — Lowellsville's Chief Meteorologist and Substitute Shuttle Pilot. She is Daniel Morris' lover and the mother of Teddy Franklin.

Linda F. Simmons — Mr. Morris' and Dr. Hudson's shared secretary. The wife of Lowellsville's Chief Structural Engineer, Ronald R. Simmons. She is also the colony's Chief Shuttle Pilot and the mother of two children—Angela and Richard. Called "Super Mom" by her

	many admirers because of her seemingly boundless energy.
James Wilcox	Lowellsville's Assistant geologist. He likes to polish colorful stones and is the colony's part-time jeweler.
Vellani Ferbratta*	A beautiful kotterbrocka alien who is the surprise neighbor of the William's Bluff ("Trailer Town") outpost.
Derron Ferbratta	Vellani's ailing husband.
Doctor Gregory Hudson	Lowellsville's first physician and the husband of radio operator Janet Hudson. He is also the father of Larry and Debbie Hudson.
Pamela Mason	Phobos Base's first nurse and a veteran of the U.S.N.A.'s Army Medical Corps. Vellani's rescuer and Warren C. Smith's lover.
Warren Cox Smith**	The handsome Chief Administrator of Phobos Base and also its Chief Robotics Technician. Beautiful Pamela Mason's lover.
Roger Harris	Lowellsville's Assistant Administrator until cancer causes his resignation. He is Chief Aerospace Engineer for Lowellsville and Robert Harris' older brother.
Thomas Saunders	Lowellsville's Head of Communications and its second shift radio operator. He is also a dentist and a painter of murals.
Ronald Reagan Simmons	Lowellsville's Chief Structural Engineer. Husband of shuttle pilot Linda Farrel Simmons and a part-time barber. He is only four years older than Sophia Collins but is like a father figure to her. He also teaches a childrens' Sunday school class on Mars.
Antwan Curtis	Lowellsville's Chief Metallurgist and an expert welder. He sometimes dates school teacher Dolores Parker.

Dolores Parker	Lowellsville's first full-time school teacher and its Chief Librarian. She is a frequent critic of Sophia S. Collins' sexual behavior and considers the occasional artist's model to be too licentious. Dolores hopes to send Sophia back to Earth.
Phillip Stewart	Lowellsville's third shift radio operator. Also the evening life guard six nights per week for the colony's swimming pool. He sometimes dates meteorologist Nancy Chan.
Nancy Chan	Lowellsville's Assistant Meteorologist and an occasional substitute secretary. She is also a skillful chess player. Nancy is romantically interested in Phillip Stewart. She eventually be-comes a friend of Kariena, a beautiful, female android.
Angela Simmons	Ronald's and Linda's daughter. She is seven years old at the start of this novel and a good swimmer. She likes to help Joseph Boswell to tend the Mars colony's hydroponic gardens.
Edward Slater	Lowellsville's Chief Vehicular Engineer and a skilled mechanic. He designs and repairs vehicles that operate on the surface of Mars. He is a widower with a son and a daughter who were born on Mars. Their mother, Catharine, died accidentally.
John Clewiston	Lowellsville's Chief Highway and Spaceport Engineer. He sometimes does similar work for Phobos Base and is Head of the Combined Colonial Transportation System.
Lawrence MacNeal	Lowellsville's first Nuclear Power Plant Engineer. Lawrence sometimes does the same job for Phobos Base, although its much smaller reactor is largely automated.

Dianne Fletcher	Lowellsville's tirelessly curious Chief of Television Program Production (and its only station's main announcer).
Alvin Lancaster	A photography expert and camera technician. He emigrated to the U.S.N.A. from England in the European Union and later came to Mars. He is Dianne Fletcher's friend and coworker in Station MLVL.
Walter Jones	Phobos Base's resident astronomer and an ardent chess player. He is especially interested in tracking comets and asteroids.
Janet Johnson	Phobos Base's Chief Radio Technician and a talented muralist. Also a gradually improving portrait painter. Popuarly known as "Jay Jay" because of her initials.
David Carlisle	Phobos Base's Resident Mining Engineer and Jay Jay's chief admirer.
Helga Svensen	Lowellsville's Chief Glazier. She installs windows in walls, doors and vehicles. Helga is also the first shift life guard for the community's swimming pool. (on weekends). Her parents brought her to the U.S.N.A. as a teenager from Sweden.
Karen Ferguson	Secretary for W.C. Smith and David Carlisle. She also monitors the radio on Phobos for three hours during most evenings.

- *Pronounced Vell-AH-nee fehr-Braht-ta.
- **Because Warren has the same first and last names as the Secretary of State of the United States of North America, the Mars and Phobos colonists often call him "Warren Cox."

CHAPTER 1

THE FOSSIL HUNT

*Monday, June 49th, 2048 MC *(1)*

Michael Edwards sat before his computer's monitor in the chief geologist's office and read with interest the latest news from Luna. The Interplanetary News Agency's article said: "Jules Verne City, Luna, June 49th. 2048. A group of lunar prospectors found a surprisingly young crater today only 35 miles from this community. Their preliminary report indicates that it is no more than a hundred years old; but an even bigger surprise occurred when they found broken bits of machinery in and around the crater. Their cautious deduction was that either a meteor had scored a direct hit on some forgotten man-made outpost or there had been an explosion inside an underground base of unknown origin. So far no nation on Earth will admit to having built an underground base in that area."

'Well' thought Lowellsville's leading rock hound (as his girl friend teasingly called him), 'who says all of the interesting news comes from Mars these days? Right now I wish that I had chosen a job on Luna instead.' The reason for this envious thought was a picture that accompanied the article. On a piece of metal debris was what looked like writing. 'That doesn't look like any system of writing that I've ever seen before' he concluded. Then there was a knock on his office door. Michael recognized the familiar "Shave and a haircut, two bits" rhythm that was often used by his pretty love interest, Sophia Collins.

"Come in, Sophia" he invited through his office's intercom system (which had a speaker out in the corridor). Michael's office was in the science section of the community and into its narrow confines came a black haired, blue eyed woman in her late twenties. Her height of five feet, six inches was six inches less than Michael's own six feet, but she was a bundle of cleverness and energy of which he never tired. She was a descendant of one of Luna's earliest explorers, but like her paramour, she had jumped at a chance three years ago to colonize Mars instead. Lowellsville had started as a group of cylindrical space craft sections that came all of the way from Earth, but a hit on one of these early shelters by a small meteorite that narrowly missed killing one of the astronauts had convinced the explorers that they should burrow into a nearby bluff for protection and most of the town had been underground since then.

"You sure do a lot for those coveralls" Michael remarked, as he admired her skillfully altered work garment. Then he rose to a standing position and greeted her with a kiss on her pretty face. She closed his office door behind her back to give them some privacy.

Sophia had left an interesting amount of the upper front part of her light green xenobiologist's uniform unvelcroed (as she often did) and her breasts' cleavage peeked out at him enticingly.

"A girl does the best she can with what's available" she explained, as they seated themselves side-by-side on a short couch that faced his desk. "Have you read the latest news from Luna?"

"I was just looking at an article about some machinery of unknown origin—if that's what you mean" her brown haired paramour replied. "Did you notice the unusual writing on that piece of tubing in the picture?"

"Yes" she replied. "I don't think the Chinese built whatever that broke off of."

"Neither do I" said Michael. Then he kissed her again (on her neck this time). "Where are you headed this morning, good looking?"

"I thought I'd have a look at that ancient stream bed that I found just before twilight yesterday" she replied. "I saw a fossil of an aquatic arthropod in a rock face beside the former stream, where it cuts into the old lake bed. I want to go back and dig it out this morning."

"I'll go with you and have a look at it" said Michael. "I think that the well drilling project out at William's Bluff can proceed without me for half a day or so."

"Good" she replied, with an appreciative smile. "We haven't had a chance to work together lately. Has Bill and his team found liquid water yet?"

"No, just ice" Michael answered, "but we're considering mining it and bringing chunks of it back here to be melted for drinking water."

"I hope it tastes better than what we have now" she said. "It always has a metallic taste—like an old copper penny."

"That's due to copper sulfate in it" Michael explained. "The waterworks people have done everything they could think of to remove it. I've even made a few attempts myself. No luck thus far.

"Anyway, let's go put on our Mars suits and check out a vehicle."

A half hour later the two scientists emerged from a large airlock in a fully enclosed vehicle that was powered by locally produced methanol. They had the luxury of a marscrete road as far as the space port (where an old lake bed had been modified with a mile and a half long, paved runway). Beyond its perimeter road they went cross country and bounced along on wide, low pressure tires. Six of these supported the weight of the cylindrical body of the 30 feet long car. The vehicle had its own small restroom and a little airlock that only two people could use at a time. The front end of the Mars car had a curved surface, the upper half of which was mostly covered by a large, convex window. Most of the body of the vehicle had been made from a rocket's fuel tank that had been modified internally with accommodations for two to four people, plus their luggage and a small amount of cargo.

Behind the vehicle there was a long, rising plume of pink dust as Michael and Sophia traveled across the old lake bed toward the fossil's site. The inhabitants of the mostly underground community of Lowellsville called the basin "Lake Lowell", although it had not contained water during all of human history. The lake bed and the community had been named for Percival Lowell, a nineteenth century American astronomer who had observed Mars through a big refractor telescope and thought he saw canals built by a native Martian civilization.

The site of what was originally called "Mars Base One" had been chosen because of the relative ease and safety of landing manned space craft on the floor of Lake Lowell. The site had originally been explored by a surface rover robot in 2014 but the huge expense of the Great Middle East War during the next four years had delayed the arrival of human explorers until August of 2030. The site proved itself to be so suitable for human use that a permanent base was begun in 2032. By June of 2048, there were 39 residents (32 adults and 7 children—four of whom had been born on Mars). Six more adults were on Mars' largest (and closest) moon, Phobos. There they operated a passenger and freight terminal for the new space liners that would begin regularly scheduled visits to Mars' orbit in July.

The United States of North America owned both Lowellsville and Phobos Base. The secession of Quebec from Canada in 2024 had resulted in ten other provinces joining the original United States of America during the next four years. At the end of that time Mars Base One was renamed Lowellsville. It was gradually enlarged as people from the new federation sought adventure and fame from making new discoveries on Mars.

Now as two of these colonists drove eastward they had a view of the summit of Olympus Mons peeking over the curvature of the planet. Fifteen miles high and as large at its base as the state of Missouri, the dormant volcano had a summit caldera the size of Rhode Island! Now its broad summit covered the travelers' entire eastern horizon (although it was slightly obscured by pink dust in the thin Martian atmosphere).

"It's difficult to believe that we are looking at a mountain 200 miles away!" Michael remarked. "What a view!"

"It looks like we could drive to it in a couple of hours" Sophia agreed. "Nature works on a grand scale here on Mars."

Soon the two fossil hunters arrived at the place Sophia had found late in the previous day. Michael parked the vehicle and rose from the driver's seat. He then took his helmet down from a rack behind the seat. Sophia obtained her helmet also and the two explorers walked along the narrow, offset aisle of the Mars car to the airlock. It could only accommodate two people if they stood close to each other, but neither person objected to the situation.

They put on their helmets and each explorer checked the other one's hermetic seals between the helmet and the suit. Then they cycled through the airlock and descended a short ladder to the ground. Sophia scanned the stony bottom and banks of a long-dry watercourse until she saw a small, bright yellow object protruding from its right bank.

"There!" she exclaimed, as she pointed toward the object. "I left that small marker flag to show me where I was yesterday." Then she walked to the spot and Michael followed her. Sophia knelt on the ground beside the little yellow plastic flag. Then she pointed to an outcropping of pale, tan colored rock.

"I searched these old strata for three hours yesterday before I found this fossil" she explained. Michael knelt beside her and saw a cream colored invertebrate animal's exoskeleton imbedded in the outer surface of the outcropping. The animal was about eight inches long and it resembled the so-called "horseshoe crab" of Earth, but unlike the latter the fossil had a lobster-like tail and a pair of slender pincers on two crab-like arms at the front end of its body. Two insect-like antennae protruded from its semicircular head.

"Congratulations, Sophia!" Michael exclaimed. "As far as I know, this is the first creature more advanced than a flatworm that has yet been found in Martian rocks!"

"Thanks" she replied, as she smiled at him proudly through the gold tinted, convex face plate of her helmet. "How old do you estimate this rock is, Mike?"

"It resembles a type of limestone that I have seen in a couple of other places along the ancient lake shore" Michael replied. "I'll need to test some samples from this site to be certain, but if it is from the same rock layer, I would guess that it's five hundred million years old—at least."

"That's an incomprehensible amount of time!" Sophia exclaimed, as a thoughtful expression appeared on her pretty face.

"God works on a much vaster time scale than the one imagined by the writers of the bible" her companion replied. "A timeless, ageless being doesn't need to hurry."

"Well, whatever age this creature is, I intend to add it to Lowellsville's fossil collection today" Sophia announced. "If God won't object, that is" she added teasingly.

"I'm sure He has plenty more fossils in His own collection" Michael replied tolerantly

For the next hour, Sophia slowly chipped away a chunk of rock from the matrix, with the precious fossil embedded in the chunk. She worked carefully with a small hammer and chisel so she would not damage her discovery. Meanwhile, Michael scanned the outcropping for other fossils. He was disappointed to see that there were none. Finally he said "I'll pick up some of these chunks that you knocked loose so I can date them in the laboratory."

"All right" Sophia replied. "I'll be finished extricating this creature's remains in a few more minutes."

Michael picked up a slab of rock and looked at both long surfaces. On the rear surface he saw a delicate tracery that resembled a thicker than usual spider web. "Well!" he exclaimed happily. A sea fan just said 'hello!' to me."

Sophia stopped what she was doing and looked at the small slab of rock that Michael was holding. "You're right!" she exclaimed. "It resembles the gorgonians of Florida's coastal waters. "What a fortunate discovery!"

"Lake Lowell may have been a small, salt water sea" Michael concluded. "Perhaps we should have named it the Lowell Sea."

"Maybe we can persuade our community to change the name" Sophia replied. Then she finished freeing the pseudo lobster from the outcropping and placed its encasing chunk of rock into a specimen bag that resembled an overgrown zip lock sandwich bag.

Meanwhile Michael had bagged his discovery and some chunks of rock lacking fossils for age and environment determination.

"Let's return to the Mars car and drink some hot chocolate" he suggested. "It will take the chill out of our limbs after this excursion into the cold, Martian air."

"Good idea" she replied. "I nearly froze my buns off when I came out here yesterday."

"That would have been a real loss to the community!" Michael teased. "You have such an attractive pair of buns." He remembered fondly how she had looked in a bikini during a recent swim with him in Lowellsville's heated, underground swimming pool. The water had come from a melted layer of conveniently situated permafrost inside the bluff.

"Thanks" she replied, "but right now they are half frozen—along with the rest of me. Let's be going." As she spoke, she picked up her tools and put them into a satchel that she wore on the outer surface of her space suit. Then she inserted the bag that contained the pseudo lobster. Afterward she followed her suitor to the Mars car and cycled through the airlock with him.

The two scientists entered a cargo compartment in front of the air lock and put their satchels inside a large bin, and then they went forward to the little galley and removed their helmets with each other's help. Michael was happy to see her pretty face unobscured by the gold-tinted face plate of her helmet. Sophia was just as glad to see his handsome face and his wavy, medium brown hair.

"You should have been a fashion model—not a scientist" Michael remarked admiringly, as he accepted her helmet from her slender fingered hands. Then he took it (along with his) to the proper racks in the driver's compartment.

"I was an artist's model on several occasions while I was in college" she informed him through an open doorway as she began mixing powdered cocoa with water in two coffee cups. "I even posed nude a few times—it was the vanity of youth—and I needed the money. You know what it's like in college if your parents are not wealthy."

"Yes, I do" Michael replied, as he returned to the galley. "During my time as a graduate student I could only afford two meals per day during most weeks. I lost about twenty pounds."

"That must have been awful!" Sophia exclaimed, as she covered each of the two cups with waxed paper and set them inside a big microwave oven. Then she set the controls for a minute and three quarters and started the heating process.

"It was" he admitted, and then he put his hands on her waist. He kissed her lips for about five seconds, as their beverages slowly heated.

"Mmmm!" she exclaimed with a happy smile. "It was worth coming all the way to Mars in that crowded little space ship to get a kiss like that!"

"At least we didn't need to pay for the voyage" he remarked humorously. "We would be washing dishes for a long time!"

"I hate washing dishes!" she exclaimed half seriously. Then she kissed his face playfully.

(*1) MC refers to "Martian Calendar." A Martian year has 687 days, so months there are longer than their counterparts on Earth. The Martian day is longer also (about 24 hours and forty minutes). This requires the use of special, digital watches and clocks by the colonists.

CHAPTER 2
The Amazing Discovery

Still Monday, June 49th.

William Schaefer was the chief hydrologist for the Lowellsville community. A bluff about ten miles east of it had been named for him and he was near it now, sitting in a trailer office and studying a ground penetrating radar chart of the local substrata. His assistant, Robert Harris (the only other hydrologist on Mars thus far), was standing beside him and looking at the same chart.

"There's water down there all right!" William declared emphatically, but it's a long way down. This permafrost layer we've been mining is too thin to supply our community's needs for more than a few months from now, so we'll need to set up a drilling rig and see if that liquid water is fit to drink."

"It can't taste much worse than what our two wells near Lowellsville are pumping now" Robert remarked. "I wish this radar of ours could tell us what minerals are in a water deposit—then we wouldn't need so many test wells."

"That would make our job too easy" William jested, as he set the chart on his desk and looked up from it. "We must earn our pay."

William was a man of average appearance and about five feet, eight inches in height. His black hair had become sparse on the top of his head at his present age of forty-six. His eyes were an unremarkable dark gray. However, his sense of humor and his thorough knowledge of a vital profession caused him to be more popular and attractive than his physical appearance alone would have done.

"I'm curious about this faint indication of something hard and straight on the radar image" said Robert, who was a handsome man in his mid thirties, with wavy black hair and gray eyes. He was five feet, eight inches in height and he reminded older women of Errol Flynn.

William was two inches shorter than his coworker and secretly envied his youthful attractiveness to women. "So am I" he said. "It appears too straight to be a natural mineral formation, such as a long, horizontal ore seam inside of a minor fault."

"It's only about twenty feet under the surface" said Robert. "Why not send down a coring bit to get a sample of the substance down there?"

"Good idea" William replied. "Then we shall see what kind of surprise Mars has in store for us this time."

"I'll go outside and tell the crew exactly where to erect the drilling rig" Robert volunteered.

"All right" William replied. "I want to talk to our friend, Mike Edwards, by radio and ask him when he can come out here. I'd like to have his professional opinion about the substrata when we have that next core sample. I'm sure he'd be interested in seeing it."

"Okay" Robert replied from the doorway of the office. "Maybe he'll bring that pretty girl friend of his with him."

"Yeah, that would be nice" said William, with a smile of pleasant anticipation. Then he looked at the radar image again. 'Whatever that straight line is, it's extending toward the bluff that somebody named after me. I wonder why that direction?' he thought, as he rose from his comfortable office chair and walked to the little radio room of the large, well insulated trailer.

'I wish Mars wasn't so damned cold!' Bill exclaimed mentally. "Working in this frozen wilderness is the worst part of my job. Those space suits never keep out the cold long enough.'

The thirty feet long walk to the radio room took him past the open doorway of his secretary's office. Barbara Waverly was—like her boss—a person of average appearance but above average competency in her job. She was typing one of the written reports that her boss had given to her orally via a recording disc. Paper was rare and expensive on Mars, so her typing normally went from one computer console to another, but this report was actually going onto sheets of paper and into a logbook that could be read without the use of a computer. Her boss considered computers to be nuisances because he hated to type, so he liked to keep a paper record of his crew's activities each day. Now the lobby of the trailer contained cabinets that were gradually filling with old fashioned notebooks. Barbara knew that these anachronisms were a waste of space, so she had ordered a microfilm machine from Earth and she hoped that it would arrive in the supply ship that was due in ten days.

Barbara doubled as a radio operator, so her office was farther back in the sixty feet long, end-to-end double trailer than Bill's was. Now, however, Bill entered the radio room and seated himself in front of the big, main transceiver. Then he picked up its microphone and scanned a digital readout to be sure that no-one had tampered with the frequency setting. He was pleased to see that the number was that of the radio room in Lowellsville. He called the radio operator there and recognized her voice immediately as that of Janet Hudson. With only 39 human residents on Mars thus far, anonymity was difficult to achieve and William was proud of his ability to match voices with names and faces. This particular voice belonged to a pretty, brown haired Canadian from Ontario (which was now a part of the U.S.N.A.).

"Hello, Janet" Bill said pleasantly. "Connect me to Mike Andrews' office please. Over."

"Wilco" she replied. Then she rang a telephone several times. Finally a computerized voice replied "This is Michael Andrews' office. I am not in it presently. Either leave a message at the sound of the beep or call me at Mars Car 4 on 220 megahertz. Thank you."

"I'm sorry, Mr. Schaefer, but Mr. Andrews is in the field" said Janet. "You may call him on 220 megahertz. Lowellsville Radio over."

"All right, Lowellsville. William's Bluff out" William replied. Then he dialed the new frequency.

"William's Bluff calling Mike Edwards. Come in, please" he requested. On the third try he heard a familiar sounding voice reply: "Mars Car Four here. Mike Edwards speaking, over."

"Mike, I'm glad I found you! This is Bill Schaefer calling. Our ground penetrating radar has found something interesting while we were prospecting for water. I'd like for you to come out here and have a look at it. Over."

"I'm fossil hunting with Sophia Collins. Can't this water prospecting phenomenon wait until tomorrow? Over" Michael's voice replied (with a tone of annoyance in it).

"Negative, Mike" Bill answered patiently. "I think someone else might have been searching for underground water before we arrived here. I want you to come have a look at what we found with our G.P.R. set. Over."

"Are you telling me that you have found evidence of a non-U.S.N.A. expedition on Mars?" asked Michael. "Over."

"There is an indication of it in a radar image of the substrata, Mike. Come out here as soon as you can" William replied. "Over."

"Let me discuss this with Sophia" said Michel. "I'll call you back in a few minutes on this frequency. Mars Car 4 out."

"Damn it!' William exclaimed mentally. How many opportunities does he think there will be like this?!' Then he added resignedly "William's Bluff out."

Chapter 3
The Secret of William's Bluff

Still June 49th, 2048

Sophia returned to the driver's compartment from the Mars car's little restroom and saw Michael looking annoyed. "What's wrong?" she asked as she seated herself in the navigator's chair beside him.

"Bill Schaefer called while you were in the restroom" he replied. "He claimed that he found some proof of a non-U.S.N.A. expedition visiting this part of Mars! What a lot of malarky! The Japanese only recently visited the moon; the Chinese are still trying to build a space station; and the European Union is still trying to decide what to do with the old space station that we sold to them to help pay for our first manned Mars expedition! Everyone knows that the Russians are bankrupting themselves with endless wars to hold onto break away regions, so who else but us could be here on Mars—the Venusians, maybe?

"I don't think so" Sophia replied with a teasing smile. "Anyway, Bill is usually a practical sort of guy. If he thinks he has found some credible evidence that we are not alone here on Mars, maybe he's right! I think if there are any more fossils in that creek bank they can wait a few more days to be found. They certainly are not going anywhere in the interim! Then she leaned toward her lover and kissed his face. Meanwhile, her cup of hot chocolate sat forgotten in a cup holder on the dashboard.

"I was hoping I could seduce you while we were out here together" Michael complained, "but here you are siding with Bill in his insanity!"

Oooh! So the truth comes out!" Sophia teased. "Call Bill and tell him we'll be there in an hour and a half."

"Hmm! Considering it's less than a 45 minutes' drive to William's Bluff, does this mean that you are willing to be seduced?" Michael asked hopefully.

"You catch on fast" she replied with a smile. Then they both began undressing . . .

Ninety minutes later Michael stopped the car beside one of five trailers that were collectively the little, ad hoc community of William's Bluff. He and Sophia could see a small group of space suit clad people gathered around a portable drilling rig beyond a flatbed Mars truck. One of the drillers waved when he saw the Mars car arrive. Michael and Sophia waved in reply, and then they picked up their helmets and headed toward the airlock at the rear end of the eight yards long car.

Slightly more than two minutes later Michael and Sophia were outside their vehicle with their helmets and pressurized suits protecting them against the harsh Martian environment. They were met by William, who shook Mike's right hand and hugged Sophia briefly. Afterward the geologist said "Well, Bill, let's see this wonderful discovery you made."

"It's on a computer printout in my office" the hydrologist replied. There are two views of the substrata—as usual—one is vertically aligned and the other one is horizontal. They both show us something unusual in the midst of the ordinary rocks, sand and ice. Come inside the office trailer with me and I'll show them to you—along with some other images that we made more recently."

"All right" Michael replied. "We'll be glad to share the civilized comforts of your trailer for a while."

So the three scientists walked to the trailer and one at a time they climbed a fold-down metal stairway into the vehicle's airlock. The little compartment could barely hold the three of them. About a minute and a half later the airlock was filled with a breathable oxygen and nitrogen mixture. Bill opened its inner door and the little group entered a suit rack room. There they removed their helmets and put them onto shelves. Afterward they shed their heavy space suits and put them onto specially made racks. Then clad in coveralls the three friends emerged from the suit rack room into a hallway that was about four and a half feet wide by thirty feet long. It extended for about half of the tandem trailers' length and had several doors along its left side. A specially made seal connected the two component trailers to each other end-to-end.

Bill led his two guests through the doorway of his office suite (which was the second door in the row). There were three rooms in the group: a reception room (which the group had just entered); Bill's private office (in the center of the suite); and beyond it was his secretary's office. The latter had a door that connected it to Bill's office and another door that provided access to the hallway.

A lightweight table with foldable legs stood in front of a couch in the reception room. Michael and Sophia seated themselves on the couch and William seated himself in an office chair at the opposite side of the table. Then he opened a large envelope on the table and took out a set of computer drawn stratographic maps.

"Here are the first images that we had made from our radar study of this former island in Lake Lowell" said William, as he handed a sheet of printer paper to Michael. The geologist placed the sheet on the table top in front of Sophia and himself. They saw two images on the sheet: the one on the left side was a circle about a hundred feet in diameter; the image on the right side was roughly a rectangular cross section of the rock and sand layers under the surface of the twenty to twenty-two feet deep circular area shown by the ground penetrating radar.

"The variations in the depth of penetration are caused by the variations in the penetrability of the rock layers by the radar beam" Bill explained to his guests.

"I'm familiar with that phenomenon" said Michael.

"It makes sense" said Sophia, as she held one of her paramour's hands affectionately.

"The set was mounted on a small cart that was pulled by a man" Bill explained further. "A computer in the cart recorded what the downward looking radar set was 'seeing' with its radio pulses." Bill pointed to a faint, narrow, straight line on the left image and said "Here is the anomaly that attracted my attention a few hours ago. It extends from about the center of the radar's field of view to the eastern edge of the image."

"I see it!" Sophia exclaimed. "It's on the other image too!"

"Are you sure it isn't just due to a radar or computer malfunction, Bill?" Michael asked skeptically.

"Yes, I am sure <u>now</u> "Bill replied. "I had the drilling rig placed directly over the anomaly and sent down a coring bit to take a sample of it. That's the resulting core sample in the narrow box on the floor. The lowest part of the sample material is to your left."

Michael and Sophia left the couch and walked several feet to a metal box that lay on the floor of the room, parallel to the front wall. The box was about five feet long, six inches wide and six inches tall. Inside of it was a mostly tan or reddish brown series of sedimentary layers lying on their sides. The two lovers knelt beside the box and scanned the layers of sediment in it.

"No wonder this world is called 'the red planet!'" Sophia remarked. "There is so much of this reddish brown rock."

"That's where the oxygen from the atmosphere went" Michael stated, "—into iron compounds in these rocks and others. We must find a way to reignite some of the Martian volcanoes and begin baking the oxygen out of these rocks. Otherwise Mars will remain a dead planet."

"I prefer to use the word 'dormant' to describe it" William remarked, "—especially since I found <u>this</u>." As he spoke he knelt to the left of the geologist and pointed to the end of the sediment core that was the nearest to them. Sophia watched from where she knelt to the right of Michael. All three people saw bits of shiny, 'white' metal and shreds of light gray plastic in a matrix of tan colored rock.

"Where did those filings come from?" asked Michael, "—and these bits of insulation?"

"They are from the straight object that you saw in the radio images" William replied with a smug smile. "It's a metal pipe covered by insulating material! Someone else was drilling for water here before we arrived."

"Oh yes! The Venusians! I forgot about them!" Michael remarked sarcastically.

"I doubt they were from Venus" William replied with an annoyed expression. "Come back to the table and look at the other evidence."

The two visitors followed him back to the card table where he took a series of radar images out of the envelope and placed them on the table top. Each image had a straight line at least part-way across it.

"Notice how short the lines are in the vertical stratigraphic images: said William, as he stood beside the table and faced his two guests.

"They should be just dots if they are being seen end on" Sophia remarked.

"Very good!" William exclaimed, "—but they are not dots because they represent about a six inch pipe that is sloping upward from a depth of about twenty-one feet in that first pair of pictures that I showed to you. They slope upward at a steady angle of thirty degrees—again, not a natural phenomenon."

"So, where are they going?" asked Sophia. "They'll reach the surface soon."

"Exactly!" William exclaimed. Then he walked to her side for the table and hugged the young woman. "They are heading directly toward <u>my</u> bluff—the one that was named after <u>me</u>."

"So if I follow your optimistic reasoning, somewhere inside that big hill someone excavated an underground community like Lowellsville" Michael deduced aloud.

"I suspect so" William replied. "My crew should be at the base of the bluff now, digging to uncover the pipe there."

"<u>This</u> I want to see!" Michael exclaimed, as he looked up from scanning the row of pictures again doubtfully.

"Why are you so skeptical, Mike?" asked Sophia.

"Because I remember Piltdown Man, the Cardiff Giant and the Tassaday People" he replied.

"What were they?" she asked, looking puzzled.

"They were twentieth century anthropological hoaxes, my dear" William interjected, "—but I doubt that anyone came the enormous distance from Earth to Mars just to create a hoax."

"Then let's go outside and <u>see what your men have found</u>!' said Sophia emphatically. "That's the only way to know for sure what those radar images were showing to us." Then she turned toward her lover and said" Come on, Mike, don't be a spoil sport!"

"All right" he replied reluctantly. "You and Bill lead the way."

About six minutes later the three truth seekers emerged one at a time from the airlock and jumped downward to the ground. The weak Martian gravity caused each of them to resemble an over-dressed Olympic athlete as he or she landed well beyond the aluminum stairway's lower end.

They walked about three hundred feet to a sandy place at the foot of the bluff where four men were digging with picks and shovels. Suddenly one of the diggers waved his shovel in the air and exclaimed loudly on the suit radios' common frequency "Yahoo! Here it is!"

Bill's group hurried to the hole in the ground and looked downward. The hole was only about three feet deep and at the bottom of it was an insulated pipe. Bill descended about four feet of excavated, dirt slope and knelt beside the pipe with a metal ruler. "Five and three—quarter inches wide!" he exclaimed happily. "My guess of six inches was nearly correct."

"Congratulations, Bill" Michael remarked. "Your Piltdown Man looks real." "But we still don't know <u>who</u> buried this pipe" said one of the diggers. Sophia and Michael saw the name *Robert Harris* on his Mars suit.

There must be an entrance close by to an underground base similar to Lowellsville" William said confidently. "When we find a way in We'll see what sort of people came here before us."

"Let me make a picture of this discovery" Sophia requested, as she opened an insulated camera bag she had been carrying on a strap.

Sure, go ahead" said Bill.

As Sophia stood beside the trench and made her photograph, Michael said "I hate to dampen everybody's enthusiasm, but if that really is a water pipe, its owners will resent us exposing it to this cold air and causing a plug of ice to form in it."

"Hmm! I suppose you are correct, Mike" said Bill. "You three men put some dirt back on top of the pipe. "Robert, I have something else in mind for you to do"

Chapter Four

The Search

Still Monday, June 49th.

"Sir, I don't want to rain on your parade, but these men and I have been working hard out here all morning" said one of the diggers, whose Mars suit had the name *Brian Mulroney* on it. We need to rest a while and eat lunch."

"All right" William replied. "Just push six inches of dirt into the hole, then go to the cantina trailer for an hour." The three men replied happily, then Bill turned toward Robert. "Bob, do you feel like hiking around the hill with me?"

"I'm afraid I don't have enough air left in my tanks to be out here more than another forty-five minutes, Bill" Robert replied, "—besides which, I think one of us had better go get the dozer and push the rest of the dirt back onto that pipe before we make its owners angry."

"I suppose you're right" said William. "You take care of that and I'll go help our two love birds to search for a way into the bluff." Then he turned toward his visitors and said ""Mike and Sophia, you go around the hill counter clockwise and I'll go the other way. Whoever finds something of interest will tell the rest of us about it by radio."

"Okay—if the bluff doesn't block the signal we can announce the find" Michael replied.

"If the hill interferes we'll get some exercise walking to places where we can call each other" William said humorously. Then he turned toward his intended route and added "Good luck, you two!"

So the searchers began walking in opposite directions around the hill. In less than a minute they could no longer see each other because of the intervening mass of rocks and soil. The bluff was "L" shaped, so the two lovers were walking toward the distant place where the long body of the letter turned eastward to form the shorter foot. The proximity of the bluff blocked much of Olympus Mons from their view, but the upper slope and summit of the enormous volcano could still be seen through the ever present, pink dust haze in the windy Martian atmosphere.

"Olympus Mons looks like it is peeking over the hill at us!" Sophia jested.

"It is an awesome sight!" Michael replied, "—but let's scan this bluff now and try to find a door to that underground settlement."

"So! You finally believe William's story!" Sophia exclaimed triumphantly.

"I'm two-thirds convinced" Michael admitted, "—but ever since NASA concluded that the great stone face in Cydonia was just a trick of light and shadows on a natural hill top, I have become wary of jumping to conclusions."

They continued to scan the base of the steep-sided hill as they neared the half-way point of the L's longest side. This main part of the big mass of sandstone was about a half-mile long and at its midpoint it was about 250 feet high.

"Look at that rock face up there!" Sophia exclaimed and pointed toward it. "That might be a good place to search for fossils."

"We'll keep it in mind for later" Michael replied. "Right now let's continue walking until we find a place where we can communicate with William. Maybe he found a door on the eastern side of the hill."

"Let's check your air supply first, Mike" said Sophia. "We don't want any unpleasant surprises."

"All right—go ahead" he replied. Then Sophia looked at the gauges which were mounted on the upper sides of the two air tanks that he wore on his back.

"You have about an hour's supply of it remaining" she announced. "How's mine?"

"You have slightly more than that" he informed her, as he checked her two gauges. Then the two explorers resumed walking and scanning the bluff's sides for an entrance. Eventually they rounded the eastern end of the foot of the "L" and saw a space suit clad figure approaching them from the northwest. "Bill, is that you?" Michael asked by radio.

"Yes, and I found something interesting" the hiker replied from a distance of about sixty feet. As the distance continued to narrow he added "There's a long, narrow rock shelf back there on the eastern face of the hill's longest ridge. It's about a third of the way up the slope. I climbed up onto it and found an area below a rock overhang where there were some gouges in the sandstone that might have been made by tools. I did not see a door up there though."

"We didn't find one either" said Michael, as he and William stopped walking about five feet away from each other. Sophia stopped beside her lover.

"If there is an entrance to an underground complex inside this hill, it must be well hidden" Sophia remarked wearily.

"Maybe Bill's mysterious diggers didn't want company" Michael teased. Then he turned toward William and asked "Did you bypass the middle part of the hill?"

"Yes" Bill replied. "I walked diagonally across open ground after I left the ledge. "I was afraid my air supply might be running low."

Sophia stepped forward and inspected his gauges. "You have about twenty minutes' worth of air remaining" she announced.

"We should start back toward the trailers now, before my air tanks become empty" Bill decided. "We can search the rest of the hill's eastern face tomorrow."

"I have some laboratory work to do then" said Sophia. "Let's try for the day after tomorrow."

"I'll try to reserve a vehicle for us to use that morning" said Michael.

"All right" William decided. "Wednesday it is. Maybe we'll be lucky then. I'm convinced more than ever that there is some kind of underground facility inside that hill."

The group began walking back toward the trailer community. As they did so, Sophia asked "What's on your agenda for tomorrow, Bill?"

"I think I'll rig up a horizontally mounted thumper and do a sonar scan of some of this bluff to learn if parts of it are hollow" he replied, "but this afternoon I must work with the drilling crew to install a well at a suitable site near the bluff. Hopefully we'll find some good tasting water."

"That would be a pleasant change" said Sophia. "Mike, how long do we have before the vehicle is due back in the garage at Lowellsville?"

"We must return it no later than seven p.m." he replied. "After that all the garages' doors must remain closed all night to conserve heat. I thought you knew that already."

"I did" she said, "—but I wondered if anyone wanted it before then."

"I think Erik Schonbaum wants to use it to go install a runway approach beacon on the rise of ground to the east of our space port" Michael replied. "If so, he will need the car all day tomorrow for his crew and himself to use, but I don't think he will need it before then."

"Good" Sophia replied. "I want to return to that stream bed where we were prospecting this morning. Maybe we can find some more fossils there this afternoon."

"All right" said Michael. "Let's go get some lunch and refill our suits' air tanks, then we shall be on our way." Michael and Sophia accompanied Bill to the airlock of a big trailer that was set at a ninety degree angle to the northern end of the administration trailer. This second trailer had been made from th opposite halves of the cylindrical rocket fuel tanks that had been sliced lengthwise with a laser beam, then welded together endwise to make the first trailer's two main components.

After Michael's small group had cycled through the little airlock they entered a closet-like suit rack room. There they helped each other to remove their space helmets and suits. Most of the well drillers had returned to their project shortly before the two lovers arrived in the trailer, so there was plenty of rack space available. The three friends hung up their suits so a robot could remove the annoying Martian dust with a vacuum cleaner. Then they went into the dining room through a connecting doorway.

The trio was greeted by Robert, who was already seated beside a small table, near the big, rectangular faces of the food dispensing machines.

"I was wondering if you three ever intended to eat" Robert teased.

"We surely do!" Michael replied, as his little group headed for the stack of trays near the automated tray cleaner machine.

"Did you find the doorway that you sought?" asked Robert, as he admired Sophia's figure from behind her.

"No, it was too well hidden—if there was one" Michael replied, as he took his tray to a food dispenser nearby. Bill and Sophia were there ahead of him.

"They'll be back the day after tomorrow, then we'll try again" Bill told the younger man.

Soon the three new arrivals seated themselves at the same square topped table where Robert was waiting for them. Sophia seated herself opposite him, while Michael sat to her right and Bill sat to her left. Michael said a short prayer, then everyone began eating.

"I wonder what sort of beings installed those underground pipes that we found?" said Sophia.

"I don't know, but I'd sure like to find out" Robert Replied, between bites of his quickly disappearing portions of food.

"I have a question for our pretty guest" said Bill, with an admiring smile.

"Well, that leaves me out" Michael teased, as he set down his spoon briefly. Everyone smiled, then Sophia said "Go ahead, Bill. I'm not shy."

"I've noticed some people refer to you on the radio network as 'Sophia' while others called you 'Sandra' he said. "Which name would you prefer that we call you?"

"I'll answer to either" she replied patiently. "My mother named me after her mother who escaped from Yugoslavia while it was tearing itself apart in a civil war, back in the nineteen eighties; but my father chose my middle name, in honor of his sister. I used to prefer the name 'Sandra' when I was a child, but when I went to high school there were three Sandra's in one of my classes, so the teacher asked me to use my first name to avoid confusion. I agreed and I gradually began to like that name. By the time I entered college I preferred it because it was distinctive and it sounded sophisticated.

"During my final year of college I became an artist's model to pay for my meals. To give myself some anonymity I asked the art teachers and their students to call me 'Sandra", since it was a common name in those days. So I was known in their classes as 'Sandra' and in my own classes as 'Sophia.' By the time I graduated I was comfortable with both names. When I was dating Mike, he preferred to call me 'Sophia,' but later some of our NASA coworkers preferred to call me 'Sandra.' I really don't have a preference any more myself.

"When I become Mike's wife, I'll just sign formal documents as 'Sophia Sandra Edwards ' and let my acquaintances decide which name they want to call me."

"That's an interesting story" said Robert. "I have a similar one to tell. My full name is Robert MacIntosh Harris, so some of my friends in college days used to call me 'Mack' for a nickname. I seldom use it on Mars, but I still see it in some of the email that I receive from Earth."

"You must hear this alot—Sandra" Bill remarked, "but why would a beautiful girl like you decide to become a scientist and a Mars colonist?"

"I wanted future historians to remember me as more than just another pretty face" she replied. "I have a high IQ and I do not want to waste it as a fashion model or an actress—although I did some of the latter for fun in high school. I didn't have time for it in college, though. I needed to get my BA degree quickly to avoid running out of money before I finished my courses."

"That's a familiar sounding story" Robert commented. "College is outrageously expensive these days."

"That's because the deans want every department to get some of your money before you graduate" Michael said cynically. His companions smiled with amusement (and at least partial agreement).

"What brought you to Mars, Robert?" asked Sophia.

"I became tired of waiting for someone to start Earth's final war and vaporize all of us" he replied with a slight smile.

"Hopefully we'll be able to create a better world here on Mars and preserve part of humanity if there is a World War Three on Earth" Bill remarked.

"Maybe we can avoid repeating mankind's past mistakes" Michael said hopefully, "—if not, we're building an awfully expensive tomb for ourselves."

Everyone nodded in agreement, then they finished eating one by one and the conversation diminished as they went to the airlock two at a time to put on their space suits. First Bill and Robert went, then Michael and Sophia. The latter two were still helping each other to put on the bulky garments while the earlier pair cycled through the small airlock of the dining trailer.

Bill and Robert went to check on the work at the well head, then Bill walked with the two lovers to the short stairway that led upward to the airlock of his office trailer.

"We'd better be leaving soon, Bill" said Michael. "Give us a call if you find anything else interesting with that thumper device."

"I'll do that" William promised. "That pipe we found leads to somewhere inside that bluff. "I'll try to trace its direction."

"Okay" said Michael. "Meanwhile I'll check the geological survey records and see if anyone else has noticed anything unusual about that hill."

"Yes, please do that" said William. "We need all the clues we can find to solve this mystery."

"We should be going now if we want to do any more fossil hunting today" said Sophia.

"I suppose so" Michael agreed. Then he turned toward William and said "Well, goodbye until our next door hunt."

"May we have better luck then" the hydrologist replied, as they shook hands.

"This planet is full of mysteries" said Sophia "and it guards their clues well."

"That it does" Bill agreed." "I'll visit you two in Lowellsville sometime soon, but right now I'd better go supervise our well drilling team." Then he walked toward the parked drilling rig.

Michael and Sophia returned to the borrowed Mars car and cycled through its airlock. They then removed their helmets and walked forward to the driver's compartment. There they put their helmets on shelves above the two seats.

"Let me drive this time" Sophia coaxed, with a gently persuasive tone.

"Alright" Michael replied with a cooperative smile. He then seated himself in the navigator's position while Sophia occupied the driver's seat. She adjusted it to accommodate her smaller size while Michael adjusted the other seat for the opposite reason. Sophia turned on the methanol and oxygen powered engine (which obtained the latter from an on board bottle). She let it idle a while to warm itself while she turned toward Michael and said "I keep feeling disappointed that we did not find the door we were seeking in that bluff. Just because Bill had less air in his tanks than we did, we went back to the trailers with him instead of following the shape of that big 'L'. We missed a chance to scan more closely about <u>half</u> of the two component ridges. I'd especially like to see if the landslide debris we noticed at the crook of them might have buried the door."

"It wouldn't surprise me if that were the case" Michael remarked, "—but if it is under all those boulders, we'll need some explosives and an earth mover to uncover it. We'll must talk to Chief Administrator Morris and get his approval before we can begin an operation that ambitious."

"Yes, and if we got his approval and we <u>didn't</u> <u>find</u> a door after moving all those rocks, we would look awfully foolish" said Sophia. She then turned on the electric motors inside the six big wheel hubs.

"Exactly" Michael agreed, as the vehicle began to creep ahead. "We must have some sort of evidence to justify the gamble. For all we know, we might have walked right past a cleverly concealed door made of natural rock, with only a razor thin gap around it."

"In that case, there should have been some tracks or scratch marks in front of it if it had been used recently" Sophia deduced.

"You're probably correct" Michael conceded. "of course, we're both ignoring that deep ravine we saw about halfway between the boulder pile and Bill's big rock ledge. The door might be somewhere along its length."

"That's a possibility too" said Sophia, as she pushed the accelerator pedal with her right foot and drove the big vehicle onto the dirt road that led to Lowellsville. Then she added with a sly smile, "I'm willing to cancel this afternoon's creek side fossil hunt if you are, Mike."

He thought for several seconds as the Mars car followed the dirt road westward, then he said "We told Bill that we would wait until he concluded his sonar scan tomorrow before we resumed the door hunt. He might be annoyed if we changed the plan without consulting him."

"To quote Yogi Bear in the old cartoon reruns that I watched as a child: "What the ranger doesn't know won't hurt us, Booboo" Sophia said mischievously.

"I'm glad to know I wasn't the only person addicted to mid-twentieth century cartoons" Michael remarked, "—but how do you propose that we sneak back to William's Bluff?"

"Just beyond that low rise of ground ahead of us, the land slopes downward to the place where Bill's men put those concrete culverts into that old, dry stream bed and laid the road across them" Sophia explained. "We'll leave the road there and follow the stream bed." By this time the Mars car was at the top of the rise and the stream crossing causeway was in view about five hundred feet ahead of it

"You sound like you've really planned this escapade carefully" said Michael admiringly, as the twin culverts came near.

"I have" she replied. "I've studied this area on maps, in case I decided to go fossil hunting here sometime." Then she slowed the vehicle and turned left near the edge of the nine feet deep gully. There were visible signs that a small river had flowed there long ago, but now only sand and rounded stones were on the bottom of it.

Sophia drove the Mars car parallel to the edge of the gully for about fifty yards, by which point the nearest bank had acquired a lower, more moderate slope. She then drove down the bank and onto the gully's floor. There she turned left again and followed the ancient water course.

"Bill must have expected water to flow through this gully again some time when he had that double culvert crossing place prepared for the road" Michael remarked humorously.

"Yes, I'm afraid he'll be disappointed" Sophia replied, as she steered the car around a boulder in the dry channel. "Water probably hasn't flowed here for many centuries."

Michael looked at the outside mounted, right rearview mirror and said "Drive a little slower—we're raising a dust plume behind us." Sophia complied and the dust's volume diminished noticeably. Soon the car was on a carpet of bare pebbles and the plume disappeared for about thirty seconds.

"I hope that anyone who happens to look in our direction will think that the wind is raising these occasional puffs of dust" Michael added.

"People tend to see what they expect to see" said Sophia, with a sly smile. "Anyway, this gully is curving toward the east now, so we shall soon be behind William's Bluff and approaching our exit point from this old river bed."

"Where do you intend to leave it?" asked Michael.

"There should be a narrower, tributary gully entering the main one from the left—that is to say, from the north" Sophia replied. "The electronic map shows it extending toward the northwest—where that ravine is in the longest ridge of the 'L' shaped hill."

Michael looked at the windshield where she had caused a translucent map to appear. "This air force technology sure is handy!" he remarked. "Nice of them to share it with us."

"Indeed so" she replied. "Ah! There's the butte now—to the north of us. We should see our gully in a few more minutes." The car was moving slower now, as Sophia scanned the left side of the old river bed.

'All that beauty and a smart brain comes with it for no extra charge!' thought Michael admiringly. 'She's a bit devious, though!'

Michael leaned to his left and read the vehicle's fuel gauge. It indicated three quarters of a tank. The other driver's instruments looked satisfactory also. Sophia noticed his curiosity, but she decided not to comment about it verbally. 'He's making sure that I'm not forgetting anything' she thought with amusement. 'The old male ego at work!' Then she switched her concentration back to watching the main gully's floor and left side ahead of her.

Soon both explorers saw what they were seeking "Aha! There's the side gully—just as I expected!" Sophia exclaimed happily. She then slowed the vehicle further and steered it into a natural trough that was just wide enough to accommodate it.

The floor of the gully had many large rocks in it, so the ride was bumpy and progress was slow. At the first opportunity, Sophia steered the big vehicle up the left side of the swallowing trough and the Mars car emerged from it at a place where rocks of many sizes lay scattered randomly on the ground.

Sophia drove beside the ancient stream bed's course to a place where the gully ended. About thirty-five feet away the narrow, sandy, dry water course led the travelers to a wide ravine that ascended the eastern side of the bluff at about a twenty-five degree angle.

Sophia slowed the Mars car to a stop at the entrance of the ravine. "Well, shall we drive further or proceed on foot?" she asked.

"Let's explore the ravine on foot first" Michael replied. There might not be any place farther up where it is wide enough to turn the vehicle around." He then stood up and added "Backing it down that narrow defile would be difficult."

"All right" Sophia replied. "Shall I pry your fingers loose from the dashboard now?" She also stood up as she spoke.

"The ride wasn't that rough" Michael replied with a smile. "You're actually a good driver, Sophia I was only scared a couple of times."

"My father used to tell me I would be a good missionary because anyone who rode with me would feel a need to pray" she jested.

"Aw, what did he know?" Michael replied humorously. "You were just practicing for the Indianapolis five hundred mile race."

They hugged and kissed for a while, then they picked up their helmets and walked to the airlock. Two minutes later they emerged from the vehicle and turned on the small lights on the upper sides of their helmets. Both helmets were attached to the upper parts of their respective suits, so their wearers needed to turn at their waists to see more than thirty degrees to either side of their noses.

Although the time of day was mid-afternoon, the deepest ten feet of the ravine was in twilight. The air in it was cold and the sky was just a narrow strip of magenta above the heads of the two explorers as they climbed the slope. They had an agreement that she would watch the left said of the narrow defile while he would watch the right side. They found some interesting deposits of metal ores but no fossils as they followed the crooked floor of the gradually shallowing ravine. Its floor ascended at angles varying from thirty to thirty-five degrees now. The ground was mostly bare rock, but a few patches of sand and dust relieved the monotony.

Michael stopped and pointed downward at an area of bare rock. "Look, honey! Something big has scuffed the surface here."

"Yes" she replied as she looked downward. "Something big and powerful—like an earthmover or a military vehicle."

"Maybe a member of Bill's drilling team has done some exploration here" Michael suggested.

"Yes—or maybe Bill himself" said Sophia. "Perhaps he couldn't wait until Wednesday either."

The two lovers walked onward about twenty feet, then Sophia pointed to a patch of sand ahead of them. "Look, Mike! A tire track!" she exclaimed.

"I see it" he replied as he walked to the track and knelt beside it. "This tread pattern doesn't look familiar. I don't think it's from the Lowellsville motor pool—I've driven every vehicle we have."

"Then who could have made it?" asked Sophia with a puzzled expression as she knelt beside him on the patch of sand.

"I don't know—unless the European Union finally got its act together" Michael replied. Then he and Sophia stood up and looked further up the ravine.

"This narrow defile looks as if it widens about thirty feet ahead of us" Michael remarked.

"Yes" Sophia replied. "I think I can see a natural basin up there. We should be able to turn the Mars car around in it."

"Would you mind going down the ravine and bringing the vehicle up it, Sophia? "I'll wait for you up in the basin."

"All right" she replied. "Don't go too far, though."

"Don't worry" said Michael. "I'll remain in the basin." So Sophia descended the ravine while Michael walked in the opposite direction.

Sophia only had about five hundred feet to walk and it was all downhill, so she soon arrived at her goal. There she cycled through the airlock and removed her helmet in the little adjacent suit rack compartment. She left the helmet lying on a wire framework shelf above one of the three space suit racks. She then walked forward through the cargo compartment, the fuel tanks and tools compartment; between the little galley and the pantry; and through the field laboratory. Finally she entered the driver's compartment at the front end of the Mars car. Over all, the vehicle was thirty feet, six inches long; eight feet wide (with the six externally mounted fenders adding a foot to this measurement on each side). The big car was eight feet tall (not including the two feet tall, rotatable radar antenna and the similar sized radio antenna that were mounted on the roof of the vehicle).

Sophia seated herself in the driver's position and started the methanol fueled engine. As she was fastening her safety harness, she heard the radio set become active:

"This is a special message to all USNA colonists on Mars; repeat to all USNA colonists on Mars. A dust storm warning has been issued by the Lowellsville Meteorological Office. This warning is being issued at 4:33 PM Olympus Standard Time on Monday and it shall remain in effect for two to five days. All personnel who are away from Lowellsville should attempt to return to the community within the next four hours. If that is not possible, park your vehicle beside the eastern edge of a mountain or hill and conserve power as well as you can. This storm is large and powerful so it should be taken seriously."

Sophia turned on the wheel hub motors and turned down the volume of the radio as the dust storm warning was repeated. Then she increased the electrical power to the motors by increasing the engine's r.p.ms. The result was that the Mars car advanced into the ravine, where the radio message faded to nothing because of the topographical obstacles. Sophia turned off the radio and concentrated on driving. There was only about a foot to spare to either side of the vehicle's fenders and the ravine gradually narrowed until only six inches of right and left clearance remained. The gully also became steep sided and darker, so she turned on the vehicle's headlights and reduced its speed.

'I hope that the car doesn't become stuck down here! That would be embarrassing—not to mention hazardous!' she thought nervously. Soon the defacto small canyon began to widen and become shallower. The Mars car gained speed as its no longer worried driver released her pent up breath and became more confident.

Soon the Mars car emerged from the ravine and entered a natural basin set in the uppermost part of the hillside. Sophia turned on the car's radio and heard Michael call her with his suit's radio: "—phia! Park the car and come see this!"

Chapter 5

The Entrance

Sophia stopped the vehicle quickly and turned off its headlights, then she flipped the radio's antenna switch to *low power/short range* and pushed the *transmit* button.

"Mike, there's been a dust storm warning issued from Lowellsville! The message advised all vehicles to return to the community within four hours—and that was about five minutes ago." She then pushed the *receive* button.

"Then we have plenty of time" Michael replied calmly, "—so put on your helmet and come outside. You'll be glad that you did!"

Sophia complied and acted as quickly as the need for safety would allow. Four minutes later she walked around the rear end of the Mars car and saw her lover standing in the rock framed; open doorway of what was apparently an airlock. A much smaller, open door to the right of the entrance revealed a set of control buttons set in a gray metal panel.

"Mike! You found the entrance to the underground base!" Sophia exclaimed, as she hurried toward him.

"Yes!" he replied excitedly. "If we had walked <u>thirty feet</u> farther together we <u>both</u> would have found it! Now come inside this airlock with me and I'll pressurize it."

Sophia quickly complied and Michael pushed an amber colored button on a control panel beside the inner door of the airlock. The outer door slid closed and a whirring sound began.

"This air pump is much quieter than any of ours" Sophia remarked.

"It's probably a better design" Michael concurred. "These sliding doors are superior to our hinged types too—although I have no idea how they can be made airtight."

"They are <u>bigger</u> than our doors are also" said Sophia, "—taller by about eight inches and six inches more in width. If these people are larger than we are, I sure hope they are <u>friendly</u>!"

"I brought a laser pistol with me in case they are hostile" said Michael. "Stay behind me in case they begin shooting."

About a minute and a half later a blue button glowed and the amber one ceased to glow. Michael pushed the blue button and the air pump stopped. The inner door slid open from right to left and no energy beam came through the doorway. Instead, a rectangular, white panel in the ceiling of a small room began to glow gently. It revealed a row of four metal doors on the far wall and two more in the left end wall. There was a larger, hinged door in the ri8ght wall, with what appeared to be an upright, high technology vacuum cleaner standing beside it.

"It looks like there is no-one here to meet us" said Michael.

"Yes, and whoever built this locker room had a problem with Martian dust, just like we do" Sophia remarked with a smile of amusement.

Michael opened one of the two lockers in the end wall and saw a space suit hanging on a rack inside of it. "Come have a look at this suit, honey!" he invited. Sophia did so and exclaimed "It's huge!"

"Yes, and whoever owns it has <u>four arms</u>!" <u>Michael</u> proclaimed. Sophia had a closer look at the suit and gasped. "You're correct!" she exclaimed," and look at the size of his helmet! This guy must be seven feet tall!"

"Yeah, the N.B.A. would love to recruit him!" Michael remarked humorously. "Think how well he could handle and pass a basketball with four hands!"

Sophia laughed in response, after which she opened the next locker. "Look, Mike, a woman's suit! She must be a foot taller than I am!"

"Yeah, and she has <u>four breasts,</u> <u>according</u> to the bumps on her suit" he remarked. "These people are definitely <u>not</u> <u>humans</u>!"

"Bill will <u>love</u> this place!" Sophia enthused. "We <u>must</u> tell him about it!" Then she hugged Michael happily.

"Let me take care of that task, honey" Michael replied. "Right now I would like for you to return to the car and get an air analyzer kit. I want to know if the air is safe for us to breathe in here."

"All right" Sophia replied. "I'll dig out my camera from the laboratory too."

"Please do find it—but don't call anyone with the radio. I don't want to have this facility over-run with curious people yet" Michael instructed. "We need some time to explore it."

"I understand" Sophia replied, "but what caused you to bring that laser pistol from the vehicle? We didn't know if we would actually find the entrance to this facility up here in this basin when we made our earlier excursion from the car."

"It was a matter of deduction, honey" he replied. "If there was a door in this hill and it was not in one of the lower slopes' then it must be in an upper part of the hill. The ravine appeared to be the only practical route to the summit, so I came through it prepared to find a door. Now please go get the items that I requested."

"Couldn't you go get them instead?" she asked, with a tone of annoyance. "I'm not a Labrador Retriever."

"I know, honey, but I don't want you to be left alone in this place" Michael replied. "Whoever built this underground base could still be here and a woman alone is a tempting target for rape."

"Oh Mike! I should have known you were just being gallant!" Sophia exclaimed with a smile. She then hugged him, and afterward she went to the airlock. Soon he heard the whir of its air pump.

Michael looked at the end wall's two lockers again and thought 'I wonder if these people have the human habit of putting pictures of their families or their lovers in their lockers? If they do, we could see in detail what they look like!'

Michel tested the door of the first locker in the row of four and found that it opened easily. 'I'm lucky! It's not locked!' he exclaimed mentally. There was no space suit inside of it, but he did find a device that resembled a metal detector with an extra long handle. When he pushed a sliding switch on its handle, strange symbols appeared on a small monitoring screen mounted near the switch. He turned off the alien monitor and closed the locker's door. Then he opened the next one in the row. It also lacked a space suit, but he found a small, metal box and what appeared to be an electronic camera. Both items were sitting on a metal shelf in the left side of the locker. When he opened the box, it was padded inside and four photographs were nestled amid the padding. The first one was a picture of an eight-wheeled land vehicle parked in the basin outside the aliens' base. The second one depicted a flying saucer parked in an apparently windowless hangar. The third one depicted the same flying saucer in the air, at a low altitude above the basin. 'Bill will be amazed to see these photos!' thought Michael.

When he looked at the fourth picture he saw an alien woman who wore a space suit similar to the one in the long row locker that Sophia had opened. She was standing beside a tall, slender, vertical rod with a series o four thick, wire loops mounted on it by way of 'X' shaped devices that caused the rod to resemble a strange ski pole. Of her body, only her face was visible as a light green, human shaped feature that looked outward through a gold tinted, translucent face plate.

This last photograph interested Michael the most of the four. It looked as if it had been made on a hilltop ('. . . perhaps the one above this base?' he thought). The woman had a pretty face and four (!) arms, with the longest pair situated above the other pair. She also had four breasts that were arranged like her arms, according to the set of bulges in the upper front part of her space suit. Her upper right, glove covered hand gripped the strange vertical rod—which was taller than she was.

'Well, she certainly isn't a bug-eyed monster!' thought Michael. 'In fact, she appears to be almost human! I'd like to meet her sometime.'

Michael returned the photographs to the box and set it back onto the shelf. Then he opened the next locker. He found only one item there: an obvious ink pen lay on the single shelf. Along the barrel of the pen were more of the strange symbols that he assumed represented a written language of some kind.

He opened the final locker and saw that it was entirely empty. A thin layer of dust covered its shelf and floor. There was no indication of recent use by the owner.

Michael left all six lockers open and went to a door at the right end of the room. It had a device near its right edge that reminded him of a pistol's trigger and trigger guard. When he squeezed the 'trigger' and pulled on the staple shaped handle nothing happened, so he pushed while maintaining his squeeze on the trigger. This time the door swung open from right to left. He stepped into a six feet wide corridor that extended from left to right. He turned right and followed the hallway to a place where it made a left turn. A small alcove was to his right and at the far end of it was a little window. Below the window was a group of wall-mounted electronic instruments. Michael looked through the window (which reminded him of an airliner's windows). He saw the Mars car parked in the basin outside the complex.

Meanwhile, Sophia emerged from the Mars car and walked toward the airlock of the alien complex. Michael saw her approaching it and decided that he had enough time to look at an alien device briefly before she arrived. He pushed a button on one of the instruments and saw symbols appear on its small screen. 'Those symbols resemble the ones I saw on that device that I saw in one of the lockers' he realized. 'I wish I knew what they meant.' He turned off the device and walked back to the locker room.

When he entered the locker room, Michael heard the whirring of the airlock's air pump, so he knew that Sophia would soon be examining the room's contents.

'I wonder where that flying saucer is now?' he thought, as he looked at the second long row locker and its small, metal box. 'I would love to find and examine it.' Other memories passed through his mind while he waited for the airlock's inner door to open: the aliens' surface vehicle, the strange, ski pole-like device, and the four armed woman. Would he find any of them? Perhaps they had all left Mars sometime before the first human explorers had arrived on the planet? Michael hoped not. He really wanted to find the four armed woman—even if she did have green skin.

The sound of the air pump ended abruptly and he turned toward the airlock. Its inner door opened and Sophia entered the room. She was carrying a brief case-like device with her left hand. A camera case hung by a strap around the base of her helmet and the handle of a laser pistol protruded from her right thigh pocket.

Sophia set down part of her load, came to him and hugged him as she exclaimed "It's so good to see another human being again! I kept wondering if the car would suddenly become surrounded by four armed, weapon carrying aliens' telling me: 'Surrender or die!'"

"They are still being shy" he assured her, as he hugged her in return. "and unfortunately we can't kiss each other while wearing space helmets."

When their embrace ended a few seconds later, he added: "I'm glad you found your camera. I want you to photograph these lockers and their contents so we'll have some proof of what we've seen here—but first let's analyze the air in this place."

"All right" she replied, "I'll begin testing it." She then walked to the brief case-like container that she had brought with her from the Mars car.

Chapter Six

Unwanted Guests

Monday Afternoon, June 49th

`Deep inside the alien complex an ambulatory robot stood impatiently while a swivel-mounted repair robot worked on its superior's detached right arm.

"You must hurry!" the two legged robot insisted. "I am neglecting my duty to our owners!"

I am working as fast as I can!" the repair robot replied electronically (in a language that no biological entity could understand). "This is a delicate item and the process must be correctly done, otherwise the functions of the arm will be impaired."

"The intruders must either be driven out or eliminated! I cannot allow them to disturb our owners!" said the ambulatory robot, as he emphasized his mission in the electronic language. "I must do my duty!"

The repair robot ignored its client's worries and concentrated on its complicated task.

Meanwhile, unaware that a reaction to her presence was about to occur, Sophia knelt beside the analyzing device. She pushed downward on a sliding switch that was on the left front part of the carrying case. The movement opened a small door which uncovered an intake aperture. A mechanical, miniature lung inhaled a tiny amount of the room's air, then compact instruments began to analyze the sample.

While Michael waited for the sample to reveal its secrets, he walked to the locker that contained the ink pen and looked at the pen again. 'I've seen writing like this before' he thought with a slight smile, 'and I think I know where.' Sophia's voice then interrupted his reverie:

"Sixty-five percent oxygen, fifteen percent carbon dioxide, nineteen percent nitrogen and one percent trace gasses—nothing toxic" she announced. "Air pressure seventy-four percent of average sea level pressure on Earth. We can breathe it, Mike."

"Good", he replied. "Let's remove these helmets." They proceeded to do so, then both people inhaled cautiously. Afterward they smiled briefly with satisfaction.

"It's a bit like hospital air—with a sort of medicinal odor. It's like we're in some type of clinic" Sophia remarked.

"It reminds me of mouthwash" Michael said humorously. "Now let me take you to some alien equipment I found."

"All right" Sophia replied. She followed him into the nearby corridor. There they turned to the right and proceeded a short distance to an alcove.

"Have a look in there" said Michael, as he pointed toward the devices that he had found earlier. Sophia did so, then she leaned forward toward a small, metal box and pushed a button that turned on a readout.

"These symbols must mean <u>something</u>—but what?" she pondered aloud.

"I don't know, but I've seen them before—some of them, anyway. You've seen them too" said Michael.

Sophia thought for a while, then she smiled and exclaimed: "That picture from Luna—of course! You showed it to me this morning!"

"Those aliens must travel a lot" Michael deduced aloud. Then he listened for a few seconds and whispered: "I hear footsteps! I think we're about to have company."

Sophia stopped pondering the alien devices and stood erect. "I hear them too—and they sound odd!" she whispered, "—sort of mechanical." She then turned around and followed him back to a place where the curving hallway straightened.

Michael looked along the hallway toward a 'T' shaped junction with a transverse corridor. The sound of footsteps was becoming louder. Michael knelt on the floor to make himself a smaller target, in case the potential alien was hostile. Sophia stood close to the right wall behind him and shifted her pistol to her left hand.

A mechanical arm appeared from the right side of the intersection and the two humans saw it was holding a weapon! As more of the shiny metal robot emerged, Michael shot at its chest. Only a slight discoloration appeared there. The robot fired its strange looking, two handed weapon and the beam passed over Michael's head. Sophia yelped with pain as she felt searing heat on her left arm. Michael aimed at the transparent bubble that served the robot as a head, then he pulled the laser pistol's trigger. The beam penetrated the bubble and seared through a slender, 'T' shaped device that supported two round, electronic eyes. One arm of the metal 'T' fell off, taking an amber eye with it. The robot made an exclamation in a strange language and retreated out of sight to the right of the intersection of the two corridors.

"That thing sure is quick for a machine!" Michael exclaimed. Then he heard footsteps retreating from the junction and said "Come with me, honey. We're leaving <u>now</u>!"

Sophia followed him quickly into the suit locker room, then Michael closed the door behind them. He looked at her and saw an expression of pain on her pretty face.

"Sophia, are you wounded?!" Michael asked in a worried tone of voice.

"Yes!" she replied. "An energy beam from that robot's weapon grazed my left arm." As she spoke, she turned her left side toward him and he saw an elongated hole in her space suit. He also saw a patch of reddened skin beneath the hole. The wound was on the upper half of her arm, near the elbow.

"It will need treatment, but at least it's not life threatening "said Michael. "That hole in your space suit will be a problem, though. We have no way to patch it here."

"I can grip my left arm with my right hand when we enter the airlock" Sophia replied. "That will cover the hole until we are inside the car."

"All right, let's be going" said Michael, "—before that robot returns."

Six minutes later Michael and Sophia emerged from the Mars car's airlock and removed their space suits in the vehicle's suit rack room. They then stowed their bulky suits in racks and went through three compartments to the little dining area. Inside one of the cabinets was a first aid kit which Michael accessed while Sophia peeled off the top half of her coveralls to free her wounded left arm.

She seated herself on one of two bar stools beside a foot wide, plastic counter top. Now she was wearing only a lace brassiere and a slender, brass chain necklace above her waist. The brassiere provided some support for her "C" cup breasts, but it only slightly obscured them.

"Are you enjoying the view?" she teased as he treated her small—but painful—wound.

"Very much" he replied with an admiring smile.

"Good, I'm glad I didn't get myself wounded for nothing" she remarked humorously, as he sprayed disinfectant on her arm. Michael bandaged her wound and kissed her face. Then he put the first aid kit back inside its cabinet. Sophia did not bother to cover herself when he turned around again.

"I was hoping you would take advantage of me" she teased. Then she winced as her left arm began to hurt again.

"I'd like to do that, but there's a dust storm coming" Michael replied. "We must return to Lowellsville soon, so I want you to let me do the driving this time."

"Don't I drive fast enough to suit you?" Sophia asked half seriously. Her wound was beginning to make her irritable.

"Yes, but we can't afford any more detours" Michael jested (with the hope of improving her mood).

Sophia reluctantly covered herself and followed him to the driver's compartment.

Meanwhile, unknown to either of them, the ambulatory robot watched their car from the same alcove that they had recently visited.

'Good fortune!' it thought happily. 'I have driven them away! There will be no need to disturb my owners about this pair of intruders. Soon I may go to the repair shop and have my missing eye replaced.'

As Michael and Sophia drove away, the robot turned around and walked to one of the video monitors to observe their departure from the basin. It felt satisfied with its victory against the two humans, even though that had cost it an eye.

"Master Vekrin, are you damaged?" asked the repair robot's voice from a nearby communications panel.

"Yes" Vekrin replied, "but the intruders have fled. I am on my way to you now to get a new eye mount. The aliens' weapons did no other harm to me, and I wounded one of them."

Chapter Seven
Departure from the Hill

Still Monday Afternoon

William stood in his pressure suit about twenty feet from where Robert and the drilling crew were working. The drilling machine was making steady downward progress and William was pleased to see that, but the mystery of the bluff's interior continued to nag at his mind and made concentrating on well drilling difficult.

"The bit's at thirty-one feet now, Bill" Robert reported by suit radio. "According to our thumper soundings we should reach porous rock and pebble stratus soon. Those areas are where we should find water."

"I hope so' Bill replied. "I'd like to complete this project soon."

"Don't worry bill" said a man named Frederick Snyder, as he watched the depth indicator. "We'll have you huntin' for aliens again in an hour or so." The other drillers laughed and the drilling machine continued to make humming and swishing sounds. Then a different sound interupted the drillers' camaraderie.

"Bill, this is Barbara" said a familiar voice through their helmets' ear phones. "I just received a weather report from Lowellsville. There's a dust storm approaching from the west, e.t.a. is about four hours from now in the Lowellsville area."

"How strong is it, Barbara?" Bill asked, as he noticed the other men's' worried expressions through their face plates.

"It's expected to be a large, powerful storm and it could last two days or more" she replied.

"Oh great! That's just what we need!" Robert exclaimed sarcastically.

"Yeah, we'll need to cap the well soon after we reach liquid water" said Bill. "Then everyone except Robert and me will need to pack the drilling equipment and head back to Lowellsville. We can hold the fort here for a couple of days until the storm passes."

"I'm willing to stay too, sir" Barbara said via a radio in the office trailer.

"All right" Bill decided. "See if you can call Mike and Sandra. I'd like to know if they got the storm warning."

"All right, sir. I'll check on them for you. Barbara out."

A few seconds later Robert announced: "Forty feet, Bill! We're at our goal."

"All right" his boss replied. "Raise the drill bit and insert the pipe."
"Yes, sir!" Robert exclaimed enthusiastically. "We'll know soon if there is water down there."

Meanwhile, Michael drove the Mars car into the the upper end of the ravine, with two powerful headlamps lighting the gradually increasing gloom. "Whew! Sophia exclaimed. "I'm glad to be away from that alien base. I was afraid that homicidal robot might shoot at us with some big weapon before we could leave the basin."

"So was I" Michael admitted," but we should be safe now. Help me to watch for boulders that may have fallen from the top part of the ravine. We don't want to damage the car's suspension system."

Michael drove the car at about five miles per hour along the gradually narrowing ravine until the narrowest point was reached. Unknown to him and Sophia, though, their recent mechanical opponent was watching them on a video screen, by way of hidden, infrared cameras mounted on ledges in the ravine. 'They are well away from here now' thought Vekrin. 'I can finish my journey to the repair room.' Then the robot left the little security office and walked further into the depths of the complex.

The Mars car passed through the narrow place and continued down the ravine. Gradually the defile widened and soon the angle of the slope lessened. Sophia looked at the right outside mirror and sighed with relief. "Well, we're not being pursued" she said.

"I can just imagine that robot wearing a policeman's uniform and riding a motorcycle" Michael teased.

"You can joke about him—he didn't hit you with a laser beam" Sophia replied with annoyance, as she glanced at her wounded arm (which now had a large, adhesive bandage and some salve on it). The arm still ached frequently.

"I'm sorry, honey. I didn't mean to offend you" Michael said earnestly.

Sophia rode in silence to the lower end of the ravine, while Michael whistled the theme song from the motion picture classic "Star Wars." He ended it with an imitation of Yoda saying "May the force be with you."

Sophia smiled and laughed. "I can't stay mad at you" she told him, "—you're too funny."

He replied with a wookie noise and she laughed again as he turned the car on open ground toward the drilling community of William's Bluff. The car bounced across some rocky ground and Michael exclaimed "Ride 'em cowboy!" Sophia laufhed while he waved his left hand in the air and whistled Aaron Copeland's tune "Rodeo." Afterward Sophia was in a better mood all the way to the trailer community and her arm seemed to bother her less. Her usual cheerfulness was returning.

They arrived near the well's site just as Robert turned on an electric pump that brought the much sought water upward through the long , vertical series of underground pipes. "A hundred gallons per minute!" he exclaimed triumphantly, as he watched a gauge at the top of the new well.

As the water flowed through an insulated hose into a big tank mounted on a trailer, Bill said" I hate to pop your balloon, Bob, but we must turn off the pump about ten minutes from now, then disconnect the hose and send the drilling equipment back to Lowellsville. That process and the trip will take us about two hours and we'll need to prepare the trailers that will remain here to endure the strong wind that the storm will bring with it."

"Hey! Isn't that the vehicle that was here earlier?!" Fred exclaimed as he pointed toward the southeast.

Bill turned around and saw the Mars car approaching at a distance of a hundred feet or so. "It surely is!" he exclaimed. "I thought Mike and Sandra were in Lowellsville by now."

Michael slowed the vehicle to a stop about twenty-five feet from the drilling rig and made a request by low power/short range radio:

"Bill, would you come inside the car, please? Sophia and I would like to discuss something with you, over."

"All right, Mike. I'll be there in a minute or two" Bill replied. "Out." Then he told Robert" Bob, you manage things here. "Make sure that the rig is well on its way to Lowellsville well before the storm arrives."

"Yes, sir" Robert replied.

William went to the Mars car and cycled through its airlock, then he entered its suit rack room. Michael met him there in a coverall garment and helped his guest to remove the awkward helmet from his suit. As Michael set it on a shelf, William asked "Where have you two been? I saw you drive away toward Lowellsville earlier."

"Sophia had a hunch that we might find something interesting in that ravine in the eastern side of the hill" Michael explained. She was driving, so I let her take us back there. Come to the dining compartment and we will explain to you what we found. I'm certain it will interest you."

"Damn it!" Bill exclaimed, "I thought we had an agreement that we would wait until Wednesday to explore the bluff together!" Then he followed Michael angrily toward the front part of the car.

"What can I say? Curiosity overcame our resolve" Michael said apologetically, as he walked through the middle part of the car.

"Now that excuse I can accept" Bill remarked humorously, as his mood gradually improved. You two may seem like the model couple, but you're still human."

"Thanks—I think" Michael replied without turning around.

They soon arrived in the little dining and laboratory area. There they saw Sophia sitting on one of the three stools. On the countertop next to her were four photographs arranged in a horizontal row. William was curious about the pictures, but he was even more curious about her left arm and shoulder, which were outside that side of her coverall garment. He noticed a bandage on her bare left arm and asked "What happened to you, Sandra?"

"I was shot with a laser rifle" she replied, with obvious discomfort in her facial expression.

"You were what?!" Bill exclaimed, as he seated himself on the stool to the left of her.

"I'll explain it to you later" she replied. "Mike, tell him what we found at the upper end of the ravine."

"Well—" he began, "we parked the car at the foot of the ravine and walked up it until we saw a basin ahead of us. I sent Sophia back to get the car because I knew we would have a place to turn it around. Meanwhile, I went ahead to the basin and found an airlock's entrance set in a cliff face. It was at the right side of the basin, near the upper end of the ravine."

"An airlock?! Do you mean like the ones we use?!" Bill exclaimed. "I was hoping for something more exotic."

"Well, it was <u>outwardly</u> similar to ours, but before Sophia arrived I cycled through it alone. The air pump sounded different from one of ours. It was quieter—and it <u>hummed</u>" Michael replied.

"Tell him about the sliding doors" Sophia prompted eagerly.

"Well, the airlock's doors did slide <u>sideways</u> to open—instead of swinging toward or away from me, like ours do" Michael continued. "They were obviously well made—they only caused a slight swishing sound as they moved. How they were made air tight, I don't know."

"When the inner door opened, did you see any of the aliens?" asked Bill, as he glanced at the photograph of the four armed woman who was wearing a space suit.

"No, I just saw a room, with locker doors set in two of its walls" Michael replied. He silently wished that Sophia had hidden the pictures for a while, so they would not distract Bill's attention. "There was a door similar to our doors set in the right wall; and there were rectangular lighting panels set in the ceiling. The room appeared unremarkable—except that the lockers' doors were unusually large—but when I opened their doors, I began to find interesting items. There were two space suits made for creatures with four arms each—and in the case of the female, four breasts."

"So I see" said Bill, as he again examined the photograph of the alien woman. "Did you make this picture of her later?"

"No" Michael replied. "I found it and those other three pictures in one of the lockers. When Sophia arrived I brought her inside the complex and showed them to her. She used her electronic digital camera to photograph the contents of all six lockers. She also photographed a device that we decided was a very advanced type of vacuum cleaner with an <u>electronic</u> filter instead of cloth filters like most of our machines use."

"So when did the shooting occur?" asked Bill, as he glanced at Sophia's bandaged arm.

"I'll let Sophia tell you about that incident" Michael replied.

"After I photographed the contents of the suit locker room, Mike led me into a hallway and along it to an alcove where he had found some alien devices" she explained. "They appeared to be sensory equipment—perhaps for monitoring the weather outside the base. Anyway, I photographed the devices, then we started back toward the suit locker room. I had told Mike about a dust storm warning that I had heard about forty-five minutes earlier, when I was about to bring the car up the ravine. So, we decided to cut short our exploration of the alien base and head for Lowellsville; but before we could reach the inner doorway of the suit locker room, an alien robot appeared around a bend of the corridor. The robot was carrying a weapon of strange design, so Mike shot its torso with apparently no effect. The robot shot at me and its energy beam grazed my left arm. Mike shot the robot's transparent dome that served it as a head. His beam severed one of its strange looking electronic eyes from a "**T**" shaped supporting device. The robot retreated out of sight and we retreated into the suit locker room. My suit had been penetrated by the robot's weapon, but I told Mike that I could cover the hole with one hand while we were outside the base, so he told me to open the airlock's inner door while he covered our retreat. I did so and we entered the airlock safely. I noticed then that he was putting those four alien photographs into an electrically heated pocket on the torso of his space suit. I was glad that he had decided to bring them with him, since we might not be able to enter the aliens' base again."

"I'm glad he brought them too said William. "Now we have more proof that there is a nonhuman intelligent species on Mars."

"Well, it appears that those green people are not interested in having us as guests" said Sophia. "They wouldn't even have the decency to come to the suit locker room and meet us. In—stead they sent their robot to scare us away."

"That is strange behavior" said William, "—unless they were not at home when you went there to visit them. That robot could be a sort of watch dog, just guarding its masters' house during their absence>"

"That theory is worth considering" Michael remarked. "They could be away visiting friends on some other part of the planet."

"Well, if so, how will we know when they come home?" asked Sophia, as she rose to a standing position and extended her arms above her head to stretch them. Then she winced due to her wound.

"I suppose we could hide a camera somewhere so that we could watch their front door" suggested William.

"They might resent that if they discovered it" Sophia replied, as Michael seated himself on the stool she had vacated. Sophia stood behind him and caressed his shoulders.

"So, we will just need to hide it well" William remarked, with an expression of annoyance. Then he looked at the two photographs of the flying saucer and asked "I don't suppose that either of you happened to see this space ship while you were up on the hill?"

"No" Michael replied. "You've been in this area longer than we have. I was hoping you might have noticed something unusual flying over the bluff—perhaps at night, when other people were asleep."

"No such luck" said William. "I'd give a month's salary to see a genuine flying saucer."

"So would I" Michael remarked, "—and a year's wages to go inside one."

"I hate to be a nuisance" said Sophia, "but there is a storm approaching us."

"Yes, I suppose we should be going homeward now" Michael replied. "We'll come back here as soon as the weather clears and explore some more. Meanwhile, though, let's all try to keep Sophia's and my adventure today a secret for a while. I don't want every human on Mars to go snooping around the bluff before we have a chance to go inside of it again."

"All right" said their guest, "but take me with you the next time you go in there."

"I promise we will" Michael replied, as William rose from his seat.

Michael stood up also and shook hands with William. Sophia gave a friendly kiss to the hydrologist, then Michael said "Please go to the control room and listen for any more weather reports, Sophia. I'll go help Bill to put on his helmet, then as soon as he's gone outside I'll drive us back to Lowellsville."

"All right" Sophia replied. "Good bye, Bill."

"Good bye, dear" he replied with a smile, then he kissed her in a fatherly manner. "I envy you, Mike" he added. "Every man on Mars does. Take good care of her or I'll steal her from you." Then he walked to the suit rack room and Michael followed him.

"Maybe I should let your helmet seal leak some" Michael teased.

"If you do, I'll haunt you" William replied with a nervous smile. "Seriously, Mike, you have a real treasure there. You'd better hold on to her."

"I intend to do just that" Michael replied. They then arrived in the suit rack room and William put on his helmet. Michael fastened the rear part of the seal between the helmet and the suit for him, while William fastened the front part. Afterward the hydrologist entered the airlock and cycled through it. Michael waited until he heard his visitor leave the little compartment, then he walked forward to the driver's compartment.

He found Sophia sitting in the navigator's seat and listening to the radio.

"—automated weather station at Castle Rock reports sixty miles per hour wind and nearly zero visibility. The storm is expected to arrive over Lowellsville in two hours" said a woman's voice from the radio.

Michael seated himself in the driver's position and fastened his safety harness.

"We should arrive in Lowellsville with more than an hour to spare" he said, as he started the Mars car's engine, "but these storms sometimes accelerate as they gain strength, so we won't take any chances. We'll head straight for home."

As Michael set the vehicle in motion he saw through the windshield that Robert's team was lowering the drilling tower onto the load bed of a parked Mars truck. Sophia noticed them too.

"It looks like they will be leaving soon" she remarked.

"Good" Michael replied. "Radio ahead and tell our two departments that we'll be in Lowellsville in about thirty minutes—with some interesting fossils."

"All right" Sophia replied. "I can hardly wait until our coworkers see that arthropod specimen. It'll cause a sensation among them-and back on Earth in NASA."

Chapter Eight
Storm Coming

Late Monday Afternoon

A half hour after Michael and Sophia drove away in what he called "the Marsmobile," William watched the truck that was carrying the drilling rig rumbling away. All of the drilling team was riding in its spacious cabin. Left behind was the capped well that William hoped would eventually be connected by a pipeline to the struggling little community of Lowellsville. He also hoped that some good tasting water would help NASA to attract more settlers to it. Lately the growing threat of a war between two or more of the newly nuclear armed, small nations of Asia or South America preoccupied the three Wealthy super powers: the USNA, the European Union and mainland China. The high cost of developing and deploying missile defense systems (and of paying for past wars) was diverting their attention from Mars. William tried not to think too much about such things as he helped Robert to rig extra tie down cables and stakes for the four trailers that remained near the drilling site. 'The last thing I would want too see would be one of these trailers flipping over' he mused, '—especially with me in it!'

The two largest trailers were the one that contained the administrative offices and the one that contained the dining facilities; but equally important was the third trailer which enclosed a small, nuclear fission powered generator; and the fourth trailer, which housed a small, state-of—the-art sewage processing plant. The latter was a mechanical marvel that Robert had helped NASA to design. The U.S.N.A.'s government was already using copies of it in some agencies' office complexes on Earth.

The use of nuclear fission power plants on Mars was still being protested by some environmental fringe groups on Earth, although the U.S.N.A.'s government had repeatedly declared that there was no longer a biosphere on the red planet for humans to potentially pollute. Bill hoped that his recently discovered, nonhuman neighbors would help his species to find a good way to dispose of the nuclear waste material.

An ominous, grayish pink cloud had appeared on the western horizon by the time the two men had completed their work. Robert sought shelter in the dining trailer, where he would be (in his words) "camping in" for the duration of the storm. He and William had rigged a safety rope between it and the office trailer to guide Barbara and themselves back and forth during conditions of bad visibility. Robert did not need it quite yet, though, as he hurried toward his temporary residence with William close behind him. William intended to carry several meal packages in one trailer to a refrigerator in the other one. That way he and Barbara would not need to be outside in the storm anytime soon.

The two men cycled through the dining trailer's airlock as quickly as they could, then they removed their helmets in a suit rack room that was twice the size of its counterpart in the office trailer. Afterward, they set the helmets on a wire grid shelf and walked into the dining room.

"I want to thank you for volunteering to take care of this trailer during the storm, Bob" said William.

His friend replied "You're welcome" as he picked up a ceramic cup from a rack and carried it to a machine that dispensed coffee and hot chocolate. Robert filled his cup with the second beverage while William went to a food dispenser and began keying in requests on a built-in keyboard. Bill used a letter and number code for each meal that he wanted, but he omitted the heating instructions deliberately.

"It's no great sacrifice" Robert added with a smile. "I have a television to watch and plenty of food near me. I must admit, though, that the prospect of sleeping on an air mattress does not thrill me. I haven't used one in years."

"I've never liked them either—at least not since I became an adult" William remarked, as he waited for the covered meal trays to emerge from the machine. Robert alternately blew on and sipped the hot beverage in his cup as he seated himself in a plastic chair with aluminum legs. The adjacent table was similarly constructed.

"What did Mike and Sandra have to say before they left?" Robert asked curiously.

"They admitted that they sneaked back to the bluff and found a way into it" William replied with some annoyance in his voice. He then set two meal trays on Robert's table and returned to the food dispenser. There he keyed in a request for two more meals (uncooked).

"I suspected something of the sort, but bravo anyway!" Robert exclaimed. "Were our mysterious neighbors at home?"

"Apparently not" William replied. "The only 'person' who greeted Mike and Sandra was a <u>robot</u> and he shot at them with a laser weapon! Fortunately his aim was bad. He slightly wounded Sandra before Mike shot off one of his eye stalks; then he disappeared and our two friends decided to leave the aliens' base. Please don't repeat to anyone what I just told you. Mike and I want to have some time to visit that place again before <u>everyone</u> on Mars hears about it."

"<u>Mum's</u> <u>the</u> <u>word</u>—as long as you take me with you" said Robert, as he watched William stack two more uncooked meals on top of the previous four.

"I intend to do just that" William promised. "Sandra may want to return to the hill too."

"I hope she does—she's pleasant to look at "Robert remarked with a smile.

"She is indeed!" said William, as he picked up two stacks of meal trays with some help from Robert and made one precariously tall stack of them in front of his space suit clad torso.

"I'd better put your helmet on your head for you" said the younger man, as he preceded William to the suit rack room.

Please do" said William, "otherwise my balancing act may be short lived." He followed his friend to the vicinity of the airlock's door, then he stooped while Robert took the helmet from the shelf and placed it over William's head. Robert turned on Bill's oxygen supply, then he fastened the seal between the helmet and the suit. Next he opened the airlock's inner door and stepped aside. The older man entered the airlock with his stack of meals, then Robert reached inside the airlock and pushed the *Air Out* button on the nearest control panel. Afterward he withdrew his arm and closed the door.

The airlock's pump began operating and when it stopped a minute later, Bill used his right elbow to turn the outer door's handle. He then shoved the door open and carefully descended the short stairway to the ground. He turned around and an awkward nudge of his helmet clad head closed the door. Afterward, he began walking across the coral red sand toward the office trailer. The wind had already begun to whistle around the trailers, while the ominous dust cloud hid most of the area to the west of them from his view.

A telephone call from Robert alerted Barbara to put on the helmet of her space suit and step into the office trailer's airlock. Next she closed the inner door and depressurized the airlock. When Bill knocked on the outer door with his helmet, Barbara was ready. She opened the outer door and accepted half of the food trays from Bill when he climbed on to the little platform at the top of the short stairway. She then stepped back and Bill entered the airlock.

While William and Barbara were cycling through their trailer's airlock, Robert stood near one of his trailer's windows and watched small dust clouds begin to swirl around the wheels of the sewage processing trailer. Then he pushed a button that electrically closed a sliding shutter. Next he went to each of the dining trailer's other windows and closed their shutters. Finally he went to the nearest food dispenser and ordered an early dinner. He had eaten lunch late and it had been too small, so he was feeling hungry again.

As Robert waited for his meal to cook, he could hear a strong wind beginning to buffet the trailer. "Well, it's started' he thought. 'I hope nothing happens to force me to go outside during the next couple of days! The television and telephone cable between here and Lowellsville is underground, so it should not be harmed by the storm. I think I'll turn on the TV. and see what is happening in the inner solar system lately.'

Robert picked up a remote control device from a shelf where the room's twenty-four inch television sat, then he walked to a chair beside one of the tables and clicked on the television set. A Solar System News Network program from Earth was in progress and instead of the usual depressing news about high unemployment or the latest war casualties; he was relieved to see a science report. The program's announcer was saying: "this news just in from Brussels, Belgium. The European Space Agency 's giant new orbiting space telescope, Kepler II, has collected the best images yet seen of the tiny, ice dwarf worldlet Make Make*[2]. This planetoid is only three quarters the size of Pluto and orbits even farther from our sun. Previous images from other telescopes have shown only fuzzy, light and dark patches resembling the old Hubble Telescope's images of Pluto thirty-eight years ago. ESA tells us that the following pictures will be much clearer than those."

Three images in succession were shown of an icy, crater-dotted sphere surrounded by the unequalled blackness of deep space. The orb was pastel pink, with small, irregularly shaped spots of brownish yellow and slightly grayish blue. Near it-and casting a tiny shadow on its surface—was a bright dot much smaller than the dwarf planet (Robert was amused by the latter's unlikely sounding Polynesian name). The announcer spoke again:

"ESA tells us that the tiny, bright dot that appears near Make Make in two of the images is a never before seen moonlet of the little planetoid. Astronomers have not yet chosen a name for it, but probably will do so in the next week to ten days . . ."

Meanwhile, William and Barbara had emerged from the airlock's inner doorway in the office trailer and had carried the six meal containers to a small lounge adjacent to the near end of William's office. There they had put the covered trays into a refrigerator. Next the two people had gone into the little suit rack room and removed their helmets. These were then placed on the usual metal frame and mesh shelf. Afterward the two coworkers had removed their space suits (or Mars suits, as they also were called) and hung them on racks below the helmets' shelf.

After the suits were safely stowed, Barbara turned toward William, stood on the balls of her feet and wrapped her arms around his neck. She kissed his lips for about five seconds, as he wrapped his arms around her waist.

When their lips parted, Barbara returned to a normal standing posture and looked slightly upward at her boss, while he looked downward from his four inch height advantage and smiled. "That was a pleasant greeting" he told her.

"I have you all to myself for at least two days" she replied. "There will be plenty more kisses for you from the same source."

"We should have dust storms more often" he remarked. Then he leaned forward and kissed her again.

*(2) Pronounced "Mah-kee, Mah-kee." It was discovered in 2005 by Michael Brown.

Chapter Nine

Homeward Journey

Still Monday Afternoon

When Michael and Sophia drove away from the trailer community, he steered their vehicle onto the dirt road that led to Lowellsville. The car's six wheels raised a plume of dust as they rumbled along the road at about thirty miles per hour.

Sophia radioed Lowellsville and got a telephone link from its radio room to the biology department. A female voice answered the telephone. "Hello, biology lab. Louisa d'Alsace speaking."

"Hello, Louisa, this is Sophia Collins. I'm heading your way with Mike Andrews in Mars Car Four. We're bringing a couple of fossils with us that you'll want to see. We should arrive in about thirty minutes, over."

"I'm glad you are returning to Lowellsville, Sandy. There's a big dust storm approaching this area and you need to outrun it:" said Louisa. "Over."

"We've heard the storm warnings" said Sophia. "We'll be inside the garage before it arrives. Mars Car Four out."

Sophia then used the same combination of radio and telephone linkage to call the geology department, but an automated recording device answered there. After it spoke, Sophia left a message on it: "This is Sandra Collins in Mars Car Four calling at 5:31 PM Olympus Regional Standard Time. Mike Edwards and I are on our way back to Lowellsville from our fossil hunt. E.T.A. about 6:00 PM, well ahead of the storm. We have a couple of interesting fossils to take to the biology lab and a couple of hungry stomachs to take to the cafeteria afterward. Mars Car Four out."

She then turned toward Michael and asked "Were my messages satisfactory?"

"Very" he replied. "No mentioning of the alien base—just the fossils and our estimated arrival time. You kept our secret well."

"Thanks" she replied, "but how long do you think we can hide that base's existence?"

"Just long enough for <u>one</u> <u>more</u> <u>visit</u> to it—<u>if</u> the drillers are <u>not</u> <u>too</u> talkative" Michael replied. "I hope Bill told them to keep quiet about it."

"What about the robot?" asked Sophia. "We'll need a way to go past it."

"We shall have one or two more people and more fire power next time" Michael replied. "If necessary we will <u>destroy</u> <u>him</u>. He is only a machine, after all."

"We would anger whoever owns him if we reduced him to a pile of charred parts" Sophia warned. "<u>Robots</u> <u>are</u> <u>expensive</u>."

"He can be <u>rebuilt</u> or <u>replaced</u>" Michael insisted. "I want to see the <u>other</u> <u>technology</u> that base contains—<u>especially</u> <u>the</u> <u>flying</u> <u>saucer</u> and whatever power source that facility uses. Maybe those aliens have found a practical way to build a small nuclear fusion reactor."

"I just hope they don't use a nuclear bomb on Lowellsville if they decide that they don't want us for neighbors!" said Sophia. "Really, Mike, couldn't we try <u>diplomacy</u>—just for a few days?!"

"That robot did not seem interested in diplomacy. He greeted us with an energy rifle-remember?" Michael asked.

"Of course I remember! I'm the one he shot!" Sophia replied angrily. Then she winced as her wound ached.

"Okay, I'm sorry. I shouldn't have said that" Michael conceded. "But how are we supposed to be diplomatic when we don't know where his masters are? How are we supposed to talk to them?"

"I don't know" Sophia replied, "But they will come home eventually. Let's just watch their access route in the ravine. When we see fresh tracks with their vehicles tread pattern in them we will know that they've returned to their base."

"Now that's a good idea!" Michael exclaimed. "You're not only good looking—you're clever too!"

"Thanks" she replied with a smile. Then she turned on a music disc player that was mounted in the car's dashboard. Soon the sound of an orchestra playing a recently composed symphony called "The Landscapes of Mars" came from four well harmonized speakers. As the first movement, "The Vast Desert," was played, the two travelers enjoyed the sounds of mystery and a vague loneliness, played by an orchestra in far away Atlanta, Georgia.

"For a guy who has only seen the surface of Mars in photographs, Theodore Jernigan creates a good rendition of it" Michael commented.

"I think he creates just the right sort of mood" Sophia replied, as she leaned her seat back slightly and relaxed.

"Music to explore Mars by" Michael remarked humorously, as he watched the coral red and medium gray landscape pass by the car's windows. The miles passed pleasantly while the symphony went through three more movements: *Olympus Mons, Valles Marineris*, and *The Polar Regions*. It was during the slow oboe theme and occasional, low pitched, horn music of the last movement that Lowell's Bluff came into view. First there was the summit, with its two secondary bluffs and several electronic antennas on top of each of them; then there were the upper, main slopes with their undulating, multitiered ramparts and occasional rock spires; then finally arose the eastward facing cliff, with its man-made, half dome facade of Plexiglas that provided insulation for the various pedestrian and vehicle doors and scattered windows (now shuttered). All of these things were like a casing for the mostly underground community and they seemed to rise out of the ground as the Mars car trundled across a long, low, rocky rise of ground about a half—mile to the east of the massif.

"Are you sure Jernigan never visited Mars?" Sophia jested. "Those dramatic *polar cliffs* bass horn sounds were very well timed."

"Maybe the guy is <u>psychic</u>" Michael replied humorously. "Anyway, here it is—home, sweet burrow—with a dramatic, setting sun background."

"You do a good guided tour" said Sophia with a pleasant smile, as the vehicle did a right turn and followed the gravel road down the western side of the ancient reef. The road then crossed the now dry floor of a long ago lagoon where the machines of man had created a small space port and a mile long airfield.

'How shall we explain my wounded arm to our friends?" asked Sophia, as they drove onto a paved perimeter road and turned right to avoid the runway where a recently assembled, solar powered, drone aircraft was landing to avoid the approaching storm.

"We'll just tell them that you had an accident with a hot object while you were cooking our lunch in the Mars car" Michael replied.

"There goes my purple heart medal for being wounded in the line of duty," Sophia teased.

Michael merely smiled with amusement and drove the car to the biggest of the three airlocks that gave access to the eastern part of the underground community. There he used a tiny, short-ranged transmitter on the car's dashboard to signal to the airlock's computer that it must depressurize the area that it controlled. About two minutes were needed to do this, then a second signal opened the airlock's large outer door. Michael drove the Mars car into the airlock and signaled for the outer door to close. When it had done so, his next signal caused the big twin electric pumps to re-pressurize the airlock. Approximately two minutes later his final signal opened the inner door and Michael drove the vehicle out of the airlock.

There was a paved driveway that went straight from the airlock to the open doorway of the main garage for the community. Michael directed the car along this driveway and into the garage. Meanwhile, a twenty-five second timer in the airlock eventually caused the inner door to close. This lag time was programmed into the airlock's activation device in case a vehicle's engine stalled and needed to be restarted, or in case another vehicle was about to enter the airlock from the area that was enclosed by the plexiglas bubble.

The airlock's tiny computer would not accept a command to open either of its doors if the other one was still open. Also the computer would not allow the outer door to be opened before the airlock's large, enclosed area had been depressurized by pumping the air back into the area under the plexiglas bubble. Oxygen was precious on Mars.

In an emergency the airlock could be rapidly re-pressurized simply by using a special command to skip the air pumping process and open the inner door of the airlock (provided that the outer door had been closed first). Under nonemergency circumstances this process was illegal because rocks and other small objects that rushed into the airlock along with the strong blast of artificial wind could damage The flexible seals on the edges of the airlock's doors and scratch the enclosure's plexiglas windows. Debris might also damage the wiring behind the thin, removable, maintenance cover plates (if the latter were blown off).

Pedestrians or drivers of small vehicles could save time by using the small or medium-size airlock instead. These things and other information about the proper use of the airlocks were taught to newcomers within two days after they arrived in the community.

Michael parked the Mars car beside a smaller vehicle that was having a damaged tire replaced on one of its four wheels. Two men were doing the procedure with the aid of a hydraulic jack and other equipment. Neither man was wearing a pressure suit, although suits and helmets hanging in a nearby suit rack room were recommended by the safety posters on the walls of the garage. A sudden, rapid depressurization of the garage area due to a meteor impacting the Plexiglas bubble was considered to be only a remote possibility by many of the inhabitants of Lowllsville, and anyway, there were hydrogen filled balloons hovering under the dome to drift to and block all but the largest holes that might occur in the tough, Plexiglas structure, so why worry?

As Michael and Sophia turned off various devices in the Mars car, Michael remarked "I'll bet those two tire changers had ancestors aboard the *Titanic* who felt safe too—until the ice berg came into view, anyway."

"I was thinking of Pearl Harbor" said Sophia, "but the same generalized lesson can be derived from both tragedies: those who do not remember the past will probably repeat it eventually." She then rose from her seat and retrieved her own helmet from its shelf.

Michael picked up his helmet also and followed Sophia through several compartments to the cargo area. There Sophia retrieved the bags that contained the two fossils which she and Michael had found. Michael picked up a bag that contained labeled rock samples, then he led her to the suit rack room and held her specimen bags for her. She then set her helmet on a shelf and put on her space suit. She then retrieved her two specimen bags and held Michael's bag for him while he put on his bulky suit.

Next the two fossil hunters picked up their helmets and tucked them under their left arms, then Michael retrieved his rock samples and Sophia opened the door of the airlock with her free right hand. Afterward she preceded him into the little compartment. When he was inside of it, Michael closed the inner door and Sophia pushed a button below the words *Safe Exit*. This allowed her to open the outer door without depressurizing the airlock first. Sophia proceeded to open the door and jumped nimbly downward to the floor of the garage.

Michael exited from the airlock and stood on the little porch platform long enough to push the outer door of the airlock closed. Then he too jumped to the concrete floor of the garage.

"We'll visit the biology lab first and leave the fossils there" he told Sophia. "I'm sure that your coworker, Louisa, will want to see them soon."

"All right" Sophia replied, "—but after that we should head for the cafeteria—I'm hungry!"

"So am I" said Michael, as he and Sophia walked toward an emergency, inner airlock which connected the garage to the first level, office area of the underground community. "It has been a long time since we ate lunch."

The interior airlock was mostly for pedestrian use and it was usually set on *normal door mode* ever since the Plexiglas "bubble" and its airlocks were completed two and a half years earlier. However, the community's security computer could restore its *airlock operation mode* if the dome enclosed area and the main garage began to decompress suddenly. Thus this small airlock was an important safety device that could preserve the entire community if a large breach of the dome or a malfunction by one of its airlocks occurred. The "old" airlock's doors were still routinely closed at night to help the community to retain heat—especially when the outside temperature plunged below zero degrees Fahrenheit.

Michael and Sophia gave only brief attention to the history of the old airlock on a bronze, wall-mounted plaque before they opened first one door, then the other. Acting according to safety regulations, the first door was closed behind them before the second door was opened. However, this precaution was sometimes ignored by some of Lowellsville's other inhabitants. One of them looked at the two fossil hunters with a condescending smile as he walked past them in the opposite direction. Michael noticed that a woman followed the man into the airlock and that he opened the far door for her before she could close the near one.

"I think I'll have a talk with the chief administrator soon about certain lapses of safety precautions" said Michael.

"I think I'll visit him with you" Sophia replied, as they resumed their walk toward the biology laboratory. "This community has become an accident waiting for a chance to happen."

Chapter Ten

Waves of Static

Monday Evening

The Martian wind whistled and howled outside the trailer while Bill and Barbara converted the couch in the lounge into a fold-out bed. When this task was completed, Barbara said "I'll put the covers on it if you'll go prepare our meals and bring out the folding table."

"All right" Bill replied. He then kissed her before he took a packaged dinner out of the refrigerator and poked some holes in the thin plastic covering with a pocket knife. Next Bill opened the door of a microwave oven that stood on a shelf near the bed. He put the plastic food tray into the oven, closed its door and set the timer. Finally he pushed the *Start* button

While the meal cooked, Bill went to a corner of the lounge and picked up a folded card table that stood leaning against a wall. He carried the table to a place near the side of the bed that faced away from the office. There he unfolded the table's legs and set it upright. Suddenly the overhead fluorescent lights began to dim and then brighten repeatedly. The humming of the microwave oven diminished then loudened repeatedly.

"Bill! What's happening?!" Barbara asked worriedly.

"I don't know!" he replied just as worriedly. "Maybe the generator is malfunctioning." Then the telephone in his office rang. Bill hurried into that room and picked up the handset.

"Hello, William's Bluff Project Office—Bill speaking."

"Bill, what's happening to the electric power?" asked a man's voice through the crackling sound of static. "Everything electrical is going crazy over here!"

"I'm not sure, Bob, but I think we may be having a generator failure. We'd better put our pressurized suits back on."

"All right but we might learn that our suits' radios are useless" Robert suggested.

"Better that than to see the life support systems fail in these trailers and head for the suit racks too late, Bob! Now put your suit on—that's an order."

"Yes, sir!" Robert replied, then he set his telephone back onto its rack. William did the same thing with his handset, then he followed Barbara to the suit rack room in their trailer. There they helped each other to put on the bulky, pressurized suits that secretly reminded Barbara of the improbable attire worn by the clowns in a circus she had seen as a child. Finally the two coworker/ lovers donned their helmets and adjusted the airflow from their metal tanks.

As William adjusted the volume of his suit's radio he winced behind the face plate of his now securely fastened on helmet. There were waves of static that made understanding an incoming message from Robert difficult. Barbara looked frightened as she encountered the same problem.

"Bob, I think we're having more than just a generator problem" Bill's voice said through the static in Robert's and Barbara's earphones. "This could be some sort of attack by the people inside the bluff—or by their robot."

"What in the name of H.G. Wells are you talking about, Bill?!" asked the younger man from his location in the dining trailer's suit rack room. "I thought you told us earlier that Mr. Andrews and Miss Collins didn't find any alien people inside the bluff and that the robot was only armed with a laser rifle—or something similar to one."

"That was true at the time when our two friends were exploring the first room and corridor of that underground base" Bill explained, "—but the aliens might have come home after their two unexpected visitors departed. They could have become angry when they found one of their robot's eye stalks shot off."

"Bill, did Michael and Sandra start some sort of <u>war</u> on this planet?!" asked Barbara , with a worried tone of voice.

"I hope not, honey" William replied, "—but it's a possibility we can't afford to ignore."

"Maybe the aliens are trying to scare us out of visiting them again" Robert suggested, "—or this radio interference could just be their robot's way of getting revenge for losing that skirmish inside the bluff."

Either option makes sense to me" said Barbara, "—unless his logic is different from ours."

"On the other hand" Robert continued, "if our generator does overload and turns itself off, we will have no choice but to go outside in the storm to restart it. Almost everything in these trailers is electrically powered—including our air filtration and humidifying equipment. We can't afford to lose power for long."

"I think we should call Lowellsville and ask someone there for help" said Barbara.

"They couldn't send anyone to us through this storm" Bill replied, "—but I suppose we should let them know what's happening here. I'll go try to telephone Chief Administrator Morris and tell him our generator is acting strangely."

"All Right" said Robert. "I'll keep my tool box near me in case I need to go work on the generator. I'm closer to it than you two are."

"I want to check on our long range radio and learn how this strange phenomenon is affecting it" said Barbara. "We might need to use the set soon."

"I doubt that it will be usable now "William replied. "You'll probably hear nothing but static from it."

"Well, let me try anyway" said Barbara.

"Go ahead" he told her.

As Barbara walked away toward the opposite end of the trailer, she wondered silently 'What sort of crisis have these men created for us? I must find a way to communicate with those aliens and ask them to stop this attack.'

She soon arrived in the radio room and removed her helmet. Afterward she set it on a vacant stool and turned off her suit's air supply. Next she seated herself in an office chair and turned it toward the countertop where a briefcase size two way radio sat. A little green LED indicated that the device was ready for use, but when she turned up the sound she heard only static. She checked the frequency setting and saw that it was the number of the station in Lowellsville. /she then picked up the microphone and pushed the *Send* button.

"Hello, Lowellsville. This is the drilling site at William's Bluff calling. Can you read me? Over." Still she heard only static. Twice more she tried and got the same result: more pulsating waves of static. 'It's no use' she thought. I can't talk to anyone on that frequency.' Then she remembered something that she had heard a North American Space Agency radio procedures instructor telling her several years earlier on Earth: "The higher a frequency is, the more likely it is to penetrate background noise and interference."

'All right' she thought. 'I'll work my way upward through the frequencies until I find one on which I can communicate with somebody.' She adjusted the frequency upward and called again:

"This is Barbara at William's Bluff calling anyone on this frequency. Can you hear me? Over." Twice more she spoke, but only static replied. She resumed working her way upward through the frequencies with the same results until she reached the highest one. There she heard a woman's voice amid the static. The woman was speaking a language that Barbara had never heard before and the secretary only recognized one word of what the mysterious speaker said; "hyoo-muns." Everything else meant nothing to her.

When the static surrounded voice stopped talking, Barbara transmitted:

"This is Barbara Waverly of the William's Bluff Community responding to your message. Do you hear me? Over." There was a pause of several seconds, then Barbara heard what she soon realized was a repeat of the earlier unintelligible message.

"Oh wonderful!" she exclaimed sarcastically. "Either I'm being ignored or I have been talking to a recording." Then she told the trailer's computer to record the stranger's message and walked quickly to Bill's office. She found him speaking to someone by telephone:

"That's right, sir. Our chief geologist and his pretty girl friend found a way to enter an alien facility inside the big hill that was named for me. The only alien they found at home was a robot, but it apparently resented their presence and a gun battle occurred. Miss Collins was slightly wounded and so was the robot. Both sides retreated and our two friends soon left the facility. They visited my operation and told me what had happened, then they headed for Lowellsville. They should have arrived well before the storm began" Bill told his listener.

"Is that the chief administrator?" Barbara asked quietly. William nodded briefly . . .

Meanwhile in Lowellsville, Mr. Daniel Morris sat in his office chair with a worried expression on his forty years old face, as he listened to William's story. "So, you are telling me that there is an underground alien base within a couple of hundred yards of your drilling operation and that our people's first encounter with the inhabitants of that base resulted in gunfire?!" Mr. Morris exclaimed in a tone of disapproval.

"I'm afraid so, sir" William's voice replied from the telephone. He was secretly beginning to regret making this call as he sat in his own office in the trailer community. "No-one was seriously injured, but the aliens may have carried a grudge afterward. There is some sort of strong electromagnetic interference with all of our electrically powered devices—and I don't think that the storm is causing more than about half of it."

"Are you telling me that you are being attacked?!" asked the chief administrator in a tone of alarm, as he sat up straighter in his chair.

"I'm not certain of it, sir, but it is a possibility" William replied, as he tried not to sound as frightened as he actually was. Then he noticed Barbara watching the erratic movements of the hands of an old fashioned, electric wall clock. Suddenly the clock began to act normally again and the static in the telephone line became much diminished.

"Uh, sir, I think that the crisis has suddenly ended!" William exclaimed when the man at the other end of the line paused for breath. "Everything is starting to act normal again!"

"Well, I intend to find Mister Andrews and have a conversation with him" said the chief administrator's deceptively calm voice from the telephone. "Meanwhile you and your skeleton crew are ordered to do nothing further to anger those aliens. Then his patience apparently ended. "Do you understand me?!" he demanded.

"Yes, sir. We'll try to act peacefully" William replied sheepishly, as he wished the conversation would end. "I'd better go check on our radio equipment and see if it's okay."

"All right, but stay away from those aliens!" said the chief administrator. "That's an order!"

"Yes, sir" William replied meekly. Then he returned the telephone to its cradle.

"Mister Morris sounded angry" said Barbara, as she stood behind William and massaged his shoulders gently.

"He <u>was</u> <u>angry</u>" Bill replied emphatically. "I shouldn't have called him."

"I learned something from using our radio recently" said Barbara, as she leaned forward and kissed the bald spot on the top of his head.

"Oh, what was that?" he asked, only half-way interested.

"On the upper-most frequency of the radio I heard a woman's voice" Barbara replied. "She was speaking a language that I've never heard before."

Bill's interest increased immediately. "Did you try to respond to her?" he asked hopefully.

"Yes, but she ignored me" Barbara replied. "She kept saying the same message repeatedly, as if she were seeking an answer from someone else."

"You could have been hearing a recording" Bill suggested.

"I suppose so" Barbara replied. "In any case, she didn't seem interested in talking to me, so I told our computer to record her message, then I came to your office to tell you what I had learned."

"Let's go to the radio room and learn if that alien's message is still being transmitted" said William. He was once again sounding hopeful. "Maybe she is saying <u>something</u> <u>different</u> by now—<u>something</u> <u>we</u> <u>can</u> <u>understand</u>."

"But what if we don't know what she is saying?" asked Barbara, as Bill stood up.

"We'll record it again and find some way to translate it later" Bill replied on his way to the radio room. Barbara hurried after him.

Chapter Eleven

Incident in Space

Still Monday Evening

Far out in space the huge space liner/ supply ship *Wernher von Braun* was hurtling toward Mars at a speed which humans could only dream about until the advent of nuclear powered rockets in the mid—two thousand teens. The state-of-the-art vessel was making its first voyage to Mars, but although it had the latest comforts and conveniences (including artificial gravity and a well furnished recreation room) only five passengers were aboard it! The recent discovery of trace remains of an apparently alien civilization on Luna had attracted the attention of space-minded people on Earth to such an extent that some of them had cancelled their plans to emigrate to Mars in order to seek careers on the Earth's moon instead.

Penelope Carter was a well known writer and a passenger aboard the *Wernher von Braun*. She was beginning to wish that she was on her way to Luna (instead of Mars) after she had viewed a recent news program. It had depicted the shattered remnants of an apparently alien, underground base on one of the big lava fields. Add to that the discovery of an abandoned mine of unknown origin a year earlier on Luna and Mars did not seem as interesting as it had been when she left Earth.

It was too late to change her destination, though. In ten days she and the other four passengers would descend to Mars from the recently constructed space port of Phobos Base. A major online news system and a television network were relying on her to send reports to them about her journey to Mars and what she found there.

The other passengers aboard the new space liner were: <u>Marvin Showalter</u>, who was Penelope's cameraman; <u>Hans Helmuth Gerhardt</u>, a structural archaeologist who had been doing comparisons among the pyramids of the Mayas and Aztecs of Mexico and those of ancient Egypt (now he wanted to study the pyramids of Mars); Douglas Bell, a famous designer and operator of drone aircraft; and <u>Mieko Kurosawa</u>, who was a promising young chemist. NASA was sending her to Mars to develop better paints than the ones that the colonists currently had (among other projects).

Penelope was brushing her hair in front of a mirror in her quarters as she anticipated a date with the ship's second officer, Peter Gordon, that evening. Her reddish blonde hair framed a pretty face with grayish blue eyes, a small nose and a delicate seeming chin. She was five feet, five inches tall and twenty-six years of age. A book that she had written about her father's adventures in the Great Middle East War had brought early fame (and large royalties) to her. "Penney's" pretty face and good figure had helped to make her a popular guest on the televised interview programs. That figure was now well displayed by the gown that she wore. It had cost her more money than most people earned in a week, but most women would have paid a month's wages to be able to fit into it.

Suddenly the room's lights began to alternately dim and brighten. Penelope rose to a standing position near the bench that she had recently occupied. She then hurried to the door of her cabin, opened it and entered the adjacent corridor. She remembered that her new friend, Shiela Graham, was the second shift radio operator. 'Maybe she knows what is happening' thought Penelope. 'I'll go ask her.'

In every part of the four hundred feet long vessel, electrical devices were acting strangely. As Shiela sat in front of the ship's long range radio, she heard waves of static and little else on the frequency that she normally used to talk to Lowellsville Radio. So, knowing radio communication principles well, she began to work her way upward through the frequencies. As she sought a clear channel, she barely noticed that Penelope had entered the room.

"This is the interplanetary vessel *Wernher von Braun* calling Lowellsville Radio" said Shiela. "Can you hear me? Over." On frequency after frequency there was no reply. Only more waves of static could be heard. Shiela heard the intraship telephone warble. She picked up the handset and said "Radio room. Shiela Graham here" as Penelope seated herself in another chair nearby and waited quietly.

"Hello Shiela. This is Captain Juan Hernandez calling "said a male voice. "I suppose you know that everything electrical aboard this ship is going crazy."

"Yes, sir, I've seen it "Shiela replied.

"I don't suppose the radio is working?" the captain asked hopefully.

"I've been trying to call Lowellsville Radio on several channels" Shiela replied. "No luck so far—just waves of static. I haven't tried all of the frequencies yet, though."

"Well, keep trying Shiela" the captain urged. If you get a reply, please call me."

"I'll do that sir" Shiela assured him, "—just as soon as I can get a reply."

"Good girl. I'll hang up now and let you go back to work" said her superior. Sheila returned her handset to its cradle and turned toward her visitor.

"This really worries me" Penelope began, without any amenities. "Our life support systems could be failing for all we know!"

"I'm trying not to think about that" the full figured radio operator admitted, as she scanned the length of Penelope's evening gown clad body. "You look <u>beautiful</u>, Penny!" she concluded.

"Thank you" her guest replied.

"Who are you trying to seduce, anyway?" asked Shiela, as she observed her new friend's breast cleavage briefly but approvingly.

"I have a date with the ship's second officer, Mr. Gordon, in twenty-five minutes" Penelope replied. "We'll be eating dinner together—<u>if</u> the food dispensers are still working."

"I'm beginning to wonder if <u>anything</u> will still be working!" Shiela exclaimed, as she observed with an odd expression the malfunctioning, wall mounted clock nearby. It was running alternately too fast and too slow as its hands performed a funny trip around its ten inches wide dial.

"I suppose I'd better start calling Lowellsville's radio station again" she said, as she forced herself to look away from the amusing antics of the old fashioned, analog time piece. Then she resumed calling her way up the frequencies. On the final channel (which Shiela had never used before because it was so new) she and Penelope heard a female voice saying "Mey bahn Velahnee riefah yaywah een Volahris. Ahblay ku hey mah? Hyoo-mons mok deyku mey sopra. Reypla bayna. Ahbo."*4 The message was repeated five times, interspersed with static. Then it ceased.

"<u>What</u> language was <u>that</u>?!" Penney asked her red haired, green eyed friend (who was an inch taller than she was).

"I don't know—I've never heard it before" Shiela replied. "Whoever she was, she sounded really worried."

"So am I "Penelope admitted. "What is wrong with the lights—and why is that clock acting so crazy?!"

Suddenly everything returned to normal. Only a faint sound of static came from the radio.

Shiela smiled slightly with relief and remarked "It must have been a large, electromagnetic energy field causing the problem. Maybe a vessel with an ion engine passed near us."

"Who would be headed for Mars at the same time we are?!" Penelope asked incredulously. "I thought interplanetary vessels were supposed to be rare!"

"I don't know! This whole incident is a mystery to me" Shiela replied. Then she returned her attention to the radio.

"Unknown station, this is the interplanetary vessel *Wernher von Braun* responding to your message" said Shiela "<u>Who</u> are you and <u>where</u> is your station? Over." For a few seconds there was no reply, then a masculine voice said "This is supervisory and guardian robot Vekrin of the *Old Sea Facility* calling the interplanetary vessel *Wernher von Braun*. Is the female being who is speaking to me by radio a hyoo-mon? Over."

"I was the last time I checked" Shiela replied humorously. "Over."

"I must say that I have found you hyoo-mons to be dangerous and aggravating creatures" said Vekrin. "Two members of your species invaded my home base recently and damaged me with an energy pistol. Fortunately another robot was able to repair me, but I am not eager to be visited by any more of you. Over."

"Please excuse my verbal intrusion" said another masculine voice. "My name is William Schaefer and I am the manager of the water drilling project at William's Bluff on the Old Sea's floor. I know the two people who visited your underground home recently and I do not believe that they went there with the intention of harming anyone. The laser fight was probably due to a misunderstanding of some sort. Over."

"Well, your associates' 'misunderstanding' cost me an eye temporarily!" the robot exclaimed. "Moreover they came here uninvited. There was no attempt to communicate with us first and ask for our permission. Over."

"They—and I—were not certain that your base was still inhabited" William explained. "Why have you been so secretive? You must have known we were here. Over."

"Yes, we knew about you" said the robot," but we did not know your intentions toward us. At the present time your species outnumbers that of my designers on Mahta Yahm*[5], the planet that you call 'Mars'. Over."

"May we speak with one of your designers?" asked Shiela. "Over."

"They are presently indisposed" Vekrin replied, "so I am having this conversation for them as their representative. Over."

"Were you—or they—deliberately interfering with our electronic devices recently?" asked a woman's voice. "My name is Barbara and I am William's friend. Over."

"Certainly not!" Vekrin exclaimed emphatically. "Our subspace transmission was not even intended for your people! My mistress was calling her people in what your species refers to as 'the Beta Centauri system.' We did not realize that you hyoo-mons were capable of receiving her message, much less that it would cause any problems for you! Over."

"Ten years ago our radios could probably not have operated on that frequency" said Barbara, "—but anyway, I am glad that those electrical problems of ours were not the results of an attack by you. Over."

"It was more like _five_ years ago!" William whispered to her. "We didn't even have a use for this frequency until today!"

"I know" Barbara whispered in reply. "I just didn't want him to think we were primitive compared to him—even if we were!"

"Good idea" her companion remarked quietly (with a smile to emphasize his approval).

Meanwhile Shiela had begun speaking through her radio: "I'm glad to hear your denial too. I'll tell my superiors that the interference was only an accident. Interplanetary vessel *Wernher von Braun* out."

Shiela glanced at her well shielded astronaut's battery powered watch and said" You should be on your way to your romantic appointment, Penney. You mustn't keep our second officer waiting—especially if this is your first date with him."

"Oh! I forgot about that!" Penelope exclaimed. I really must be going! Thank you for reminding me."

"You're welcome" Shiela replied, as she watched Penney rising to a standing position. "Now you and Tom will have something interesting to discuss over dinner—besides your physical appearance."

"Do you really think that was an alien robot talking on the radio a minute ago?" asked Penney.

"Shiela laughed and replied "Probably not. Those Mars colonists like to play tricks on visitors. Those six jokers in Phoobos Base are especially mischievous I suppose they have too little else to do between ships' arrivals."

*(4) In the Kotterbrocki language this means: "I am Vellani Ferbratta. Calling anyone in space transit. "Can you hear me? Humans may find me soon! Reply please. Over."

*(5) "Mahta Yahm" translates as "Our World," a name for Mars used by its Kotterbrocki inhabitants. Kotterbrocki from other planets and moons call it "Rahz Plavin"—"Red Planet."

Chapter Twelve
Angry Mister Morris

Still Monday Evening

". . . I have other duties to perform now" said Vekrin. I suggest that you hyoo-mons call us before you come to visit our base again. Old Sea Base out."

"Message understood. William's Bluff Community out" William replied.

"This is amazing!" Barbara exclaimed. "We've been having a conversation with an alien!"

"Yeah, it'll be something to tell your grandchildren about someday" said William, as he hugged her happily. "I think I'll call Mike and Sandra. They'll be interested in hearing about this and the technicians seem to have our new telephone system debugged now."

"I hope so" Barbara replied. "The radio can be so difficult to use during these big storms! I feel cut off from the world then."

"Oh, a little isolation is not such a bad thing" Bill teased, before he kissed her face playfully. Anyway, I can think of some interesting things to do to pass the time while no-one else is here."

Barbara laughed and said "I suppose isolation does have <u>some advantages</u>."

Suddenly the telephone in Bill's office rang. He reluctantly stopped fondling Barbara and went to his desk. There he picked up the handset and seated himself in his office chair.

"Hello" he answered, "William's Bluff Community here. This is Bill Schaefer speaking."

"This new system does work!" a familiar sounding female voice exclaimed. "I just wanted to tell you that Mike and I have arrived safely in the Lowellsville Biology Lab with our fossil discoveries."

"It's good to hear your voice, Sandra" said Bill, as Barbara reached toward the *Speaker* button on the telephone's base/cradle. William nodded, so she pushed it.

"Mike and I are with my coworker, Louisa, and the two fossils that we found this morning are being examined by all of us now" said Sophia Sandra's voice from the little speaker grid.

"These are really exciting specimens, Mister Schaefer!" exclaimed a female voice that he and Barbara assumed was Louisa's. "One of them is like a horseshoe crab with pincers. No native life form this complicated has ever been found on Mars before!"

"I'm glad you have something interesting to study" Bill remarked with a smirk. "We have some news for you too!" Then he made a head gesture from Barbara's direction toward the telephone's base set.

"You three will never guess who we talked with by radio a few minutes ago" Barbara said into the telephone.

"Was it Ray Bradbury's estate manager authorizing you to write a sequel to *The Martian Chronicles*?" Michael's voice teased from the telephone.

"Nothing that exciting!" William teased back, "—but we did have a conference call by ultra high frequency with a couple of women aboard the *Wernher von Braun* and with the robot who wounded Sandra! He said you must call him first by radio before you visit him again."

"Yeah—and wear a suit of armor!" Sandra's alto voice teased from the treble speaker. "His hospitality leaves a lot to be desired!"

"He wasn't too happy about Mike shooting off one of his eye stalks" William remarked wryly. "He suggested that you two adventurers should leave your arsenal at home next time."

"Maybe all of you should meet on neutral ground until you learn to trust each other" Barbara suggested, "—and leave the weapons at home!"

"Those are probably good ideas" Michael agreed. You should have worked for the State Department, Barbara."

"I agree with both of you" said Bill. "I also suggest that all of us meet with that robot and his mistress here in the William's Bluff Community. Perhaps in the dining module."

"Did you say 'his mistress'?!" Michael exclaimed, "—such as a real person?"

"That's right" Bill replied. "She was sending a subspace message to her people in the Beta Centauri System and her transmitter wreaked havoc with everything electronic both here and aboard the *von Braun*—even though the ship is still far out in space."

"Did her transmitter cause any <u>lasting damage?</u>"_Michael asked worriedly. "We need the supplies aboard that vessel—and I don't want to lose any of our people either—especially you, Robert and Barbara."

"We're safe enough" Barbara assured him, "—but would you please tell me what <u>time</u> it is now? All of our clocks went crazy for a while."

"Yeah, even my watch is looney!" exclaimed Bill.

"It's six oh eight PM" Michael informed them.

"Thanks" said Barbara. She then went to the nearest clock to reset it.

"You're welcome" Michael replied. "Has the *von Braun* recovered from the accidental electronic assault too?"

"They <u>seem</u> to be <u>okay</u>" William assured him. 'I hope' he added mentally. "Uh, Mike, you might be receiving an irate 'phone call from Chief Administrator Morris soon about that laser fight with the robot. I spoke with the C.A. about twenty minutes ago and he was really steamed up, so be on your best behavior for a while."

"All right—thanks for the warning" Michael replied.

"Uh, Mister Edwards, he's here <u>now!</u>" said Louisa worriedly, from the doorway of the laboratory room.

"Hmm. Maybe I'd better hang up now, Bill" said Michael. "I don't want your 'phone to melt on your hand."

"Okay" Bill replied. "Good luck."

"Thanks—I'll need it" said Michael. He then turned off the base speaker of the laboratory's main telephone.

Chapter Thirteen
A Meeting With The Chief

Still Monday Evening

"I wonder if it's too late to get a reassignment to Luna?" Sophia whispered, as Louisa's short legged form arrived in the specimen examination area. Close behind the plain faced xenobiologist was an angry looking Chief Administrator.

"There you are, Mister Edwards!" exclaimed their distinguished visitor. "What sort of devilry did you and Miss Collins do inside that alien base today? Start a war?!"

"Almost, sir" Michael replied contritely, as he rose to a standing position and Sophia followed his example. "But Bill Schaefer just called and told us that he had a radio conversation with the alien robot and ended the crisis" ('I hope!' he added mentally). "It was all just a misunderstanding."

"For your sake I hope so" the Chief Administrator replied, "—otherwise you and Miss Collins will be going to new jobs in Phobos Base soon. It's bad enough that China and Taiwan are threatening to go to war with each other and drag the U.S.N.A. into it; without you and that robot starting an interplanetary crisis here! I want to know exactly what happened." As he spoke the C.A. seated himself on a barstool that Sophia had used earlier. Michael motioned for Sophia to use his stool, while he remained standing. Louisa went to the front room of the Biology Department and brought back an office chair. She offered it to Michael, but he declined, so she seated herself in it.

"All right, Mr. Edwards, we're ready to hear your story" Mr. Morris told him.

"Well, sir, "said Michael, "Sophia and I were searching for fossils this morning along an ancient creek bed about three miles to the northeast of here. We got a radio call from Bill Schaefer late in the morning inviting us to come to his drilling outpost to examine some interesting ground penetrating radar images that he had recently gotten there. He said that they would prove there had been some non-U.S.N.A. group seeking good drinking water in that area before his team arrived. So Sophia and I went out there in the middle of the day and saw radar images in the office trailer of what appeared to be a pipe that led from a place near Bill's drilling rig to the big hill known as William's Bluff. The pipe appeared to slope upward toward the bluff, so some of Bill's drillers dug a hole next to the foot of the hill and uncovered an actual, insulated water pipe that entered the hill mass there."

"That must have been an exciting discovery!" Louisa remarked.

"It was" Michael replied, "because I had been skeptical about it until then." He glanced at the plain faced, bespectacled young woman before he resumed his narrative. Louisa seemed spell bound by his account, and even Mr. Morris sat quietly while he listened raptly.

"We—meaning Sophia, Bill and I—decided to walk around the base of the bluff so we could see if there was an entrance to a foreign base there." Michael resumed. "I, at least, was still thinking in terms of some unpublicized group from Earth tunneling inside the hill-perhaps as part of an old mining operation. Anyway, Bill explored in a clockwise direction while Sophia and I walked on a counter-clockwise course.

"As it turned out, Bill did not go far. He became interested in a long, horizontal gouge in the eastern face of the main hill mass. When he climbed up to it he found marks in a rock face that appeared to have been made by machinery. Sophia and I could not communicate with him then, because of the intervening hill mass. So we continued walking and found nothing unusual along the way. We eventually rounded the place where the hill angled sharply toward the east, like the lower part of a big 'L'. Bill in the meantime walked southeastward toward the eastern-most end of the secondary ridege He wanted to meet us there and tell us what he had found He gave little attention to the rest of the hill."

"That sounds foolish" Louisa commented. I would have scanned every foot of its slopes."

"We would have done that too" Sophia replied, "But his remaining air supply was smaller than ours. We didn't know about his concern for it until later."

"In any case, Sophia and I walked to the far end of the hill and when we rounded it, we saw Bill hurrying toward us cross country" said Michael. "He soon told us by suit radio about the artificial ledge he had found, gouged out of the northern ridge and of his preoccupation with some tool marks in the rocks there. We told him that we had seen no signs of any digging operations on the western or southern slopes of the hill, but we wanted to see what he had found. He admitted to us then that he needed to hurry back to the trailer community because his air supply was low. We reluctantly agreed to accompany him and leave exploring the rest of the hill until the following Wednesday, when all of us could do it together. We did scan the slopes from a distance, though, and saw the debris of a landslide in the crook of the 'L.' We also saw what appeared to be the lower end of a ravine that had been gouged out by water action long ago. All of us wanted to have a closer look at those places later, but Sophia and I decided that we would spend this afternoon fossil hunting where we had found two specimens that morning. Bill told us that he needed to resume supervising the water drilling project after lunch. So we all went to the dining trailer and ate lunch together. Afterward, Sophia and I drove away westward in Mars Car Four while the drillers went back to their work. I'll let her tell you what happened next."

"All right" said Sophia. "I was driving and we went as far westward along the road as the place where it crosses the old, dry riverbed. I then got the idea of exploring the ravine in the eastern part of the hill, instead of returning to where we had been that morning. I thought we might find some fossils in the ravine and if we were really lucky we might even see some aliens there. So I took us onto the old river bed, then we followed it and a tributary stream bed back to the eastern side of the hill."

"What did Mr. Andrews have to say about that course reversal?" asked the Chief Administrator.

"She talked me into it" Michael replied, "—sort of like Eve offering the apple to Adam, I suppose. Anyway, I secretly wanted to go back to the hill, although I had told Bill that we would wait until Wednesday and search the eastern slopes with him accompanying us."

"And <u>men</u> say <u>we're</u> duplicitous!" Louisa muttered (only half in jest).

"<u>Anyway</u>" said Sophia, "we went back to the ravine and explored it on foot. We found some recently made tire tracks about halfway up it. Mike told me that they did not look like they were made by any of the vehicles from Lowellsville. We were <u>really</u> hoping to see aliens after that—or at least, some European astronauts. We could see that the ravine widened ahead of us, so Mike sent me back down it to get the Mars car. "He believed that we would be able to turn it around safely if we needed to leave the ravine in a hurry."

"Had you seen any sign of the aliens themselves yet?" asked Mr. Morris (who was beginning to enjoy the story enough to calm his mood some).

"No" Sophia replied, "—just the tire tracks, "—but there was no reason for us to expect a hostile reception at that point. We were both curious to see what sort of beings they were. Mike, would you like to continue the story?"

"All right" he replied. Meanwhile, Sophia looked at the Chief Administrator appraisingly. She decided that Daniel Morris was not impressive to look at—he was only about five feet, seven inches in height and average in build. He had light brown hair and hazel colored eyes. There was a small moustache on his upper lip and his voice was in the tenor range. Sophia thought he looked more like a new car salesman than the leader of a group of scientists, engineers and explorers.

Michael knew better than to judge the man by his appearance, though. He was aware that Daniel Morris had the courage and tenacity of a terrier when he was solving a difficult problem.

"While Sophia went down the ravine to get the car, I walked up the defile to a place where it entered a natural basin" Michael began.

"Weren't you afraid of being ambushed while you were *zehr* alone?" asked Louisa, with her slight French accent sounding stronger than usual, due to her rising excitement. Sophia knew that her friend had a French mother and an American father. The latter had brought his young family from Europe to the then United States of America when Louisa was only five years old. The child had continued to learn the French language, though (mostly from her mother, Adrienne). Her father, Marcel d'Alsace, was a first generation American and a moderately successful diplomat who worked for the State Department. His parents had been French émigrés to the old U.S.A., before it had absorbed most of the Canadian provinces to become the U.S.N.A. in 2026.

"I was slightly worried, but I still thought at that time that the 'aliens' would turn out to be from the European Union or Japan, rather than being members of another intelligent species" Michael replied to Louisa's question. "Any way, I soon noticed an air lock's door set in the right wall of the basin. I knew I had about twenty minutes to spend before Sophia returned with 'our' car, so I decided to try to open the door."

"Don't you think now—with the benefit of hindsight—that you should have informed me of the existence of that base you found, before you decided to go in there uninvited?" Mr. Morris asked diplomatically. Michael noticed that his earlier anger seemed to have abated to annoyance.

"Yes, sir, I probably should have done that "Michael conceded. "I let my curiosity overcome my caution."

"You certainly did!" the Chief Administrator remarked, "—but continue your story."

"Well, sir, since the airlock's controls were marked with pictographs I was able to deduce quickly how they functioned. I opened its door and cycled through it" said Michael. "Incidentally, those airlock doors slid open and the aliens' air pump was quieter than our design is. We could learn some things from them about airlock designing."

"I'll make a note of that" the C.A. replied. Louisa left her chair and went into the office room in the front part of the biology department. She returned a minute later with two pieces of paper and a writing pen on a clipboard. She handed these items to Mr. Morris (who murmured "Thank you"), then she returned to her chair.

"What did you find beyond that smoothly functioning airlock, Mr. Edwards?" Daniel asked in a more normal tone of voice.

"A locker room, sir" Michael replied. "There were six lockers built into its walls and in two of them I found space suits. Both resembled our suits, but they were more flexible and they were designed for people who were about a foot taller than us. Each of them also had four arms on it."

"Four arms?!" Mr. Morris exclaimed. "Those people really are aliens! But go on—what happened next?"

"Well, I also found some photographs in one of the six lockers" Michael replied, as he reached into a pocket of his coverall garment and pulled out four pictures. Louisa left her seat and stepped closer to Mr. Morris so she could look over one of his shoulders. Michael placed the items on the counter top where both people could see them.

"I was surprised to see that the woman in this photograph had green skin—just like the old stories about Martians!" Michael remarked humorously, as he pointed to one of the four strange photographs.

"Her skin might not be green" Louisa suggested politely.

"Oh? Why do you say that?" asked Michael, with a mixture of humor and annoyance in his voice and facial expression.

"We're looking at her face through a golden yellow face plate, like the ones we use to filter out harmful radiation" Louisa explained. "The face behind her radiation filter could be light blue."

"Hmm, I never thought of that" Michael said thoughtfully.

"It makes sense!" Sophia remarked. Blue plus yellow makes green."

Suddenly the telephone rang in the office and Louisa went to answer it. She returned less than a minute later with the cordless handset. "It's for you, Mister Morris" she announced. She then handed the telephone to him as he stood up to receive it.

"Thank you" he replied, as Louisa returned to her seat.

"Mister Morris, this is Cesar Guerrero" said a man's voice from the handset. "I'm Lowellsville's substitute radio operator for this shift and I have a radio/telephone call for you from Anne Jordan. She's the First Officer of the *Wernher von Braun.*"

"All right" said Daniel, as he seated himself again. "Put her on the line, please."

"Before I do, sir, please remember to say 'over' when you want to change from talking mode to listening mode and 'out' when you want to end the conversation" said Cesar.

"I'll remember" said the C.A., with a trace of annoyance in his voice.

"Go ahead, Miss Jordan. Mr. Morris is ready to take the call, over" said Cesar's voice from the telephone.

"Hello, Mr. Morris. I'm glad we have a good connection" said an attractive, alto voice. "We had some troublesome radio interference for about ten minutes. It apparently originated near Lowellsville and it was so strong it interfered with almost everything aboard our vessel. Over."

"I'm sorry to hear that" Mr. Morris replied. "I hope that it did not damage your navigation computer. Over."

"No. Fortunately the computer is well shielded" Anne replied. "We've needed to reset most of our clocks, though (with some help from Cesar). Over."

"I presume you'll be arriving on schedule at Phobos then" said Mr. Morris. "Over."

"Yes, but we'll only have five passengers transferring to the Mars shuttle this time. The two Korean scientists and the Swede cancelled their reservations with us and sought transportation to Luna instead" Anne explained. "They might regret it soon, though, if we really did get a call from an alien robot today, as our radio operator claims. Have you found any evidence of an alien civilization on the red planet? Over."

"We certainly have!" Mr. Morris replied proudly. "Two of our scientists have met that robot who called you! He regarded them as intruders in his home, apparently, but I hope to arrange a friendlier meeting—perhaps on neutral ground—with at least one of the people who built him. Over."

"Wow! I wish I could be there to see that event" Anne exclaimed. "Some lucky humans will get a chance to make history. Over."

I'll ask the aliens to let us make some photographs of them" Mr. Morris promised, "—but we already know that they have either light green or light blue skin and they are generally humanoid in shape. They also have four arms! A little photograph that one of our people obtained recently of one of them wearing a space suit shows that to us—and Cesar, if you are eavesdropping, <u>none</u> of what you are hearing is to be repeated to <u>anyone</u> or I'll have you vacuuming Mars dust off of space suits for a month. Over."

"Understood, sir" Cesar's voice replied from the 'phone. "I must listen, though, to know when to switch from 'transmit' mode to' receive.' I'll be quiet now."

"Good" said the Chief Administrator. "Miss Jordan, I'd like to know who your remaining passengers are, over."

"There's a television reporter named Penelope Carter" Anne replied, "—and her cameraman, Marvin Showalter; a structural archaeologist from Austria named Hans Gerhardt; a Japanese born chemist named Mieko Kurosawa who works for NASA; and a drone aircraft expert named Douglas Bell. The latter has what look like two big model airplanes with him—and a lot of spare parts! He took advantage of two other passengers' cancellations to bring the extra drone with him. Over."

"Good. You may bring everyone but the two reporters to us, then put sedatives in their soda pop and take them back to Earth—just kidding" said Daniel. "We don't need any trouble with the networks. They might complain to their friends in Washington and cause our budget to be cut again by the congress. Over."

"Understood!" the First Officer remarked humorously. "Our company doesn't need any bad publicity either. I must go back to work now, so I'll say a temporary good bye. *I.S. Wernher von Braun* out."*(6)

"Lowellville administrator out" said Mister Morris. Then he turned toward Luisa and remarked "I'm glad that the North American Space Agency and the Interplanetary Transport Service are paying for that call! Otherwise Miss Jordan would owe a month's pay for it!" As he spoke he turned off the telephone's *Talk* function and returned the handset to Louisa.

Mister Morris turned toward Michael and said "That was the *Wernher von Braun's* first officer. She said that they had some electronic problems aboard their ship recently but that they could be corrected. She also said that they had a passenger named Douglas Bell who was bringing a couple of drone aircraft with him to help us explore this planet."

"Hallelujah!" Michael exclaimed enthusiastically. "He's probably the leading expert on drone technology in the entire solar system! Now we can finally explore the Cydonia region and learn for certain what is there."

At this point Sophia's digestive tract made some growling and squirting sounds. "Oops! Excuse me. I think it's been too long since I ate lunch!" she exclaimed humorously.

"I think we're all becoming hungry" said Mr. Morris. "Let me hear a condensed version of how you and Michael met the robot, then we will all head for the food dispensers."

"You tell him, Mike. You've done a good job so far" said Sophia.

Michael nodded, then said "Well, sir, after Sophia and I finished snooping through the aliens' lockers and she had finished photographing their contents, we decided to explore a little further into their base. So we left the locker room and entered a hallway that curved back toward the ravine which we had climbed earlier. We found an alcove which had a little window in it and some devices of unknown purposes. We saw alien symbols on their read-out screens, but we could only guess at what they meant."

"Did they perhaps resemble the writing on some of the debris from that alien base on Luna?" asked Mr. Morris.

"Now that you mention it, I believe they did!" Michael replied thoughtfully. "It could have been the same language in both cases."

"I wish we could ask those four armed aliens about that Lunar base" said Sophia. "They could tell us for certain."

"We'll do that when the weather improves" said Mr. Morris. "Anyway, what happened next in that William's Bluff Complex?"

"Sophia and I heard mechanical sounding footsteps, so we drew our laser pistols as a precaution" Michael replied. "The aliens had not tried to communicate with us, so we did not know how they would react to our presence in their base. Anyway, we saw a mechanical arm protrude beyond the bend of the corridor and as soon as we saw it was holding an energy beam weapon, we began firing at its body as that came into view. Its torso was made of a shiny metal that our laser beams could not penetrate, so I soon aimed for its bubble-like head. I heard Sophia yelp with pain, so I knew she had been hit. I fired at a metal, 'T' shaped device that supported the robot's eyes and the right eye fell off. The robot retreated deep into the complex, then Sophia and I returned to the locker room. You talk for a while, honey. My throat is dry." Sophia nodded and Michael took a plastic cup to a nearby bathroom to get some water.

"My left arm was wounded, but fortunately the wound was shallow" said Sophia. "I told Mike that I could use my right hand to cover the hole in my suit while we hurried to the car, so he picked up the aliens' photographs and put them into a pouch, then we put on our helmets. Afterward we retreated to the airlock and cycled through it. When we walked quickly to the car the aliens did not pursue us, so that was the end of the encounter. Mike drove us to the well drillers' community and we hosted William for a while in 'our' vehicle. We told him what had happened to us since we left him earlier in the day. He was annoyed that we had not waited until Wednesday to explore the hill, but he was a good sport about it after we showed the aliens' pictures to him. He left the car then to help his men cap the well and we returned to Lowellsville ahead of the big dust storm. That's the end of the story."

By this time Michael had returned to his seat with the cup of water. "I think she told it well enough" he remarked, as his own stomach began growling.

"All right" said the Chief Administrator. "Let's go to the dining facility and eat some dinner. Don't anyone talk about the aliens while we are there. Let's keep their existence a secret for a while longer until we know more about them. Otherwise the television networks will be pestering us for information and we will not know what to tell them."

"That's a good idea, sir" said Michael. "It will avoid a lot of pointless speculating by the news media."

"I suppose we can keep the aliens' existence a secret for a few more days" said Sophia.,"-if no-one aboard the supply ship tells the networks about them."

"I told the *von Braun's* radio operator not to divulge my conversation with her to anyone unless I gave my consent" Said Mr. Morris.

"What about you, Louisa? Can you keep a secret?" asked Michael.

"Yes, Mister Andrews" she replied. "I don't want to start a network feeding frenzy either." Then she turned toward Daniel and asked "Would it be okay if I told NASA about the two fossils that he and Sandra found today? That would give the news media something to talk about for a week or so."

"Go ahead" the Chief Administrator replied. "Now let's go get some dinner."

"I'll call Bill Shaefer and ask him to keep his drillers minds off of aliens for a few days" said Michael, as he followed Mister Morris and Sophia out of the office and into the adjacent corridor. Louisa turned of the lights in the office and joined her colleagues in the hallway. The group walked along a series of corridors to a pair of elevator shafts and a stairwell. They decided to ride one of the elevators upward two levels and emerged from it into another hallway. Walking along it and parts of two more corridors finally brought them to the community's dining room.

Mr. Morris' group was glad to see that there were only three other people still in the big room. Everyone else had eaten already and departed. The two big viewing screens on the wall at the eastern end of the chamber would normally have provided scenes of the Martian desert to the east of Lowellsville and of the space port respectively, but now they were blank. The cameras that would have provided their images had been safely retracted into small niches with ceramic shutters to await the end of the storm.

The four late arrivals went to adjoining restrooms and washed their hands. The two women also took hair brushes from their purses and tidied their hair. Afterward everyone met at the food dispensers and keyed in their meal selections, which were paid for electronically via plastic debit cards that accessed each of the diner's computerized financial records. While the food was being microwave heated, each person got his or her utensils and a beverage in a plastic cup. Afterward the group seated themselves around a small, round table and waited for their food to be ready.

*(6) The prefix I.S. meaning "Interplanetary Ship" was used to distinguish the vessel from a planet—to-orbit shuttle. It also identified the *Wernher von Braun* as a commercial vessel owned by a corporation, rather than being owned and operated by a government agency such as N.A.S.A.

Chapter Fourteen
The Proposal

Mon. Evening, June 49th.

Before any of the microwave ovens could beep, Michael gathered his courage, left his chair and knelt on his left knee beside Sophia. Everyone in the room (especially Sophia) stopped talking and watched what he was doing.

"Sophia" he said, "I think you are the prettiest woman on Mars and I would feel like the luckiest man on this planet if you would consent to marry me."

"Of course I will!" she replied. "I was beginning to wonder if you would ever ask me!" She turned ninety degrees to her left, leaned forward and kissed his forehead. All of the spectators applauded. When the sound had nearly ceased, Daniel Morris asked "Well, you lovebirds, do you want a civil ceremony or a religious one?"

"Whatever Mike wants is okay with me" Sophia replied, as her paramour rose to a standing position.

"I'd like to have Pastor Boswell preside" Michael replied, "—although I'm sure you would do a good job sir."

"Thank you for your vote of confidence" Mr. Morris remarked with a smile. Then one of the microwave ovens beeped. Sophia saw it was hers and went to get her meal.

"There is a beautiful woman, Michel! You're a lucky man!" said the Chief Administrator.

"I know, sir" Michael replied. "She has a good personality too" he added, as he noticed Louisa frowning slightly. Another microwave oven beeped and Michael was relieved to see it was hers. As Louisa left the table,

Sophia returned, carrying her meal tray and utensils. Michael left his seat and pulled his fiancée's chair back for her. She sat down as he pushed the chair under her bottom. "Thank you" she told him.

"You're welcome "he replied." Then his own oven beeped and he went to it.

"Louisa, will you be my bridesmaid?" Sophia asked, as her friend returned to the table. Daniel left his chair and pulled Louisa's seat back for her.

"I would be happy to do it" she replied, as she seated herself with the Chief administrator's help. "Just tell me the day." Then she thanked Mr. Morris as Michael returned to the table. Mr. Morris helped his tray carrying subordinate to seat himself, then he heard his own oven beep. He went to it and opened the door on the front of it, while Michael said a prayer of gratitude for their meals. Daniel waited until the prayer was completed, then he carried his meal tray to the utensil rack and got his tableware. Afterward he returned to the table, where Michael helped him to seat himself. The geologist was glad to see that the C.A.'s mood had improved greatly during the last half-hour.

"Thank you, Michael" said Mr. Morris. "I believe that you and Sophia will be an ideal couple. "When do you plan to have the ceremony?"

"I don't know, sir" Michael replied. By this time he was seated again, to Sophia's left and Daniel's right. "When do you want to do it, Sophia?"

"Well, I suppose there will be no need to wait until our families can be here" she replied humorously. "It's a long drive from Earth."

"Yes, and my parents don't happen to own a flying saucer" said Michael, just as humorously. "About all we can do for the people we know on Earth is to send television pictures of our wedding to someone at NASA who can put them on video discs and mail them to our parents. Our other relatives can make copies of the discs' recordings."

"I suppose that's the best we can do" said Sophia, with a trace of regret in her voice.

"You two should eat your food before it becomes too cold" Louisa coaxed.

"Good idea" Michael replied. "We can choose our wedding day after we eat."

The other three people in the room (who were seated around a different table) rose to leave and as they filed past the table where Michael's group was eating, each of them congratulated the two lovers. Michael recognized them as Erik Schonbaum, Karl Richter and Joe Standing Bear (who was a Cherokee Indian). Erik was Lowellsville's senior electrician and Karl Richter, who was his first cousin, worked with him as his assistant. Both men had emigrated to the U.S.N.A. from Germany when the Mars Base was still in an early planning stage. Their original home in Europe had been the city of Bonn, where Ludwig van Beethoven had been born. Like his nineteenth century hero, Erik was a skillful pianist, but Erik had never developed Beethoven's genius for composing. Also, whenever he had played for an audience larger than a few friends he had suffered from stage fright, so he had never become a concert pianist.

Joe Standing Bear had been born on the Cherokee Reservation in Western North Carolina. He was a lighting expert who was not afraid of heights. He was often seen working on a scaffold or a tall ladder where other people preferred not to be. Sophia knew who Erik was and she had heard him play Lowellsville's only piano—an expensive baby grand.

Erik, would you play some music for us during our wedding?" she asked hopefully, as he approached her at the rear end of his group's single file line.

"Foah you, liebchen, I vill do anything" Erik replied, "—but I hate to see dis guy take you out of suhculation." He then smiled to cause his statement to seem like a joke, but no-one in the room was entirely convinced.

When Erik and his companions had left the room, Michael's group resumed eating. At the end of their meal, Michael and Sophia decided to adjourn to his apartment's little living room to resume planning their wedding. Mr. Morris decided to go to the colony's meteorology Department and consult Patricia Franklin, the Chief Meteorologist, about the storm. Louisa decided that she wanted to study the two fossils which Michael and Sophia had found. So the four colleagues scattered, although the two lovers had first promised to inform their recent fellow diners about the day chosen for the wedding. In fact, the couple still had only vague ideas about its schedule themselves.

Michael and Sandra walked through a series of corridors to his apartment and went inside of it. The first room that they entered was the small living room. There they seated themselves close together on the couch and began discussing their wedding ideas.

"I really don't know what would be the best day for our wedding" said Sophia, "but I suppose it could be soon. There aren't a lot of relatives' work schedules and traveling times to consider."

"No, fortunately not" Michael agreed. "All of our coworkers' residences are conveniently close by and we only have one pastor to consider as a presiding official."

"I know we both like Pastor Boswell, so that's no problem" said Sophia. "What really baffles me is where will we go for our honey moon?"

"How about to a moon?" Michael suggested.

"A moon? Do you mean Phobos?" she asked.

"Exactly!" Michael replied. "There should be a Mars Shuttle supply flight going to Phobos soon after this storm ends. We could go along with it."

"That would be some place really different—and the view of Mars from there would be spectacular!" Sophia exclaimed. "Oh, Mike, that's a wonderful idea!" Then she kissed his face.

Michael Smiled and said "We can make the arrangements for it tomorrow."

Chapter Fifteen

Wedding Plans

Tues. Morning, June 50th.

By the next day Michael and Sophia had decided that they wanted to marry on Wednesday afternoon. The storm was expected to leave the area sometime Wednesday evening and the two lovers hoped to get another chance to visit the aliens' base when the weather cleared.

Michael had decided to ask Daniel Morris to be his best man. When the geologist visited the Offices of the Chief Administrator at about ten o'clock that morning, he found Daniel's pretty secretary, Linda Simmons, busily typing on her computer's keyboard in the outer office. Linda was about five feet, eight inches tall when she was standing. She was also slender and well groomed. Her hair was brownish blonde and her eyes were light gray. She wore a knee length dress and comfortable low heeled shoes. Michael was glad to see that the wearing of high heeled shoes with pointed front ends was finally ending among most women. This trend was caused by the most recent health warning that the U.S.N.A.'s Surgeon General had issued. It had described a host of foot problems that such shoes were causing for women.

"Good morning, Linda" Michael said cheerfully. "Is Mr. Morris available? I need to speak with him for a few minutes."

"I'll call him with the intercom and ask" she replied. She then picked up the handset of her desk top telephone and pushed two buttons on its base unit. "Sir, Michael Andrews is here. He wants to speak with you for a few minutes" she announced. After a few seconds Linda turned her office chair toward Michael and said pleasantly "Go ahead—he's waiting for you."

"Thank you" Michael replied, as he walked toward the connecting door between Linda's office and that of her boss. Then he reached outward and pushed it open.

"Good morning, Michael. I've been expecting you" said Mr. Morris, speaking from behind his expensive, real wooden desk (most of the furniture on Mars was made of aluminum alloy and/or plastic).

"Good morning to you too, sir" Michael replied, as he walked into the office and briefly admired a photograph of an attractive girl of about twelve years of age that stood on the Chief Administrator's desk.

"You really love your daughter, don't you sir?" asked Michael, before he seated himself in an arm chair in front of the desk.

"Yes, I do" Mr. Morris replied. "I loved her mother too, before that helicopter crash that took her from me."

Michael was familiar with the story. Caroline Morris had been a member of a statewide charity organization in Kentucky. At the age of twenty-seven she had been on her way from Lexington to Frankfurt to receive an award from the governor for her efforts on behalf of sick former energy company workers. The state owned helicopter in which she was riding had collided with a privately owned, twin engine air car that was flying above its authorized altitude. Everyone in both aircraft was killed (seven people in all). Daniel had been working in a NASA administrative job in Huntsville, Alabama at the time. He was about to watch the award presentation on a television news program when he saw instead that Caroline's over-due helicopter had crashed only five miles from its destination. The wreckage of the helicopter had fallen onto a soccer field near a school, but fortunately the field was not in use at the time.

Ever since the tragedy seven years ago, Daniel had devoted his time increasingly to his N.A.S.A. career while his wife's parents raised his daughter, Julia. Daniel had visited her during weekends until he was chosen to become Lowellsville's Assistant Administrator five years ago. Now he could only see and talk to her by way of videophone "conversations." These were awkward ways to communicate because of the ten minute time delay while the electronic signals traveled from one planet to the other.

"She's almost twelve now" said Daniel. "I made this 'portrait' of her by 'freezing' this image from one of her videophone messages, printing it onto high quality paper and having it framed with plastic that looks like wood. I asked her grandparents to send some more still photographs of her to me in real wooden frames. They should be aboard the *Wernher von Braun*."

"Sir, why don't you go back to Earth aboard the *von Braun*?" Michael suggested gently.

"Because Caroline's parents <u>don't</u> <u>want</u> me to return to Earth!" Daniel replied. They see Julia as a substitute for their daughter. Caroline came from a wealthy, respected family. They never really accepted me as one of them—and they can do much more for my daughter than I can. She can go to the best schools and marry a wealthy man." Then Daniel began to weep silently.

"Sir, I can see that I've come at a bad time for you" said Michael. "I can come back later."

"Yes, please! In about an hour" Daniel replied, "—and please! Don't tell anyone that you saw me like this!"

"I understand, sir. I won't tell anyone" Michael promised. Then he rose to a standing position and left the room. Then he quietly closed the door behind himself and told Linda "See to it that no-one disturbs him for the next hour. He's very busy." Linda nodded knowingly and replied "I'll make certain of it."

Michael smiled briefly and thought on his way out of the office suite: "A secretary like her is a priceless asset. He's lucky to have her.'

Chapter Sixteen
Wedding Preparations

Still Saturday Morning

Outside of the colony the Martian wind still shrieked and howled as it assaulted the rocky hill and the Plexiglas half dome with strong gusts carrying sand and pink dust.

Inside Lowell's Hill Michael sat in his office and thought about the incident in Mr. Morris' office. "I never realized before what a strain it is to be in charge of a community of thirty-seven adults and five children who are more than one hundred thirty-six million, four hundred thousand miles from Earth at this moment, according to the electronic astrometer on my desk top. Any wrong decision by a manager in this remote place could cost people their lives and end their hopes, their accomplishments—everything that makes them unique individuals. I don't know if I could cope with a job like that!

Michael thought about some of Lowellsville's history (particularly an incident that happened four years before he and Sophia arrived on Mars). 'Our previous chief executive officer returned to Earth as a nervous wreck six years ago, after two people were killed in a newly dug room. A volatile gas pocket seeped into it and exploded. The boss chose the location of that room because he liked the view from there! A tunnel digger warned him that a small gas deposit had been encountered nearby and advised against digging any further in that direction . . .'

Then the telephone on Michael's desk top rang. He picked up the handset and said: "Hello, Geology Department."

"Hello, Mike" Sophia's voice replied. "Did you ask Pastor Boswell to conduct our wedding ceremony tomorrow afternoon?"

"Not yet, honey. I must go see Mr. Morris soon" he replied. "Would you call Pastor Boswell instead, please?"

"Yes, I'll do that" Sophia promised. "I wish you could have Bill Schaefer as your best man, though. He would probably love to do it for you."

I wish I could have him here too" Michael replied, "but the storm will prevent that. You've heard the morning weather report, darling."

"Yes: 'strong winds and five to ten feet of visibility outside of Lowellsville today and tomorrow—uncertain for Wednesday'" she quoted gloomily, "'but probably bad.'"

"Exactly" said Michael. "So I'll ask Mr. Morris—and if he is not available I shall ask my fellow geologist, James Wilcox, to be my best man instead. I'm sure he would say 'yes.' In any case, we'll go to Lowellsville's best jewelry shop this afternoon at one o'clock to choose our wedding rings"

"You mean Lowellsville's only jewelry shop" Sophia remarked with a smile. "Lunch at noon as usual?"

"Yes. I'll meet you in front of the dining room's main entrance" said Michael. "Right now I see I have a call waiting."

"All right, I'll hang up now and call Reverend Boswell" said Sophia. "Good bye temporarily, dear."

"Bye" Michael replied, then he switched to the other call. "Hello, Geology Department."

"Hello, mike" said a familiar sounding male voice. "I heard you're about to marry Sandra. Congratulations."

"Thanks, Bill. We'll be doing it tomorrow afternoon. I wish you could be here" Michael replied diplomatically.

"Why so soon?" asked Bill. "Couldn't you wait until the weather improves?"

"Sophia and I want to visit the aliens' base then—if they will allow it" Michel explained.

"That's another reason why I called" Bill said cheerfully. "Barbara and I got a short range radio message this morning. Barbara recorded it so I will let her play it for you. Are you ready, dear?" Michael heard faintly her reply from another room. "I'm ready. Here it is." There was a click, then Michael heard the following conversation by radio:

"Hello William's Bluff trailer dwellers. This is Vellani Ferbrata. I heard that you and one of my robots had a brief skirmish. Over."

"You are mistaken about me—I wasn't there and neither was my er, my boss. However, two of our friends were involved. Bill can explain it to you better than I can—let me call him. Hey Bill! Come to the radio!" Barbara's voice shouted.

"I'm coming! Who is calling us?" Bill's voice replied faintly.

"One of the aliens—a woman!" Barbara replied loudly. "Vellani something. Hurry!"

A few seconds later Bill could be heard entering the radio room. After a few scrambling noises he could be heard speaking into the microphone: "Hello, Vellani, this is Bill Schaefer. Over."

"Your female employee told me that you knew the people who shot and injured my robot" said Vellani. "Can they be trusted not to damage it again?" There were some coughing sounds, then the word "Over."

"I'm sure it was all a mistake" Bill replied. "They thought he was about to shoot them—and he did slightly wound one of them. Over."

"Vekrin might have acted overly protective" Vellani conceded. "It would not be the first time. I should have been there myself to greet your friends, but my husband and I have been ill with a disease I believe originated on your planet. I have partly recovered from it" (coughing) "—but he is still very ill. He needs the aid of one of your human doctors. Over."

"Why do you think the illness is from Earth?" Bill asked (after some indignant prompting by Barbara in the back ground).

"Four weeks ago my husband found a robotic space probe from your world and brought it home to study it. I would not allow him to bring it beyond our vehicle maintenance area, so he took it apart there. Two weeks later he was sick and I was ill a week afterward." More coughing, then: "A medical robot has treated both of us, but our medicines have mostly been ineffective. Over."

"Let me talk with her. I've treated plenty of sick children" Barbara requested in the water project's office.

"All right" Bill replied skeptically.

"What are the symptoms of this illness?" she asked, as she received the microphone from Bill and settled into a chair beside him.

"Derron's forehead feels hot and he seems alternately hot and cold" Vellani replied. "We both feel weak and tired—constantly—is that the right word? Over."

"If you mean 'on all occasions', yes" Barbara replied. "These symptoms sound like influenza, although other things can cause them too. Bill and I have some medicines here that might help you—if we had any way to take them to you. As for a doctor, the nearest one is in Lowellsville, fifteen miles from here. There is no way to bring Doctor Hudson to you during this dust storm, though. Over."

"If I were not so sick I could go there in our 'Mars car'—as you call such vehicles (cough!)-and take my husband to him" said Vellani. "Our ground radar is much more advanced than yours is." Then she resumed coughing and her transmitted message stopped abruptly.

"That was all that we heard from her" said Bill. "She must have been too sick to continue."

"She probably pushed herself too hard and relapsed" Michael commented. "That's a common mistake among influenza sufferers."

"Well, at least we know now that she and her husband exist" said Bill. "Their base isn't just inhabited by robots."

Michael heard footsteps in the hallway in front of his office, then the door opened and Daniel Morris entered the room.

"Mister Morris!" Michael exclaimed happily. "You're just the man I wanted to see! Bill Schaefer and I have been talking by telephone. He and Barbara Waverly received a telephone call from an alien!" By this time Daniel had closed the door behind him and crossed the room to Michael's desk. Michael turned on his telephone's conference feature while his guest rolled a chair close to him and seated himself in it.

"Hello, this is Daniel Morris speaking. Did you two just receive a message from the aliens?" he inquired.

"Yes, sir!" Bill's voice replied from the conference speaker. "Barbara, play it back for him." She did so and afterward, Daniel exclaimed "Oh great! Now we have two sick aliens to worry about! All that we need right now is a flu epidemic to really complicate matters!"

"I'm willing to go visit them and try to cure them. I'll leave as soon as the weather will allow me to do it, sir" said Barbara's voice from the conference speaker.

"If you go, keep your space suit on and use the suit's speaker system to talk to them" Mr. Morris instructed. "Take some medicine to the aliens and we'll hope it cures them, but don't bring any germs to Lowellsville. "We can't afford to have everyone sick here."

"I understand, sir" Barbara replied respectfully. "Let me speak to Michael now, please."

"He is right here beside me" Daniel replied. "We're all on conference call."

"Hello, Barbara" Michael said cheerfully.

"Hello, Mike" she replied. "Is Sandra there?"

"No, just Mr. Morris and me" said Michael.

"Well, tell Sandra that I envy her" said Barbara. "Maybe one of these days Bill will make an honest woman out of me" she added teasingly.

"I think he should too" Michael agreed playfully. "Barbara, seriously, I don't think you should visit those aliens alone. Doctor Hudson and I should go with you."

"No way, Mike!" Daniel objected. "We can't afford to risk our only doctor to treat what could be an alien disease that is unknown to us! He might be killed or incapacitated by it—and you're about to become a married man. I don't want any serious illness for you either."

"He's right, Mike" said Barbara. "I can take a videophone with me and show the aliens' symptoms to Doctor Hudson that way. Besides which, my late husband was a doctor. I learned a lot about treating the flu and other common illnesses from him."

"This might <u>not</u> be <u>the flu</u>!" Michael protested. "It could be something that no human being knows how to cure!"

"In that case, it would be better to risk <u>me</u>, rather than <u>Dr. Hudson</u>" said Barbara. "Anyway, my decision has been made—so don't argue with me."

"All right" Michael replied reluctantly. "Good luck."

"Thank you" said Barbara. "Good luck with your marriage to Sandra. It's about time for some Lowellsvillians to start marrying each other and show some confidence in our future."

"Thank <u>you</u> "said Michael. He then turned toward Daniel and asked "Is there anything else that you want to say to Barbara or Bill, sir?"

"Yes" his guest replied. "How is everyone in our William's Bluff outpost faring during this big storm?"

"We had a scare yesterday when we thought our generator was failing" Bill's voice replied from the conference speaker. "When we learned that the aliens' radio transmitter was causing our electrical problems we complained to them about the interference. Since then our electrical devices have returned to their normal working condition."

"I'm glad to hear that" said the Chief Administrator.

"Robert is in the meal trailer taking care of things there" Bill continued. "He and I have been playing chess by way of our telephone land line to help pass the time."

"Who is winning?" Daniel asked with a tone of amusement.

"He's ahead three games to two so far, sir" Bill replied.

"Maybe you'll win the next one" said Daniel. "Mike wants to talk to me now about something , so I'll hang up. Call us if you hear anything from the aliens again."

"We will, sir. Good bye" Bill replied. Michael's group heard a dial tone, so Daniel turned off the telephone's conference function. Michael had already returned the hand held receiver to its rack, so the telephone became silent.

"Well, Mike, what do you think of their situation?" asked Daniel.

"I don't like it" Michael replied. "We don't know enough about those aliens' illness or their internal anatomy. Hell, we don't even know what foods they eat! How is Barbara supposed to heal them of a disease we can't even diagnose properly?!"

"I don't like it either" Daniel admitted, "—but we cannot risk our only doctor there. Barbara's idea of taking a videophone with her might not work, but a camcorder probably would. I would be willing to let one other person go with her to carry it, but I won't risk more people than that. We're way out on a limb here, Mike, and I won't risk anything sawing it off! Even with those new nuclear powered rockets, Earth is still about four months' traveling time away. By the time help arrives from there, we could all be dead from this unknown disease!"

"I <u>know</u> <u>that</u>, sir, and a disease organism that can survive Martian surface conditions frightens <u>me</u> too! We just don't know what sort of microbe it is! Hell, we don't even know if it's from Earth!"

"Well, <u>wherever</u> it <u>originated</u>, it must be <u>eliminated</u>!" Daniel stated emphatically. "I think I know the right person for the job."

"Who is that, sir?" Michael asked curiously.

"<u>Pamela</u> <u>Mason</u>" Daniel replied. "She's the resident nurse practitioner of Phobos Base. She was in the U.S.N.A.'s Army Medical Corps during the Great Middle East War when we fought the Iranians, their Syrian allies and the terrorist groups. I've seen her military file and it's impressive! I don't think any disease could frighten her after the war wounds and biological warfare effects she has seen."

"She does sound impressive, sir" Michael commented, but how will you persuade Warren Cox Smith to part with her? She's the only medical person he has."

"It'll only be a <u>temporary</u> <u>absence</u>" ('<u>I</u> <u>hope</u>' Daniel added mentally, "—and she's due for some muscular regeneration time in Mars' surface gravity conditions.

"Meanwhile, you and Sophia might consider a sort of working honeymoon on Phobos. Warren has been pestering me for a week or so to lend one of my geologists to him to do a mineral survey up there. He's hoping to find some more useful metal ores than his mining engineer has identified so far. As for Sophia, she could be your secretary. I've seen her office skills and she is a better office manager than you or me. She types faster than we do too."

"I know, sir" Michael replied. "I teased her once about her needing a water cooled keyboard, so the keys would not melt!"

Both men laughed, then Michael said "Sir, I'd like for you to be the best man during our wedding—if you could spare the time from your busy schedule."

"I'd be happy to do that for you" Daniel replied with a smile.

"Thank you, sir" Michel said gratefully.

"You're welcome" Daniel stated, "—and Mike, I want you to forget the incident in my office this morning. We all have our weak points and my relationship with my daughter is mine."

"What incident, sir?" asked Michael.

"Thanks, Mike—and you may call me 'Daniel' from now onward—when nobody else is with us—except Sandra."

"All right, sir—er, I mean Daniel" Michael agreed awkwardly.

"That's all right, Mike. It takes a while to end old habits. Have you and 'Sophia' talked with Pastor Boswell yet about the details of the wedding?"

"Sophia is talking to him this morning, sir—er, Daniel" Michael replied. "I'll confer with her during lunch about what they have tentatively planned—unless one of them calls me before then."

"Okay, just let me know as soon as you can when I will be needed" said Daniel. Then his expression became more somber. "By the way, Mike, there is something else I need to discuss with you. As you know, Roger Harris has been my assistant administrator since I was promoted six years ago, but last Friday Doctor Hudson diagnosed him to have a slow growing type of cancer that will require better treatment facilities than we have here. Roger has decided to return to Earth aboard the *von Braun* and he has asked me to accept his resignation from the assistant administrator's job as soon as I could find a replacement for him. I have agreed to do so and I am offering the job to you now. I realize this is a surprise, so I can wait a couple of days for you to consider my offer."

"I'm flattered, Daniel-I really am" Michael replied, "—but why choose a scientist like me? I haven't held any kind of elective office—except President of the Lowellsville Chess Club—more recently than my college days."

"I know, Mike, but I have been reviewing the records of several people recently and I prefer yours to anyone else's. You are a hard worker and you are calm in a crisis. You have managed our Geology Department well and you are devoted to the task of making Lowellsville a successful, permanent community. I like those qualities."

"Thank you, sir." Said Michael. "I appreciate your confidence in me—especially after that encounter with Vellani's security robot."

"Well, at least the damage that you did to him was repairable" Daniel teased, "—and his owner said he was sometimes overzealous about protecting her and her husband. What do you say, Mike? Do you want the job?"

"Yes, sir, I'll take it!" Michael replied, "—as long as it doesn't take up all of my time. "I'd still like to be a geologist part-time."

"I think that can be arranged" Daniel remarked with a smile. "I will ask Roger to delay his resignation until a week from today so you and Sandra can have a short honeymoon on Phobos before you begin the duties of your new office."

"Thank you, sir-Daniel, I mean" Michael replied awkwardly. "Wait until Sophia hears about this promotion!"

"I'll let <u>you</u> tell her about your new job" said Daniel. Meanwhile I'll go talk with Roger and arrange for him to fill in for you during the remainder of this week." As he spoke he rose to a standing position and Michael did the same.

"I'd like to send a radiogram to my parents on Earth to tell them about my new promotion" said Michael.

"Feel free to do so" Daniel replied. "I'll be going now. Let me know about your wedding plans as soon as you can."

"I'll do that" Michael promised. Then he followed Daniel out of the Chief Administrator's offices. Daniel went in search of Roger and Michael went to the geology laboratory to catalogue some rock samples that he had gathered during the previous week. Knowing what minerals they contained and where they were found was helping him and James Wilcox to map the natural resources of the region around Lowellsville.

A few minutes later James arrived in the laboratory and smiled happily. "Hello, Mike" he said as he seated himself beside his boss and placed a catalogue in front of him. "I got some refined gold from the metallurgist this morning. He's done good work with that gold dust that I found in the old creek bed where we were exploring last Wednesday morning. I can make a pair of wedding rings for you and Sandra as soon as you two choose their details."

James was a year younger than Michael's twenty-eight journeys around the sun. James was about five feet, seven inches in height, with blond hair and brown eyes. He had a small moustache and a generally attractive appearance. He was usually cheerful and Michael found him to be a pleasant, knowledgeable assistant.

"All right" Michael replied. "She and I will look at these pictures as soon as we can view them together. "It will probably be around midday. May we keep the catalogue for a few hours?"

"Sure" said James. "Oh, I almost forgot, I was talking with Mr. Morris in one of the corridors and he told me you'd had some more good fortune—besides Sandra accepting your proposal, you lucky guy!"

"Yeah, Daniel—as he wants me to call him now—was in here about four minutes ago. He wanted me to become Roger Harris' successor as the Assistant Administrator for the District of Lowellsville! I told him I would take the job" Michael modestly informed his friend.

"Congratulations!" James exclaimed. "He couldn't have made a better choice! Have you told San—er, Sophia, as you like to call her?"

"No, I'll wait until she and I are together during lunch" Michael replied. "Sophia is talking with Pastor Boswell this morning to arrange the details of our wedding. I may get a telephone call from her at any time."

"I'm happy for you Mike—even though Sophia has been the favorite fantasy woman of every man in Lowellsville—including me. I suppose it was inevitable that she would choose someone to marry eventually" said James. "Anyway, you had a head start on the rest of us because you and she both went to Duke and you entered NASA training together."

"Yes, as a twentieth century hero driver, Richard Petty, used to say: 'All I want when I go racing is an unfair advantage'" Michael joked.

James suddenly looked and sounded more serious as he inquired "Say, Mike, is it true that you and Sandra found an alien, underground base inside that big bluff fifteen miles east of here?"

"<u>Who</u> told you <u>that</u>?!" asked Michael, as he tried not to sound affirmative.

"A member of the well drilling team" James replied. He and I were playing Gin Rummy together recently."

"Was he drinking some of that bootleg wine I've heard about?" Michael asked (in his best Assistant Administrator's voice).

"No comment" James replied defensively.

Michael smiled and said "I rest my case. Anyway, you are still invited to my wedding—as soon as <u>I</u> know where and when it will occur."

"Thanks Mike. I'll be there" James promised. Then he and Michael returned to their routine geology work, while the storm continued to swirl dust eddies around Lowell's Hill.

Chapter Seventeen

Rumors of War

Still Tuesday Morning

A half-hour after his narrow escape from James' questioning, Michael heard the telephone near him ring. He picked up the handset and said his usual greeting: "Hello, Geology Department."

"Hello, Mike" Sophia's voice replied from the telephone. "I'm in Pastor Boswell's office and we need to discuss some things with you. Can you come up here now?"

"I suppose so" he replied. "I'll tell James where I'm going and leave him in charge here."

About five minutes later Michael walked into the Botany Office of the Biology Department. This was on a different floor than the latter's main office and as Michael approached the Head Botanist's desk he saw Sophia sitting in front of it in a light weight plastic and aluminum chair. She was wearing a short sleeved blouse and a pair of Bermuda shorts. An empty chair stood to the right of her.

The Reverend Joseph Boswell sat behind a wooden desk that had been imported from Earth (as had the office chair in which he sat). He was nervously trying not to glance at Sophia's attractive bosom or legs too often. Even her pretty face caused him to feel uneasy. "I feel like a long tailed cat in a room full of antique rocking chairs whenever she's near me" he thought self consciously.

Joseph was wearing his green botanist's coveralls with a small, brass cross suspended by a slender brass chain around his neck. He had dark brown hair, a face that was of average appearance and dark gray eyes.

"Hello, Mike" he greeted as he part-way rose from his chair, leaned across his desk and shook hands with the newly arrived Head Geologist. Joseph felt relieved of an awkward situation, now that he was no longer the only person in the room with the beautiful Sophia.

"Hello, Pastor Joe" Michael replied, then he seated himself in the vacant chair beside his fiancée. "Will you help us to 'tie the knot'?"

"I think so" said the clergy man with a smile. "I'm glad you could join us this morning, Mike. I've been talking with San—er, Sophia—about your desire to be married either tomorrow or the next day. That's rather sudden, don't you think?"

"Yes, pastor" Michael agreed, "but we would like to have the ceremony while our community's members are unable to wander around outside the bluff. That way we should have plenty of viewers on closed circuit TV." Michael smiled humorously, and then he added seriously "This should be a convenient opportunity for most of our friends to attend the ceremony—if they want to be there."

"Our fellow citizens do tend to scatter on various errands when the weather is good" Joseph agreed, as he steepled his fingers, with his elbows resting on the desktop. "Anyway, I'm glad that you and Sandra—as I prefer to call her—are asking for God's approval of your marriage."

"I just hope you won't get into trouble with your fellow Baptists for performing a ceremony for a couple of heathen Methodists" Michael teased.

"Oh, I think that we are far enough away from Earth for it to avoid their notice" the pastor replied, with a humorous smile, "—but my fellow N.C. State alumni may be annoyed that I joined together two Duke graduates."

"Yes, especially when our women's softball team is representing the conference going into the big tournament" Sophia teased.

"The Lord works in mysterious ways!" Joseph replied, as he glanced heavenward. "Anyway, will four o'clock tomorrow afternoon be soon enough for you two lovebirds to wed?"

"Yes" the couple replied in unison, with happy smiles and voices.

"Good" said the pastor. "We can have a rehearsal at two p.m. so everyone will know what to do. Will that be all right?" The couple assented.

"Fine" said Joseph. "Now I'm a bit curious. Where do you two plan to have your honeymoon—or should I ask?"

"It's all right to ask, pastor" Michael replied. "Chief Administrator Morris suggested several days on Phobos as a suitable honeymoon for his soon-to-be Assistant Administrator and I agreed."

"Oh Mike! That's wonderful!" Sophia exclaimed, as she leaned toward him to give him a hug and a kiss.

"Congratulations!" Reverend Boswell exclaimed, as he left his seat and came to where Michael was sitting. The two men shook hands while Sophia sat up straight again in her chair.

"I'll see you two tomorrow afternoon in the main conference room" said the pastor, "—provided that no-one has reserved it already. Let me do a computer check and I'll let you know by telephone in five minutes or so. Where May I telephone you?"

"We'll be in the lunch room" Michael replied. "Just leave a message on each of our email sites—unless you are feeling hungry, that is. Then he and Sophia left Joseph's office and went to Lowellsville's main dining room.

Meanwhile, Daniel Morris was in the radio room, from which he had temporarily ousted the daytime operator, Janet Hudson. Daniel knew how to use the big transceiver and he was soon talking with Warren Cox Smith, who was the Chief Administrator for the District of Phobos (and a favorite chess opponent).

"Hello, Warren. I have a favor to ask of you. Over" Daniel Began.

"How much do you want to borrow?" Warren teased. "Over."

"It's not money—it's Pamela Mason. I need her medical skills for about a week" Daniel replied. "Over."

"I'd rather lend you money, Dan" said Warren. "Seriously, you already have a doctor, so why do you need my nurse too? "Over."

"Some of my people have made a <u>great</u> discovery, Warren!" Daniel explained. "We have a couple of <u>sick</u> <u>aliens</u> <u>to treat</u>—we think they might have the flu and we need to treat them in their residence to reduce the risk of a pandemic in Lowellsville. Over."

"So! The rumor <u>is</u> <u>true</u>!" Warren exclaimed. "There is a native Martian intelligent species! Congratulations for your discovery. Over."

"Thank you, but I'm trying to keep it quiet for a while—I dread a flood of questions from Earth" Daniel explained. "Anyway, I will lend my best geologist and his pretty wife to you in exchange for Pam Mason's help to heal those two aliens. Over."

"What's the wife's specialty—besides looking pretty?" asked Warren. "Over."

"She's a xenobiologist" Daniel replied. "Over."

"I doubt we'll need that skill up here" said Warren. "The only <u>life</u> on this rock is <u>human</u>. Over."

"She's also a <u>fast typist</u>" said Daniel. "She can serve as her husband's secretary up there. Over."

"All right, <u>send</u> them <u>both</u> up—but what I really need right now is <u>a good plumber</u>!" Warren exclaimed. "This low gee system we have <u>isn't worth ten cents</u>! Over."

"I'll send Bob Harris with them when this awful weather leaves our area" said Daniel. "He can persuade <u>any kind</u> of plumbing system to function well! Over."

"That sounds good to me!" Warren enthused. "He will have plenty to do up here. Do you have your next chess move ready? Over."

"Yes, knight takes king's pawn" Daniel replied. "Over."

"I was afraid you would do that!" said Warren. "Knight to queen's bishop three. I need to go now. One of our cargo carrying robots is malfunctioning and we'll need him when the *von Braun* arrives. Phobos Base out."

"Lowellsville out" said Daniel. Then he turned the frequency dial back to the setting for William's Bluff (where it had been when he arrived in the radio room) and left the room. "It's all yours again" he told the regular radio operator (who was drinking canned apple juice in the corridor).

"Sir, why do you persist in trying to hide the truth about those aliens?" asked Janet (who was a small, slender, brown haired woman with gray eyes and a soprano voice). "The truth will come out eventually."

"Since you've overheard so much, come into the radio room with me and I'll try to explain it to you" Daniel replied. Janet reluctantly followed him into the room and closed the door most of the way behind herself.

The two people seated themselves in front of the table where two radios sat (one for short range and one for long range communication).

"Janet, <u>those aliens are sick</u> and I don't know what the disease is!" Daniel explained. I don't want a bunch of our people trying to visit them and by doing so bringing the disease back to Lowellsville. It could jeopardize our entire community!"

"I didn't realize that, sir" she replied shyly (with a worried expression on her moderately attractive face).

"Also" said Daniel, "when the news that there is a nonhuman, intelligent species on Mars reaches the Earth eventually, we won't have a moment of peace for six months afterward! Every scientist, reporter and politician will be pestering us for information and we actually know little about the aliens so far. I don't want to be reduced to the level of speculation just to give the reporters something to write about!"

"I understand, sir" said Janet. "I'll wait for you to choose the best time to tell the public about the aliens—but just from personal curiosity; do they look anything like us?"

"Their faces do and so do their arms and legs—but they each have four arms" Daniel replied. "The only picture I have seen of one of them reminded me of a multi-armed Hindu deity, but she was wearing a space suit, so I could only see her shape in general. No details were visible to me."

"Thank you for telling me sir—I've been very curious about those creatures. Do you think we'll have an opportunity to see one in person soon?" Janet asked in a tone of child-like wonder. She was only about five feet tall, so she was looking upward at an awkward angle to see Daniel's face. Her soprano voice added to the illusion of childhood.

"I honestly do not know" Daniel replied. "It will depend on how long they remain ill. We must rely on our medical people to advise us when a meeting with the aliens would be safe. I must attend to my duties now, so if you will excuse me, I'll be going."

"Of course, sir" Janet replied, as she watched him leave the room. 'What awful luck!' she added mentally. 'I've learned that there are intelligent aliens on Mars, but I'm not allowed to tell anyone about them!"

While Janet was fretting about her misfortune, Michael and Sophia were seating themselves in the community's main dining room, with their meal trays in front of them.

"Well dear, how did your morning go?" Michael asked pleasantly.

"It went well" Sophia replied. "Louisa has agreed to be my bridesmaid and Linda Simmons is preparing something special for me to wear."

"That's nice of her—especially since she's also taking care of two children and a secretary's job" Michael commented.

"Linda is a genuinely nice person" Sophia replied with a happy smile.

"James left a catalogue with me so we can choose our wedding rings from it" said Michael. "It's in my office now."

"Good" said Sophia. "We can look at it after lunch."

The two lovers began eating their meal, although they were interrupted several times during the next twenty minutes by well-wishers. After lunch Michael and Sophia walked to the Geology Department's office. They spent a pleasant half-hour choosing their wedding rings from the catalogue. Finally they showed their choices to James (who had been working in the nearby laboratory).

"I promise to have the rings molded and the gems mounted by the time of the wedding" James assured them. "Even if I must work through lunch tomorrow."

"Thanks, James-you're a real friend "said Michael. Sophia kissed James on his face, then she went to her own work place.

Chapter Eighteen
Phobosian Interlude

Still Tuesday Morning

On the small moon, Phobos (or to be more precise, <u>inside</u> <u>Phobos</u>) Pamela Mason walked into the robot repair chamber of the mostly underground base. Phobos Base was in its infancy, having been established only two years earlier. It was chronically understaffed, so every one of its six inhabitants had at least two jobs. Therefore Pam did not think it was unusual to see the base's Chief Administrator repairing a robot. The room was full of parts, tools and the odor of machine oil.

"You sent foah mih, chief?" asked Pam (who was from South Carolina and proud of it).

"Yes, I did" he replied, as he slid out from under a big, two legged robot with a partly disassembled left leg. While he rose to a standing position, Pam admired the five feet, nine inches tall repairman. He had a military haircut for his pale yellow hair and a pair of light blue eyes scanned the length of Pam's shapely figure. She had custom fitted her white, Medical Department coveralls and the upper front part of the garment had been left unvelcroed to reveal most of her breasts' cleavage. The two attractive objects were at the smaller end of the C cup range, but in the weak, artificial gravity of Phobos Base they stood outward proudly from her upper chest, without the need for a brassiere to support them.

Pam had curly black hair, a pretty face and emerald green eyes. Her height was only three inches less than Warren's was, but she was more slender in build and weighed about forty pounds less than he did.

"I have a special job for you, Pam" he informed her. "Let's go into the office and I will explain it to you."

"Okay" she replied, and then she followed him carefully across the c cluttered repair room. Both people move with little physical effort, in spite of the nickel weight augmentation plates in their shoes.

They entered the small office of the Machinery Repair Department and Pam closed the door behind them. Then they kissed each other's lips while Warren caressed her shapely bottom through her coveralls and thin panties. After about ten seconds their lips parted.

"Ah liked that assignment" Pam said with a mischievous smile. "What's the next one?"

"Pam, honey, what I am about to tell you is not to be repeated to anyone else in this base" Warren replied seriously.

"Okay, Ah won't tell anybody" Pam promised, with her own tone of voice becoming serious.

"Good" said Warren, "—because it would really anger Dan Morris if you did. We need to keep him happy, because until NASA headquarters sends some more people to help us, we must borrow even a master plumber from Lowellsville to keep Phobos Base's commodes functioning! Right now the U.S.N.A.'s government is taking funds away from the space agency to help pay for a weapons buildup to deter China from invading Taiwan. That situation could really become frightening because there are rumors that the Taiwanese have secretly built a small nuclear arsenal with the help of the Israelis. If that's true, we could see something similar to Israel's nuclear retaliation against Iran for that atomic bomb that the Iranians smuggled into Eilat's harbor and exploded there back in 2013. That—as you know—started the Great Middle East War and left Iran's economy crippled for two decades after that Jericho Two missile destroyed the Iranian's biggest oil refinery complex.

"Ah remember all of that" Pam assured him. "The Syrians decided to help Iran by usin' a missile with a Bubonic Plague wahhead to staht an epidemic in Tel Aviv and the Israeli's ayuh foahce responded by destoyin' the Syrians' ayuh foahce—mostlih on the ground. Then the new Iraqi Republic sent its ahmih into Damascus an'arrested Syria's dictatah foah sponsorin' terrorism in Iraq. A bunch of U.S. ahmih raynjuhs helped them to captyuh him an' put him on trial—befoah they hanged him! Ah knew some of those boys!"

"You have your facts straight" said Warren. "Later the U.S.A. and Great Britain invaded Iran and overthrew its government—after a lot of fighting. That war caused many grudges against us in the Moslem nations and resulted in more terrorist activity by various groups of jihadist fanatics. Today the U.S.<u>N</u>. A. and Great Britain are still hunting them."

"All kinds of compli-cay-shuns can result when even a small nucleah exchange occurs" Pam remarked, "—and evrih wah oah threat of wah results in NASA's budget bein' cut!"

"That seems to be the case" Warren agreed. "It's a wonder we <u>ever</u> reached Mars!—but anyway, some of Dan Morris' people have found some <u>sick</u> <u>aliens</u> somewhere on Mars and the Lowellsville medical staff needs your help to cure them! This mission could put your name into the history books eventually, so do your best, honey."

"Gee! Little ole <u>me</u> becomin' fay-<u>mous</u>?! Ah thought mah assign-ment ta Phobos Base was a one-way ticket to ob-scur-itih" Pam declared, in her best deep south accent.

Warren smiled with amusement and said "There will be a shuttle rocket coming up here in a couple of days to take you to Lowellsville's space port. Dan Morris will be loaning <u>three</u> <u>people</u> to me in exchange for <u>you</u>! That's how important you have become!"

"Ah do de-clayuh!" Pam exclaimed. "Thih-yus could become as excitin' as mah stint in I-ray-un durin' the big wah!"

While Pam was enjoying the idea of escaping from Phobos for a while, the matrimonial countdown was continuing in Lowellsville . . .

Chapter Nineteen
Wedding Gown and Bikini

Tuesday Afternoon

Michael and Sophia divided their Tuesday afternoon between doing their normal jobs and making various wedding preparations. They spent little time together until dinner—which they ate in the main dining room.

As they sat facing each other across a small, plastic table top, Sophia exclaimed "I heard an interesting item of news today!"

"Oh? What was it?" asked Michael (between bites of rare, made-on-Mars cornbread).

"My long-ago college friend, <u>Penelope Carter</u>, is coming to Mars!" Sophia announced excitedly. "I haven't seen her since she got that World Network News job four years ago—well, I have <u>seen</u> her, but only on television or a videophone screen. Now she's a passenger in the *Wernher von Braun*! I don't know how she was able to hide it from me for this long. I suppose she's been wanting to surprise me and she <u>certainly has</u>!"

"I'm happy for you, honey" said Michael (with little real emotion in his voice).

"Well, you don't sound like it" Sophia remarked. "What's wrong, Mike?"

"The *von Braun* is scheduled to arrive nine days from now" Michael replied. "After that, with a reporter snooping around this community, we won't be able to keep <u>any secrets</u>. I hope Dan Morris knows about her imminent arrival."

"He probably does" said Sophia, with a tone of annoyance in her voice. <u>Really, Mike</u>! Penny <u>doesn't snoop</u>! She's a <u>nice person</u>!"

"Yeah, so was Attila the Hun" Michael replied cynically. "Now I'll need to put locks on all of my filing cabinets."

"Ja, und puhaps ve should all begin using aliases instead uff owah real names" Karl Richter remarked humorously from a nearby table.

"Well!" Sophia exclaimed angrily. "Maybe I should dine <u>alone</u> tonight!" She then gripped both ends of her tray and pushed her chair back.

"I'm sorry, honey. Please stay" Michael coxed. "I shouldn't be so cynical. Your friend is probably all right."

"Just don't criticize someone you don't know!" Sophia exclaimed, as her anger slowly waned.

The two lovers finished eating their dinner with a minimum of conversation. Afterward they put their trays and utensils into an automated cleaning machine and left the dining room. As they entered an adjacent corridor, Michael asked "Would you like to go swimming—say around seven p.m.?"

"Oh, all right" Sophia replied reluctantly, "—but right now I want to go to my apartment and rest a little while."

"Okay. We'll meet beside the pool at seven" said Michael. He then kissed her face and added afterward "I'd better go talk to the second shift radio operator about something now." He walked with Sophia to the junction of two hallways, then they went their separate ways.

Michael walked to the radio room and found the door open. Thomas Saunders, who was the second shift radio operator, sat in his chair near the radios. He set down a sandwich as Michael approached him.

"Good evening, Tom" said Michael. "I have a request to make."

"Oh, hello, Mike" Tom replied, as he wiped some crumbs off of his lips. Michael saw a handsome young Canadian from Ontario. Tom had short, blond hair, blue eyes and a baritone voice.

Michael remember him being about five feet, ten inches in height when he was standing, but for the present he was relaxing with his feet propped up by an empty supply box.

"Have a seat" Tom invited cordially.

"Thanks" Michael replied, then he lowered himself into a low gravity type of aluminum and plastic chair.

"Tom, have you heard anything about a reporter named Penelope Carter?" Michael inquired.

"I sure have!" Tom replied enthusiastically. "A crew member of the *von Braun* told me today that she was aboard the ship. It'll be interesting to have a celebrity visiting us."

"I suppose so" Michael said without enthusiasm. "Are there any other reporters travelling aboard the *von Braun*?"

"None that I am aware of—but she does have <u>a</u> <u>cameraman</u> with her—or so I've been told" Tom replied helpfully.

"Well, in that case I'll be careful about my appearance when I meet her" Michael remarked humorously.

"Excuse me while I go close the door" Tom requested. Michael nodded and Tom went to the doorway. He leaned through it and peered in both directions along the corridor. He saw a woman enter another room about twenty feet away, after which the corridor was empty. Tom stepped back into the radio room and closed its door. The he returned to his chair.

"Michael is it true that you and Sandra Collins made some kind of important discovery recently?" asked Tom.

"Yes, it is" Michael replied (as calmly as he could pretend to be). "In fact we made <u>two</u> important discoveries. <u>Sophia</u> found an <u>arthropod</u> <u>fossil</u>—the first one ever discovered on Mars—and I learned that <u>I</u> will become the next <u>Assistant</u> <u>Administrator</u> of Mars' largest community! The <u>promotion</u> will happen in about <u>a</u> <u>week</u>."

"Oh" said Tom (with obvious disappointment). "I thought it was something else. Well anyway, congratulations for your promotion."

"Thank you" Michael replied. Now I must be going. Tune in to Sophia's and my wedding tomorrow at four p.m."

"I will sir—and congratulations for that as well. Sophia is a beautiful woman" Tom declared, as he forced himself to smile. 'You lucky bastard! Every man in Lowellsville wants to marry her!' he added mentally.

"Yes, she is lovely" Michael replied happily. By this time he was standing near the entrance of the room. He opened the door and stepped into the corridor. "Shall I leave this door open?" he asked.

"Yes, sir. Please do" Tom replied. "The heat from these radios causes the place to become uncomfortable sometimes."

So Michael walked away and left the door ajar. He went next to Daniel Morris' apartment where he rang the door bell. It was an old fashioned, two tone type and sounded pleasant. After a few seconds, the door opened and Daniel stood in the entrance.

Good evening, Michael" he greeted.

"Hello, sir" Michael replied, as he unintentionally reverted to an old habit of address. "May I come in?"

"Yes, please do" Daniel replied. He then stepped back from the doorway. Michael entered the living room and saw Lowellsville's Chief Meteorologist, Patricia Franklin, seated on the small couch.

"Hello, Michael" she greeted pleasantly as she rose to a standing position.

"Hello, Patricia" he replied just as pleasantly. Michael liked the attractive, five feet, four inches tall woman with medium brown hair and dark brown eyes. Her cheerful personality and generally accurate weather predictions had made her a popular person in Lowellsville.

"Have a seat, Mike" Daniel invited, as he motioned toward an armchair that faced the couch in the narrow—but cozy—little room. Michael accepted the offer and enjoyed the view of Patricia's shapely legs as she seated herself along with Daniel on the couch.

Patricia was wearing a knee length, sleeveless dress that outlined her body's shape without revealing too much of her pale complicated skin. A rising rate of skin cancer during recent decades had caused many North American women to dress more modestly during this fifth decade of the twenty-first century. Some women continued the habit on Mars (although they spent much of their time underground now).

"Pat and I have been talking about your wedding tomorrow-among other things" Daniel remarked. "How are your preparations going?"

"Well enough so far, sir" Michael replied, "—but Sophia told me that she learned today about a famous television reporter and her cameraman being aboard the *Wernher von Braun*. I wondered if you knew anything about them?

"Yes, Mike. I learned about Penelope Carter from our second shift radioman. Her imminent arrival has caused me to make a decision about your discovery at William's Bluff. I've decided not to keep it a secret much longer. Rather than wait for Miss Carter to discover the truth, I shall only wait until you and Sophia are safely on your way to Phobos Base before I make an announcement to our colonists and afterward to NASA's headquarters. I've already told Pat because I know she can keep a secret."

"In that case, Pat, how long will it be before Sophia and I can have our rocket ride?" asked Michael.

"You should be able to leave our spaceport by Thursday morning at the latest—possibly even late Wednesday afternoon" Patricia replied. "This storm is a small one and it is moving fairly fast."

"That's a relief" said Michael. "I hate not being able to go outside the base. "Now I have no excuse not to catch up with my office work."

The two listeners laughed, then Michael said "Well, I'll leave you two so you can resume whatever you were doing before you heard the doorbell." As he rose to a standing position Daniel stood up too and followed him to the entrance of the apartment.

"Mike, I have one question for you before you leave us" Daniel said, as they entered the hallway together. He closed the door behind them and asked:

"Is Sophia as good in a bedroom as she is beautiful? Every man in Lowellsville has wondered about that."

"She's as much fun in bed as she usually is out of it" Michael replied with a smile.

"In that case I predict a long, happy marriage for the two of you" Daniel stated (with a smile of his own). He then returned to his apartment and Michael walked away toward an elevator that would take him downward to his office's level. He wanted to complete some work there before dinner and his evening date with Sophia.

Meanwhile, Sophia was not alone in the two bedroom apartment that she and Louisa called home. Louisa was working late in the Biology Department, but Linda Simmons was with the soon-to-be bride. Linda was the wife of Lowellsville's Chief Structural Engineer and she was the mother of two children. She was also the best seamstress in the community and she was presently pinning together a beautiful wedding gown made of parachute nylon. Sophia stood patiently in her bedroom while the gown slowly took shape on her curvaceous body.

Sophia was wearing only a thin pair of panties beneath the temporarily pinned together prototype of the white gown. The long, translucent sleeves had not yet been made and Linda was in the process of marking where the low, wide, U-shaped neckline would be in the front. Sophia's nipples and large (but irregularly shaped) aureoles made two small bumps and light pink spots in the thin material of the gown's bodice.

"I'd better fasten some lace to this bodice to obscure your nipples, dear" said Linda, "—otherwise they'll be overly exposed."

"All right, but don't use too much of it" Sophia replied. "I don't want to hide them entirely."

"You are a bold, young woman, Sandra; planning to wear this nearly negligee thin gown without a brassiere beneath it!" Linda remarked. "I hope you'll at least wear panties."

"I will—especially since Pastor Boswell will be there" Sophia promised with a smile of mirth.

"Good, dear, otherwise he might forget his lines!" Linda teased.

Linda Simmons was an attractive, married woman, thirty years of age, with blonde hair and light brown eyes. She was an inch shorter than Sophia's five feet, six inches and her figure was not as spectacular as Sophia's was, but men still turned around to view Linda from behind when she walked past them. Due to her many talents and seemingly boundless energy, she was referred to by many of the colonists as "Super Mom."

"You might have had a great career as a cinema actress, Sandra. What caused you to become a scientist?" Linda asked, as she held a piece of lace across Sandra's bosom to test the visual effect of it.

"I suppose it happened because I'm an early lunar explorer's grand niece" The younger woman replied patiently. "As far back as I can remember I wanted to explore another planet and search for alien life forms. So I was thrilled three and a half years ago when my application to become a Mars colonist was accepted by NASA."

"So was I when I was accepted four years before that" Linda remarked. "I'm happy just to be on Mars and away from all the problems of Earth, but you seem to have achieved more than that already!" As she spoke, Linda set aside the lace and began shaping the gown's left sleeve.

Sophia smiled proudly and said: "I won't ask if you can keep a secret—because Mister Morris would not have chosen you for his secretary if he thought you couldn't—so I'll confide in you. Mike and I <u>did</u> find evidence that there is <u>another</u> <u>intelligent</u> <u>race</u> on Mars! I must leave it at that for now, though."

"I thought as much, from overhearing bits of my boss's telephone conversations" said Linda. "I just hope that those aliens are not <u>hostile</u>. Janet Hudson told me that something was interfering with her radios this afternoon and she didn't seem to think it was just the dust storm."

Before Sophia could think of what comment to make the apartment's doorbell rang.

"I'll go see who that is" said Linda, as she stood up and turned toward the outer door.

"Tell whoever that is that I cannot come to the door right now, Super Mom" said Sophia. "If it is Mike tell him that I will see him at seven o'clock." The doorbell rang again and Linda almost forgot to close the bedroom door behind herself as she entered the living room. She turned halfway around and closed the door quickly, then she hurried to the apartment's outer door.

As Linda opened the door, she saw Michael Edwards standing in the hallway.

"Oh, hello Michael" she greeted. "Sandra can't come to the door right now."

"Well, just remind her of our date at seven o'clock for me" said Michael. "Tell her I'll be in my office for a while if she needs to call me."

"All right" Linda replied. "Am I invited to the wedding tomorrow?"

"Certainly!" Michael replied. "I'll be emailing some invitations from my office's computer tonight."

"Okay, now you'll have one less to send" Linda remarked cheerfully.

Michael walked away and Linda closed the door, then she hurried back to the bedroom. When she arrived there, she finished shaping the sleeves of the gown. She pinned each of them onto it briefly, so she and Sophia could see how the whole garment would appear (although its neckline had not yet been shaped).

"It's strange to think that I've known Mike for several years, yet I sometimes feel like I don't know him at all" said Sophia.

"Men are complicated creatures" Linda remarked, "—but then they say the same thing about us! I've been married to Ronald for eight years, but he still surprises me sometimes. I recently decided to surprise <u>him</u> with a broccoli and cheese casserole, using broccoli recently grown hydroponically here on Mars. I went to a lot of trouble to prepare it—then when I served it to him and the children, I learned that he hates broccoli! Richard wouldn't eat it either, so Angela and I ate the casserole while the two males went to the food dispensers! I was so angry for a while I was tempted to dump the casserole on Ronald's head, but I eventually forgave him."

Sophia laughed and said "That would have been funny to see, but I'm glad you decided to eat the broccoli instead. Growing food here on Mars is still awfully expensive! Pastor Boswell told me some of our terrestrial vegetables won't grow in the local soil unless he adds a lot of nutrients to it. They grow better in sawdust from wood that is shipped here from Earth!"

While Sophia's gown was slowly taking shape, Michael went to the Geology Department and emailed wedding invitations to several people via the computer in his office. He glanced frequently at the old fashioned, circular, wall mounted clock that he preferred to a digital, desktop clock. The hands seemed to his love struck mind to be moving at half of their normal speed. He finally finished sending the wedding invitations, after which he decided to telephone Bill Schaefer. Michael hoped that Bill had been able to communicate with the aliens again, but Bill had nothing new to report about them. Michael told Bill about his coming promotion and received congratulations from him, then Bill asked "Do you know yet what you want to do for a honeymoon?"

"Yes" Michael replied. "We're going to Phobos Base for a sort of mixed business and pleasure trip. We'll be gone about a week."

"That should be an interesting change of scenery" said Bill. "I'd like to go there myself someday, but it won't be anytime soon. "Dan Morris wants me to build a heated well house around the well head here when the weather improves. A bunch of volunteers in Lowellsville will be building a big tanker truck to carry water from here to there. You should have some decent tasting water within a week and someday there will be a pipeline to facilitate delivery."

"That's good news" Michael remarked. "It will be like receiving a shipment of champagne from Earth." Bill laughed, then Michael said "By the way, Bill, have you been told yet that Warren Cox wants to borrow Bob Harris to improve the low gee plumbing system on Phobos?"

"No, you're the first person to tell me about that" Bill replied. "I hope Dan Morris said 'no.' I need Bob here on Mars."

"No such luck" Michael remarked. "Bob will be going to Phobos at the same time that Sophia and I do."

"Oh hell! I was planning to have Bob study the feasibility of using an underground volcanic hot spot five miles east of here for a source of electricity" Bill complained.

"You'll probably have him back a week from whenever the weather clears" Michael said consolingly.

"Well, there's that much hope, anyway" said Bill. "I have something I need to do now, Mike, so I must end this conversation."

"All right, Bill. Call me if anything changes about the aliens' situation" said Michael.

"I will. Good night, Mike" Bill replied. Then he put his telephone's handset back on its rack and Michael did the same.

Michael left his office and locked the door behind himself. He walked to his apartment and watched television until 6:30 p.m., then he turned off the set and went to his bedroom. There he undressed and put on his swimming trunks. Next he donned a beach jacket and a pair of sandals. He put a set of keys into a pocket of the terry cloth jacket and went into the bathroom. There he got a large towel from the linen closet.

'I hope Sophia isn't still angry about that incident during lunch' he thought as he emerged from the bathroom with a towel. Then he heard the telephone ring and he went to the bedroom's nightstand to answer the extension 'phone. To his relief the caller was Sophia. She told him she was about to leave her apartment and go to the pool.

"All right, honey. I'll meet you there" he replied. Then he and she ended their telephone conversation and went to the swimming pool chamber. Sophia's apartment was closer to it so she arrived there first. When Michael arrived he found her sitting in a lightweight folding chair on the patio between the big room's entrance and the pool itself. She wore a beach jacket over her bathing suit and there were a pair of sandals on her feet.

"Good evening" said Michael, as he seated himself in a similar chair to the left of her.

"Hello, Mike" she replied with a friendly smile. "I was just sitting here watching young Angela Simmons. She has a lot of youthful energy and she really loves swimming! Her father is over there teaching her how to swim under water."

"So I see" said Michael, as he looked in the direction that Sophia was pointing. He saw a lively seven years old girl with dark brown hair and black eyes. She was standing beside her father in about three and a half feet of water. Both people were dripping wet and the girl soon dove beneath the surface. She submerged about two feet and swam to the concrete wall at the shallow end of the pool. She surfaced there and rubbed the water away from her eyes.

"Hello, Ronald" Michael called. "Your daughter swims like an otter now."

"She is making good progress" Ronald replied, as he wiped some water off of his own dark brown hair with his right hand. "I hear you're about to become a married man."

"I'm afraid so" Michael replied humorously. "I think Sophia put something in my coffee a couple of days ago. Before I knew what had happened I was down on one knee proposing to her."

"Women are tricky" Ronald replied with a smile, as his daughter swam back to him below the surface and gripped his legs before she use her own to push herself upward.

Ronald Simmons was six feet tall (like Michael) and had a moderately handsome face. He had the same clor of hair as his daughter, but his eyes were slate gray. He was Lowellsville's Chief Structural Engineer and a member of Michael's chess club (as was his son, Richard).

"Daddy's been teaching me how to swim under water—with my eyes open!" Angela announced proudly. "So I see!" Michael replied (with pretended admiration). "You're learning fast."

"She's a good student" Ronald remarked with a proud smile.

"Where is Richie this evening?" asked Michael.

"He's doing his homework" Ronald replied. "He spent most of the afternoon playing video games instead of doing his school assignments, so he must do the latter now instead of being in the pool." Angela's face formed a 'Serves him right!' smile, but she said nothing.

"Yes, he must learn to take responsibility for his own actions" said Michael. "Well, Sophia, are you willing to get wet now?"

"Yes, I'm ready" she replied. She and Michael rose to standing positions in front of their chairs and draped their towels across the arm rests. Afterward the two lovers removed their beach jackets. Within a few seconds the eyes of everyone in the pool—or near it—were gazing at Sophia. She was wearing an aquamarine colored bikini with little yellow fish printed all over its four triangular panels. Two of these panels served as brassiere cups (although they left about a third of the surface area of each breast uncovered). These two panels were supported by narrow back and shoulder straps, while the two panels of her bikini's bottom half were supported by two slender hip cords each, with one at each upper corner. These hip cords were joined by a bow knot on each side, while the lower corner of each panel was connected to its counterpart by a narrow crotch strap.

"Wow!" Michael exclaimed in admiration (while the other men had similar thoughts). "That's the most revealing bikini I've ever seen you wear, Sophia! Please don't decide to dive into the pool."

"I won't" she promised. "I would soon be searching for the bottom half of my suit if I did. By the way, Ronald, your wife made this bikini for me as a wedding present. This is the first time that I have worn it."

"I should thank Linda later on behalf of everyone now present" Ronald replied with a smile.

"Yes, please do" Michael remarked with enthusiasm. He then led Sophia by one hand to a set of semicircular, concrete steps that descended into the left corner of the swimming pools sixteen feet wide near end.

"Golly, Sandra, you look beautiful!" Angela exclaimed from the central part of the pool's near end. "I wish I looked like you do!"

Sandra smiled and said" Thank you, dear" as she and Michael descended the steps.

"In about ten more years you might look like her, Angie" Michael said encouragingly, as he released his fiancée's left hand. Then he looked at the bikini clad beauty and said "Let's swim underwater to the far end, honey."

"All right" she replied. She and he then breathed deeply in and out three times and inward for a fourth time to oxygenate their blood. They then did a surface dive to within a few inches of the bottom of the pool. There they followed the gradually downward-sloping contours of it for the entire forty-eight feet length of the basin. Finally they kicked upward from the bottom of it and swam to the surface.

By this time the other four people who were in the pool had resumed their own swimming and diving activities. In addition to Angela and her father there was Lowellsville's only metallurgist, a Negro man named Antwan Curtis, and his date, a negro woman named Dolores Parker. She was Lowellsville's only full-time school teacher and a part-time librarian.

There was one other person near the pool. He was Phillip Stewart, who was the third shift radio operator and the evening life guard. He sat in a chair that had legs five feet tall, with a steep flight of aluminum stairs leading up to it. The chair was situated between the high and low diving boards, beside the deep end of the pool. Phillip was a handsome, athletic man with blond hair and brown eyes. Because of his nocturnal job he was seldom seen by most of Lowellsville's inhabitants before four o'clock in the afternoon.

Sophia and Michael rested their arms on the ledge of the overflow drain. It was about two inches above the tops of the wavelets in the pool and it provided a convenient resting place for tired swimmers in the eight feet of water at the deepend.

Phillip enjoyed the downward view of Sophia's breasts. Her bikini left an interesting amount of them exposed and its material had molded itself to the contours of whatever it did cover.

"You two swim well" said Phillip. He was two years younger than the lovers and about three inches shorter than Michael whenever they were standing near each other.

"Thanks" Michael replied. "I used to be on my university's swimming team. In later years, when Sophia and I went to a NASA astronaut training school in Florida, I introduced her to scuba diving during the weekends. She learned quickly."

"So I see" Phillip said (with an approving smile).

"I'm sure that's not all you can see" said a female voice from Phillip's right vicinity. He and the two lovers looked in that direction and saw Nancy Chan, Lowellsville's assistant meteorologist. She had arrived in the swimming pool room unnoticed by the little group. Nancy was a Chinese American and she had been dating Phillip for several weeks during Sundays (which were his only days off).

"Try to notice the other people in this room, Phillip—one of them could be drowning" she added in a tone of mild reproach. Nancy was a pretty woman the same age as Phillip (who was twenty-six). She was six inches shorter than his five feet, nine inches and had a good (but small breasted) figure. Her eyes were a chocolate brown color and her hair was black.

"Nobody has ever drowned on my watch" Phillip replied with a tone of annoyance. He forced himself to look away from Sophia longer than he would have liked to do, in an attempt to placate Nancy.

"Well there could be a first time" said Nancy ('or I might drown you!' she added mentally).

Nancy was wearing a yellow bikini that was almost as revealing as Sophia's had been when it was dry. Nancy resolved silently to soak her attire soon so she could compete better with Sophia's present appearance.

"Let's swim back to the other end of the pool—on the surface honey" Michael coaxed his fiancée.

"All right" she replied, with a brief glance at Nancy (which indicated that she understood Michael's reason for the change of location).

The two lovers swam toward the shallow end of the pool while Nancy entered the deep end by way of an aluminum ladder. Nancy's bra had no shoulder straps and she did not want to risk losing it by jumping into the water.

Michael only needed to slow his Australian crawl stroke slightly to let Sophia stay close to him. Despite the water resistance against her breasts, she had become a faster swimmer than most women during her many visits to the pool and gymnasium with Michael.

When they arrived at the shallow end's wall, Michael and Sophia stood up. They noticed that Ronald and his daughter were about to leave the pool area. "Leaving already?" Michael asked humorously.

"Yes, I think we've swam enough for one evening" Ronald replied. He glanced toward the far end of the pool with an annoyed expression.

"Good night, you two" said Sophia.

"Good night" said Angela. "I hope you have a nice wedding."

"Thank you, dear" Sophia replied. The Simmonses then exited through a doorway that led to a main corridor. Michael guessed that they intended to follow a circuitous route to the dressing rooms (to avoid Nancy and Phillip).

Michael and Sophia noticed next that Antwan and his date were following the right pool-side walkway toward the main corridor.

"Good luck with your wedding" called Antwan as he and Dolores approached the patio area and their chairs.

"Thanks" Sophia replied. "It will be on the community channel at four p.m. tomorrow if you want to watch it."

"We might do that" Antwan hinted with a smile. Then he and Dolores gathered their possessions and left the pool area.

"There appears to be a general exodus" Michael remarked humorously, as he seated himself on one of the concrete steps in a corner of the pool.

"I can guess why" Sophia replied, as she seated herself beside him. She looked toward the far end of the pool, where Phillip was trying to placate Nancy. She was floating on her back in the pool as she looked up at him with an expression of disapproval.

"Maybe we should leave too" Sophia suggested quietly.

"Good idea" Michael replied. "Let's go to my apartment and make love."

"That sounds like a good way to spend an evening" Sophia agreed, as she noticed a bulge in the front part of his swimming trunks. She smiled at him invitingly and stood up. Michael stood up also and followed her up the stairs. He admired the way that her wet bikini clung to her body. He patted her bottom with his right hand while he walked beside her. The lovers crossed the concrete patio to the two chairs where they had left their beach paraphernalia.

"I think that bikini may be the best wedding present we'll receive" he remarked playfully.

"I think so too" she replied, as she arrived at her chair and picked up her big, fluffy towel.

Ten minutes later they arrived in the bedroom of Michael's apartment. There they undressed and went into the bathroom to hang their damp bathing suits on towel racks. The towels were moved to the counter top beside the lavatory. Their large, damp towels that had been beside the swimming pool were spread temporarily on the tile floor. Then the two lovers entered the shower stall and bathed together. Afterward Michael turned off the water and followed Sophia onto the towel covered bathroom floor. They dried each other with fresh towels, then they hung these on the rim of the shower stall and went into the bedroom. They had sexual intercourse twice on the bed (in different positions). Afterward Michael turned off the lights before he joined her beneath the covers of the bed. "That was wonderful!" she exclaimed, as he lay down beside her. "Let's do it <u>again</u> tomorrow night—<u>after</u> we're married."

"You are <u>full</u> of good ideas lately!" Michael remarked humorously. Then he kissed her pretty face playfully.

"That's not <u>all</u> that I'm <u>full</u> <u>of</u>—thanks to you!" she complained mildly.

Michael just smiled and kissed her several more times. Afterward he said "C'mon, Sophie, admit it. You enjoyed serving under me tonight."

"Oh, <u>all</u> <u>right</u>!" she conceded playfully. "You're a <u>good</u> <u>lover</u>—in <u>both</u> <u>positions</u>."

"That's better" he said with mock firmness. He kissed her again, then he went into the bathroom to pee. Afterward he picked up the damp towels from the floor and took them into the bedroom, where he dropped them into the laundry hamper.

In the dim glow of a night light's red bulb he saw Sophia lying nude and prone on top of the bed covers. He climbed onto the bed and lay down on his left side to the left of her. Then he placed his right hand on her bottom. He caressed the smooth twin objects for a while, then he remarked "Nancy sure was annoyed with Phillip for looking at you so much tonight."

"Maybe I should have worn one of these 1890s bathing suits" she replied humorously. Then he couldn't have seen anything interesting."

"Neither could I, though" Michael reminded her, "—and you are sexy in that skimpy bikini."

"Linda did a favor for both of us when she made it for me as a wedding present" said Sophia, "—even if it did make Nancy jealous of me."

Michael kissed her left shoulder and patted her bottom again, and then they went to sleep.

Chapter Twenty
The Bare Facts

Wednesday, June 51st.

When Michael awoke, his bedside clock indicated 1:37 a.m. He felt Sophia shivering slightly, so he slapped her bottom to awaken her.

"Ow!" she exclaimed as she awoke. "Why did you do that?"

"We're both cold" he replied. "Let's go beneath the covers.

"I think you left a hand print on my bottom!" she complained mildly, as they slid beneath the covers. "I hope that you set your alarm clock so we won't be late for work."

"I think I forgot" he replied. He then rolled onto his right side and turned on the lamp on the night stand. The lamp was a lathe turned, aluminum item of local manufacture*(7) (to avoid high shipping costs for more attractive furnishings from Earth). When Michael checked the digital alarm clocks *wake up* time it indicated 6:30 a.m. He turned on its *enable* switch, and then he turned off the lamp and said "The clock should buzz at 6:30 in the morning."

"That's early enough" she muttered, as he lay down beside her. They enjoyed the pleasant, mutual warmth and both lovers quickly went to sleep again.

When the alarm clock buzzed eventually, Michael felt as if he had only slept an hour or so; but when he opened his eyes he saw 6:30 on the face of the clock. Sophia sat up, yawned and stretched her arms above her head. Meanwhile the coves slid downward to her waist. Michael enjoyed the view of her breasts while she looked at him with a happy smile. Then her yawn became contagious and he copied it while she lowered her arms to her sides.

Sophia glanced at the bedside clock and exclaimed "Oh damn it! I forgot to go to my bedroom last night and get a set of clothes to wear! All that I have with me are my beach jacket and bikini, plus my sandals and towel."

"Just put on the garments you have with you—they should be enough for this early hour" Michael suggested.

"I suppose so" she replied drowsily. They both left the bed and Sophia put on her beach garments of the previous evening. Meanwhile Michael donned his usual office attire of khaki trousers and a short sleeved shirt over an under shirt and boxer shorts. Afterward Sophia kissed her fianc'e a temporary 'goodbye' and left the apartment.

Sophia only passed two people on her way to the apartment that she shared with Louisa. Both were men and after saying "Good morning" they each turned around to admire her legs as she walked past them. Sophia simply smiled briefly each time and continued walking.

Sophia soon arrived safely at the door of her apartment and reached into the low placed, right pocket of her beach jacket to find her keys. She was relieved to find them still there and she quickly pulled them out. As she leaned forward to insert her key into the lock, she heard the door of the apartment across the hall from hers opening. "Hello!" said a familiar sounding male voice.

"Oh! You startled me!" Sophia exclaimed, as she felt the right bow knot of her bikini's bottom loosening (because she had not tied it firmly enough). She slapped her right upper thigh with her right hand and was able to catch the skimpy garment when it was most of the way down her buttocks. Sophia straightened her body as she turned around and recognized an older man. Ronald Simmons was standing only three feet away.

"Excuse me!" she exclaimed with embarrassment. "I almost lost my bikini bottom!"

"Pardon me if I don't express regret" Ronald remarked humorously (while wishing that the beach jacket wasn't present). "In fact, I was wondering last evening what was holding that item in place. My guess then was that it was mostly accomplished by will power on your part."

"Maybe you were right" she replied with a slight smile. "Anyway, I've been wanting to talk with you and Linda about married life and what it is like."

"It's mostly about sharing and caring" Ronald replied earnestly, "—and not spending more than twenty-five dollars from a joint savings account without consulting your spouse first."

"Oh" said Sophia, with a real smile. "I thought it was more complicated than that."

"It can be sometimes" Ronald admitted. "Linda and I argue sometimes about what is best for our children. She wanted to have the extra amount of webbing removed from between Angela's fingers by surgery when she was four years old. I told both females that I thought it would help Angie when she swam (and it does). I decided it should be left in place until she became at least sixteen. She could decide then for herself if she wanted to keep it."

"I suppose that makes sense" Sophia said (without conviction in her voice). "Anyway, I must enter my apartment now and dress for work." She then turned around and opened her apartment's door. As she entered the right bedroom, she could hear someone having a shower bath in the bathroom between the two bedchambers. Sophia closed the entrance's door behind herself and went to the closet. She opened its door and selected her outer garments for that day.

'I'm lucky that Linda did not come to her apartment's doorway and see what her husband was seeing!' she thought with relief. She then let her bikini bottom fall to the floor in front of the closet. Afterward she selected a blouse and skirt, took them to her bed and placed them on it.

'This is my wedding day' she mused, '—and I don't want anything to spoil it! I also want to appear especially beautiful!'

Sophia returned to the closet and removed her hip length beach jacket; then she put it onto a hanger. Next she removed her bikini's brassiere, after which she stooped and picked up the lower garment from the carpeted floor. Finally she went to a chest-of-drawers and placed both bikini halves in one of its drawers.

Now wearing only her sandals, she entered the narrow hallway that connected the two bedrooms and passed behind the small living room. The door of the bathroom was midway along the right side of the hallway and it was not locked. When Sophia opened the door she looked diagonally across the bathroom and saw the blurred form of Louisa's nude body. It could be seen through the frost patterned, water streaked glass of the shower stall.

"Don't use all of the hot water" Sophia chided mildly. She spoke loudly enough to be heard above the sound of the shower of water droplets.

"I won't" Louisa promised. "I'm almost finished." After a short pause she asked "Did you spend the night with Michael?"

"Yes!" Sophia admitted (loudly enough to be heard again), as the shower contined its noisy hissing. "I'm sorry I didn't call you and let you know where I was."

"Mr. Simmons told me that you were in the swimming pool with Michael yesterday evening, so I deduced the rest" Louisa said with a teasing tone of voice. Then she turned off the water and opened the sliding door of the shower stall.

"Hand that big, pink towel to me please" she requested and pointed. Sophia did so, , then she watched her friend dry much of her body. Afterward Sophia dried her back for her.

"You need to visit the gym more often" said Sophia, "otherwise you'll ruin your figure with too much office work."

"Maybe if I had a handsome man to go fossil hunting with me I'd get more exercise" Louisa replied teasingly, as she turned around to face Sophia. She then kissed the top of the taller woman's left breast playfully. Afterward her mood became more serious. "Really, Sophie, it isn't fair to the rest of us females that nature gave you such a head start on us!"

"Don't you begin being jealous of me—I encounter enough of that everywhere else I go!" Sophia replied with annoyance. Then she placed her hands on Louisa's shoulders and looked at her face with an earnest expression. "Really, Louisa, you and Linda are the only two <u>female</u> friends I have—that are <u>near my age</u>, anyway. I <u>need</u> <u>both</u> of you!"

Louisa smiled and said "Don't worry; I'll still be in your fan club when you marry Michael—unless you begin neglecting me, that is."

"We'll still be friends" Sophia promised, as she hugged her admirer. "I'll visit you often."

"Good" said Louisa. Then she kissed Sophia's lower chest (below her breast's cleavage) and exclaimed "Really, Sophie! I'd give ten years off my life to look like you!"

'You wouldn't say that if you knew how lonely I've been sometimes' Sophia thought, as Louisa left the bathroom. Afterward she turned toward the shower stall and entered it. Soon the hissing of the water and the fogging of the big mirror above the lavatory resumed.

Ten minutes later Sophia left the shower stall and dried herself with a large towel. Afterward she hung the towel on a wall mounted aluminum tube and left the bathroom.

She walked into her bedroom and stood near the left side of the bed. She had left a brick red, short-sleeved blouse and a black skirt lying on it earlier. She chose a black lace brassiere and matching panties from her bureau's drawers and put them on. Next she went to her vanity table and seated herself on its bench. There she spent fifteen minutes skillfully applying makeup. She used it sparingly so she would seem not to be wearing any. Afterward she brushed her foot long, jet black hair thoroughly. Its soft, wavy tresses were among her favorite physical features of herself.

She rose from the bench and returned to her bureau. There she chose a pair of black, fish net stockings and two grayish blue garters. She took them to the bed, seated herself on its edge, and pulled on her leg wear. Next she stood beside the bed and donned her outer garments. Finally she stood in front of her bedroom mirror and gathered her hair behind her head in a large pony tail.

"Louisa, come here and tie my pony tail in place for me, please" she called loudly. Her friend (and admirer) soon came through the partly open doorway and picked up a brick red ribbon from the top of the vanity table. Louisa happily wrapped the ribbon around the base of the pony tail and tied it in place with a large, attractive, bow knot.

"Thanks, Lou, you're really good at that!" Sophia complimented, as she admired the result by way of the big mirror above the vanity table. Afterward Sophia seated herself on the bench and put on a pair of grayish blue, low cut shoes. "I'm ready to go now" she announced.

The two women left the apartment and Louisa locked the outer door behind them. They walked together toward the communal dining room, with several men's heads turning to watch them as the passed by. Near the dining room's main entrance the two women met Michael Edwards and James Wilcox, who were going in the opposite direction.

"Well, girls, we were wondering if you two were planning to eat this morning" James teased. "I thought you might be dieting."

"You men don't need to put on a new face every morning" Sophia replied enviously, with a slight frown.

"The old ones looked good to me" James assured the two women. Sophia's frown disappeared.

"Shall we meet at noon for lunch, Sophia dear?" Michael suggested.

"No, I cannot do that today" she replied. "I have some things that I need to do before the wedding rehearsal."

"All right, I'll see you at two o'clock for that" Michael said calmly. Then he and James walked away and disappeared around a corner.

Because of considerable flexibility in their schedules, Sophia and Louisa were able to eat breakfast at a moderate pace and still not be penalized for arriving at their work place twenty minutes later than the two geologists arrived at their department. Sophia spent a half-hour trying to choose a Latin name for the arthropod that she had discovered, after which she finally asked Louisa (who was seated to her left) "What do <u>you</u> think we should call it?"

'Why not call it a <u>false</u> <u>crab</u>?" Louisa suggested. "It has pincers like one."

"A <u>crab's</u> <u>pincers</u> are not <u>this</u> <u>slender</u>" Sophia replied. "It reminds me more of a trilobite, because it has a true thorax instead of a cephalothoraxes like a crab."

"Then call it a false trilobite!" Louisa enthused. "That would sound okay."

"I think I shall!" Sophia decided. "<u>Pseudotrilobitus</u> <u>collensis</u> shall be its name."

Next Sophia worked on the scientific description of the creature for about an hour. Louisa was a great help to her with this task, because she had examined the fossil during the previous afternoon while Sophia was making wedding preparations. Louisa had even made some useful notes of what she had seen and these were included in the final description (with some modifications or additions by Sophia). Finally Sophia said "Let's stop for a while. I've stared at this computer screen so long I'm about to become cross-eyed!"

"All right" Louisa replied, as she stood up from her laboratory stool and rolled her shoulders (to remove some of their stiffness). "Speaking of staring at something, Mr. Simmons told me that <u>you</u> attracted plenty of attention with your skimpy new bikini last night!"

"Yes, <u>I</u> <u>did!</u>" Sophia replied, with a lop-sided smile. "**<u>Everyone</u> in the pool**—or <u>anywhere</u> <u>near</u> <u>it</u>—<u>was watching</u> **<u>me!</u>** I haven't attracted that much attention since I posed nude for an art class during my senior year in college!"

"That must have required a lot of courage" Louisa said admiringly.

"It sure did!" Sophia replied. "If a psychologist had not taught me a biofeedback technique to prevent panic, I never could have completed the first session! After that, the next posing session was less stressful. It was really kind of flattering to have six art students and their instructor painting pictures of my naked body. OH! I almost forgot my college roommate, Penelope. She accompanied me to the studio for morale support during that first session."

"That was nice of her" said Louisa. "By the way, I noticed this morning in our bathroom that you appeared to be blushing—or was it a rash of some kind that went away quickly? My father had high blood pressure for about a decade before his death last year. He used to become red all over his head, neck and upper chest area sometimes."

"Well, **I** don't have high blood pressure!" Sophia assured her friend. "I was blushing because of an incident in the hallway earlier. My bikini bottom <u>ties</u> <u>together with bow knotted cords</u> at its upper <u>cor</u>ners, but one of the knots came loose this morning while I was unlocking the outer door of our apartment. I had hoped that I was alone in the hallway, but I soon noticed that the door of the Simmons' apartment was opening. I just had enough time to pin my bikini's bottom half against my right thigh with one hand to prevent it from falling off completely!"

"Wow! That <u>was</u> an embarrassing moment!" Louisa exclaimed. "What did Mr. Simmons say to you about it?"

"He told me that he thought <u>will</u> <u>power</u> was the main thing that had held my bikini's lower half together originally! I suppose he was hinting that I had a momentary lack of will."

"More likely it was a lack of attention to how well the knots were tied" Louisa remarked humorously. "Did he see anything interesting?"

"Yes, he did! He saw most of my derriere! I hope he didn't think that lapse was intentional!" Sophia exclaimed worriedly.

"<u>Who</u> <u>knows</u> <u>how men think?!</u>" Louisa exclaimed. "<u>I</u> certainly don't! Otherwise I would know how to get a date with James."

"I'm afraid I can't help you with that problem" said Sophia, "—but <u>I'll</u> <u>tie</u> <u>stronger</u> <u>knots</u> the next time I wear that bikini! I'd rather break a finger nail while removing that lower part at home than lose the darned thing in a crowded swimming pool room the next time it falls off!"

Meanwhile, Michael and James spent almost an hour studying and photographing a small meteorite in the geology laboratory. James had found it five days earlier in an area about five miles to the west of

Lowellsville. The two men agreed that it was a carbonaceous contrite as they examined a small, thin slice of it under a microscope. James had already marked the site of its discovery on a large, wall mounted map of the Lowellsville Administrative Region.

"This looks like it broke off of a larger object" said Michael, as he hefted the reminder of the meteorite with his right hand. Nearby James used an ultraviolet light to cause some of the minerals in the slice to fluoresce under the microscope.

"That was what I thought when I found it" James replied, without looking up from the big microscope. "I tried to find the parent object but I had no success. I would like to return to that area sometime and search for it again, but this dust storm has probably blown away my site markers."

"Yes, it undoubtedly has" Michael remarked sympathetically. "This storm is a real nuisance!"

"I can understand why you're annoyed" said James, as he finally looked up at his supervisor. "It could delay your honeymoon with Sandra on Phobos."

"That's <u>one</u> of the reasons why I'm annoyed" Michael replied. "It has probably also obscured the site where Sophia and I found two interesting fossils during our Monday outing."

"I'd like to know <u>what</u> <u>else</u> you and she found that day" said James. "There's a rumor that you found proof of another intelligent species existing on Mars and that for some reason Mr. Morris wanted you to avoid telling the rest of us."

"I found some tire tracks that <u>might</u> <u>not</u> have been made by a vehicle from Lowellsville" Michael replied, "but the storm may have obliterated them by now. Sophia and I would like to examine that area again."

"Oh" said James, sounding disappointed. "I suppose the C.A. told you not to excite everybody with such inconclusive evidence. Am I right?"

"Something like that" Michael replied evasively. "Anyway, I'm not supposed to tell anyone about it yet, so don't reveal to anyone else what I told you just now."

"Mum's the word" James promised.

The door bell rang and James said, "I'll go see who that is. I'm tired of looking through this microscope."

"All right" Michael replied. "I think I'll resume studying those rocks that I brought in on Monday evening."

James walked to the office's outer door and opened it. He saw the six feet tall, Negro metallurgist, Antwan Curtis, standing in the hallway.

"Mind if Ah come in?" asked the visitor, with a deep south accent.

"Please do" said James, as he stepped aside. "How is Lowellsville's best basketball player feeling today?"

"Ah'm doin' just dandy" Antwan replied, as he entered the office. "Mah wrist that Ah huht in that game last weekend ain't sore no moh. Anyhow, man, you shoulda been in the swimmin' pool room last night! Miss Sandra was wearin' a bikini with bra panels about the size of a playin' card! Ah almost scorched mah eyeballs!"

Antwan was a slender, Negro man from Birmingham, Alabama. Michael and James both knew that he had played point guard for the University of Alabama's men's basketball team. A slow-to-heal foot injury during his senior year had prevented him from being drafted by an N.B.A. team, so he had decided to learn metallurgy from a film in his home city that had contracts with N.A.S.A. After two years of learning and practicing his new profession on Earth, he had learned that the Mars colony needed a metallurgist. His application for Mars Conditions training had been accepted by the space agency. After a year of instruction (half of which had been spent on Luna to accustom him to working in weak gravity), he had made the long journey to Mars. He and a recently recruited school teacher named Dolores Parker had traveled together aboard the small, prototype, atomic-powered vessel "Prometheus." During the four month space voyage, a friendship had formed between them. It resulted in their dating each other often after they arrived on Mars. They were currently the only members of the negro race on that planet (although the space agency had tried to recruit others)

"I wish I had gone swimming with you" James remarked enviously, "but I was in my apartment instead, reading an actual book with paper pages! Fred Snyder loaned it to me. Its title was: *The First Lunar Colony* by Mark Albertson. It was really interesting! I got some ideas from it that I would like to try here on Mars. Anyhow, what may I do for you in our humble establishment?"

"Ah want to ask Mike Andrews to spend some time away from Miss Sandra while he's up on Phobos, so he can see if theyah is ennih molybdenum up theyah. Ah shuah could use some down heah" Antwan replied.

All right, he's not doing anything vital right now, so I'll let you go to the lab and ask him in person" said James.

"Thanks" said Antwan. He went into the laboratory and James was about to follow him when the telephone rang on top of the office's desk. James picked up the hand set and said "Geology Department, James Wilcox speaking."

"James, this is Daniel Morris. Tell Mike Andrews that I want <u>all</u> <u>department</u> <u>heads</u> to come to a_meeting in the main conference room at <u>nine</u> <u>a.m.</u> It's <u>important</u>, so <u>no excuses</u> will be accepted for missing it" said a familiar sounding voice from the telephone.

"Yes sir! I'll tell him" James assured the C.A. He heard the dial tone and set down the hand set. 'Well, that was a short conversation" he thought. Then he walked into the laboratory and found Antwan there telling Michael: "—but that's enough talk about what <u>Ah</u> <u>need</u> from Phobos. You'll be takin' with you what <u>you</u> <u>need</u>. Miss Collins is one <u>amazin'</u> <u>woman</u>!"

Michael smiled and replied "She is indeed!"

"Far be it from me to disagree with either of you about Sandra—I wish I could <u>clone</u> <u>a</u> <u>copy</u> <u>of</u> <u>her</u> for <u>me</u> to marry!" James exclaimed humorously. "But right now I must tell you that our Chif Adminis trator wants all of the department heads to meet with him in the main conference room at nine o' clock—with no excuses accepted for being absent."

Michael looked at his watch and exclaimed "<u>Nine</u> <u>o'clock</u>! That's only <u>ten</u> <u>minutes</u> from now!"

"Well, Ah'm just a lowlih Section Leadah—an the onlih puhson left in that section—so Ah guess Ah'm not invited to the big pow wow" Anton jested. "But <u>you'd</u> bettah be on youah way, Mistah Edwahds."

"I'm on my way" said Michael as he finished returning some rock samples to a drawer and closed it. "Hold the fort, James!"

"Yes sir!" the younger man replied, with a mock military salute.

As Michael picked up a small recording device in the office, he heard James say "It's too bad that other metallurgist returned to Earth to inherit his family's business. I know you've been as busy as a one armed paper hanger, Antwan!"

*(7) One of the reasons for Lowellsville being created where it was the discovery of the first known Bauxite (aluminum ore) deposit on Mars. It was found in the now much diminished rise of ground where the eastern end of the space port was presently situated.

Chapter Twenty-One
Survival Planning

Still Wednesday Morning

The floor indicator above the shaft's door said that the elevator was two floors above him, so Michael chose to use the stairway instead. He spent the next forty-five seconds rising two levels by muscle power, then he entered a hallway and turned to his left. A brief walk took him to a large, open doorway in the right wall of the corridor. As he passed through it and entered the meeting room, he saw that most of Lowellsville's department heads were already seated around a pair of tables set end-to-end. Sophia was seated halfway along the left table's near side (which put her fairly near the podium). She had saved the seat immediately to her left for him, so Michael headed toward it.

He was pleased to see that Sophia was wearing a short sleeved blouse and a knee length skirt instead of her laboratory coveralls. He kissed the left side of her face, then he seated himself. He noticed that only three seats were still vacant and one of them was behind the podium. He glanced at a wall mounted clock and hoped that the Chief Administrator would arrive soon. 'I wonder what this meeting is about?' he thought. 'Daniel has always given us more notice than this before.'

Daniel Morris arrived exactly at nine a.m. He was carrying a small television set, which he placed on a wall mounted shelf facing the group. Afterward he plugged the set's power cord into an electrical outlet and its antenna cord into a cable t.v. outlet.

Meanwhile, Linda Simmons prepared a big, pedestal mounted camera and a conference telephone at the other end of the room. A wireless microphone sat on the podium's lectern, waiting for Daniel. Mr. Morris walked to the podium and said "Good morning!" Several people responded with the same words, then the C.A. resumed speaking. "This equipment will enable us to talk with Bill Schaefer and John Clewiston, who are at William's Bluff and on Phobos, respectively. The t.v. has an audio-visual recorder, which will, in effect, be our secretary for this meeting."

Daniel took a remote control device from one of the pockets of his coveralls and pushed a series of buttons. A split screen pair of images appeared on the t.v., with Bill Scaefer's image on the left side of the screen and John Clewiston's image on the right side. Both pictures were grainy looking and lines moved across them occasionally, due to the static electricity in the dust storm outside the hill.

"Good morning, Bill and John. Can both of you hear me?" asked Mr. Morris. Both electronic participants replied "yes."

"Good" said Mr. Morris. "Let the record show that this meeting is being convened on Wednesday, the fifty-first day of June, Martian Northern Hemisphere Summer, Terran year 2048. Daniel Morris is presiding as Chief Administrator of the Lowellsville District, at nine oh eight a.m. in the Olympus Time Zone.

"This morning a radio message arrived from NASA's headquarters at eight-thirty, our time. The message says that the air force of the People's Republic of China attacked a fleet of U.S.N.A. warships this morning in the Tai Wan Straits and sank one destroyer, for the loss of five Chinese airplanes to interceptor aircraft and missiles. A U.S. Navy cruiser was moderately damaged by a missile but remains afloat. Our fleet continues to patrol the strait, although the cruiser *Admiral Dewey* withdrew to a Tai Wanese port for repairs, escorted by a T.W. destroyer.

"At the same time as these events, the People's Republic of North Korea bombarded the South Korean capital city of Seoul with long range artillery, causing extensive damage to buildings and loss of lives among the city's inhabitants.

"The U.S.N.A. has retaliated for these attacks with a bombardment of a Chinese naval base by conventionally armed cruise missiles and by the use of deep penetrating tactical nuclear warheads on air-launched missiles to destroy the North Koreans' underground artillery batteries that had fired at the city of Seoul. President Theodore R. Kerrigan has also asked Congress for a formal declaration of war as soon as possible against the People's Republic of China and the P.R. of (North) Korea, due to their recent unprovoked attacks against U.S.N.A. naval vessels and the Republic of (South) Korea's capital city.

"The mainland Chinese have since used a conventionally armed missile of some sort to damage the U.S.N. A.'s *Progress Space Station* with the loss of five people's lives and three astronauts wounded. The latter are returning to Earth in an escape capsule for a landing at an undisclosed location.

"President Kerrigan, Vice President Warner, the Congress, the Supreme Court and the Joint Chiefs of Staff have all left Washington, D.C. to go to undisclosed underground bunkers and our armed forces are all on a wartime alert status. The Tai Wanese government has also gone into deep bunkers and the government of Australia is sending a fleet of war ships from a new island base in the Indian Ocean to assist our navy in the Tai Wan Straits. In short, it looks like World War Three may be starting on Earth if any more nations become involved, so we must take care of ourselves for an indefinite period of time.

"I want every department head to write a list of recommendations for ways to make Lowellsville and Phobos Base together as self sufficient as possible. You may work on them in your offices after this meeting and I want to see them as soon as they are done.

"Michael and Sophia, I must ask you to reduce the list of participants in your wedding to the minimum number needed. Michael, I still want you to visit Phobos after your wedding and advise me of any useful minerals that you can find there that have been overlooked by the people of Phobos Base. Sophia, you will be needed here on Mars for your duties as Head of the Biology Department and Director of Life Support. I must ask you to postpone your honeymoon on Phobos."

"All right, sir, I understand the situation" Sophia replied earnestly. Michael discerned that she was bravely trying not to sound distraught.

"As for the rest of you" Daniel said sternly, "it has been brought to my attention that some of you have been ignoring the list of air loss precautions at the inner doors of the main parking garage. If I see that happening, some people will begin losing parts of their paychecks. I should not need to remind you how far away from Earth we are. Mars is still a hazardous place to dwell on and we are at least five months of traveling time away from any help sent from either Earth or Luna. Moreover, we don't know how long this latest war in Asia will last. We <u>do</u> <u>know</u>, however, that while it occurs, it will <u>reduce</u> the amount of <u>help</u> that the U.S.N.A. can send to us and Phobos Base."

"Sir, if I may speak bluntly, don't you think it's time you were honest with us about <u>another possible source</u> of help?" asked Linda Simmons (who was present because she was the senior Mars-to-Phobos shuttle pilot and the Head of the Administrative Support Service*(8). "I think you know who I mean."

Daniel sighed and said ""yes, I <u>do know who you mean</u>. I suppose I might as well make the announcement <u>now</u>, while everyone is gathered here. I've been dreading the flood of questions that this revelation would cause, but the secret is gradually leaking out anyway. <u>We are not alone</u> here on Mars! <u>Another intelligent species</u> was here ahead of us."

Every eye in the room was watching Daniel intently now. If a pin had been dropped during the next few seconds, everyone would probably have heard it.

"<u>It's true!</u>" Dolores, the brown-skinned school teacher finally exclaimed, ending the silence. "<u>I</u> "<u>knew</u> it wasn't just a rumor!"

"I don't know how you heard about it, Miss Parker—and it would be better for everyone involved if I never did—but Michael Andrews and Sophia Collins <u>did find</u> an <u>underground base</u>" said Daniel. "It was within the proverbial stone's throw of our water drilling outpost at William's Bluff. "<u>But</u>, even before our two intrepid explorers found it, I was privy to a series of photographs which a secret Defense Department orbiter made two years after the briefly famous, ape-like face in Cydonia Mensae was discovered by a NASA orbiter.

"The Defense Department's probe had much better, top secret instruments in it than that Viking Orbiter had. It's camera revealed <u>bipedal creatures—and their ground vehicles</u>—around the controversial, pyramid-like objects to the northeast of Olympus Mons" Daniel continued. "But during its next orbital pass over the Cydonia Region the satellite registered a brief flash, then it stopped transmitting. It has not been seen or heard from since then."

"Do you suppose that the aliens might have destroyed it, sir?" asked the Head of the Highways and Space Port Transportation System, John Clewiston.

"It's a possibility" Daniel replied, "—or the satellite might have been hit by a meteor in a coincidence of timing. We just don't know.

Anyway, no subsequent orbiter has revealed any signs of life around those pyramids—and I believe that they probably are pyramids."

"I never thought I would hear a NASA trained manager admit the obvious about those structures!" said Lawrence McNeal, who was Lowellsville's only nuclear power plant engineer.

"Miracles do happen sometimes!" joked Edward Slater, the colony's only vehicular engineer.

"Well, what I just told you was my opinion—not the N.A.S.A. director's policy line" Daniel explained. Now, about the aliens inside the big hill known to us as William's Bluff, there seems to be only one male and one female—plus some robots. Unfortunately, I learned recently that they are both sick with a disease that might be a strain of influenza brought to Mars by an unmanned space probe from Earth. So, I have asked Nurse Pamela Mason to come down here from Phobos Base and try to cure them. She will be assisted by Radio Technician Barbara Waverly and advised from a distance by our own community's Doctor Hudson."

"What's to prevent the disease from spreading to Lowellsville?" asked Chief Structural Engineer, Ronald R. Simmons.

"Pam and Barbara will wear space suits whenever they visit the aliens" Daniel replied. "That way, whenever our two medical ambassadors go outside the aliens' base, natural ultraviolet light should sterilize the suits—but they will use a u.v. lamp inside their vehicle's airlock to be sure their suits are decontaminated."

"You can't properly treat or diagnose someone like that! Especially aliens!" Doctor Hudson objected. "What do we know about those beings? You haven't even told us what they look like."

"Michael, tell the good doctor—and the rest of us—about the aliens' appearances" said Daniel.

Michael stood up and said "Well, judging by their space suits, they are about a foot taller than we are. They have four arms—one pair above the other—and the women have four breasts—also one pair above the other. Their faces appear light green through a space suit's yellow tinted visor, so their skin might be light green—or maybe light blue. We just don't know yet."

"Green skin!" Doctor Hudson exclaimed, "—just like the old cartoon pictures of aliens! I suppose they have antennae on their heads too."

"Sophia and I did not see any evidence of such appendages" Michael replied (with slightly strained patience).

"What do their faces look like?" asked Linda Simmons, "—if they have faces." Several people laughed at her remark, but Michael and Sophia just smiled briefly.

"They look like our faces—except for their skin color" Michael replied. "That's really all I can tell you. I've never seen one of them outside of a space suit."

"That's enough talk about the aliens for now" said Daniel. "I want each of you to think about what you and your department—or section—can do to make this base as independent of Earth as possible. Afterward, send your recommendations to me by email, or bring them to me in person—after you make a reservation with my secretary. I can't have all of you in my office at the same time."

The group laughed, then Bill Schaefer's voice came from the television set: "I know of one thing we can do to make ourselves more independent right now."

"Oh? What's that, Bill?" asked Daniel. "Your ideas are needed too—and yours, John."

"Thanks" said John's voice from the set. "Let's hear your idea, Bill."

"There is an underground, volcanic hotspot about five miles to the east of here that I believe could be used to generate electricity. I'd like to borrow Antwan and Erik when the weather clears so we can do a feasibility study of this idea. It would involve a trip to the site."

"All right, Bill. I want you to write a detailed report of what such a project might require and send it to me by computer." Daniel replied.

"I have a suggestion too, Daniel" said John. "Since the Chinese have damaged the *Wernher von Braun*'s home space port once already and could do so again, why don't we ask NASA's director to let us keep the ship and its crew out here at Phobos for the duration of the war? We could use the crew members' skills to make Phobos more habitable."

"That's an interesting idea, John—although it would involve changing several people's personal plans" Daniel replied. "You should make the suggestion to Warren Cox and see what he thinks of it, though, since you are on his territory."

"Yes, sir—I'll do that" John replied.

"Good" said Daniel. "Unless someone has some urgent issue to discuss, I will ask the following people to remain here a while longer: Doctor Hudson, Michael Edwards, Sandra Collins and Ronald Simmons. Tom Saunders, I want you to go call the *von Braun* to be sure that its captain knows about the war and about the Chinese missile damaging the Progress Space Station. The rest of you may return to whatever you were doing before this conference. Meeting adjourned."

Ten of the fifteen attendees left the conference room and Daniel closed the double, simulated wood doors behind them. Afterward he turned toward Ronald Simmons and said "Ronald, how long would you need to design and build a blast resistant door for the entrance of our main vehicle garage?"

"Do you mean to augment the present door or to replace it?" asked Ronald, with an engineer's attention to details.

Whichever proved itself to be the most feasible idea" Daniel replied.

"I don't know exactly" Ronald said carefully. "I would guess at least two weeks—provided we could find enough titanium to make it at all. Our present automated mine north of here is nearly depleted."

"Well, considering that a guided missile launched from Earth would require about five months to reach us, that should give us enough time to find another lode—if necessary" said Daniel. "See what you and Michael can do. This will be a high priority project."

"Yes, sir" his two subordinates chorused: then Michael added: "—but considering that a dangerously large meteor could hit this region of Mars before then, even <u>two</u> <u>weeks</u> for a completion date would really be none too soon. I've long believed that our big garage's door should have been made much thicker."

"I believe you would look both ways before crossing a one-way street, Michael" Ronald teased.

"You're right—I would" Michael replied with a slight smile. "Drivers don't always notice the **one-way** signs."

"Well said, Mike" Daniel commented. "I'd rather err on the side of caution too, but my predecessor didn't think that way. He always wanted to save money and please the bureaucrats in Wash-ington, D.C."

"Your predecessor was sent back to Earth as a broken man, sir" said Sophia. "I believe you are doing the right thing about the garage door. Our lives are more important than saving some money."

"Thank you for your support, Sophia" Daniel replied with a sincere smile.

"You have my endorsement too, Dan" said Doctor Gregory Hudson. "It won't do the colony any good if we save a few thousand dollars only to be killed by a meteor or a missile afterward."

"Thank you, doctor" Daniel replied. "Now tell me when you can examine Michael and Sandra to see if they were exposed to a dangerous disease when they explored a small part of the alien base two days ago?"

"I could invite them to my office and do blood tests for each of them" Doctor Hudson replied. "My medical computer should be able to detect any unusual microbes in the blood samples that I take from them."

"But <u>when</u> can you <u>do this,</u> doctor?" Daniel asked with a tone of annoyance. "I need to know if they should be quarantined."

"I can do it <u>now</u>, <u>sir</u>" Doctor Hudson replied ('although it may aggravate my regularly scheduled patients' he added mentally).

"Then <u>please</u>, go and <u>do it!</u>" Daniel said impatiently. "We need to know <u>if</u> the disease is <u>already</u> <u>among</u> us. If it is, there will be little benefit from taking elaborate precautions in the aliens' residence."

"<u>Yes</u>, <u>Mister</u> <u>Chief</u> <u>Administrator</u>" Doctor Hudson replied. He sounded as if he were becoming annoyed also. "Will you two intrepid explorers come with me, please?" he added, as he tried to sound humorous rather than sarcastic.

"Yes, doctor" Michael replied jestingly. "We'll go quietly."

Sophia giggled at Michael's surrendering felon act and followed him as he followed the physician out of the conference room. Sophia closed the door behind herself and accompanied the two men to a stairwell. None of them wanted to wait for an elevator near the conference room, with Mr. Morris still in a bad mood. On the next lower level they did go to an elevator shafts door, though and Dr. Hudson pushed the level selector button to summon the elevator.

Gregory Hudson was a small, slender, handsome man with a narrow, somewhat Germanic head. His hair was light yellow, his eyes were light gray and his voice was tenor. He was only five feet, six inches in height (the same as Sophia) and very intelligent. He had a good 'bedside manner' and most of the colonists liked him (except for those who tried to avoid doctors and dentists in general).

The little group soon entered the elevator and rode it downward four levels to a hallway where there were signs on the walls that pointed toward the various medical treatment and physical rehabilitation facilities. The three people turned leftward and walked along the corridor to a door in its right wall that had **Gregory Hudson, M.D.** engraved in a small, brass plaque that was fastened to it with four screws made of the same metal.

As Michael and Sophia followed the doctor into his waiting room, they saw only one other person there ahead of them—Louisa Monique d'Alsace.

"Well, Louisa, I didn't expect to see you here" said Michael. "What's bothering <u>you</u>?"

"If you <u>must</u> <u>know</u>, I have a yeast infection and my vagina itches" Louisa replied, while she tried to sound calm like a clinical technician.

"Go ahead and take care of Louisa, doctor" said Michael. Sophia and I can wait a while."

"All right" Doctor Hudson replied. "You and Sophia have a seat while I check in Louisa."

The two lovers went to a small couch and seated themselves on it. Meanwhile, Doctor Hudson went to a computer's data entry keyboard in what was normally his secretary's work area. He seated himself in front of her desk and thought: 'I hate only having a secretary during the afternoon hours.' He found Louisa's file with the computer, then he typed her arrival time and the reason for her visit into the appropriate spaces on the monitor's screen. Afterward he closed the file and led Louisa to one of the examining rooms.

As soon as Doctor Hudson was out of sight, Michael said to Sophia" Our doctor has an English surname, but he looks more like a German."

"His wife told me that he had an Austrian mother" Sophia replied. "His father was a doctor too and he met Elsa during some sort of medical convention in Vienna."

"Well, that solves the mystery" Michael joked.

"What do you plan to do to make our colony more self-sufficient, Mike?" asked Sophia. "All I can think of is 'Ask aliens for help.'"

"That may be all I can recommend too" Michael replied. "It's not like there is a wide variety of options available to us. Our resources are too few."

"Ow! Be more careful, doctor!" Louisa's voice exclaimed from beyond the examining room's door (which was about twenty feet from where Michael and Sophia sat).

"I'm sorry. I didn't realize that the infection had made your labia so sensitive" the doctor replied, with his voice muffled by the door.

"Louisa sure is in a bitchy mood today" Michael commented (in a tone just above a whisper).

"I think she's a little bit jealous of me because I found a husband and she hasn't" Sophia replied just as softly. 'Well, that's one of the reasons anyway' she added silently.

"Hell, that's not your fault!" Michael remarked with mild annoyance.

"I know, but her biological clock is ticking and she hasn't been able to interest James in dating her yet" Sophia explained.

"Oh? Is that why she's been exposing more cleavage lately?" Michael asked (with a smile of amusement).

"I think so" Sophia replied (also smiling). After a short pause she added "Maybe after I'm married, men will notice her more."

A few seconds later the examining room's door opened and Doctor Hudson emerged. He crossed a corridor and unlocked a door, then he entered a small supply room. It had six shelves on each of three walls and he scanned them until he found what he was seeking. He took a tube of ointment from a little bin and walked into the hallway. Once there he turned toward the waiting room and said "Michael, come to the second room on the right. I'll be with you soon."

"All right" Michael replied. He stood up and walked into the twenty-four feet long corridor behind the secretary's work area.

Doctor Hudson opened the door of the first examining room and was about to enter it when he heard a man's voice call to him from the waiting room: "I'm sorry I'm late for my appointment, doc. Can you still fit me in?"

Doctor Hudson turned toward the waiting room again and Michael stopped quickly to avoid colliding with him. Michael rotated toward his right to let the doctor see the person in the waiting room. In turn, Michael looked past the doctor. He saw Louisa sitting facing him on the near end of an examining table. She was naked and her legs were well separated.

Louisa emitted a shriek of embarrassment and quickly moved her legs toward each other. Her hands sped to her breasts, then Doctor Hudson closed the door quickly, with his face becoming as red as Louisa's countenance was.

"I'm sorry I exposed you, Louisa! Please forgive me!" he entreated sincerely. "Oh, where is my secretary? Things like this never happen when she's here!"

"You're lucky there aren't any lawyers on Mars yet or I'd sue you!" Louisa exclaimed through the door. "Now hand that ointment to me and tell Michael to go away!" The door opened slightly and a small, feminine hand reached outward with its palm turned upward. Doctor Hudson motioned for Michael to step behind him, then he handed the tube of hydrocortisone to Louisa. She quickly took it and withdrew her hand, then she slammed the door.

"Oh hell, doc! I didn't mean to cause any trouble!" Brian Mulroney's voice exclaimed from the waiting room. "I just wanted to get another type of athlete's foot ointment from you. My feet still itch."

Sophia placed her right hand over her mouth in an effort to stifle her laughter as she observed the six feet, two inches tall Texan's expression of boyish embarrassment. A pair of blue eyes blinked nervously at her green ones from beneath a Kennedy-like shock of red hair.

"What's so goldurned funny?!" Brian demanded with righteous indignation. In reply, Sophia laughed so loudly that her breasts bobbed up–and-down within her blouse. Every time she tried to stop laughing and apologize to him her laughter would resume. Sophia fell onto her right side on the couch's seat and laughed until Brian left the waiting room. As his footsteps faded away in the corridor that led toward the elevators, Sophia finally reduced her laughing to occasional giggling and sat upward erect.

Meanwhile Louisa sat, still naked, on the end of the examining table and carefully applied some of the ointment to her most feminine area. Afterward she closed the tube and set it aside.

'Of all the days to decide to go braless!' she exclaimed mentally, '—and why is Sandra laughing so much?! I didn't laugh at her this morning when she told me about Ronald Simmons seeing her bare buttocks!'

Louisa stood up beside the table and began dressing herself as fast as she could. While she pulled on her panties and coveralls she listened to the doctor typing information into his computer. Farther away she could hear her female coworker still giggling. Finally Louisa pulled on her warm socks and shoes, then she stood up. As she left the little room and entered the hallway as she said loudly: "Please control yourself, Sandra! You're prolonging my embarrassment!"

I'm sorry, Louisa—I really am! I apologize to you too, Doctor Hudson. "It's just that Brian reminded me in some ways of a little boy—even though he's much taller than I am" Sophia stated. Her giggling finally ended and she tried to appear more serious.

"Well he reminds me sometimes of that guy on the cover of *Mad Magazine*" Louisa admitted humorously, as she arrived in front of the couch. Then she and Sophia both laughed. Even Doctor Hudson smiled with amusement at the comparison and relief at Louisa's improvement in mood.

"All right" said Doctor Hudson. "I will go and check Michael's blood now. Your turn will be next, Sophia."

"Don't hurry" she replied sincerely, as the doctor walked to the second examining room. As soon as its door closed behind him, Louisa said "Now I know how you felt this morning, Sandra. Your fiance' just got an eyeful of me stark naked with my legs spread! I felt even worse when you began laughing—I thought it was directed at my situation until you told me about Brian. Why was he here, anyway?"

"He just wanted some athlete's foot ointment" Sophia explained, "—but he looked just as embarrassed about your situation as you were. I suppose his untimely arrival did help to cause your exposure to Mike, though."

"Yeah, I guess Doc Hudson did have too much to cope with at that point" said Louisa. "I just hope that Michael won't tell anyone else what he saw today."

"Don't worry—he's a nice guy. That's why I'm marrying him" Sophia consoled, "—but I wish you could have heard Brian speak with that cowboy accent of his: 'Oh hell, Doc! I didn't mean to cause any trouble!' "she mimicked. "He reminded me of Will Rogers from the nineteen thirties."

"He does sound like that!" Louisa realized with amusement. "And you make him sound so <u>penitent</u>! You'd think <u>he</u> had just seen <u>your</u> <u>bare</u> <u>bottom</u> instead of <u>Ronald</u>!"

"What's all this talk about <u>Ronald</u> looking at <u>your</u> <u>bare</u> <u>bottom</u>, Sophia?!" asked Michael, who had just emerged from the interior hallway with a cotton puff pressed against the inner surface of his sore right elbow.

"Your silly fiancée was retrieving the bottom half of her bikini after it fell off in front of Mister Simmons' apartment" Louisa explained smugly.

"It was an accident, Mike—like what happened in this medical suite's hallway ten minutes ago" Sophia added. "I was unlocking the door of Louisa's and my apartment when the right bow knot of my bikini bottom came loose and I almost lost the garment! I leaned forward and caught it almost off my bottom, then the door of the apartment behind me opened and Ronald Simmons glimpsed some of what every man in Lowellsville has been wanting to see! Fortunately my beach jacket covered some of what my bikini bottom didn't."

"That must have been embarrassing for you "Michael sympathized, as he sat down to the right of Sophia on the small couch.

"<u>It</u> <u>was!</u>" Sophia assured him, "—but at least it was <u>Ronald</u> who saw me then , instead of somebody who would tell everyone about it."

"I'm glad to see that everyone is in a <u>good</u> <u>mood</u> now" said the doctor (who had entered the secretary's work area unnoticed). "Come with me please, Sophia."

As Sophia stood up, Louisa exclaimed "I vant your blahd, mortal!" in her best vampire imitation.

Sophia made a lopsided frown of disapproval as she followed Doctor Hudson to the examining room that Michael had recently visited.

Meanwhile Louisa had seated herself in an arm chair across the waiting room from Michael. There were a few awkward seconds while she composed her thoughts, then she said calmly "All right, Michael, now that you have seen what you wanted to see, did you like it?"

"Yes" Michael replied sincerely. "you have a good looking body, Louisa."

"I'm glad <u>you</u> think so" she replied. "I could walk <u>naked</u> past most of this colony's <u>other</u> <u>men</u> and <u>they</u> would just go on yakking about how they would like to <u>go to bed with Sandra</u>! Honestly, Michael, <u>she is a nice person</u>, but she is driving the rest of us girls <u>crazy</u>! <u>We</u> keep wishing that <u>she</u> would <u>go</u> <u>back to</u> <u>Earth</u> and join a nunnery <u>so</u> <u>we</u> <u>could</u> <u>get</u> <u>some</u> <u>attention</u> <u>from</u> <u>the</u> <u>men</u> <u>around</u> <u>here</u>!"

"Well, you <u>certainly</u> <u>got</u> <u>my</u> <u>attention</u>" Michael declared, "but I am sorry if I embarrassed you, Louisa."

"It's all right" she replied. "To tell you the truth, I wish now that I had not brought my legs together so quickly! I was just startled. It was what we biologists call a *conditioned reflex*."

"I understand" said Michael (who really did not know what else to say in this type of situation).

"Any way, I can't stay mad at you." You're such a nice guy—<u>most of</u> <u>the</u> <u>time</u> anyhow" Louisa said with a slight smile. 'He's so <u>handsome</u>!' she thought, 'and he's <u>actually</u> <u>talking</u> to <u>me</u>!'.

Sophia emerged from the second examining room with a cotton ball in the same place that Michael's was. She walked into the secretary's work area and heard some of her fiancé's conversation with Louisa.

"Of course he's a nice guy—that's one of the reasons why I'm marrying him" she remarked humorously, as she emerged through the little exit gate into the waiting area. Michael and Louisa stood up to greet her and Louisa appeared slightly embarrassed.

"let's not tell anyone else about the incident this morning, okay?" Louisa asked her two friends. Both people agreed, after which Sophia said: "I'm glad to see that you two have made peace. The last thing I need are two friends of mine quarreling shortly before my wedding."

"I agree" Louisa replied. "Now, will someone please tell me what that meeting was about this morning? Mr. Morris didn't invite me to it."

"The U.S.N.A.and our Australian allies are at war against mainland China and North Korea" Michael explained. "So far it has been mostly a naval war on the Tai Wan Straits, but there also has been some fighting on land along the border of the two Koreas."

"Oh hell!" Louisa exclaimed. "Now everybody on Earth will forget about us here on Mars!"

"I, for one, hope that they do forget about us until the shooting stops!" said Sophia. "That way there won't be any missiles launched toward us!"

"I have an idea, girls" said Michael. "Since Mr. Morris wants the various departments' recommendations about what Lowellsville should do to survive the war, Let's all three go to the Geoogy Department. There we and James can combine our brain power and write a joint set of recommendations for me to take to the Chief Administrator's office today before noon." Both women agreed that this was a good idea, so the three friends left Dr. Hudson's office and walked to the elevator. They went upward one level, then they walked to the Geology Department. There they and James began making plans together.

An hour later, Michael and Sophia walked together to an elevator and went upward one more level. As they rode, Sophia said "Thanks for taking the time to apologize to Louisa, Mike. It caused her to feel important." She then kissed his face. Michael just smiled happily as the elevator stopped and its door opened.

The two lovers walked together to Daniel Morris' office suite and found his secretary, Linda Simmons, seated in he work station adjacent to the waiting area.

"Good morning. May I help you?" Linda asked pleasantly.

"Yes" Michael replied. We have a computer disc with the combined survival plans of the Biology and Geology Departments on it. My fiancée and I would like to present it to Mr. Morris in person—<u>if</u> he will <u>allow</u> us to do that."

"I'll ask him if that is all right" Linda replied. Afterward she used her telephone as an intercom and called her boss, while Michael admired her pretty face.

'She's such a good secretary, it's difficult to believe that's not her only job' Michael thought, 'but I remember her piloting the landing craft when Sophia and I arrived on Mars . . .'

Mr. Morris says it's okay to go in" Linda announced with a slight smile.

"Thank you said Sophia, as Michael preceded her toward Daniel's office. "Can you and I still meet at one-thirty today in my apartment?"

"Yes, I'll be there" Linda promised. "I'll be at your wedding too. Thank you for the invitation."

Sophia smiled and followed Michael into Daniel Morris' office. She had noticed her fianc'e ad-miring the view through Linda's thin, nylon blouse (which had a brassiere under it). Sophia thought: 'Wait until he sees me in my wedding gown—he will forget there are any other women on Mars!'

"Good morning, love birds! Today's the big day!" Mr. Morris greeted merrily.

"Yes, Sophia is reeling me in" Michael teased.

"Well, he took the bait willingly enough" she remarked with a patient smile.

"I'll bet you are right about that! Go ahead and have a seat" said the amused Chief Administrator, as he gestured toward a pair of light weight arm chairs in front of his desk. His two guests complied and both of them noticed a slight strain behind his smile.

"I've been talking to N.A.S.A. headquarters by radio" the C.A. told them. "I suggested that we could use someone to manage our growing fleet of manned and unmanned flying vehicles here on Mars—especially with a drone aircraft expert due to arrive in the supply ship with some of his creations about a week from now. Our Director reluctantly agreed to ask the I. T. S. to transfer Juan Hernandez to us and let his First Officer take the *Wernher von Braun* back to a lunar orbit to sit out the war. She would be a tempting target for the Chikoreans in an Earth Orbit."

"No doubt" Michael replied. "Sir, Sophia and I have brought a comp disk with us which has our recommendations for a combined Geology and Biology Department list of emergency methods on it for improving Lowellsville's security and autonomy during the war on Earth."

"Good" Daniel replied. "How about summarizing your suggestions for me verbally?"

"All right" Michael replied, as he placed the envelope containing the disc on his boss' desk-top. "First of all, Pastor Boswell recommends that the food gardens be at least doubled in size and that he be given an assistant."

"I've been considering expanding the gardens already" said Daniel, "but I think about fifty percent is as much as we can practically extend them any time soon. As for an assistant, I don't know where we could get one—unless Sandra could spare the time to do it" he added (using the name for her that he considered to be less formal). While he spoke, he was admiring the exposed lower halves of her shapely legs. 'She could have been a hosiery model!' he thought. 'What caused her to come to Mars?! Whatever it was, I'm glad she's here.'

"Sir, Louisa and I recommend that the *Wernher von Braun* be kept in a Mars orbit for the duration of the war and that its crew be divided between Lowellsville and Phobos Base" Sandra stated, as Daniel's gaze traveled slowly back up to her face.

"I like that idea!" Daniel replied,"-but I doubt that our agency's Director, Mr. Dobson, could persuade the I.T.S. to allow it. The ship belongs to them, after all."

"It would be worth a try" Michael remarked. "The *von Braun's* crew has skills that we and Phobos Base could put to good use."

"All right, I'll ask the Director to request an indefinite duration loan of the ship and we'll see what happens" Daniel promised.

"Our two departments also recommend that a defensive military alliance be created as soon as possible between the human colonists on Mars and Phobos as one group and the six limbed alien race as the other signatory" said Michael. "The latter group could probably provide the technology needed to destroy approaching enemy space craft."

"A couple of other departments have already made that suggestion by computer and I intend to implement it" Daniel replied, "—provided, of course, that the aliens do have the necessary technology and that they are willing to share it with us."

"They might not be able to share it with us" Sophia cautioned. "The disease that is afflicting them could become fatal."

"If that happens, we will study their machines and try to understand them without the aliens' help" Daniel replied, "—but it would be much easier for us if at least one of the creatures survives the illness."

"Pardon me, sir, but do we really know how many aliens there are—and if we do, how many of them have the disease?" Michael asked.

"Based on recent radio conversations between the aliens and the crew of the *Wernher von Braun*," Daniel replied, "I believe there are only a few of those four-armed people in their William's Bluff underground base—plus some robotic servants. Their culture may be in decline—at least in this region of Mars."

"In that case, maybe they need our help as much as we need theirs" Michael suggested.

"That would be the ideal situation" Daniel replied. "It would provide some bargaining power for us and they would still have something worthwhile to offer."

"Sir, I have a favor to ask of you" said Sophia.

"Oh? What's that" he asked. 'She's so gorgeous!' he added mentally. 'Why is she marrying a geologist?!'

"I don't think we're in immediate danger of attack—except by some stray meteor, perhaps. The Chinese have not even demonstrated the ability to reach Mars with a robotic lander—much less a weapon with the accuracy to hit Lowellsville from as far away as Earth. They can interfere with our interplanetary supply line, though. I think that is the greatest danger from them or the North Koreans."

"I hope you are correct" said Daniel, "but anyway, what are you leading up to?"

"My impending wedding to Mike is a special time for him and me" Sophia replied, "and I want our marriage to last. It needs to be constructed on a firm foundation of mutually shared experiences that will build respect and love between us. What I'm trying to say, sir, is that we need a honeymoon together on Phobos! Would you please allow that to happen?"

"I never knew you were such a good speech maker, Sophia" Daniel replied. Then he added humorously "Maybe you should have my job?"

"I don't want it, sir" Sophia assured him. I just want a proper wedding and a honeymoon! After ward, I'll be contented just to become Lowellsville's Life Sciences Director. I think that would be a better title for my job than Head Xenobiologist or whatever. After all, I'm as much involved with keeping our life support systems operating properly as I am with studying newly discovered alien life forms on Mars."

"What about you, Mike?" asked Daniel. "Do you have anything to add to her argument?"

"Well, sir, I know that the other women here in Lowellsville would probably like to send Sophia to Phobos for a week—or longer—just so they could get more of our men's attention" Michael replied (only half in jest). He and Daniel both laughed at this remark.

"If you two men would just <u>be</u> <u>serious</u> for <u>one</u> <u>minute</u>" Sophia said with annoyance, "—even if the Chinese do send a missile toward us, it will require several months to reach Mars and then it will probably <u>miss</u> <u>us</u>."

"All right, Sophia. I'll gamble on your being correct" said Daniel. "I'll let you and Michael go to Phobos together and do a series of experiments there in low gee sexual maneuvers. Maybe you'll write a book for the rest of us to read later, such as *Recommended Sexual Techniques for Low Gee Moons and Planetoids* by Michael and Sophia Edwards. It could become a best seller after the war ends."

"We'll give your idea serious consideration, sir" Michael replied. He noticed that Sophia's patience was wearing thin, so he stifled an urge to smile broadly and laugh.

"Okay, you two" said Daniel (more seriously than before), "when do you want me to go to the conference room this afternoon for your wedding ceremony?"

"The rehearsal will be at two o'clock and the wedding will be at four" Sophia replied. "May we have at least a few guests, sir?"

"All right, I'll let you invite two spectators each" said Daniel, "—provided that their recommendations for our colony's survival have been completed and sent to me by then."

"Thank you sir!" Michael and Sophia said in unison, then they exchanged a few pleasantries with Daniel and left his office. In the corridor Michael asked "What's next on your agenda, honey?"

"I must go consult with Pastor Boswell about what items he will need to enlarge the gardens' area by twenty-five to fifty percent" Sophia replied. "What do you need to do next?"

"I will go find James and ask him when he can have our wedding rings ready" Michael replied. I know that the war alert has delayed his work some. I also want to ask one of our meteorologists when she thinks the weather will improve. That way we will know when to begin packing for our trip to Phobos Base."

"All right" said Sophia. "Let's meet in the lunch room at noon."

An hour later, with their errands completed, Michael and Sophia met in the lunch room and ate their meal together. The room was crowded with people and most of them were talking about the war—or topics related to it. The two lovers soon tired of hearing this talk, so they ate quickly. When they finished eating they rose from their seats and left their table. Michael and Sophia took their trays, glasses and utensils to the automated cleaning system, then they left the noisy lunch room. They walked to a place in a corridor where they were about twenty feet away from the lunch rooms nearest entrance. There the lovers stopped walking and stood close to each other.

"I can finally hear myself think!" Michael exaggerated. "I'm tired of hearing all of that noisy speculation about the war."

"So am I!" Sophia agreed. "Now that we can hear each-other speak, what did James say about our wedding rings?"

"They won't be ready until two-thirty or so" Michael replied. "So we will just pretend that we are putting them on during the rehearsal."

"That's annoying, but I suppose there is nothing we can do about it" said Sophia. "Did you get a weather forecast?"

"Yes. I spoke with Nancy Chan in the Meteorology Department" Michael replied. "She thought the weather would begin clearing tomorrow evening, so you and I should have our rocket ride on Friday morning."

"Good" said Sophia. "We will have plenty of time to pack after our wedding night. "I talked with Louisa before lunch and she is willing to trade apartments with you so that you and I may have the big apartment together. We could start moving your things and hers tomorrow evening and she could complete the process for us while we're on Phobos—that is, if it's all right with you."

"If it's okay with her, its fine with me" Michael replied. "I need to re-decide who I will invite to the wedding now—and do a few other things, so I will see you at two o'clock."

"All right, dear" Sophia replied. "I need to do some errands too." They then kissed each other and went in different directions.

*(8) This was Daniel Morris' grandiosely bestowed title for the secretarial pool.

Chapter Twenty-Two
A Joyous Occasion

Sophia entered the waiting room of Dr. Hudson's office suite and saw Linda Simmons seated in front of a computer screen in the secretary's work area. Linda looked upward from the medical record that she was augmenting and smiled at the younger woman. "Hello, Sandra. Are you here for an appointment?" she asked.

"No" Sophia replied, as she approached the three feet high, simulated wooden railing between the waiting room and the work area; "—although Dr. Hudson suggested this morning that I should let him give me a physical examination some time soon. Honestly, Linda, everyone wants to see me naked!"

"Can you blame them?" Linda asked humorously. "I know you have a mirror in your apartment, so you <u>do know</u> what your <u>body looks like</u>, don't you?"

"Yes, I'm well acquainted with its appearance—after all, I've been wearing it for twenty-eight years" Sophia replied with strained humor. "<u>You're</u> the one people should admire, though. You are pretty, intelligent, and able to take care of the office work for <u>two part-time bosses</u>; in addition to being a <u>part-time shuttle pilot</u>, a <u>seamstress</u> and the <u>mother of two children</u>! Honestly, Linda, I don't know how you find the time to <u>eat</u>!"

"Sometimes I don't" Linda admitted humorously, "—like today, for instance. I finished sewing together the parts of you wedding dress during my lunch hour and left it lying on your bed."

"Thank you, Linda!" Sophia exclaimed. She then pushed her way past the little swinging gate in the barrier and went to where her friend was sitting. Sophia leaned toward Linda and kissed her face.

Linda smiled and said "That's a nice partial payment for a dress. Thank you, Sandra" (using the name that she and most of the other colonists preferred).

"You're welcome" the young beauty replied. "Incidentally, where is Doctor Hudson? I want to know if Mike and I are harboring some kind of alien disease organism after our discovery of that alien, underground base."

"As a matter of fact, I was just typing a summary of Doctor Hudson's findings so I could email them to you and Michael" Linda replied. "The doctor has gone to report them directly to the Chief Administrator. They are probably discussing the tests' results now."

"Oh God!" Sophia exclaimed. "I might as well hear the bad news from you, Linda."

"That's the strange thing about those test results—there is no bad news!" Linda declared. "According to the medical computer's analysis, you and your fiancé are in perfect health! No live pathogens of any type were discovered. Whatever made those aliens sick seems not to have been able to infect you."

"Thank God!" Sophia exclaimed. "I would have felt terrible if Mike and I had caused an epidemic here in Lowellsville—or on Phobos, for that matter." "Well, you don't need to worry about that" said Linda, "—however, there is a hormonal indication that you need to know about, Sandra—you may be carrying a passenger. The doctor wants to give you a different kind of test to be sure."

"Do you mean I'm pregnant?!" Sophia exclaimed.

"There's a possibility that you are" Linda replied, "—so it's a good thing that you are about to be married. Your child will have both parents to take care of it."

"Thank you for this news!" Sophia exclaimed. "Please don't tell anyone about it, though. "I'll decide when I want people to know about it."

"All right" Linda replied. "I know how you feel. My first pregnancy came as a surprise too."

"There's something else I need to discuss with you" said Sandra, with a slight frown. "Mister Morris told me that I could only invite two spectators to my wedding! So I want you to be one of them and Louisa or your husband to be the other one—I have not decided about that yet."

"Thank you dear. That is very kind of you to invite me!" said her pretty benefactress with a happy smile.

"I invited several other people originally" added Sophia. "Now how do I disinvite them?"

"I don't know of any easy way to do that, dear" Linda replied. I suppose all you can do is just tell them that our Chief Administrator forced this choice on you and that you reluctantly did it."

"Sophia considered this advice for a while, then she said "All right, I suppose there's no other choice." She added a temporary "goodbye" to her friend and went to her apartment to try on the new wedding gown.

When she entered her bedroom six minutes later, she removed her brassiere, then she picked up the gown. Sophia put it on eagerly and saw that it fit her well. The thin, clingy material outlined the shape of her body from the hips upward. Some of the color of her skin could be seen through the light weight, parachute fabric—especially on her breasts and shoulders.

Sophia stepped before a large mirror on her closet door and felt almost nude when she saw the flesh colored silhouette of her body created by the room's electric lights shining through the gown.

"Hmm! Perhaps it's just as well that there will be few spectators!" she said to herself. She then carefully removes the gown and laid it on her bed (where she had found it when she arrived in the room).

Clad only in her thin, lace panties and light weight shoes she went into the apartment's long, narrow living room and turned off the video function of the vidphone. She then electronically substituted a pre-recorded, stationary image of herself for the real thing. The fully clad image would be seen by her responders as she telephoned the people whom she could no longer allow to attend her wedding.

One by one the disinvited guests reacted with disappointment—and sometimes anger. The angriest person was Louisa, but Sophia was glad to learn that her tirade was mostly directed at Daniel Morris. 'He deserves it, rather than me!' Sophia thought, as she called the last person on her *must call* list. This was Ronald Simmons in his work place. When she heard him answer she said:

"Hello, Ronald, this is Sandra. I'm sorry about the recorded image, but I'm not dressed."

"Oh, I wondered about that" he replied. "What may I do for you?"

"I would like for you to bring a digital camcorder to my wedding and record <u>all of it for</u> me!" she replied (as she tried to restrain her emotions after the stormy conversation with Louisa).

"Sure, I'll be happy to do that" Ronald assured her. "You sound unhappy, Sandra. What's the problem?"

"Mr. Morris <u>forced me</u> to shorten the guest list!" she explained,"—but <u>you are still on it</u>".

"<u>That rat!</u>" the normally calm engineer replied. "I'll have a few words with him!"

'This is one of the few times I ever heard him insult someone' thought Sophia. "He has always reserved name calling for the greedy corporate bosses on Earth!'

"Would you like for me to record the rehearsal too?" Ronald asked, as he forced himself to sound calmer. Inside him his emotions were still boiling though.

"No, just the main event" Sophia replied. "It will be much smaller now. Mr. Morris will only allow Mike and me to invite <u>two</u> spectators each, so everyone else will need to see it on closed circuit T.V.—if Daniel doesn't cancel that! Honestly, I don't know why he wants to spoil my wedding day! We're millions of miles away from that war on Earth."

"<u>I'll go ask him</u> what his reasons are—and he's better have a <u>good explanation!</u>" Ronald exclaimed. "If he thinks I can only design structural supports for buildings and tunnels, he has another thought coming! I'm not one of his damned robots!" Ronald paused for a moment, then he added: "Anyway, I'll be in the conference room at four o'clock—<u>if</u> I'm not under <u>house</u> arrest by then."

"Make that about ten minutes before four o'clock, please, so you can be sure to record all of the guests as they arrive" said Sophia. "Maybe Mr. Morris will relent and let us have a few more people there by then. I really feel bad about disinviting Louisa, for instance."

"Okay, three fifty it will be" Ronald replied, "—and thanks for being such a good sport about that incident this morning. Some women would have sulked about it for several days."

"I possed <u>nude for an art class</u> when I was <u>twenty-two</u>" Sophia explained, "so it's not the end of my world if a friend sees me when my bikini bottom falls off. Just out of curiosity, though, what caused you to open your door at that precise moment?"

"I heard your flip-flops in the corridor and I wanted to ask you how your wedding preparations were going" Ronald explained. "I didn't expect to see a preview of your honey moon, though. Mike is a lucky man."

"Thank you for your flattery!" said Sophia. ":A girl likes to know she's appreciated."

"Well, <u>you</u> certainly are!" he assured her. "Now, if you'll excuse me, I want to go visit our esteemed Chief Administrator . . ."

Shortly before two o'clock Michael, Sophia, Pastor Boswell, and Daniel gathered in the main conference room for the rehearsal. They were not yet formally clad, but someone had already removed the two tables and placed a large group of chairs in several rows at the right end of the room. There were vases full of artificial flowers decorating the left end of the room and a narrow red carpet led in a 'tee' shape from the group of chairs to the area in front of the lectern.

"Why are there so many chairs?!" Sophia asked Daniel (who appeared sheepish in his behaviour and expression).

"Because I've been <u>forced</u> <u>to</u> <u>rescind</u> <u>my</u> <u>restrictions</u> on the number of spectators" Daniel replied (with a mixture of resentment and embarrassment in his voice). "Some of our citizens—led by Mr. Simmons—have threatened to <u>declare</u> <u>a</u> <u>republic</u> and <u>elect</u> <u>a</u> <u>new</u> <u>leader</u> if I didn't!"

"I must say that I've been surprised by the amount of threatening email received recently by our Chief Executive" Pastor Boswell remarked half humorously.

"Hi everybody! Am I on time?" asked a cheerful female voice from the main doorway. Michael glanced at his watch and replied "No, Louisa, you are right on time. Welcome to the rehearsal. We've just been discussing the reasons for this last minute change in the number of guests." Louisa entered the room with a silly, lop-sided grin on her freshly made up face. She was wearing a pink, knee length dress with a wide skirt and a crinoline beneath it. Its thin sleeves and bodice were covered with lace, but an interesting amount of skin peeked through the thin material.

"Well, <u>I</u> <u>must</u> <u>say</u> that when <u>a</u> <u>preacher</u> sends an letter to me saying that 'I believe your zeal for war preparations is excessive' I suppose I should expect a public reaction to my policies that is little short of armed revolt!" (his listeners noticed a trace of humor in their leader's voice at this point). "So, I shall make a public address system announcement shortly after this rehearsal to tell our irate citizens that I am willing to risk allowing a direct hit by a large warhead to collapse the upper floors of our community with most of our colonists crowded onto them."

"Oh, for heaven's sake!" Louisa exclaimed, with her hands on her hips. "Stop acting like a martyr, Mr. Morris! A nuclear warhead would require at least five months to reach our community from China or North Korea—that is, if a strategic missile assault by the U.S.N.A. doesn't erase these two troublesome Asian nations from Earth's maps in the next few days."

"Please, everyone!" Pastor Boswell exclaimed. "May I remind all of you that we are here to rehearse a wedding—not to debate wartime policy!"

"That's a good point, reverend" Michael remarked. "We can debate later—if anyone still wants to do it. Meanwhile, Pastor Boswell is the man in charge of the present proceedings."

"Thank you, Mr. Edwards" said the clergyman. "Because of the awkward way that this room's main doors are located, I think that the bride and groom should use the service doors at the eastern end of the room—that's why the red carpet begins there. Are there any objections from anyone?"

"Not me, pastor" Michael replied, "—although I have not seen my fiancée's wedding dress yet. Would it be too wide to pass through that narrow doorway, honey?"

"No, dear" Sophia replied. "The gown is close fitting most of the way down."

"All right" said Pastor Boswell. "That eliminates a potential problem. "I'v already been informed by the groom's 'phone call a half-hour ago that the two wedding rings are not quite ready yet, so we'll just pretend to have them during this rehearsal. Let's begin with the arrival of the groom and his best man . . ."

About twenty-five minutes later the rehearsal was completed and everyone left the conference room. Michael and Sophia met with Mr. Morris afterward in a transverse, third floor corridor, near the main entrance of the conference room.

"Thank you for changing your mind, Mr. Morris" said Sophia. "It means a lot to us."

"I hope that I'm doing the right thing" Daniel replied contritely. "The Chinese have been purchasing Russian-made missiles for at least the last four years and their leaders could have been planning this war that long. If so, they might have launched a missile—or perhaps several—toward

Mars before their air force attacked our country's warships on the Tai Wan Straits."

"Or maybe this entire war is due to a series of miscalculations by the Chinese and the North Koreans" Michael countered. "Anyway, Russian-made rockets have never succeeded in landing a functioning Planetary probe on Mars, so I doubt that they could hit a small target like Lowellsville this far away from Earth with any kind of warhead."

"I hope you are correct" Daniel replied, "—but I'd rather see our people busy building a pair of blast doors for Lowellsville's main entrance than having most of us close together in—or near—a single room. If a missile destroys that one room, we will lose most of our community's best scientists and engineers."

"Tomorrow will be soon enough to start worrying about a war that's millions of miles away" said a familiar sounding male voice from close to their left. The group turned and saw James holding a rolled up piece of soft cloth. He unrolled it and revealed a pair of golden rings. Each ring had a small diamond set in it.

"These diamonds are man-made, since no-one has ever found a naturally made diamond on Mars" James explained.

"They're beautiful!" Sophia exclaimed. "Thank you, James!" Then she kissed his face briefly.

"You're welcome" he replied, as Sophia stepped back two paces. James looked at her admiringly and thought: 'I wish <u>I</u> was the one <u>marrying her</u>! Instead I have that plain faced Louisa wanting to date me. <u>Her body</u> is <u>attractive</u>, but <u>her face</u> could use a visit to a <u>plastic surgeon</u>!'

James gave the rings to their intended recipients, then he went to his apartment to put on his only formal suit.

By a quarter 'til four, fifteen people were seated in folding chairs in the eastern half of the conference room. There were seventeen chairs arranged in three rows. A five feet wide aisle divided each row into two sets of two or three chairs and each chair was highly valued by the person who sat in it. One chair was no t yet occupied in the back row and one was being saved by Linda Simmons in the right half of the front row. Ronald soon entered the room with his camcorder (he head been standing in the corridor and recording the guests' words and images as they arrived). He scanned the crowd with his camcorder as he approached his chair, then he finally seated himself in it.

The last guest to arrive was Brian Mulroney and he was the first of them to see Sophia in her wedding gown. The sight of her standing in the corridor, with Michael to her left and Louisa and Daniel to her right, nearly took his breath away! Sophia's all white gown was as thin and soft as a man's undershirt. Its low, wide, U-shaped neckline revealed a fascinating amount of the most beautiful pair of breasts that Brian had ever seen!

"Reel your eyeballs back in, Brian" Michael teased. "You might need them again later." Brian smiled sheepishly, and moved his lower jaw briefly, but no words would emerge. He then entered the wedding room and went to the last empty chair, which was in the back row. It was at the right end of the row, beside a television camera, the operator of which was standing in place of another chair there. Each long row of chairs curved forward slightly at its outer ends, which helped to provide enough space for the bulky television camera and its tripod.

"If I live to be a hundred, I'll never see a more gorgeous woman than I have just seen!' thought Brian. 'Compared to her, these other women—with the possible exceptions of Linda and Dianne*(9)—are a flock of plain faced sheep!'

Precisely at four o'clock, a music disk began playing the wedding march from Wagner's opera, *Tanhauser,* through four shelf-mounted speakers in the glorified conference room. Michael and Daniel entered the room and followed the red carpeted aisle to its T-shaped end. Both men were formally clad and handsome (especially Michael). Close behind them came Sophia and Louisa, both of whom were wearing beautiful, low-cut gowns. Louisa had a partly suppressed grin of triumph on her face—especially whenever she glanced at Daniel. The latter just frowned slightly and looked away whenever he noticed her attention.

Sophia immediately felt the gaze of every man in the room. She also noticed that the adjustable, overhead lights were at their maximum brightness (which was seldom used, due to the glare). This unusually bright light caused her gown to seem even thinner than it normally appeared. 'I wonder <u>whose clever idea that was</u>?!' she wondered. 'Probably one of the <u>men</u>!'

Several people (mostly women) actually gasped as the wedding gowns material revealed an unintended amount of physical details. 'Thank God I decided to wear <u>panties under</u> this gown!' Sophia thought, as she bravely advanced along the aisle. 'Right now I feel like they are <u>all</u> that I'm wearing!'

Michael whispered emphatically to Daniel: "Go turn that damned rheostat <u>down!</u>" Daniel nodded and walked to the device (which was mounted on the south wall of the room, beside the big, double doors). Daniel backed the circular light control knob about fifteen degrees, then he returned to his assigned place beside Michael. The rest of the wedding went well and Michael happily kissed his new bride at the end of it.

The unmarried women from the audience gathered in the corridor and the newly wed couple walked through a hastily made gap in their group. From about eight feet beyond them, Sophia turned around and tossed the bridal bouquet toward the group. Patricia Franklin caught the bouquet and the other unmarried women reluctantly applauded. Patricia looked hopefully at Daniel as he approached her. Daniel put his left arm around her shoulders and kissed her face. His right hand was busy loosening his tie to admit some of the corridor's comparatively cool air under his collar.

"Well, Daniel, you're Lowellsville's most eligible bachelor now" Linda Simmons remarked with a pleasant smile from a few feet away.

"Maybe so—if these good people don't start <u>sticking knives into me</u> like <u>Caesar's foes</u>!" he replied with grim humor. "Hopefully I will arrive safely at the reception party for today's couple." He then looked at his pretty companion and whispered "Let's go now, Pat." She nodded and the two of them walked together to an elevator shaft where they waited for the car to reach their floor.

"I think you saved yourself with that concession message that you sent to everybody by email an hour or so ago" said Patricia. "That was quite a feat of diplomacy, dear."

"Thank you" Daniel replied. "I tried to lose gracefully."

"I think you succeeded admirably, sir" Michael commented, as he and Sophia waived to the right of the other couple. Soon the elevator arrived and the group rode downward two levels to a hallway that gave access to the recently decorated dining room.

"The Chinese missed a golden opportunity today" Daniel remarked as the elevator's door opened. The two couples emerged from the car and joined a crowd of people who had used the stairway to arrive at the area near the dining room. Soon all of the celebrants entered the dining room, with the two newly weds in the lead. Everyone received a piece of the huge, multitiered wedding cake that some of the women had spent several hours preparing during the previous evening. Several people made photographs of the new couple and of the distribution of the cake as the latter gradually disappeared. Soon several couples began dancing to recorded music in an open area near the left end of the room. Daniel and Patricia were among them, as were Michael and Sophia.

After about half an hour of celebrating with their well wishers, the newlyweds left quietly and went to Michael's apartment. He put a 'Do Not Disturb' sign on the door and closed it, then he picked up Sophia and carried her into the bedroom. There they kissed each other a while before they undressed and went to the bed. They spent the next half-hour making love to the accompaniment of a recording of Ravel's erotic composition *Bolero*.

Meanwhile, frame able prints of Sophia in her very revealing wedding attire became much in demand among the unmarried men of the Lowellsville community. However, no-one would admit to being the person who had secretly turned up the rheostat in the conference room before the wedding ceremony began.

The women of the colony were eagerly awaiting an improvement of the weather, since Mr. Mor-ris' announcement in the dining room that he had decided to allow Sophia to accompany her new husband to Phobos Base for a week's assignment there. This was the realization of the ladies' fondest wish and it gave them an additional reason to celebrate for another forty-five minutes after the newlyweds had left the dining room.

*(9) Dianne Fletcher was the attractive—and still unmarried—manager of Lowellsvilles only television station, LWVL. She had only one full-time assistant, her camera man, who was not present at the wedding.

Chapter Twenty-Three
A Busy Wedding Night

At six-thirty in the evening, the naked newlyweds heard the apartment's doorbell ring, then a familiar sounding female voice announced through the private intercom: "Room service! I brought dinner on a cart for you two love birds."

The newlyweds recognized Louisa's voice, so Sophia replied "I'll be right there!" As she started toward the living room, Michael asked "Don't you want to put something on?" Sophia shook her head and replied, this is Louisa, remember?"

Sophia went to the apartment's door and unlocked it. As she opened the door, she stepped behind it. "Come in, Lou" she invited.

Meanwhile, Michael had quickly stepped into his boxer shorts and went into the living room. "Hello, Louisa" he greeted, as she pushed a four wheeled, stainless steel, meal cart into the apartment.

"Hello, Tarzan!" she replied humorously, as she scanned his handsome, scantily clad body appreciatively.

Sophia closed the apartment's door and stepped boldly naked from behind it, while Louisa parked the car in front of the couch. Louisa then turned around and smiled.

"You might as well have <u>gotten</u> <u>married</u> <u>like</u> <u>that</u>!" she teased. "You made all of the men happy in that see-through wedding gown of yours! I would never have had the courage to wear <u>that</u> in public!"

"It wasn't <u>meant</u> to be <u>completely</u> <u>transparent</u>!" Sophia repled.

"I think that initial room lighting was someone's perverted idea of a joke" Michael remarked testily, then he and Sophia seated themselves on the couch. As they picked up their utensils from the cart in front of them Sophia remarked: "I wasn't expecting Florida Keys-like lighting*(10) in that room. My wedding gown was meant for Lowellsville's usual gloomy amount of lighting."

"That's the price you pay for having a <u>televised</u> <u>wedding</u>" said Louisa, as she seated herself in an armchair that faced the couch. "People will be talking about your <u>Lady</u> <u>Godiva</u> <u>act</u> for a <u>long</u> <u>time</u>!." As she spoke, she leaned forward and took her own plate and utensils from the lower shelf of the cart.

"Let them talk!" Sophia replied with a mixture of defiance and resignation. "The men have <u>long</u> <u>wanted</u> to see <u>me</u> naked and they <u>almost</u> got their wish!"

The three friends ate in silence for a while, then Sophia said "Those blood tests of ours came back <u>negative</u> this morning, Mike, in case you were haven't heard about it already. Doctor Hudson said that he and his medical computer could not find <u>a</u> <u>trace</u> of an <u>active</u> <u>disease</u> <u>organism</u>!"

"That's good news" Michael replied, "—but it leaves me wondering <u>what</u> <u>made</u> those <u>aliens</u> <u>sick</u>?"

"Maybe it was an organism that <u>we</u> <u>humans</u> long ago learned <u>to</u> <u>tollerate</u>" Louisa suggested. "<u>We</u> might not consider it to be an infectious agent."

"<u>That's</u> a <u>possibility</u>!" Sophia agreed.

"This whole situation reminds me of what happened to the American Indians when Columbus and his men arrived" Michael remarked. "European diseases killed most of the Arawak people of the West Indian Islands that the Spanish explored."

"The process could also operate in reverse" Louisa cautioned.

"Yes, but so far it has not" Michael replied, between bites of food. "I wonder why."

"I don't know" said Sophia, "—but that space probe that the aliens were examining needs to be removed from <u>all</u> <u>contact</u> with people of <u>either</u> <u>species</u>."

"Agreed" said Louisa. "We don't need a repeat of something like the AIDS pandemic that is plaguing much of Earth now."

"Speaking of <u>contact</u>" said Michael, "I've bee curous about something concerning you two women. During two years of sharing an apartment, did you two ever have any recreational sex with each other?"

"<u>How</u> <u>did</u> <u>he</u> <u>know</u>?!' Louisa wondered silently. 'This could ruin everything!'

"We did it a few times" Sophia admitted reluctantly, "—just for fun. Are you jealous, Mike?"

"No, not at all" Michael replied. "<u>Everyone</u> <u>needs</u> to do it <u>with</u> <u>somebody</u> occasionally. I was just wondering if either of you would object to some <u>three</u> <u>way</u> bed sport tonight."

"I thought you would <u>never</u> <u>ask</u>!" Louisa replied with a smile. "Any way, <u>I'm</u> <u>a</u> <u>bisexual</u>, Mike. You might as well know it now. I hope that doesn't bother you."

"No" he replied, "—in fact, <u>it</u> <u>may</u> <u>simplify</u> <u>things</u>. What's your vote, Sophie?"

"I have <u>no</u> <u>objection</u>—<u>if</u> you <u>use</u> <u>a</u> <u>condom</u>, Mike" Sophia decided mildly. "All of us are mature adults, after all—and I want us to remain friends—as well as lovers."

"All right, nature boy! Let's see what's been hiding under those shorts!" Louisa exclaimed playfully. Then she quickly divested herself of her shoes while the object of her desire emerged—as if on a signal—from the slit in the front of the offending garment. Michael and Sophia pushed the cart aside and stood up. Louisa wolf whistled as Michael dropped the under garment to his ankles and stepped out of it.

"Sophie should have gotten married sooner!" Louisa exclaimed happily. Then she stood up and her female lover helped her to undress . . .

An hour later, a recently reclad Louisa left the newlyweds' apartment and pushed the meal cart back to the dining room. Pleasant memories of Sophia's and Michael's intimate interactions with her nude body accompanied her. So did a request from Sophia for a medium-size suitcase of hers, with a dress, grooming items, and some underwear packed inside of it.

Meanwhile, Michael and Sophia walked naked from their bedroom into the living room and seated themselves on the couch. Sophia leaned against him affectionately while he picked up the remote control. Device for the television and summoned the most recent news program from Earth. As they had expected, the crisis in Asia had a prominent role in the reporting segments. The Tai Wanese government had declared complete and permanent independence from China and had demanded a seat of its own in the United Nations. The U.S.N.A. had urged the world's governments to recognize the new nation and allow it to be seated in the U.N.

The Tai Wanese had used a U.S.N.A. provided Patriot III missile to intercept and destroy a Chinese ballistic missile that was apparently aimed at their capital city. A Tai Wanese Navy destroyer had used an antiaircraft missile to shoot down a Chinese warplane that had ventured too close to the ship.

On the Korean Peninsula, a tank battle was being fought in an area just south of the so-called 'Demilitarized Zone' and the two opposing Korean governments were each claiming to be winning it. U.S.N.A. Air Force jet fighters were reported to have shot down two north Korean aircraft near the ground battle, with no loss to themselves.

"It looks like things are going better for our team today" Michael remarked.

"Let's hope that continues" Sophia replied.

The television picture shifted toward the top part of a large map of the two Korean nations. A small, red dot near the Chinese border glowed brighter. Next the news anchorman spoke:

"We have just received word from the U.S.N.A.'s Space Command that one hour ago two missiles left this camouflaged launch site near the Yalu River. At first Space Command thought that these were offensive missiles headed toward Japan or perhaps Guam, but instead their upper stages went into space! Space Command is now trying to determine what the real objective is. So far there is no def—inite answer."

A commercial advertising life insurance came on then and Michael laughed at the grim relevancy of it before he turned off the television set. "I think they waited a bit too long to offer those policies" he remarked.

"Probably so" Sophia replied with as brief smile, "—but I wonder where those two North Korean rockets are going?"

"I think I know the answer" Michael replied grimly. "Those two missiles were aimed at either our lunar clony or <u>us</u>."

"Or <u>both</u> <u>colonies</u>" Sophia suggested, "—one warhead for each place."

"<u>That's</u> <u>a</u> <u>possibility</u>" said Michael, "—but <u>if</u> one of them <u>is</u> on its way <u>to</u> <u>Mars</u>, it will require <u>several</u> <u>months</u> to make the journey, <u>then</u> it must try to find and hit <u>a</u> <u>tiny</u> <u>community</u> on a planetary surface as large as <u>all</u> <u>of</u> <u>Earth's</u> <u>continents</u> <u>combined</u>."

The apartment's door bell rang, with two short rings close together, like Louisa had promised to do. "I'll answer it" said Michael. He picked up his boxer shorts from the back rest of the couch and put them on, while Sophia remained seated on the couch. Michael went to the door and opened it. To his surprise he saw Linda Simmons instead of Louisa. She was wearing a knee length dress and a pair of shoes—plus a worried expression.

"Michael, have you heard the news?!" she asked excitedly.

"Do you mean about the <u>North Korean missiles</u>?" he asked, as he stood facing her in the apartment's doorway.

"Yes!" she replied. "Do you suppose that one of them <u>might be aimed at us</u>?"

"It's possible" he answered, "but I doubt it can <u>find us</u>—we're a <u>very small target</u> and <u>the distance</u> it must travel <u>is enormous</u>! I doubt that it will hit us."

"I hope you are correct" Linda stated. "Any way, I think I left my best pair of scissors in your bedroom when I finished making Sandra's wedding gown."

"You did" Sandra replied, as she rose to a standing position. "I found them and put them in the top drawer of the night stand. I'll go get them." She went into the bedroom, while Michael invited Linda to come into the living room and wait for her. Linda was about to politely decline the invitation, but the telephone in the bedroom rang and Sanra answered it.

"I suppose I shouldn't keep you standing here at the door" said Linda as she stepped past Michael and he closed the door behind her.

"I want to <u>apologize to you</u> for making Sandra's wedding gown out of <u>such thin material</u>" said Linda. "I should have <u>sown more lace</u> onto it, <u>but I ran out of time</u>!"

"<u>Don't worry about it</u>!" Michael replied. "Sophia has the sexual boldness of a legendary Greek nymph! It's one of the things I like about her."

Sophia returned to the living room and smiled with amusement at her husband's remark as she handed the scissors to her seamstress. Linda accepted them with only slight embarrassment as she briefly scanned the figure of her nude customer.

"Honestly, Sandra! I thought <u>I</u> had a good figure until I met <u>you</u>!" Linda exclaimed. "Michael is correct—you do look like a nymph from the ancient Greek legends!"

"I'll take that as a compliment" the younger woman replied humorously. Afterward she turned toward her husband and said "Mr. Morris just called. He wants you to come to his apartment as soon as possible!"

"All right, I'd better get dressed" Michael replied with some annoyance. "I'm sorry to rush off, Linda—and thank you for helping Sophie and me with our wedding."

"You're welcome" Linda stated. I was glad to be of assistance. Anyway, I need to be going too. I promised my son I'd help him with his math homework."

"I guess I'll just watch t.v. and hope that Louisa will bring my overnight suitcase to me soon" Sophia decided.

Michael and Linda left the living room of the apartment. He went to the bedroom and she went to her own residence. About ten minutes later Michael emerged from the newlyweds' bedroom fully dressed. He went to the couch and briefly kissed Sophia goodbye, then he left the apartment.

Sophia went into the bedroom and decided to put on her panties, since she did not know if someone might accompany Michael back to the apartment. Afterward she admired her beautiful wedding dress as it hung in the walk-in closet. 'That was a wonderful ceremony!' she thought, '—but it went by so fast! Now I'm a married woman—and probably a mother to be! So much has happened during the last few days!'

Meanwhile, Michael walked to Daniel's apartment and rang the door bell. Daniel soon opened the door and Michael entered the living room. He was not surprised to see Patricia Franklin there. Every—one in Lowellsville knew by this time that the pretty little weather predictor and their Chief Administrator were in love with each other. However, he was surprised to see Louisa d' Alsace, who looked up at him from her seat on the couch and smiled briefly. Louisa still wore the same vee-neckline dress that she had put on after the wedding ceremonies and the party ended; but Patricia wore a short bathrobe and a pair of house shoes. The bathrobe required frequent pulling together at its lower front area to avoid revealing too much of her body. Her hastily brushed hair was still in some disarray, so Michael thought 'It's obvious to me that she and Daniel have recently been doing something more interesting than discussing the weather!'

Patricia was sitting to the right of Louisa on the couch and she too smiled in a friendly way when she saw Michael arrive. 'He's such a nice guy, I doubt he will tell anyone that he saw me wearing so little here this evening' she thought hopefully.

Michael smiled back at the two females and seated himself in one of the two armchairs, from which he had a good view of the women's legs and breast cleavages. 'I wonder why Louisa is here?' he thought with casual interest. Meanwhile Daniel seated himself to the right of Michael in the other big, comfortable armchair.

Once again Michael noticed how the little imperfections of Louisa's nose, moth and chin caused a potentially pretty face to appear plain. 'A plastic surgeon could do wonders for her!' he thought. Then he noticed a medium sized suitcase standing beside her end of the couch and close to the door of the apartment. He recognized it as an item that Sophia often referred to as her "over night luggage."

"I'm sorry to interrupt everyone's post wedding frivolity" said Daniel, "but there is the small matter of a war to discuss, along with our role in it." Everyone looked at him with a resigned expression. When Daniel saw that he had their attention, he resumed speaking. "As each of you has probably heard by now, North Korea seems to have launched two missiles into space recently. N.A.S.A.'s director sent a coded message to me a short time ago to inform me that there are some indications that one of those missiles is beginning a long, interplanetary journey through space toward Mars. While I am skeptical of its ability to find Lowellsville, the possibility remains that it might. Director Dobson suggested to me that the missile could have a guidance system that is designed to home on our radio transmissions to Earth. Therefore I have decided to reduce the lengths of those transmissions and I am considering building a transmitter at a decoy location to try to lure the missile to a false target during the last couple of weeks that it is in flight. "However, I shall wait until Douglas Bell arrives and ask him to advise me about unpiloted vehicles' guidance systems."

"Those sounds like good ideas to me, sir" Michael remarked. "Mr. Bell should know more about guidance systems than anyone in Lowellsville does at the present time. We want to make sure that the missile does not outwit us somehow."

"Shouldn't we warn the people in <u>Phobobs Base</u>?" asked Patricia. "The missile <u>could</u> <u>hit</u> <u>them</u> <u>instead</u> <u>of</u> <u>us</u>."

"I have considered that possibility" her lover replied. "That's why I want Michael to take this warning message to Warren Cox Smith for me." He removed a recording disk from his shirt's breast pocket and handed it to Michael in a clear plastic container.

"I'll give it to him, sir" Michael promised.

"Good" said Daniel. "I don't want anyone in this room to tell <u>anyone else</u> about this disk's message—in case we have <u>a spy</u> in our community."

"Do you suspect someone?" asked Louisa, with a worried tone of voice.

"No-one in particular, but the most effective type of spy is the one who is able to blend with the community that he—or she—is harming" Daniel replied. "We cannot afford to assume that <u>everyone</u> in this colony <u>is loyal</u> to it. To do so might put the entire community in danger."

"Why would the North Koreans or the Chinese plant a spy in Lowellsville?" asked Patricia. "We don't have any hidden weapons of mass destruction here—do we dear?"

"No, but those two nations' leaders are small, paranoid groups of idealists" Daniel replied. "They don't always act in ways that we would consider rational."

"As is evidenced by this war that they recently started" Michael remarked cynically.

"<u>Exactly</u>" Daniel replied. "They probably <u>can not win</u> it, but they can cause misery or death for <u>tens of thousands</u>—or <u>even millions</u>—of people before they lose it."

"<u>I wish we could help our people</u> back on Earth" said Patricia, as she fidgeted nervously and moved her legs slightly farther apart. Michael smiled briefly as he had a glimpse of what she had been trying to conceal earlier, then she rotated her body a few degrees to the right and the center of her womanhood was hidden again by her left leg.

"<u>We can help them</u>—<u>indirectly</u>" Daniel stated (without seeming to notice his lover's brief discomfiture). "<u>We can outwit that missile</u> and prove to our nation's enemies that it is time for them to <u>negotiate an end</u> to this war." Then he looked toward Louisa and asked:

"Louisa, are you ready to <u>direct our Biology Department</u> while Sandra is on Phobos?"

"Yes, sir. <u>I can do it</u>" she replied confidently.

"The life support machines for this entire community are in your area" he reminded her. "you'll need to keep a close watch on them, in case of an attempt at sabotage."

"Should I wear <u>a gun</u>?" she asked (sounding slightly less confident.

"It wouldn't hurt" Daniel replied.

"I'll ask Sandra to loan her laser pistol to you if you don't have one" Michael told Louisa.

"Thank you" she replied, "—I'll accept your offer, Michael." Then she looked toward Daniel and asked: "Do you want me to take any other precautions, Mr. Morris?"

"Just be alert and patrol the life support machinery room occasionally" he replied. Don't let anyone else go down there, unless I tell you it's all right."

"I understand" she replied.

"In the meantime, I'll review everyone's background file, in case there is anything suspicious in it" Daniel continued. "Michael and Pat, if you notice any suspicious activity, report it to me as soon as you can and I'll take action immediately to stop it." Both of them nodded.

"I hope you won't suspect Nancy Chan, just because her parents emigrated to the U.S.N.A. from China" Patricia told the group. "I've never heard her say anything disparaging about our country."

"I'll try not to be biased" Michael replied, "—but I hardly know her, so I don't have your immediate confidence in her."

"I'd like to know more about her" said Louisa. "I've only talked with her a few times."

"She is a graduate of U.C.L.A. and she has a master's degree in meteorology" said Daniel. She was in the air force for three years, then she was accepted for N.A.S.A. training. So far she has worked competently as a meteorologist during her two years in Lowellsville. That's about all that is in her N.A.S.A. file. The F.B. I. report told me that she has never been a member of any radical group and she has only visited China once, for five days, so she seems to be an unlikely spy. I try not to let her Chinese ancestry bias me toward her."

"Thank you for this information, sir" said Louisa. "Now, if you don't mind, I promised Sandra that I would bring a few things to her from her wardrobe."

"All right" Daniel replied. "You may go, now—and thank you for coming here this evening."

"You are welcome, sir" said the biologist. Afterward she picked up the suit case and left the apartment. She walked to Michael's temporary apartment and gave the suit case to Sophia. The two women seated themselves facing each other in the living room and Louisa told her friend about the meeting in Daniel's residence. She omitted only the message disk from her story.

"Well, it seems that I have missed an important meeting" said Sophia. "I wonder why I was not invited to it."

"You will need to ask Mr. Morris about that" Louisa replied, as she observed her friend's scantily clad body enviously. 'I'd give <u>ten years</u> off of my life span to look like her!' thought the little brown haired biologist. She mentally compared her own five feet, four inch body to Sophia's two inches taller one. In every physical category she felt inferior to her beautiful supervisor. 'The only way I can compete with her is in **I.Q.**—and that doesn't seem to impress the men much!' Louisa realized.

The door of the apartment opened and Michael entered the living room. "I'm glad to see you are still here, Louisa" he said, as he seated himself on the couch to the left of Sophia. He kissed his wife's face before he spoke again. "Honey, I want to ask a favor of you. Would you let Louisa wear your laser pistol while we are on our honey moon?"

"Sure" Sophia replied. "I doubt I will need it on Phobos. Then she looked across the narrow room at their gray eyed guest and asked "Do you know how to use it, Louisa?"

"I had <u>one practice session</u> with that type of weapon before I left Earth" Louisa replied, "—but I have not used one since then."

Sophia turned toward Michael and asked "Would you object to me giving a shooting lesson to Louisa on the practice range <u>tonight</u>, dear? We may not have another opportunity."

"Not as long as you put some clothes on first" her husband replied with a teasing smile.

"I shoot a pistol better <u>when I'm nude</u>, but I'll humor you this time" she teased back. She kissed his face and added: "I'll take my suit case into the bedroom and see what Louisa brought to me."

"I'll wait for you out here" said Louisa, "—if you trust me not to run away with your husband."

"Ill risk it" Sophia replied humorously. Afterward she entered the bedroom and closed the door.

"That was an impressive scientific description you girls did of Pseudotrilobitus collensi" Michael remarked (although actually he had only scanned the work on a computer's screen one time). Louisa happily described her and Sophia's joint brain storming session while Michael silently observed the talkative guest. 'She's much more impressive academically than she is physically' he thought. "Her grade point average in college was higher than Sophia's or mine, but for some reason N.A.S.A.'s management thought Sophia was better management material.'

Physically Louisa was not an impressive person. She was small, short legged and small breasted. Whereas Sophia had done some acting in school plays during high school and artists' modeling in college, Louisa's only extracurricular activity had been tutoring other students in the French language and customs occasionally.

'She's not bad looking, but she certainly isn't beautiful, like Sophia!' he thought, as he compared Louisa's short, light brown hair to her boss's long, black tresses with bluish highlights. 'Her eyes can't compete with Sophia's either' he decided, as he compared Louisa's light gray irises to her friend's medium blue ones. 'On the other hand, her I.Q. is ten points higher than Sophia's 120 and eight points above mine' he remembered from reading her personnel file once. 'She should do a good job of operating the Biology Department while Sophia is gone.'

Sophia emerged from the bedroom in a light green, coverall garment with a name tag reading 'S. S. Collins' on its upper right front and a U.S.N.A. flag bearing fifty while stars and six small, red maple leaves on its left sleeve. The abbreviation 'N.A.S.A'. was sown on in the form of big, white letters across the upper back. Michael recognized the garment immediately. It was the same Biology Department uniform that Sophia had worn during their brief exploration of the aliens' base. A rectangular patch had been sewn in place to cover the laser slash in its left elbow area.

Around her waist Sophia wore a black, leather, pistol belt with a set of large, cylindrical devices on the front of it which held spare energy packs for the laser pistol. The latter occupied a matching black holster that was suspended beside her upper right thigh.

Sophia was still velcroing the front of the coveralls, so her two admirers could briefly see a blue lace brassiere and matching panties before she closed the gap in her main garment from its crotch to her upper breast cleavage. The latter was almost never concealed (unless she was wearing a space suit). A pair of white socks (with rolled down tops) and a pair of black, imitation leather shoes completed her mostly modest attire.

Michael rose from his seat on the couch and kissed Sophia, while Louisa left her seat in an armchair and exchanged kisses with him playfully. Afterward the two women left the apartment and went into the corridor. Sophia handed a set of keys to Michael through the doorway before she and Louisa walked away. Michael knew that Sophia's key to the apartment she had shared with Louisa would be on the metal key ring, so he gathered some of his belongings and took them to the living room of his new residence. He decided that he would leave them there wait and wait until Louisa began moving out before he put his possessions into her bedroom.

Michael made three trips to the women's apartment before they arrived in it and carried some of Louisa's belongings to the living room of Michael's apartment. The two women made two round trips, with Michael helping them; then Michael and Sophia said "Good night" to Louisa. Afterward, they returned to Michael's apartment for what would be their last night in it.

*(10) Sophia was remembering a scuba diving trip that she and Michael had taken during a weekend away from their N.A.S.A. training regimen. Although she was wearing sun glasses then, the harsh glare of the subtropical sunlight on the white coquina rock of the islets had been uncomfortable for her.

Chapter Twenty-Four

The Storm Ends

Thursday Morning, June 52ⁿᵈ.

Michael and Sophia were awakened on Thursday morning by the noise of his bedside alarm clock. Michael turned it off, then he and his new wife sat up, yawned and stretched. Both of them were nude and Michael reminded himself for the sixth time since the wedding how lucky he was to have such a beautiful woman for his marriage partner. He pulled her to him playfully and they copulated happily for ten minutes before they finally left the bed.

Their workday morning passed routinely as did their lunch time. At one o'clock Sophia went to an appointment she had made with Doctor Hudson, A physical examination indicated that she had gained five pounds recently and needed to be more careful about what she ate, but otherwise she was in good health. A pregnancy test revealed that she was indeed pregnant and might be carrying twins. When she returned to her job at 1:45, Sophia told Louisa about her condition.

"Oh, Sandra! That's wonderful news!" Louisa exclaimed. "When do you plan to tell Michael?"

"This evening, after dinner" her friend replied. "Have you checked the life support machinery this afternoon?"

"No, I was hoping you would go with me and tell me what a couple of those gauges meant" Louisa replied.

"All right" said Sophia. "I could use the exercise. "I've gained a little weight recently from eating too much dessert."

"Maybe it's due to your pregnancy" Louisa suggested.

"That could be, although Doctor Hudson thought I was only about eight weeks into it" Sophia replied. "Now let's go down into 'the catacombs' as I call them."

"Don't say that! It sounds creepy!" Louisa exclaimed (with an attempt at humor).

The two friends left their laboratory by way of a back door that gave access to a stairwell. They followed the stairs downward to a landing in front of a door which had **Life Support—Authorized Personnel Only** painted on its white surface with inch and a half tall, red letters.

Louisa unlocked the door with a key that she had seldom used until recently. Afterward, she opened the door and entered a large room. At first, only the lights in the stairwell illuminated it, but Sophia followed her friend through the doorway and flipped a light switch. Vaguely seen machinery cabinets and conduits full of electrical wiring came into clear view, as did water pipes going in several directions. The nearest pair of pipes protruded from the floor and went across the ceiling to the right wall. Both women knew that one of these thickly insulated pipes carried hot water from a nuclear reactor's cooling jacket down into a well where it melted underground permafrost. The other pipe carried the partially cooled jacket water from there back through a set of cooling fins in the next room to yet another room where the reactor was situated. The heat from the middle room was carried away through air ducts to warm the entire community.

As the two women approached a pair of gauges on the downward flowing hot water line, something small and fast startled Louisa as it ran past her. "Eek! What was <u>that</u> <u>thing</u>?" she asked as Sophia turned around quickly to watch it scurrying into the shadows behind yet another water pipe.

"Just a roach" Sophia replied, with a brief smile of amusement. "I've seen a few of them down here before."

"You could have warned me!" Said Louisa in an accusing tone of voice, as her heart beat rapidly.

"I'm sorry, I forgot" Sophia replied. "We'll rest here a minute . . ."

Meanwhile, Michael was visiting the Meteorology Department, which was about as far away from the life support machinery's area as a person could go in Lowellsville. The fist area was on the community's lowest level, while the second was on its uppermost level, near the summit of the hill. Inside twelve feet by fourteen feet room, Michael found a row of four television screens with views of various regions of the planet from space, a large doppler radar screen, an instrument console, and a computer the size of a brief case.

Seated in front of the console in a swivel chair was Nancy Chan, who wore a light pink*(11) coverall garment and a pair of comfortable, soft soled shoes. She looked upward from the set of instruments' gauges that she had been scanning and greeted Michael as he closed the door behind himself.

"Hello, Michael. How is married life?" she asked.

"Good, so far" he replied pleasantly. "Is the weather improving any?"

"Not yet in our area, but it's clearing to the west of us" she replied. "Have a look up there at Monitor Number One."

Michael did so and saw that about a hundred miles to the west of Lowellsville the planet's surface features could be seen again. "Well, that's good news!" he remarked. "How long will it be before our area looks like that?"

"Maybe by six or seven p.m." Nancy replied.

"Hallelujah!" Michael exclaimed. "I'll be glad to see the sun again."

"So will I—if it doesn't set before the sky clears" Nancy remarked. "There was a brief, awkward silence, then she said "I'm sorry about the way I acted in the swimming pool room when you and Sophia were there. I must have spoiled your fun."

"You're forgiven" Michael replied. "I suppose all of the single women of Lowellsville are glad that I have taken Sophia out of circulation since then."

"We certainly are!" Nancy admitted. "I know this may sound childish to you, but we can't get much attention from the men when she's around."

*"Well, you will be happy to know that Mr. Morris has decided to let her go with me to Phobos" said Michael. "We will be up there from five to seven days."

"That will be an interesting honey moon" said Nancy, with a teasing smile. "A honey moon on a moon! The view of Mars from there will be spectacular!" . . .

Meanwhile, back in Lowellsville, Sophia and Louisa completed their inspection of the life support machinery without finding any attempts at sabotage or any malfunctioning machinery. They left what Sophia had called "the catacombs" and Louisa locked the door near the foot of the stairs behind them. Afterward, they climbed the stairs and returned to the Biology Department, where they resumed doing more normal work. Unknown to them, Michael finished his visit to the Meteorology Department and resumed his normal workday routine at about the same time.

At five-fifteen the three friends ate dinner together, after which they decided to finish the exchange of residences by Louisa and Michael. The group spent about an hour and a half moving various items from each apartment to the other one. Afterward, they spent an hour setting up house keeping for both transferees in their new homes. Meanwhile, Daniel helped them in a different area.

Daniel Morris was the colony's leading expert in the workings of its largely automated telephone system and he was kind enough to spend about twenty minutes reprogramming the two apartments' telephone numbers and testing them. Louisa received the telephone number that she had formerly shared with Sophia, while Michael and Sophia would be listed together in the community's computerized telephone directory along with the telephone number from Michael's previous apartment. Their new listing had the entry Michael and *S. Sandra Edwards.* Their telephones had two distinct rings (one for each person) that were activated by dialing an extra digit of 1 or 2 following the main number.

The newlyweds' first visitor in their shared home rang their doorbell at 8:30 that evening. Michael and Sophia had just finished testing their new telephone service (with the help of Daniel, who was in the switching room near his office suite), when they heard the door bell. Michael opened the door, with Sophia standing close behind him. They were surprised to see former Assistant Administrator Roger Harris, but they invited him to enter their still cluttered and disorderly living room. Roger accepted their offer and seated himself in an armchair, while the newlyweds sat down together on the couch.

'She certainly is beautiful!' Roger thought, as he admired Sophia visually, '—even in those cover-alls! She looks happy too.'

Michael smiled and said "I think you've gained another admirer, honey."

"Oh, I've been the president of her fan club for the past two and a half years" said Roger, who was a moderately attractive man in his early thirties. "I was admiring pictures of her before she even arrived on Mars. She reminded me of photographs I had seen of Ava Gardner, the famous Hollywood actress of the nineteen forties and fifties."

"I've always thought she looked more like Elizabeth Taylor did when she was in her twenties" Michael remarked.

Oh, hush, you two!" Sophia objected mildly. "You'll give me an inflated ego."

Michael replied "Okay, we'll change the subject." He kissed Sophia's face then he asked their guest "What's the latest news about the war, Roger? I haven't had time to watch t.v. this evening."

"It has abated some, thank heavens!" Roger replied. "The Secretary General of the United

Nations is trying to broker a cease fire between the Chinese and the U.S.N.A.; but a regiment of North Korean tanks entered South Korea behind a mine clearing barrage about twenty miles to the northeast of Seoul. After a lot of fighting against allied tanks and tank killer aircraft it was finally driven back across the border. It had about sixty percent casualties during the battle. Now the United Nations is trying to stop the fighting in Korea too."

"What about those two North Korean missiles?" asked Sophia. "Has anybody done anything about them?"

"North Korea's dictator claims they are just space probes!" Roger replied, "—but nobody believes him. N.A.S.A.'s headquarters told our lunar colony not to transmit on any long range frequencies during the next four days, in case the missile that is on its way toward them can home on a radio transmission."

"That's a wise precaution" said Michael. "We'll need to do something similar."

"Are you still planning to go back to Earth, Roger?" asked Sophia.

"Yes, I must" he replied, as his medium gray eyes looked at her turquoise blue ones briefly. "I need a treatment that I cannot obtain here, so I have increased my number of exercise sessions in our gymnasium to strengthen my muscles for Earth's strong gravity."

"I'm glad that I'm not returning to Earth!" said Sophia. "I'm so accustomed to point three eight gee that I doubt I could stand up and walk if I were back home in Durham, North Carolina now."

"I'll probably need a wheel chair for the first month that I'm back home in Louisville, Kentucky" Roger admitted.

"What caused an engineering professor from the University of Louisville to emigrate to this first human colony on Mars?" asked Michael.

"I suppose it was the same thing that caused a former artist's model and a former mining company ore prospector to come here: <u>curiosity</u>" Roger replied. "I wanted to walk on the surface of an alien world and see what it looked like before people began terraforming it—and I wanted to <u>design</u> <u>real</u> <u>aerospace</u> <u>craft</u>."

"I doubt that the terraforming of Mars could begin soon" Michael stated. "The U.S.N.A. has a hasty military buildup and <u>several</u> <u>wars</u> <u>to</u> <u>pay</u> <u>for</u> first and all that the other nations do is <u>talk</u> <u>about</u> <u>colonizing</u> <u>Mars</u> eventually."

"There always seems to be <u>something</u> <u>happening</u> to distract people on Earth from President Kennedy's 'new frontier'" Sophia complained. She turned toward Roger (who was seated in an armchair) and asked "How did <u>you</u> know that I was <u>an</u> <u>artist's</u> <u>model</u> <u>six</u> <u>years</u> ago on Earth, <u>Mister</u> <u>Harris</u>?! I don't remember telling <u>you</u> about it." Both men noticed that she sounded annoyed.

"It's in your F.B.I. background check" Roger explained (with a brief half-smile). "Reading about it caused me to wish I'd been an art student then, <u>Mistress</u> <u>Edwards</u>."

"Oh? I don't suppose you obtained any of the paintings for which I posed?" asked Sophia (sounding slightly worried).

"As a matter of fact, <u>I</u> <u>did</u>" her brown haired guest replied. Both newlyweds noticed (with casual interest) that his hair was a few shades darker brown that Louisa's was). "It's hanging in my bedroom now. I bought it when I was visiting a cousin of mine in Carrboro*(12) three years ago. I'll give it to you tonight as a wedding present—if you <u>promise</u> not to destroy it."

"<u>I'd</u> <u>like</u> <u>to</u> <u>have</u> <u>it</u>" Sophia replied, "—and of course <u>I</u> <u>won't</u> <u>destroy</u> <u>it</u>!—even if it shows me <u>naked</u>! Would you object to us having it, Mike?"

"As long as it is in good taste, it would be acceptable to me" Michael replied carefully.

"I'll go get it and let you judge it for yourself" said Roger, after which he left the apartment. Five minutes later he returned with a framed painting covered by a towel. He unwrapped it on the couch in the Edwards' couple's living room. Meanwhile Sophia closed the door quickly and went to stand beside her new husband in front of the couch.

The portrait depicted Sophia at the age of twenty-two. She was kneeling nude on a small couch in front of a thinly curtained window. Her body was depicted as it was seen by the artist from the left rear, with her upper torso turned toward the left. One breast was visible, as was almost all of her derriere. The portrait was about two and a half feet tall and sixteen inches wide.

"It's beautiful!" Sophia exclaimed, "—don't you think so, dear?"

"Yes, I do" Michael replied sincerely, "—but <u>what</u> <u>was</u> <u>outside</u> that window?" He spoke as Roger carefully handed the painting to him.

"A big pasture, with a herd of Black Angus cattle on it" Sophia replied with amusement. ""The painting was done in the artist's house, which was out in the country. He and his daughter painted pictures of me from opposite angles in their den that day. She was one of his best students."

"What did <u>his</u> <u>wife</u> think of <u>you</u> <u>posing</u> <u>nude</u> in her home?" Roger asked curiously (with a trace of amusement in his voice).

"She didn't object" Sophia replied. "There were a couple of <u>nude</u> <u>portraits</u> of <u>her</u> and <u>their</u> <u>daughter</u> in the master bedroom."

"How old was her daughter?" Michael asked curiously.

"She was seventeen, I think" Sophia replied. "Where shall we hang this portrait, dear?"

"<u>In</u> <u>your</u> <u>bedroom</u>, I suppose" Michael replied, as he glanced at the picture with some misgivings. "At least it will be <u>your</u> <u>room</u> until we can get a <u>larger</u> <u>bed</u> for one of these rooms. We let Louisa keep my old bed, remember? You said you wanted a wider one with a built in bookshelf."

"I think we should put the picture in <u>our</u> <u>bedroom</u>, Mike" Sophia suggested. "We will need the other one for <u>a</u> <u>nursery</u> about seven or eight months from now."

Michael's eyes opened widely with surprise. "When did you learn this?!" he asked, as he set the painting in an armchair.

"<u>Today</u>, <u>for</u> <u>certain</u>" Sophia replied. "Doctor Hudson did a test this morning that confirmed an earlier one. He said I may even be carrying twins!"

Michael smiled broadly and embraced his new wife. "This is <u>great</u> <u>news</u>!" he exclaimed happily.

"I shall leave you two to discuss your plans for a nursery" said Roger. "Congratulations!" He kissed Sophia briefly and left the apartment.

"Now we will <u>really</u> <u>need</u> some <u>new</u> <u>furniture</u>!" Michael exclaimed, as he and Sophia seated themselves close together on the couch.

A few seconds later the telephone on the end table rang. Michael went to it and picked up the handset. "Hello? Edwards' residence" he said.

"Good evening, Mike. This is Dan Morris" said the caller. "Pat just told me that <u>the weather is clearing</u>! You and Sophia will be on your way to Phobos base tomorrow morning at nine o'clock."

"That's <u>good news</u>, sir! Michael exclaimed. "I'll tell Sophia. Thank you. Goodbye for now." Michael returned the telephone's handset to its cradle, then he pulled Sophia to himself with a firm, left armed hug. She snuggled against him and asked "Did Mr. Morris just call?"

"Yes" Michael replied happily. "He said Patricia assured him that <u>the weather will improve</u> enough by dawn tomorrow for the *Pometheus* to take you, me, and Roger up to Phobos!"

"Hooray!" Sophia exclaimed, after which she kissed her new husband's face. Next she rested her head on his left shoulder.

"Are you <u>happy</u>?" he asked with a smile, as he stroked her wavy black hair with his right hand.

"<u>Very</u>" she replied, matching his smile. "I love you, Mike."

"I love you too, honey" he assured her.

"Just think! Tomorrow we will fly up to Phobos Base and their nurse will come down here to treat the aliens" said Sophia. "If she succeeds in <u>curing them</u> I'll be allowed to <u>visit them</u> and <u>study live aliens</u>! It will be a <u>dream come true</u> for me!"

"<u>I want to meet them as much as you do</u>" Michael reminded her. "<u>Everyone</u> who joins NASA hopes to <u>meet intelligent aliens</u> somewhere eventually. It's the <u>main objective</u> of the <u>manned space program</u> now! So let's <u>be nice to the Phobosians</u> and don't give them <u>any reason to change their minds</u> about <u>loaning their only nurse</u> to the Lowellsville District for a while."

"Right, dear. She's our ticket for admission to a whole chapter in the history books!" Sophia exclaimed. "Maybe someday someone will make a movie about us exploring that big hill and finding the entrance to an underground communit7 inhabited by four armed aliens."

"<u>That would be pleasing</u> for our children to read!" Michael enthused. "Now let's get some rest. We will have an exciting day tomorrow on Phobos."

*(11) Light pink was the usual color of the Martian sky and was therefor a suitable color for the Meteorology Department's uniforms.

*(12) Carrboro is a small town in central North Carolina. It adjoins the larger college town of Chapel Hill.

Chapter Twenty-Five
A Thrilling Shuttle Flight

Friday Morning, June 53ʳᵈ.

At eight-thirty on Friday morning Michael, Sophia, Roger Harris and the versatile Linda Simmons were driven to the space port's small terminal building by Ronald Simmons. The short journey was done in the now familiar Mars Car Four.

John Clewiston, the colony's Transportation Director, was waiting for them beside the marble structure's main entrance. He had gone to the space port an hour earlier on a little tractor which had towed the shuttle craft with a yoke. The shuttle had been taken to its fueling place (a safe distance from Lowell's Hill) and had been loaded with fuel and oxidizer. Afterward it had been towed to the parking apron in front of the terminal building. Now the shuttle was on the parking apron where he had left it. An accordion pleated, air filled, boarding tube connected it to the terminal's departure doorway.

Edward Slater, the colony's ground vehicular engineer and Chief Mechanic, was John's companion this morning as the two Mars suit clad men brought a walkway tube out on four wheeled, supporting frame carts from the roadside doorway of the terminal to the Mars car's airlock door. They quickly connected the docking collar with the aid of a pair of four wheeled, ladder carts that were brought to them by two man-size robots. Soon a green light glowed on the Mars car's dashboard.

"Okay folks, end of the line! Everybody out!" Ronald instructed cheerfully from the car's driver's seat. Afterward he unfastened his safety harness and stood up. His four passengers left their seats also and each of them went to the cargo compartment to pick up a suitcase or two. Roger had a second suitcase which Ronald carried for him as the group walked to the car's small suitrack room. There Michael and Sophia obtained their Mars suits' helmets. Ronald and Linda had brought theirs from the driver's compartment and were carrying them left handed.

All five people were already wearing their protective suits in case of a small meteor hitting the terminal building or the access tube and causing an air leak. All of them were silently aware that if a large meteor arrived at a vulnerable moment, the shock wave and ejected would immediately kill them, so they tried not to let their minds dwell on that possibility.

The group walked through the air filled tube in a single file line and entered the marble terminal building. Its material had come from the only such rock outcropping that the settlers had yet found on Mars. Its completion about two terrain years ago had been a source of pride to the entire colony since then. Michael and Sophia's fellow travelers and they had been the first new arrivals to use it.

In the waiting room there were six pairs of chairs and two video screens. The right screen had Robert Harris' image on it; while John Clewiston's now familiar face was on the left one. As most of the soon-to-be space travelers seated themselves in plastic and aluminum chairs inside the terminals otherwise sparsely furnished lobby, Linda Simmons went to a communications console that stood on a small, rectangular dais.

"Good morning, John" she greeted as she held a microphone with her right hand in front of her temporarily helmetless face. "How does the runway look?"

"Ed and I went all over it with the sweeper trailer before I brought the shuttle out here" John replied via his suit radio. "That big storm blew a lot of dust and pebbles onto the pavement, but we removed the stuff for you."

"Thank you" said Linda. "Good morning to you also, Robert. I recognize your face because you were on a local news program recently. Our t.v. lady, Dianne Fletcher, said you were the man who found the water pipe that led to the aliens' underground base."

"Yeah, I got lucky" Robert replied humorously, "—but it was Mike Edwards who found the actual entrance to their base."

"Your modesty is commendable" Linda remarked with a smile. I will let you talk to your brother now, while I go inspect the shuttle's interior. I can't risk anything going wrong while we're in space." Linda then relinquished the microphone to Roger.

"Hello, Bob" Roger greeted. "I'm glad that we can talk one more time before I leave town. How did your outpost fare during the last day of the storm?"

"It endured the wind well" Robert replied, "—although the local landscape has had some minor rearrangements. There are piles of pink dust and sand against the foundations of the trailers. I needed to dig the stuff away from the well head this morning. Some workmen have just arrived from Lowellsville. They are here to help me build a small well house to protect the pipe and the valve better."

"Have you heard any more from the aliens?" Roger asked hopefully.

"No—nothing we could understand, anyway" Robert replied. "They sent what must have a maintenance robot been out to inspect the place where our well diggers dug up their water line (and Bill later reburied it). The 'bot seemed satisfied with the reburrial. I tried to talk to it, but it didn't seem to understand our language and I certainly couldn't understand its words! It seemed kind of bored with me after a while and just went away."

"So, its owners didn't make an appearance, huh?" asked Roger.

"No, and that was a strange looking 'bot!" Robert replied. "Its skin was some sort of blue metal! It wasn't painted, though. The color was in the metal itself! That's enough about 'bots, though.

"We're expecting a nurse to come down from Phobos soon and find out what's ailing the live aliens. I sure want to meet one of them! (when they are well, that is)."

Meanwhile, out on the dusty parking apron Dianne Fletcher was interviewing Edward Slater. The t.v. cameraman, Alvin Lancaster, alternately recorded scenes of them and the sixty feet long, delta-plus—canard winged Mars shuttle that was parked nearby. Alvin was six feet, two inches tall and of slender build. His medium brown eyes frequently scanned the sleek, streamlined, aerospace rocket plane that would soon be on its way to Mars' closest (and largest) moon.

Dianne, however, was carefully extracting as much information from Edward as she could about who was going to Phobos and why. She wished that she could be inside the terminal building, but the only airlocks were presently covered by walkway tubes and there was no other way to enter the structure.

In contrast to Alvin's imposing size, Dianne was a mesomorph who was five feet, four inches in height, with reddish brown hair and slightly grayish green eyes. She also had a good—but not spectacular—figure (although this was presently mostly hidden by her bulky space suit). Alvin's hair was a less interesting, light sandy brown and his complexion was slightly darker than his coworker's pinkish cream color. Dianne (and most other women) considered him to be fairly handsome (in a boyish sort of way).

At the moment, however, Dianne's thoughts were centered on her desire to interview either Michael Edwards or his new wife, whom she preferred to call 'Sandra.' She was acutely aware that so far they were the only human beings who were known to have entered the aliens' underground base. Mr. Morris, however, had been keeping her away from them for some reason. The reporter had, however, obtained an informative interview yester day afternoon with Sandra Edwards' plain looking, frequent companion, Louisa d' Alsace. Dianne intended to interview her again soon . . .

Meanwhile, inside the terminal building, Roger was still conversing with his younger brother by videophone, but Michael wanted to talk with Robert too. Roger finally relinquished the microphone to Michael and went to one of the lobby's chairs, where he seated himself awkwardly in this Mars suit*(13).

"Hello, Robert" said Michael. Mr. Morris told me this morning that you would not be going to Phobos with us today."

"That's right" Robert replied. "There are a lot of little things that need to be repaired here—especially beneath the trailers—because of the storm. I persuaded our Chief Administrator to let me wait another five days to go to Phobos and work on the plumbing system up there."

"I suspect Bill was glad to keep you with him" Michael said with a knowing smile.

"Yeah, only I'm not with him right now' Robert informed his new friend. "He's gone to Lowellsville on a Marscart*(14) to get some supplies that we need. He hopes to return early this afternoon."

"Well, I'm sorry I missed him" said Michael. He then noticed Linda's image replacing those of Dianne and Edward on the other monitor.

"This is your pilot speaking" Linda's voice announced from the t.v. and some wall mounted speakers. "The preflight inspection has revealed no problems, so everyone who is scheduled to go to Phobos today, please come aboard the shuttle craft."

"We're on our way!" Michael replied enthusiastically, then on the same frequency he said:

"Goodbye for a while, Bob. I'll call you from Phobos this evening." Michael pushed a button on the small, black console under the monitors and Robert's image was replaced by the words *No con-nection. Available for use.* Afterward he pushed the corresponding button for the other screen and went to the chair where he had left his helmet.

Each person in the lobby picked up his or her helmet and a suitcase, then the travelers formed a single file line and walked through the exit tube to the small passenger cabin of the shuttle vehicle.

Outside on the parking apron Ed Slater saw John Clewiston beckoning to him and told Dianne "I must go help John to load the cargo now."

: All right. Thank you for the interview, Mr. Slater" said Dianne.

Ed walked to the twenty feet long Mars truck that he had brought from the community's main garage almost an hour ago. John was inside the presently unpressurized cabin and sitting on the driver's seat. John went to the passenger's seat and closed the door behind him. Then John drove the truck forty yards and parked it beside the big, white shuttlecraft. The two men emerged from the cabin and climbed a short ladder onto the load bed, where several cargo pods and a work robot awaited them. John pulled a lever on the small console beside him and the truck's load bed rose to the level of the shuttle's cargo hatch. Ed opened the hatch, then the two men and the vaguely human-like robot began loading cargo pods into the shuttle's cargo bay with the help of the ship's 'resident robot.' The two men used electrically powered pallet jacks to lift and move the big, box-like, white pods; but the two robots simply lifted the orange pods by hand

The cargo bay was sixteen feet long and eight feet wide, so it occupied approximately a fourth of the shuttle's length. The methanol powered Mars truck had been backed close to the shuttle's fuselage, in the gap between the right canard wing and the right delta wing of the titanium skinned, aerospace plane. A tiny, rearward facing radar set and a camera on the truck's rear end had guided John to a safe docking with the shuttle's cargo area.

On the top of each of the two big delta wings was a circular emblem. The light blue, left circle bore two smaller circles. The upper, dark blue circle had a white star on it. The lower, equal size, white circle had a red maple leaf on it. The big, salmon pink circle on the right wing bore a gray, volcanic cone above the white letters USNA. A yellow, four pointed star below the nation's abbreviated name was above the dark red letters of the word MARS. A dark green silhouette of the North American continent was to the right of the two sets of letters.

The shuttle's name, *Prometheus*, was written in dark red letters on each side of the fuselage, between the two wings. To symbolize the meaning of the name, *Prometheus*, in its original language (ancient Greek), a saffron colored comet was depicted on the lowest part of each wing's big roundel, and above the name of the shuttle on each side of the vehicle. The titan, Prometheus, had brought the useful gift of fire to the first humans in an ancient Greek myth.

Dianne and Alvin watched from the northern edge of the parking apron while the shuttle was loaded with cargo, then the truck's load bed was lowered and four stabilizing, outrigger legs on the truck's chassis were retracted. Afterward Ed went to the tow tractor and towed the thirty tons (Earth weight) shuttle to the head of the mile long runway. There he disconnected the towing yoke and wished the *Prometheus*' crew and passengers "Good luck" by radio.

"Thank you. I will see you again this evening or tomorrow" Linda's pretty, alto voice replied in his headphones.

Edward drove the tractor back to the terminal and parked it beside Mars Car Four where the building would shield both vehicles in case of a fuel explosion aboard the *Prometheus*. John arrived in the freight truck, then the two men and a robot assistant went to the northern passenger assistance tube, disconnected it from Mars Car Four and detached the other end from the building's northward facing doorway. Afterward, the tube was stored inside an unpressurized room at the eastern end of the building. Next the other tube was detached from the building's southward facing doorway and stored in an unpressurized room at the western end of the building. Finally, one robot went into each tube storage room, closed the door behind itself, and powered down.

Ed drove the tractor halfway back to its home in the shuttles' hangar, while John drove the freight truck halfway back to the town's main garage in the eastern third of the hill. Afterward both men emerged from their vehicles to watch the shuttle's departure. Ed was now about six hundred feet away from the big aerospace plane and John was half again as far.

Liquid oxygen and liquid hydrogen had been pumped into their respective fuel tanks in the shuttle earlier at the refueling point. The actual fueling process had been done by two robots while John and Edward were doing other things at the terminal building a safe distance away. Edward had once referred to the fully fueled shuttle as "a big artillery shell" and this had remained a private joke between him and John ever since then. The fuel and oxidizer came from big, thickly insulated, armored storage tanks near an automated fuel making plant to the south of the runway. For safety reasons the shuttle's two main engines would be started well away from these storage tanks (and away from the terminal building).

Meanwhile, Ronald had not stayed aboard the shuttle. Instead he had helped Roger to carry his luggage aboard it and had said "Good bye" to the other passengers. Afterward he had left the vehicle before it was towed to the western end of the runway. Next he had walked to the terminal building, and as soon as the southern doorway and its airlock were disencumbered, he had cycled through the latter and entered the building. Now he was sitting in front of the two television monitors in the terminal's lobby and was watching the shuttle's image on both screens. He was holding a remote control device that could operate both monitors and two rooftop cameras.

Suddenly twin jets of flame shot out of the shuttle's rear end and the aerospace plane dashed along the runway. When most of the pavement was behind it, the shuttle rose into the air and climbed at a thirty degree angle toward the pink Martian sky. Ronald had turned on an infrared tracking device that enabled the rooftop cameras to follow the exhaust plumes of the shuttle. Now the two t.v. screens showed the shuttle's angle of climb steepening as the vehicle sped eastward away from Lowllsville and toward a distant rendezvous with Phobos.

Aboard the shuttle Michael looked through a small window to his right as the Martian landscape quickly receded below him. With only three passengers among four rows of seats, and three seats per row, a window seat was easily available for each person.

"Wow! What a ride!" Sophia exclaimed. Her two male companions smiled in agreement as the shuttle passed through the hazy, pink Martian sky at a steadily increasing rate of speed. Soon the big vehicle was into a clearer, darker colored part of the atmosphere. A few wispy ice crystal clouds were above the shuttle briefly, then they too rushed past the windows.

On the front bulkhead of the passengers' compartment a viewing screen showed an image of huge cliffs approaching the shuttle. Beyond them was a gentle upward slope that extended to the horizon.

"There is the Olympic Pedestal on the viewing screen" said Michael. "That seemingly endless slope standing on the top of it is the western side of Olympus Mons."

"That slope does seem to <u>go</u> <u>onward</u> <u>forever!</u>" said Sophia, "—and look <u>how</u> <u>dark</u> <u>the</u> <u>shaddow</u> <u>of</u> <u>those</u> <u>cliffs is</u>! It's like looking <u>at</u> <u>night</u> <u>approaching!</u>"

"Those cliffs do block a lot of sunlight at this time of the day" Roger commented.

"That's because they are more than <u>3,000</u> <u>feet</u> <u>high!</u>" Michael explained.

What could make a plateau <u>large</u> <u>enough</u> for that <u>enormous</u> <u>mountain</u> to stand on it?!" Roger asked with amazement.

"I wish I had the answer to that question" Michael replied. "We geologists are still baffled by it."

The cliffs could soon be seen through the windows of the shuttle as it climbed rapidly above them. Next the vehicle and its human occupants passed over a broad, gently rolling landscape beyond the huge natural ramparts. An occasional wide gully crossed the vast pedestal to the edge of the cliffs.

After several minutes Roger exclaimed "That looks like the great plains of North America down there! With some grass on it it would resemble Nebraska."

"That plateau could easily hold the state of Missouri on top of it" Michael commented.

"The gods of ancient Greece would have loved this place!" Sophia exclaimed. "Everything was created on an enormous scale here!"

"It would have been a fitting home for the Olympians" Michael agreed, as the onward rushing shuttle's course finally began to traverse the gargantuan western slope of the mountain. Enormous hardened lava flows could be seen passing below the little aerospace plane and its tiny human riders. The volcanic landscape continued for several minutes.

Now the sky to either side of the shuttle was becoming steadily darker shades of violet. As Olympus Mons' summit finally passed a thousand feet below the shuttle, Michael told his companions "That huge volcano's crater is the size of Rhode Island."

Sophia's eyebrows rose with astonishment. For once she could think of nothing to say that seemed adequate.

"<u>It</u> <u>is</u> a fitting home for the <u>gods</u> of ancient Greece!" Roger remarked appreciatively, as he observed the enormous crater below them. He could see the tiny shadow of the shuttle rushing across its multicaulderaed floor.

"I don't see any <u>new</u> <u>volcanic</u> <u>activity</u>, but that mountain is still <u>an</u> <u>awesome</u> <u>site</u>!" Sophia exclaimed finally. "I want our children to see this view some day!"

After many more minutes the mountain of the gods finally receded behind the shuttle. Ahead of it, three comparatively smaller—but still impressive—dormant volcanoes appeared. For a while they thrilled the travelers with their own vast sizes, then the shuttle passed them too and entered the realm of eternal night. As the sky became black, hundreds of stars appeared, as did the planet Saturn. With its rings barely visible to the unaided eye, its faint, yellow glow still pleased the travelers.

The roar of the two rocket engines suddenly ceased and Linda's voice came from a speaker on the forward and aft bulkheads of the passenger compartment.

"Lady and gentlemen, we are in space! In about a half hour we should see our destination ahead of us. Enjoy the flight!" The shuttle rotated sixty degrees counterclockwise on its longitudinal axis and the salmon pink disk of the planet Mars came into view again through the left row of windows. Through the right row, the tiny, bright oval of the moonlet, Deimos, became visible against the starry backdrop of the void.

"Some day I'd like to explore Deimos" said Michael, as he looked across the aisle and beyond an empty seat. "It might have some useful mminerals."

"Look out <u>this</u> <u>side</u>!" Sophia exclaimed, from the seat behind Michael's. He did not need to look where she was pointing though, because the entire left row of windows displayed the same view—a maze of giant canyons.

"That's *Noctis Labyrinthus*-the 'maze of night' to our left'" Michael stated. "The Martian surface slumped long ago in the early part of the Hesperian Age*(15) and created that bunch of huge chasms."

"I must see those!" exclaimed Roger, who had been recording images of Deimos and the star field with his digital camera. As he crossed the aisle, Sophia was already using her camera to photograph the spectacular view of the canyons. Roger seated himself behind Sophia and exclaimed "What a strange landscape!"

"It was caused by the movement of two crustal plates as they drifted away from each other" Michael explained. "You'll see an even more dramatic result of that process soon."

"Wasn't any of that maze carved by flowing water?" asked Sophia.

"Water erosion probably played a secondary role in creating that landscape, but crustal faulting was the main cause" Michael replied.

A few minutes later, Sophia emitted a brief shriek of astonishment. "Mike! Look at that!" she exclaimed.

"Oh my god!" Roger enthused. "That looks like the Grand Canyon on steroids down there!"

"That's Valles Marineris" Michael explained. "It's believed to be the beginning of an ocean basin, although now it has no liquid water in it."

"It's enormous!" Roger exclaimed.

"It's main chasm is about <u>sixty miles</u> wide in some places" Michael stated with enthusiasm, "—and <u>three to four miles deep</u>! The only thing similar to it on any of Earth's continents is the Great Rift Valley of Africa. The eastern coastal region of that continent is slowly tearing loose from the main land mass and eventually ocean water will pour into the gap. Then there will be a long chain of islands paralleling the new coastline of the continent."

"I'm glad you came along with us" said Roger. "It's good to have a geologist to explain these things to us."

"Didn't you see this canyon when you were making a shuttle descent from your transport vessel six years ago, Roger?" Sophia asked.

"No, it was on the night side of the planet then" Roger explained. "Everyone in my shuttle was disappointed by that fact."

"Part of the canyon system was in darkness when Mike and I came to this planet two years ago" said Sophia. "I hope we can see <u>all of it</u> during this flight."

"That's not likely" said Michael.

"Why not?" asked Sophia.

"Because that main chasm is <u>as long as the forty-eight contiguous states of the old U.S.A. are wide</u>!" her husband replied. "It would <u>span four different time zones</u> on Earth!"

"That's amazing!" Roger exclaimed (while Sophia's eyebrows rose to express the same opinion). "What could make such an enormous gash in a planet's surface?"

"An even larger convection cell, rising from the planet's deep interior" Michael replied. "At its top the cell widens and acquires the shape of a mushroom. The outward expansion carries the planet's crust in two or more directions. That is what is happening beneath the Atlantic Ocean on our former home planet, although at least two cells are at work there."

Then Linda's voice came from the speakers mounted on the forward and aft bulkheads: "We will be arriving on Phobos in fifteen minutes. Please remember to awaken any sleepers then."

"As if anyone could sleep with the scenery we've had below us!" Sophia remarked humorously.

"It's difficult to believe that our shuttle pilot is a self effacing secretary most of the time" Roger commented admiringly. "She's really the person in charge here."

"She's kind of like Clark Kent stepping into a closet and changing into Superman" Sophia remarked humorously.

"That's a good comparison" Roger remarked. "You're not only beautiful, you're clever too! I can see why Mike loves you."

Meanwhile in Phobos Base, four of its six permanent residents were taking turns forming pairs to cycle through its small, main pedestrian airlock in expectation of the Prometheus' arrival. John Clewiston and a pair of work robots were already outside working to enlarge the space port's facilities in preparation for the much larger Wernher von Braun's arrival on the following Wednesday. After five minutes, all four members of the greeting party were standing on the six feet wide concrete strip that led to the much larger landing platform. Strips of magnetized steel were imbedded in the concrete surfaces to attract magnets in the shoes of the Phobosians' space suits. These strips helped people to keep their muscle tone and to anchor themselves in the moonlet's artificially enhanced—but still weak—gravitational field.

Phobos was an irregularly shaped moonlet which had been orbiting Mars for an unknown amount of time. Only 16.2 miles long by 11.4 miles wide, Phobos was an inhospitable little world, but its inhabitants had the best view in the solar system of the planet Mars. In fact, it was difficult to ignore the ever present, brownish pink orb that was an average of 5,640 miles away. Mars filled one side of the sky, as seen from Phobos Base's landing platform. The moonlet's tiny shadow could be seen moving across the planet's sunlit face.

The four Phobosians (as they liked to call themselves) looked at the huge orb and smiled. Mars was an anchor to sanity on a tiny, light gray rock (with a few pink spots). Most of Phobos' sky was eternally black and dotted with stars that were unimaginable distances away.

The little group of people was led by Warren C. Smith, the Chief Administrator of Phobos Base. He was accompanied by Walter Jones (who was normally the little community's only resident astron-omer): Janet Johnson, the communications technician: and David Carlisle, the mining engineer (who often referred to himself as the "Chief Burrower"). All of them were watching the disk of Mars to see which one of them would detect the approaching shuttle first.

Walter's many years of observing asteroids and comets gave an unfair advantage to him in this type of contest. Thus, no-one was surprised when he exclaimed "There it is! About halfway along Mariner Canyon." Everyone looked where he was pointing and saw a tiny white speck approaching a place where the giant chasm encountered a large patch of dark gray, volcanic terrain.

"I win the first bottle of cola from the shuttle's supplies!" Walter announced happily through his suit's radio. "I'm so tired of drinking water I could barf—especially when it's Lowellsville's water!"

"I've heard they found a new source of water recently" said Janet. "It is supposed to taste better than their first source's water does."

"They'll probably keep the good stuff for themselves" said David (who had often been pessimistic lately).

"Well, their <u>worst water</u> is better than what we have found <u>inside</u> Phobos!" Warren reminded him. "I remember <u>your comment</u> 'This stuff is only good for flushing toilets!'"

"That does sound familiar" Janet teased.

John Clewiston looked at thae approaching shuttle and told the two nearby robots "Finish laying that new slab, then waits for further orders." The robots complied, then John walked to where the four Phobosians were standing.

"Well, John, it looks like you'll have our space port ready for the *von Braun* in a few more days" said Warren.

"I will if I don't lose my grip on this rock and float into space!" John replied half seriously.

The *Prometheus* seemed to grow rapidly from a speck on the disk of Mars to a recognizable shape. The shuttle's approach became slower as it neared its objective, but soon it loomed above the waiting group of Phobosians.

Linda did a radar and television guided approach to the recently enlarged space port. Soon she used the maneuvering thrusters to bring the ship to a computer assisted stop above the well marked landing pad. A brief use of the upper thrusters caused the big shuttle to descend slowly to a nearly perfect landing on its three slender legs. Its tires were prevented from freezing and cracking because of hot air sent down the hollow, stainless steel tubes of the landing gear legs and by the electrically heated disc brakes near them. The magnetized steel strips in the landing apron helped to hold the thirty ton shuttle in place when its descent ceased.

The five humans on the pad strapped heating jackets to the landing gear to further protect it, while the passengers and the one person crew of the shuttle left their seats and picked up their space helmets from the overhead racks. Soon they heard a woman's voice come from the bulkhead speakers at each end of the passenger area:

"Welcome to Phobos, all of the passengers and crew of the shuttle *Prometheus*. We hope you enjoy your visit with us." Afterward they heard their pilot pick up a microphone and say:

"This is your pilot speaking. For your safety, please put on your helmets and turn on your suits' air supplies. Remain on board until I depressurize the passenger compartment and the hold."

In the pilot's compartment, Linda flicked two switches on a control panel and two red lights glowed. The throbbing sound of air pumps could be heard throughout the shuttle. Then Linda put on her own helmet and secured it in place.

Outside of the shuttle, Warren, Walter and John pushed a four wheeled, portable stairway across the concrete surface of the landing pad until the stairway's padded leading edges contacted the left side of the shuttle's fuselage. Then John set the odd little vehicle's parking brake so that the steel framed contraption would no longer roll. The upper part of its framework now bracketed the shuttle's paint outlined passenger door.

The shuttle's passengers were by this time standing in the aisle of the passengers' compartment with their helmets on, while the faint hissing of their space suits' air supplies could be heard by each of them. Linda went into the passengers' compartment and asked Roger to check her helmet's seals, which he did. Afterward, she went to the door in the rear bulkhead that provided access to a short hallway and the baggage compartment to the right of it. Linda unlocked a door and went into the baggage compartment, then she handed the suitcases through the doorway to their owners, one at a time. The last suitcase that she picked up was her own.

The two big air pumps stopped abruptly, then Linda walked to the exit door of the passengers' compartment and opened it. There was a small puff of residual air and condensed moisture escaping, then a view of the portable stairway and of the electrically lit concrete surface of the landing area appeared.

"Please take this into the base for me" she told Michael, as she handed her suitcase to him.

"All right" he replied, then he and the other two passengers descended the portable stairway to the pavement on which a group of Phobosians stood waiting to greet them. Linda could soon hear (by radio) the Phobosians introducing themselves to the newcomers:

"Hello, I'm Warren Smith, the C.A. here."

"Hello, I'm Dave Carlisle, the mining engineer and Chief Burrower."

"Hi, I'm Jay Jay the radio tech."

"I'm Walter Jones the astronomer. I make sure we don't collide with any comets."

"I'm Dave Carlisle. Some of you know me already. I bounce back and forth between here and Lowellsville to keep the transportation facilities up to date."

Linda smiled as she listened to these familiar sounding voices, then she went into the windowless baggage compartment again and scanned it to be certain that no personal items remained in it. Afterward she left the compartment and went to a metal door at the right end of the short corridor. She unlocked the door with a magnetic card, then she opened the portal and entered another short corridor. At the far end of it was another door, which she opened. Linda looked into the cargo hold. The four feet long cargo pods appeared to be in good order, so she pushed a button on a small control panel to her right. A long, narrow section of the hold's floor swung downward on hinges near her feet. The hatch-become-a-ramp would have been too fragile to support the weight of the cargo pods (that were standing in a row along its length) if it were on Earth, but it easily supported them in the slightly enhanced microgravity of Phobos.

Linda did a u-turn to her right in the cargo hold, then she opened the metal door of a small compartment. She unstrapped the shuttle's resident robot from its storage position. Afterward she activated the bipedal machine and sent it to help the Phobosians and their two robots to unload the cargo from the hold.

Meanwhile, the female Phobosian who had introduced herself as "Jay Jay," led the passengers down a long, narrow ramp that was just wide enough for two people to walk side by side. It had been carved out of Phobos' natural rock (which was mostly various shades of gray, with a few scattered patches of pink or tan). At the bottom of the ramp were the open double doors of a large room, which was presently unpressurized. As they entered it, cargo pods were being brought into the room from the ramp behind them. The pods were being placed in neat rows on the floor of the room by the three robot stevedores, directed by a female human in a space suit. An aisle space was left intentionally to give access to the door of a small, pedestrian airlock in the far wall of the room.

The three guests followed their guide to the closed door. Then Jay Jay turned around and said "This is our main pedestrian airlock. It is only large enough for two people to use it comfortably at a time, so Miss Collins, if you will cycle through it with me first, the two men can wait to use it next."

"I'm <u>Mrs. Andrews</u> now" Sophia corrected mildly. "No-one has had the time to change the name on my suit yet. Michael and I were just married two days ago."

"All right" Jay Jay replied. "Congratulations! Now follow me please." As she spoke, Jay Jay opened the door of the already depressurized airlock. The two women entered it and cycled through it.

Meanwhile, Michael and Roger watched the space suit clad female with a name tag that read 'K. Ferguson.' She was using a small, portable calculator to check in the cargo pods (by referring to their black, inch tall, serial numbers). She spoke occasionally to the robots to give instructions to them, but she was obviously too busy to introduce herself now. Neither newcomers said anything to distract her from her work and she efficiently continued doing it.

Soon it was the two men's turn to use the airlock. It was so small that it reminded them of the one in Mars Car Four. When Michael and Roger emerged after a minute or so from what Michael humorously referred to as "the broom closet," they saw that they were in a long hallway with doors in either wall at irregular intervals. Jay Jay beckoned to them from a doorway in the right wall. She was already helmetless, so she could not speak with them yet. She motioned for the two men to remove their helmets in the hallway, so they stopped walking long enough to do so.

It had been easy for each of the new arrivals to guess what the origin of the nickname "Jay Jay" was. On the right front part of her space suit was a name tape with *J. Johnson* printed on it in black letters. She had told them outside on the tarmac that the *J.* stood for *Janet*, "—but people seldom call me that here on Phobos" she had added good naturedly.

When the two men had removed their space helmets in the hallway, Jay Jay told them "Wait here a few minutes while we girls desuit, then you may take your turn." Her male guests agreed, so she disappeared into the suit rack room. Sophia soon emerged from it in her coveralls and towing a large suitcase with a pair of wheels at one end. "Your turn, Mike" she said. Michael stepped past her and entered the room. He could see why his guide had kept Roger and him waiting for several minutes. The room would have been annoyingly crowded with more than two people helping each other to desuit in it at a time.

"They obviously don't have company very often, judging from these facilities" Michael remarked humorously. His eyes scanned the little room to make his point.

"It is a good thing that neither of us has claustrophobia" Roger agreed with equal mirth.

"We're working on a new entry point with a larger airlock, but it isn't quite ready for use yet" Janet informed them patiently from the doorway. "We'll have it ready by the time the big space liner arrives on Wednesday."

After their helmets were placed on shelves and their space suits were safely hung on specially designed racks, the two men returned to the hallway, where their luggage was waiting for them. With the latter in tow they and Sophia followed their female guide to the inner end of the corridor. There they passed through a doorway and entered another corridor, with more doors to either side of it. They turned right and walked past some of these doors to another corridor. They turned left into it and Jay Jay stopped the group after they had gone only a few yards.

"Mister and Mistress Edwards, this will be your apartment while you are visiting Phobos Base" said Jay Jay, as she pointed to a numbered door in the right wall. "Mr. Harris will have the apartment across the hall from yours and Mrs. Simmons will have the one to its left. Please memorize the numbers on the doors and the capital letters painted beside the arrows that point into the corridors. That way you will avoid becoming lost. When you think you can find these apartments again, put your suitcases inside of them. Afterward I'll take you on a tour of the community and show you where its inhabitants work."

The guests followed her instructions and as they did so, they noticed murals of landscapes on either Earth or Mars painted on the walls of their apartments' living rooms. Each of these paintings was signed *Janet Johnson*, with a date below it. When the newcomers had left their luggage in their apartments and had gathered in the hallway again, Sophia remarked "You're a good artist, Jay Jay."

"Thank you" Janet replied. "It gives me something to do when I'm not working."

Janet Johnson was a small, slender woman of undistinguished appearance. In spite of this, she had a lively, optimistic personality that made her popular. She was about five feet, five inches in height, with medium brown hair and slightly grayish blue eyes.

"She has an intelligent, creative mind and everybody seems to like her—even though she doesn't appear to seek popularity' thought Sophia. 'I think I like her too.'

"Where did you learn to paint like that, Jay Jay?" asked Roger.

"Art was my minor in the University of Cincinnati" she replied. "My major was in electronic communications and that's mostly what I do here."

"You look like you are in your early twenties—you couldn't have been out of college longbefore you came here" Michael remarked.

"Thank you, but I'm twenty-six" Jay Jay replied with a slight smile. "Now let's begin our tour, starting in this residential area, where most of the apartments are . . .

*(13) The terms "Mars suit" and "space suit" were used interchangeably by the colonists, since the same attire was used in both hostile environments. Although these suits were more advanced than those of the late twentieth century, they still left much to be desired in terms of their weight and bulk.

*(14) A Marscart is an unpressurized, four wheeled vehicle that resembles an enlarged dune buggy with a small load bed added.

*(15) The Hesperian Age of Mars' geologic history began about 3,500,000,000 years ago.

Chapter Twenty-Six
Excitement in the Dome

(Also Friday Morning).

Meanwhile, back in Lowellsville, Dianne and Alvin had returned to their office two floors above the ground level. While Alvin was unloading his digital, motion picture camera's images into a com-puter, Dianne telephoned the Biology Department. After five rings, as a recorded voice started to answer the caller, a woman's live voice interrupted it:

"Hello, Biology Department. Louisa d'Alsace speaking" she said (with a slight tone of annoy-ance in her voice). Dianne guessed that she had been busy with some project that she did not want to have interrupted, but the reporter spoke anyway:

"Hello, Louisa. This is Dianne Fletcher calling from Station MLVL. Remember me?"

"Yes" Louisa replied, "but I don't have time for an interview right now. Could you call me back later today?"

"I just wondered if we might have lunch together? I'm buying" Dianne said pleasantly (as she ignored the question).

"Well, all right. Maybe around eleven-thirty?" Louisa suggested.

Dianne glanced at a wall clock. It said 10:32 a.m., OST (Olympus Standard Time). "That would be good" she replied. "I'll see you then . . ."

Louisa put the little, portable telephone back into a pocket of her coveralls and resumed looking through a binocular microscope. She was examining a specimen slide that she had prepared from some dust which she had vacuumed off of Sandra Edward's Mars suit during the preceding afternoon. The dust contained a surprising amount of a bacterium that was normally found growing on the dead, outer layer of human skin. The microbe had mutated slightly, but it was still recognizable.

'I believe this organism <u>came</u> <u>from</u> <u>Earth</u>—and I don't think it came by way of a shuttle bringing it down from a manned transport ship' thought Louisa. I'd be <u>willing</u> <u>to</u> <u>bet</u> that it came aboard an <u>unmanned</u> <u>rocket</u>, from some nation that wasn't as concearned about environmental contamination as the U.S.N.A.is.'

Louisa removed the slide and set it aside. Next she put another slide on the little stage of the microscope and peered at it through the eyepieces. What she saw were some dead skin cells that she had scraped off of her own right arm. The skin cells were slowly being eaten by microbes similar to the ones on the other slide.

'This second type of microorganism traveled to Mars on human skin, where it breaks down the epidermis in competition with mites and is shed by us with our dandruff as the latter flakes off' thought Louisa. 'The mucous membranes in our respiratory systems trap and kill the microbe—o the mites—as either contaminant enters a human body, but the aliens might not have the right chemicals in their nasal membranes, sinuses, and throats to do the job. <u>If</u> they <u>don't</u>, this microbe could be <u>attacking</u> <u>the</u> <u>living</u> <u>tissues</u> <u>of</u> <u>their</u> <u>respiratory tracts</u>! <u>I'd</u> <u>better</u> <u>call</u> <u>Doctor</u> <u>Hudson</u>!'

Louisa took her portable telephone out of one of her pockets and keyed the physician's number. On the fourth ring he answered and Louisa explained her theory to him. She identified the microbe by its scientific name (Staphylococcus aureus) and explained that its cell membrane had thickened and strengthened to cope with the harsh Martian surface environment, which it had encountered when the space probe in which it had ridden had landed on the red planet. Louisa concluded her argument by saying "I'll bet that alien base is teeming with this germ right now! If it is, I know of a chemical that might kill it. She named the drug, which had the trade name *Epinecrosol*, then she explained "NASA requires its spacecraft assemblers to clean their skin with it, now that we know that this bacterium hitch hiked to Luna when our first base there was being built."

"Thank you for this information" said Dr. Hudson. "Please send a detailed presentation to my email address as soon as you can."

"I'll do that this afternoon" Louisa replied, "and I'll bring him a sample of *Epiecrosol* to your office—say in about an hour or so."

"Yes, please do" Dr. Hudson requested. They then ended their telephone conversation and Louisa went to a sink where she decontaminated her hands and arms with the chemical. Afterward she washed these areas with soap and water, then she used a hot air dryer. Feeling clean, Louisa emerged from her department, put an 'Out To Lunch' sign on the door and locked it. Afterward she walked to-ward the lunchroom. Along the way, Louisa wondered why Dianne wanted to see her again so soon. The previous interview had mostly been about Sophia's and Michael's wedding and the origin of the by now famous gown. The latter seemed likely to remain a popular topic in Lowellsville for weeks (as was the speculation about the identity of the notorious rheostat "saboteur").

'I like Sandra most of the time, but right now I'm a member of the group that is glad she's on Phobos!' thought Louise, as she approached the double doors of the dining room. She opened one of them and scanned the big room to find Dianne. A voice from behind her startled Louisa.

"Looking for me?" it asked humorously.

"Oh! You startled me!" Louisa exclaimed. "You caught me off guard."

"I'm sorry" said Dianne. "Shall we go in?"

The two women entered the big room together. Six other people were already there, so Dianne suggested "Let's get our food and take it to your office where we can have some privacy."

"All right" Louisa replied. "I'd like that."

Ten minutes later Louisa was pushing an aluminum cart loaded with food and beverage containers toward her office while Dianne opened doors for her and watched for obstacles. However, their roles were reversed when they came to Louisa's locked office door. Soon afterward the two women were transferring the trays and lidded cups onto the office's desk top. Afterward Louisa brought an extra office chair from the laboratory and the meal/interview was ready to begin.

"All right, ask your questions" Louisa said in a tone of mild resignation (between bites of food).

"May I use a voice recorder and a still camera?" asked Dianne.

"Go ahead" Louisa replied reluctantly.

"You told me yesterday that you were Michael's and Sandra's friend" Dianne prompted. "Am I right?"

"That's correct" Louisa replied. "Sandra and I are like sisters."

"Did you ever hear them talk about <u>what</u> they found in that big hill called *William's Bluff* last Monday?" Dianne asked, "—or <u>how</u> they found it?"

"Yes" Louisa replied. "They and Bill Schaefer went hunting for an entrance to a suspected alien base inside the hill early that afternoon. They had found a water pipe that led from the area where our people had been drilling to the northern end of the bluff. That was what caused them to believe—" then suddenly there was a loud '**Bang!**' and an alarm sounded from somewhere nearby.

"What was <u>that</u>?!" asked Dianne, as she turned toward the first sound.

"I don't know, but it sounded like <u>trouble!</u>" Louisa replied. "If there has been <u>an</u> <u>explosion</u> of some kind, it <u>could</u> <u>cause</u> <u>an</u> <u>air</u> <u>leak!</u> We should put on our <u>pressurized</u> <u>suits!</u>"

"<u>My</u> <u>suit</u> is in the News Department—<u>on</u> <u>the</u> <u>next</u> <u>level</u> <u>upward!</u>" Dianne replied.

Louisa noticed fear bordering on panic in the newswoman's voice. The biologist thought quickly, then she said: "All right, we'll go to a place where we'll be safer. <u>Follow</u> me." Then she led Dianne to the back end of the Biology Science Laboratory and unlocked the heavy metal door there. Louisa turned the 'L' shaped handle and opened the door, then she reached through the doorway and flipped a light switch beside it. Afterward she stepped onto a metal landing and said "Come in here. I'll secure this door behind us." Dianne complied and Louisa closed the door, then she locked it.

"<u>Where</u> <u>are</u> <u>we</u>?!" Dianne asked in bewilderment.

"We're about to go down those stairs to the Life Support Machinery Area" Louisa replied, as she remembered a sign she had seen there during an earlier visit with Sophia. "Just stay close behind me . . ."

Joe Standing Bear was slowly raising himself toward the ceiling of the main garage where a troublesome electric light was flickering annoyingly. There was a replacement for it on the hydraulic lift with him and he had risen about six feet into the air when he heard the loud noise. He thought at first that a transformer in a chamber near the garage had exploded.

"Oh hell! I can't complete one job before another one needs to be done!" he thought with annoyance. He then noticed that all of the other lights in the garage were still shining steadily. He finally stopped the platform's ascent within reach of the flickering floodlight, about sixteen feet above the floor of the garage. He then heard a low pitched; whistling sound and the platform began to sway. Joe hastily pushed the 'Down' button of his hand held control device and watched an oil stained rag scooting slowly across the Marscrete floor of the garage.

Joe heard an excited voice coming from the built-in speakers of his Mars suit's helmet as the latter lay on the floor of the lifting platform. He stooped and picked up the helmet as an unusual wind fluttered his shaggy black hair. "I don't like this situation!" he told himself.

". . . meteorite impact near the big airlock!" a man's voice exclaimed from the earphones. "It's made a hole about eighteen inches wide in the dome!"

Joe held his helmet upside down with his left hand while his right hand gripped the handrail of the swaying lifting device. The platform's control box now lay forgotten on its floor as the swaying worsened.

"Who is this speaking?" asked Joe, as the platform descended too slowly for his liking. Before he could get an answer, the platform toppled toward his left and he leaped away from it. Joe landed on his feet for a moment, but his momentum was too great and he toppled onto his kees and right hand. He felt a strong pain in that hand and hoped he had not broken any bones. Suddenly he felt another pain in the upper part of his head and he lost consciousness.

Sometime later Joe returned slowly to consciousness. As he did so he became aware that he was in the little infirmary beside Doctor Hudson's office suite. A door at the far end of his room opened and Dr. Hudson entered the room. Close behind him was William Schaefer. Joe smiled and sat up on his bed.

'That was a mistake!' he realized belatedly.

"Well, Joe, how are you feeling?" asked the doctor.

Joe winced as his head began to hurt again. He also felt dizzy and lay back down.

"Lousy, Doc! Did someone get the license number of that truck?!" asked the Cherokee.

"It wasn't a truck, Joe, just a runaway tool cart. It was responding to the pull of escaping air" the doctor replied with a smile of amusement. "The back end of it wedged the old, inner airlock's outer door open until Bill here dragged you aside and pulled the cart free. Afterward he stuck your helmet onto your head and turned on your suit's air supply. If he hadn't you would have suffocated when more than half of the garage's air was lost."

"Oh, I just happened to come along at the right time" Bill remarked modestly. "If Helga Svensen had not closed the garage doors—in spite of being pummeled by debris—our air loss would have been <u>much</u> <u>worse</u>."

"I suppose it pays to have a strong woman who is five feet, ten on the payroll" Joe remarked humorously. The doctor smiled again as he sprayed a soothing liquid onto the amerind's upper forehead and Joe added "Thanks, doc."

"You're welcome, Joe" said the physician. "I'll let you take some Tylenol with you when you are ready to leave, but first I want to check your vision."

While the doctor was doing his test (which partly consisted of asking Joe to count the number of fingers that the physician raised), the door of the infirmary opened and a young woman entered the room. She was taller than any of the three men who were present and all of them recognized her as soon as they saw her.

Helga Svensen was a pale complicated woman in her late twenties. She had light yellow hair and light green eyes. "She looks like a <u>big</u>, <u>porcelain</u> <u>doll</u>!' Bill thought as he observed her arrival.

Helga was small breasted and she had a lender, boyish shape, but her pretty face and a voice that was pitched in the lowest part of the alto range left no doubt in the men's minds about her gender. As she seated herself on the vacant, second bed in the room, Bill greeted her.

"Hello, Helga" he said. "You were quite a heroine today!"

"Ay yust did vot needed to be done" she replied modestly in her thick, Swedish accent.

"Well you probably saved my life" said Joe. "Thanks, Helga."

"You're velcome" she replied with a pleasant smile. "Ay yust came to see if you vur okay."

"He seems to be all in one piece" said the doctor, humorously, "but he will have a headache for a while." "How long was I unconscious, doc?" asked Joe.

"I'd guess about an hour" Dr. Hudson replied. "You have a bump on your head the size of a golf ball. "Bill told me it was caused by a collision with that runaway tool cart that some careless person left parked in a corridor without setting the brake lever in '**Park**.' We lost a lot of air when it rolled into the old pedestrian airlock and jammed the outer door open."

"I hope our chief administrator learns who left it unattended and fines the person plenty!" Bill exclaimed angrily. "Some people seem to forget that we're not on Earth any more. They take this artificial atmosphere for granted." The doctor and Helga frowned in agreement but did not comment.

"Well Joe, I think you'll be all right now" Bill said in a milder tone. "I need to do some errands, so I'll be leaving now. Wear a football helmet the next time you go up on that wobbly platform" he added humorously.

"I'll do that" Joe replied with a patient smile as he watched Bill leave the room. Then the amerind turned toward Dr. Hudson and said "I'm hungry, doc. Is it lunch time yet?"

The physician glanced at his watch and said "It's ten 'til twelve. I'll get some Tylenol for you, then I'll let you go."

"Good" Joe replied. I'd like to eat lunch with Helga—if she doesn't have other plans."

"Aye vud like dat" she replied with a friendly smile. "My verk can vait a bit . . ."

Louisa had begun taking Dianne on a guided tour of the main life support machinery room when a man's voice came from a wall mounted loudspeaker:

"This is your Chief Administrator speaking" it said. "The bang that you heard five minutes ago was a small meteorite that punched a hole in our protective dome. An emergency blocker balloon has been sent up to seal the hole until our repair people can make and install a patch. Also, the old pedestrian inner airlock has been reactivated and must now be used to enter the main garage because the latter has become sixty percent depressurized. Do not go there unless your duties require it!

"Helga Svensen, please pickup your pressure suit and report to the Dome Repair and Maintenance Vehicle immediately! Thank you for listening everyone. End of announcement."

"Well, I guess it's safe for us to return to the Biology Department's Office now" said Louisa (with relief in her voice).

"I suppose so" said Dianne (as she followed Louisa toward the exit stairway), "—but what were you studying so intensely when I visited you yesterday?"

"Just some blood samples from two of our fellow colonists" the biologist replied. "They visited the aliens' underground base and I wanted to see if they brought back any unusual germs with them."

"Well, <u>did</u> <u>they</u>?!" asked Dianne, as the two women began climbing the noisy metal stairs.

"Nothing that would <u>make</u> <u>a</u> <u>human</u> <u>sick</u>" Louisa replied carefully, "—but it's difficult to determine what might be a pathogen to <u>an</u> <u>alien</u> <u>species</u>."

"So, do you believe the aliens <u>really</u> <u>are</u> <u>sick</u>?" asked the reporter, with her professional curiosity aroused.

"Yes, but <u>I</u> <u>don't</u> <u>know</u> <u>from</u> <u>what!</u>" Louisa replied emphatically , as they arrived on the upper landing. "I need to confer with Dr. Hudson about that." Louisa unlocked the metal door to the laboratory and opened it, then the two women entered the laboratory.

"I'll need to cut short our interview" said Louisa. "I must try to restore a normal atmosphere in the hallways. You may telephone your cameraman and ask him to bring your pressurized suit to you."

They went into the office and Louisa watched while Dianne used the telephone. The air in the room was uncomfortably sparse and by the time Alvin brought Dianne's suit to her, Louisa was glad to go to the nearby suit rack room and put on her own protective garment. Afterward, she said goodbye to her two visitors via her suit's radio. As soon as they left the Biology Department, Louisa closed the door behind them and locked it from the inside. As she returned to her laboratory work, she only felt slightly guilty about sending the two reporters away. She had known at the time that the air creating machines in the big room below her had been automatically activated and that they would already be replacing the amounts of oxygen and nitrogen that had been lost to the dome puncture. Air filters would just as autonomously be removing any outdoor Martian dust that might have been tracked in by repairmen returning from errands outside the dome.

As the air pressure gradually rose, Louisa glanced occasionally at a gauge on the right sleeve of her pressure suit. When the air pressure was close to normal, she walked back to the suit rack room and removed the bulky, pressurized garment. Afterward she hung it on a rack. Finally, she went to the computer terminal in her laboratory and began composing a report about the bacterium for eventual transmission to Dr. Hudson. When it was finished, its main body of text said:

Dear Dr. Hudson,

I want to bring to your attention the terrestrial bacteria Staphylococcus aureus and Tubiformium militaris. The former is fairly common on many parts of Earth and the latter was brought back to the homelands of both Russian and NATO soldiers who fought a series of small wars in Afghanistan during the last quarter of the Twentieth Century. Please notice the photographs of the two organisms as they appear in their terrestrial forms and the second pair of pictures which show an obviously Mars adapted form of S. aurueum and what may be a more altered form of T. militaries. The latter two organisms were present in samples of blood from our friends, the Edwards couple, which I examined late yesterday afternoon.

About a week ago another variant of T. militaris was found flourishing inside our nation's moon base. It appears in the last picture, along with the name of the medical examiner who found it there—a physician named Chang Lee Hwan, who is a naturalized citizen of the U.S.N.A.

Apparently all of these organisms are extremely hardy—especially in the form of spores. S. aureus—as you may be aware—is found on some parts of the skin of most people and normally does no harm. However, a person whose immune system has been weakened by something else may become dangerously sickened by the staph organism. T. militaris was originally found living on the skins of some Afghans, where it devoured the dead cells of the epidermis without causing any harm to the host. In a few cases, though, the host was allergic to the germ and it caused a painful rash on the parts of the body where it was present. The organism caused similar problems in our country when it migrated there.

This afternoon I did a microscopic study of a dust sample that I took from S. Sandra Edwards' pressurized suit. As I suspected, a microorganism was present that no-one had detected before in this community—Tubiformium marsium (which was the name that I tentatively gave to the suspected relative of T. militaris).

I suspect that Sandra—and perhaps Michael as well—encountered the altered Tubiformium in the Alien Base and that our medical assistance team will find traces of it there. Sandra told me that she had learned recently that one of the aliens had examined some kind of space probe two weeks ago and that they were convinced it came from Earth. That may have been how they became ill.

It is possible that either S.aureus or T. militaris (or both) might have been able to enter the aliens' respiratory tracts where it caused flu-like symptoms. I would like to test that possibility sometime soon.

Yours truly,
Louisa d'Alsace

Louisa sent the letter to Dr. Hudson's computer, but she retained a copy of it in her own electronic files. She knew several people were likely to show an interest in what she had found.

'I wish that I could discuss these microbes with Sandra!' she thought, '—but I don't know if she has a secure email site on Phobos yet. I'd better wait until she communicates with me so I will know more about her situation.'

The telephone in her department's office rang and she went there to pick it up. Louisa had never really trusted the security of wireless telephones and she expected the chief executive to call her soon. She was not disappointed.

"Hello, Biology Department. Louisa d'Alsace speaking" she greeted.

"Hello, Louisa, this is Daniel Morris" her caller replied. "What's the situation in your area?"

"None of the life support equipment was damaged by the impact" Louisa reported. "Sir, I think I know what might have caused the aliens to become sick. I'd like to have an opportunity to confirm my hypothesis."

"Have you told Dr. Hudson about this hunch of yours?" asked Daniel.

"Yes, sir, I just finished sending an email to him" the brown haired biologist informed her boss.

"Well, I want a copy of your message too" said Daniel. "I want to know what we might be encountering—in case it spreads to our base."

"I don't want to alarm you, sir, but I think it already has" said Louisa. "I don't think it poses much of a threat to humans, though."

"Just send your report, Miss d'Alsace" Daniel ordered mildly. "I'll draw my own conclusion."

"Yes, sir. You will have it in a few minutes" Louisa assured him. Then he hung up and she did the same.

Chapter Twenty-Seven
A Low Gee Honeymoon

Midday Friday

"You people have done an amazing amount of tunneling during the last two years!" Michael exclaimed, as he and the other three visitors followed their guide through the maze of chambers and corridors inside the moonlet.

"I'm impressed too" said Sophia. "Your team has burrowed like a bunch of moles through this big rock, Jay Jay."

"Well, it gave us something to do to pass the time" she replied humorously, as the group stopped temporarily in an unfinished room. "Seriously, though, we were hoping to receive some additional people aboard the *von Braun*, so we made plenty of room for them. Some natural caves assisted our work, since Phobos' interior is not tightly packed together."

"Even so, the gravity in here is stronger than I expected" Michael remarked. "It feels more like Luna's gee force than that of a tiny moonlet."

"That's because we obtained the original prototype, gravity generator's plans from its designer on Luna" Jay Jay explained. "Then our electronic genius of an administrator modified our spare electrical generator to create gravity waves! Pretty clever, huh?"

"It's amazing!" Sophia exclaimed, "—but how did Mister Smith pry loose the plans from Arnold Webber's tight grasp?!" I've heard he is really protective of his patents."

"Warren wrote a computer program for him that made Mr. Webber's mechanical design for an automated, shallow deposit, mining machine feasible" Jay Jay replied. It made a huge amount of helium three available to fusion reactor designers and builders on Earth. That, in turn, created an important export market for the colonists on Luna."

"I didn't know he was involved in <u>Lunar mining</u>" said Michael. "He's a man of many talents!"

"Mr Smith sounds like an interesting man to know" said Sophia, "—but what's he like away from his work?"

"He's a bit of a womanizer, actually" Jay Jay replied with a humorous smile. "I'd be careful around Warren if I were a beautiful lady like you" she added semiseriously.

"Let's go to your lunchroom now" said Roger. "<u>I'm feeling hungry!</u>"

"All right" Jay Jay replied. "Follow me, everyone." The tour group compled, while Sophia wondered silently how seriously she should take her guide's warning.

After the group had meandered through a confusing series of hallways it finally entered one end of the lunchroom. "As you can see, we recently enlarged this room, in anticipation of the Wernher von Braun's arrival" said Jay Jay. The group noticed that a different style of ceiling tile had been used in the new section. "We ran out of the original type of ceiling tiles" Jay Jay explained, after noticing their upward glances.

"Our food dispensers are the same design as those in Lowellsville—or so John Clewiston tells us, anyway" said Jay Jay. "Just pull your debit cards out and help yourselves." The two male visitors promptly did so. Sophia was about to ask her guide a question about Warren Smith when another attractive, black haired woman entered the room. Michael and Roger looked up from their recently acquired cups of hot chocolate as the new arrival introduced herself.

"Hello, evrihwun. Ah'm Pamela Mason" she drawled in a nearly exinct, deep south accent.

"We've heard about you!" Roger exclaimed happily, "—but nobody told us you were this pretty!"

Pamela smiled and replied "Thank yew, Mistuh Harris!" as she read the name tag on his light gray, engineer's coveralls. "Ah'm flattuhed. Yew folks may call mih **Pam**." Then she seated herself beside the two men's table, after Roger rose briefly and pulled a chair out for her.

Roger seated himself again and said "Dan Morris wants to borrow you so you can treat a coouple of sick aliens. We hope to make friends of them afterward."

"That's the plan, anyway" said Michael. "Are you ready to spend some time in Mars'stronger gravity?"

"Ah'd be glad to visit Mahz foah a while" Pamela replied, as Michael pulled the last chair outward for Sophia (without standing up). Both men admired what the unvelcroed, upper six inches of Pam's white nurse's coveralls revealed. Pam noticed their attention to her cleavage and smiled briefly.

"Ah'd lahk ta meet some moah people an' walk on a planitarih suhface without takin' precau-shuns against floatin' away inta space" Pam added humorously.

"There is <u>that</u> <u>advantage</u> on Mars" said Michael, "—but our people want to see a new face there too, accasionally."

'And some <u>new</u> <u>cleavage</u>!' thought Sophia, with a mixture of annoyance and amusement.

"Weh-ull then, we'll all benefit from mah new assign-munt" Pamela said happily.

"I love the way you talk" Roger commented admiringly.

"Thay-uts good, bihcause Ah'm not about ta change it" Pamela replied, "—especiallih since Cong-ress finalih passed the *Regional Accents Presuhvay-shun Act* two weeks ago. Ah'm a '<u>national</u> <u>ass-et</u>' now!" she added humorously, as she pushed her chair back. Afterward she stood up and walked to one of the beverage dispensers. She ordered a cup of artificially sweetened tea for herself from the machine, which was part of a row of similar vending machines. They covered a whole section of wall in the trunk portion of the 'L' shaped room.

"Well la dee dah!" Jay Jay remarked teasingly. "It isn't enough that she's <u>physically</u> <u>attractive</u>—now we must help her to preserve her '<u>cultural uniqueness</u>!' I think I shall volunteer to go explore an asteroid!"

"Don't let us fool yew—we ac-tu-allih <u>lahk</u> <u>each-uthah</u>—<u>most of the tahm</u>!" Pamela told her guests. Jay Jay just formed a humorous half-smile.

Michael and Roger had been happily admiring Pamela's physical appearance, but they also enjoyed her and Jay Jay's playful banter. Michael decided that he definitely liked both women and he noticed that Roger seemed to share his opinion of them.

Even Sophia felt at ease with her two new acquaintances. She was confident enough of her own attractiveness to men to not be jealous of

Michael's and Roger's admiring glances at Pamela (especially since her own exposed cleavage was receiving frequent glances too).

Linda Simmons was also sitting beside a table in the newly enlarged room. She had arrived there before the other Lowellsvillians did, but she had been content just to listen and had said nothing so far. Instead she quietly sipped a Diet Pepsi and scanned a mural of the gray, crater pocked surface of Phobos on the room's longest wall. A star spangled, black sky filled most of the upper third of the painting, although a small part of Mars was visible at its right end. Linda noticed the signature: 'Janet Johnson—2047' near the pink, hazy curve of Mars' edge.

"I like your painting of Phobos, Jay Jay" Linda remarked, "—it's very realistic. "Do you ever paint portraits?"

"I'm learning how to do it, but I need some more practice" the artist replied. "People are more complicated subjects than a small, airless, gray moon."

"Oh, listen to huh makin' excuses!" Pamela chided. "She's reallih quite good at paintin' pictyuhs of people! She recentlih painted a big, nude portrait of mih foah Wah-ren's buthday next week. Ah gave it to him uhlih because Ah won't be heah then. Enihway, it looks just lahk mih."

"I think it's a good likeness too" said Warren, as he walked into the room through its other doorway. Every head in the lunchroom turned to look at him. He was a handsome man in his early thirties. Michael estimated that he was about five feet, ten inches tall, with light brown hair and hazel colored eyes. His hair was cut short and he had a neatly trimmed, handlebar moustache.

Warren seated himself at the nearest vacant table to where Pam was and scooted his chair close to hers. They kissed each other for a couple of seconds, after which he said "Karen Ferguson took a radio message from Lowellsville about ten minutes ago and played it back for me. It said that a small meteor punched a hole in the dome that protects the eastern entrances to Lowellsville. It happened while you four guests were on your way up here."

"Was anyone injured?" asked Linda.

"Apparently two people were" Warren replied. "An Indian-Joe somebody—fell from a scissors lift and had a mild concussion, while a Scandinavian woman was badly bruised in several places by flying debris. Both people are expected to recover fully, although they will need a few weeks to do so."

"Maybe this accident will <u>finally</u> cause our people to follow <u>proper</u> <u>safety</u> <u>procedures</u>!" Michael said hopefully.

"In any case" Warren continued, "A repair crew is busy patching the dome now, after which Daniel wants to do <u>a</u> <u>thorough</u> <u>testing</u> of <u>all</u> <u>the</u> <u>airlocks</u> and electrical wiring in Lowellsville proper and between the hill and the space port before shuttle flights resume at the latter; so Linda must wait until <u>tomorrow</u> to fly back to Lowellsville with Pam as her passenger."

"That's no problem" Linda replied. "I always bring a suitcase with me in case something like this happens. My family can cope without me <u>for</u> <u>one</u> <u>night</u>."

"Good" said Warren. "I'll get some decaf coffee, then I want Pam, Michael and Sandra to come with me for a conference in my apartment. Roger, I would like for you to suit up and go see how the shuttle's systems fare during the recent flight up to here. We can't be too careful with a manned aerospace vehicle. Linda, if you haven't yet been introduced to our chief-and only—computer operator and secretary, Karen Ferguson, I'd like for Jay Jay to take you to visit her now. You could probably be of help to Karen with your office skills. I'll see most of you later at lunch time."

A few minutes later Pamela, Sophia, and Michael followed Warren into the living room of his apartment. As Michael closed the door between the apartment and the corridor, he noticed a large, crudely framed portrait of Pam hanging above the couch. The painting was not quite as lifelike as the one that Michael had of Sophia, but it was still adequate to display Pam's attractive face and figure in a standing position. She was seen from a right front viewpoint. Her genital area was depicted realistically, rather than by the blank, sexless style of earlier centuries. She had an amused smile on her face that indicated she enjoyed posing nude for the portrait.

"Well, I think Jay Jay has good potential as an artist" Michael said admiringly.

"I think so too" Warren remarked. "I just wish I could have gotten better wood than that baseboard material to use when I made the frame for that picture."

"Well, we are a long distance from the nearest lumberyard" Sophia remarked humorously. "I think you did okay under these circumstances, Mr. Smith."

"Thank you—and please call me 'Warren. 'We are not formal here on Phobos" said her host.

"All right" Sophia replied. "May I ask if you are related to Warren Parker Smith, the U.S.N.A.'s secretary of State?"

"You may, but we are not related as far as I know. It is just a coincidence that our names are similar" Warren answered.

"May Ah call yew 'Sandra'?" Pam asked Michael's new spouse. "'Sophia' sounds like the queen of some country." 'Sandra' just smiled and nodded. She had long ago become accustomed to most people preferring her middle name.

Warren and Pamela seated themselves in a pair of arm chairs, while their guests used the small couch in front of them, at the opposite side of the narrow room.

Michael noticed some interesting similarities between Sophia and Pamela. Both young women had black hair and Pam was only an inch taller than Sophia's five feet, six inches. They both had pretty faces, but Pam lacked Sophia's spectacular figure. Michael decided that Pam's body was beautiful, but not gorgeous.

"You two girls look like you could be sisters—or at least, first cousins" Michael remarked.

"Ah'm flattuhd, but Sandra is in a class bah huhself foah appearunce" Pam replied. Then she turned toward the stunningly beautiful visitor and asked "Why did you come out heah to the fron-teah, Sandra? Yew should have become a movih stah on Uth!"

"Thank you" Sophia responded, "But I've always wanted to explore another planet and search for native life forms there. Ever since I saw those late twentieth century Mars rover pictures in books as a child, I've wanted to come to Mars."

"So have I" Warren remarked, "and every time I stand outdoors in a space suit and look toward the planet I'm glad I made the journey."

"You do have a spectacular view outside!" Michael enthused. "It's worth the long flight up here from Lowellsville."

"Well, you two saw something that I wish I had seen, when you ventured into that alien base near the William's Bluff drilling camp" said Warren. "I'd like to hear an account of how you found its entrance and what you saw there."

"So would Aih—especiallih if yew met some of the aliens" Pam prompted.

The two guests proceeded to tell their story in turns (similarly to the account that they gave to Daniel Morris earlier). Pam and Warren listened in fascination.

Afterward, Warren remarked "I wish I could have been there! You two actually saw a robot made by alien hands!"

"We really did!" Sophia replied. She then calmly unvelcroed her coveralls downward to midtorso and withdrew her left arm halfway out of its sleeve. "—and it left me this" she added , as she untapped a large bandage from just above the elbow; "—as a souvenir of our meeting." She had uncovered a pink wound that was about two inches long and a quarter of an inch wide.

"Ooh! They-ut looks painful!" Pam exclaimed in sympathy.

"It is painful—whenever the spray-on medicine loses its effect" Sophia replied.

"Do you use Decaminol?" asked Warren.

"Yes, but its effect is wearing off" Sophia responded, as she noticed him scanning her lace brassiere covered left breast. The bra was more decorative than concealing (as Warren had quickly noticed).

"Pam, honey, would you go to my medicine cabinet and get some decaminol for me?" asked Warren. "Bring some bandaging material too."

"Ah'm on mah way" she replied, as she picked up the old bandage and left the couch.

As Pam disappeared into the bedroom (on her way to the adjoining bathroom), Warren told Sophia "That is the most beautiful breast I've ever seen!"

"Thank you" she replied with a slight smile. "I wish I could be rid of that ugly burn wound, though. "Dr. Hudson told me it might take six weeks to heal!" "You're lucky it was just a grazing wound" said Warren. "It could have been much more serious."

"I know" Sophia replied with a brief frown. "I have a nightmare sometimes about receiving a chest wound instead of an arm wound in that skirmish. The imaginary pain always wakes me."

Pam returned with a fresh bandage, a roll of tape and a bottle of Decaminol. She sprayed some of the latter onto Sophia's wound, then she began bandaging it.

"Thanks, Pam" said Sophia.

"Youah welcome" Pam replied. Then she added "Ah'd pay a plas-tic suhgeon a month's wages if Ah could have mah bosom changed to look lahk youahs. Ah those na-tyur-al?"

"Yep, it's all me!" Sophia replied proudly, as she lowered the right shoulder portion of her coveralls. These breasts helped me to pay for my living expenses during my senior year in college. I used to pose nude for artists in central North Carolina back then."

As she started to pull up her left upper sleeve, Warren said "<u>Please</u> don't do that!" Sophia complied. "I'd like to have Jay Jay look at you and tell me what she would charge me to paint a nude portrait of you. I want to hang it beside Pam's—<u>if</u> neither of you girls or Michael objects, that is."

"Ah don't mind" Pam replied (although this was not entirely true).

"I suppose not" said Michael (who was becoming accustomed to Sophia's nonchalance about revealing her wispily clad breasts to a friendly admirer). "As long as Sophia is willing to pose for Jay Jay and you pay her for her time."

"All right" said Warren. "I'll pay Sandra <u>fifty</u> <u>dollars</u> to pose for the painting until Jay Jay completes it."

"<u>A</u> <u>hundred</u>—and you know <u>I'm</u> <u>worth</u> <u>it</u>!" Sophia countered confidently.

"Oh, all right. A hundred" Warren conceded. "I'll call our artist and ask her to bring her sketch pad to my apartment. She can sketch Sandra in several poses in the bedroom and I'll decide which one should become a portrait." He then went to an end table, picked up a telephone and dialed Jay Jay's portable 'phone number. When she answered, he said to her:

"Hello, Jay Jay. I have an art project for you! Do you have time to do some sketches of a beautiful model?"

"I suppose so" she replied (as she deduced who it would be). "Things are slow in the radio room, now that the Mars shuttle has arrived here."

"Good. You can work with her in my bedroom" said Warren. "Michael, Pam and I will wait in the living room until you two are finished."

"Okay. I'll be at your place in about fifteen minutes" the artist assured him. I need to finish cleaning some brushes and gathering my equipment."

"She'll be waiting for you. Goodbye" Warren told her. He then hung up the telephone.

Meanwhile, Pam had returned from a quick trip to the nearby infirmary and was seated beside Sophia on the couch. To make room for her there, Michael had moved to the armchair that Pam had vacated earlier. Pam injected some pain killer into Sophia's wounded arm.

"Does youah ahm huht ennih now, San-dra?" asked Pam, as she finished her work.

"Just a little" her guest replied. "I can tolerate it now."

"You mentioned some photographs that you found in that alien suit locker room, Mike" said Warren, who was once more seated in the other armchair. "Do you happen to have them with you?"

"Yes" Michael replied. He then reached into one of the front upper pockets of his coveralls and pulled out an envelope, which he handed to Warren.

Warren studied one of the pictures while Pam left the couch, went to her lover's chair and leaned over his right shoulder.

"A flying saucer!" Warren exclaimed. "Has either of you adventurers actually seen it yet?"

"No" Michael admitted. "I hope it is inside that bluff somewhere in an underground hangar. I'd love to see it myself!"

Warren showed the picture to Pam, then he returned it to the envelope facing away from the other photographs. When he took out the next picture, he saw the flying saucer in flight.

"Here it is again!" Warren exclaimed. "It's flying this time. I'd love to know what powers it!"

"I've been wondering the same thing" said Michael. "I'd give a month's pay to know the an-swer. There's no visible exhaust plume."

"Maybe Ah kin puhsuade the aliens to tell us how it wuhks" Pam said hopefully.

"Yes, please do an extra good job of healing them, Pam!" Warren urged, as he returned the picture to the envelope.

The group looked at the photograph of the aliens' ground vehicle next and Pam commented "It doesn't look much dif-erent from owah Mahs cahs—except foah those an-tenna-lahk thangs on its roof."

"Well, I have a suspicion we'll see some really sophisticated electronic equipment inside that vehicle" Michael remarked. Sophia and I could only guess about the functions of most of the devices we saw in an instrumentation alcove that we found in that alien base."

"That's the truth!" Sophia exclaimed. "They were bewildering!" She then added "I'd better go to the bedroom now and undress."

"<u>Please</u> <u>do</u>" Warren urged. "Jay Jay will be here soon."

Sophia went into the bedroom and shut the door, then the rest of the group examined the fourth of the alien photographs. "Mah wuhd!" exclaimed Pam. "Look at those foah ahms on thayut alien wo-mun! She looks lahk a pic-tyuh in a Hindu temple!"

"I see them!" Warren exclaimed with amazement. "She is <u>definitely</u> <u>not</u> <u>human</u>! I'd like to see what <u>the</u> <u>rest</u> <u>of</u> <u>her</u> looks like."

"So would I" Michael remarked, "—especially her <u>real</u> <u>skin</u> <u>color</u>. That helmet's sun visor probably changes it."

"Ah'll trah ta make some photo-grah-uffs of huh when Ah visit huh home" Pam promised.

"Well, just be careful not to contract whatever illness she has" Warren Cautioned. "I want tyou back here healthy in a week or two."

The telephone (which was lying on a small end table near the couch) rang and Pam picked it up.

"Hello?" she said.

"Hello, Pam" said a female voice. "I need you to come to my office quickly! I think Mr. Harris is having an adverse reaction to some medicine he took!" the worried caller added.

"All raht, Keh-ren" Pam replied. "Ah'm on mah way!" She then turned off the 'talk' circuit and set the telephone back on the end table. She quickly explained the situation to the two men, then she added "Yew men stay heah. Ah'll tell the medical robot to assist mih. It knows what to do." Afterward she picked up her briefcase size medical kit from the floor (near the couch) and hurried out of the apartment.

A minute after Pam left the living room, the doorbell rang. Warren opened the door and in came Jay Jay with her drawing kit. Warren directed her to the bedroom and opened the door for her. He had a glimpse of Sophia sitting nude on the left edge of the bed, then Jay Jay pushed the door closed with her right elbow.

"You are a lucky man, Mike" Warren remarked, as he went to his favorite armchair and seated himself. He was now near an amused looking Michael (who had chosen the other chair).

"I know—I hear that a lot!" Michael replied with a slight smile. He then took the message tape out of a pocket of his coveralls and said "Daniel sent this to you." He then handed the tape to his host.

"It's a private message" Michael added.

"Thanks for delivering it" Warren told him. Afterward the two men began discussing the situation on Earth and Phobos' supply needs during the war.

About an hour later, Pam returned to Warren's apartment and saw Jay Jay showing four drawings to the two very interested men.

"Hi, Pam. Is Roger okay?" asked Warren.

"Yay-uss" she replied. "His condih-shun is back undah control now. Ah found an antinausea drug in owah phahmacih thet makes the can-suh drug moah tol-lerable."

"Good" said Warren, as he beckoned to her. "Come help me to decide which of these positions to have made into a painting."

"Oh-kay" she replied. She then seated herself on the right armrest of his big, comfortable chair. On Earth, the chair might not have supported both people's weight, but on Phobos—even with augmented gravity—their bodies only weighed one-sixth as much as thy did on Earth.

"Are you sure Roger is all right, Pam?" asked Michael (who felt guilty about not being able to help the engineer himself).

"He is foah a while" Pam replied,"—but he real-lih needs to be in a can-suh clinic on Uth—and as soon as possible!"

"Well, that's the *von Braun's* responsibility—not ours" said Michael. "All we can do is to make sure he's aboard the ship when it leaves."

"Ah know thah-ut" Pam replied (sounding slightly annoyed), "—but what if those foah ahmed ay-liens have a bettuh treat-munt foah can-suh than we have? Thah-ut could save Rojuh's life—with-out sen-din' him back ta Uth!."

"Maybe—if we knew their type of medicine would work on humans" said Michael. "Otherwise it might kill him instead!"

"Michael's right, honey. We can't afford to gamble on an alien drug or device" said Warren, "—unless we have no other choice. Besides which, right now they need our help to stay alive!"

"Yay-us, and they'll be grate-ful if we succeed in curin' they-um" said Pam. "Thay-uh ah risks in-volved in a long space flight thay-ut Ah wish Rah-juh could avoid—ray-diation, foah instance."

"I'll ask the *von Braun's* crew if they can take some extra precautions in Roger's case" Warren promised. "Now which of these drawings do you like most?"

Pam scanned the drawings and said "Ah prefuh this wun," as she pointed to a drawing of Sophia lying on her right side, with her right forearm propping up her head.

"I like that one too" said Warren. He then handed the drawing to Jay Jay as Sophia entered the living room once more fully dressed.

"They want me to paint a portrait of you in this position" said Jay Jay, as she showed the drawing to her model. "Will you pose for me at two o'clock this afternoon?"

"Yes" Sophia replied. "May I bring my disk player with me? I like to listen to classical music while I'm posing. It prevents me from becoming bored."

"That's fine with me" said Jay Jay, "—as long as it's not too loud."

Warren glanced at his watch and said "There is till about an hour before lunch. I'd like for you to identify a mineral for me in our newest tunnel, Mike. It's pretty stuff, but I'd like to know if it has any practical applications."

"All right" Michael replied. "Is the tunnel pressurized yet?"

"No, we'll need our space suits" Warren replied. He then turned toward the three women and said "We'll see you ladies in the dining room at noon."

They replied affirmatively, then the two men left the apartment.

Fifteen minutes later they were in their space suits and walking through a tunnel with a circular cross section that had been bored through solid rock. The two men's footsteps echoed from the bare walls that were briefly lit by the explorers' flashlights and helmet lights. Soon they arrived at the rough rock end wall of the nine feet high passageway. They stopped there in front of a large seam of light orange rock with a large number of black specks in it.

"Well, Mike, do you recognize this orange rock?" Warren asked hopefully.

"I certainly do!" Michael replied with a smile. "It's Aresite*(16)—some of the prettiest mineral of its type that I've ever seen! But until now I've only seen it on Mars. How far underground are we now?"

"I checked the depth by sonar after we stopped tunneling yesterday" Warren replied. "It's about a hundred and twenty-five feet."

"This looks like a well embedded, naturally occurring seam" said Michael, "—rather than a meteor-itic intrusion. For this type of sandstone to be found here—with no trace of partial melting—indicates that <u>Phobos</u>

was once a part of Mars, rather than being a captured asteroid. It looks like this entire moonlet may have been blasted loose from the surface of Mars in chunks by a large commentary or asteroid impact—like the one that made the Hellas Basin. The pieces orbited the planet for a few thousand years, then mutual gravitational attraction brought them together to form Phobos.

"Congratulations, Warren! You have made an important discovery!"

"Well, lucky me!" Warren commented with a smile, "but if this orange material is sandstone, what are these little black specks?"

"They are probably either fragments of the meteorite or volcanic soot from one of the Martian volcanoes" Michael replied. "I'll take a chunk of this rock to a laboratory and do a thorough analysis of it. Afterward I might be able to tell you what kind of meteorite—or which volcano—made the soot."

"That's great!" Warren exclaimed. "I'll show you where your lab is, now that you are on assignment to Phobos Base."

"Okay" said Michael, as he picked up a fist size, Aresite rock from the floor (where the drilling machine had left it earlier). Afterward he followed Warren through a series of tunnels, an airlock and some corridors to a well equipped geology and metalurgy laboratory. Michael thought "This place looks like it has seldom-if ever—been used!" Then the two men desuited and placed their helmets on a shelf. They hung their space suits on a crude-but sturdy—improvised rack.

"I had this equipment brought here from Earth by the previous supply ship, with the hope that our community could get its own geologist and/ or metalurgist soon—but no such luck!" Warren explained. "We got an astronomer instead! Not that I have anything against astronomers, mind you, but right now I'm more concerned with what's happening here on Phobos than with what comets and objects in the main asteroid belt are doing."

"That's understandable" Michael remarked, with a brief, sympathetic smile, "—although we might need to mine the asteroids for useful ores eventually."

"I doubt that will happen anytime soon" Warren said skeptically. "We have a whole planet to mine that is much closer to us."

"That's true—up to a point" Michael stated, "but there could be minerals in the main asteroid belt that we cannot find on Mars."

"Well, for the present I just want to know what the best uses for this ariesite rock are" said Warren, "—in your professional opinion."

"It's a good building material" Michael replied, "and it's decorative when it's polished. "We covered the walls and floor of our swimming pool room with it. It's also common—on Mars, anyway—so we won't exhaust our supply of aresite anytime soon."

"Thank you" said Warren. "We'll use it in the walls of our conference room—when we get around to building one." Warren looked at his watch and remarked "It's about lunchtime. Let's go so-cialize with the other Phobosians."

"All right" Michael replied. "I'm starting to feel hungry."

The two men walked to the lunchroom and found most of the rest of the little community's people there already.

"These people must love to eat" Michael remarked humorously.

"There's not much else to anticipate around here" Warren replied, "—except chess and low gee basketball during the evenings and on Saturday afternoons. Pam and I will introduce you and Sandra to our version of basketball tonight. It's our own unique invention."

"That sounds like it could be fun" Michael remarked. He then turned his attention toward greeting the other diners and choosing his meal. Warren did the same and soon each man was seated with a small group of his friends. Michael sat with Sophia and Jay Jay, while Warren was with Pamela and Roger at another table.

Warren soon stood up and said "I have an announcement to make. Our borrowed geologist has made an important discovery! He has identified a light orange sandstone in our newest tunnel as *Aresite*—a rock found previously only on Mars! That may mean that our little moon was once a part of the planet below us!"

David Carlisle had recently entered the room and was selecting his food. Now he enquired loudly enough for everyone to hear: "How would an object as big as Phobos be torn loose from Mars and sent flying way up here?!"

Michael calmly pushed back his chair and stood up. Then he said "It is just a theory so far, but I propose that a huge asteroid—or a comet—struck Mars at some time in the past and blasted lose some large chunks of Mars that later clumped together to form Phobos."

David got his beverage and said "I suppose that's possible, but it sounds like an idea that will need some more evidence to be convincing." Then he seated himself beside Jay Jay.

"Your theory is interesting, Mr. Edwards" said Walter Jones, as he rose to a standing position beside his table. Michael estimated that Walter was about five feet, nine inches tall. He had black hair, bluish gray eyes and a slender build. He was in his late thirties and already his hair was becoming sparse on the top of his head. Until now, Walter had been sitting alone contentedly beside the third table of the four, with a technical drawing beside his food tray. "I'd like to see this orange sandstone of yours" he added. "Any ideas about the origin of Phobos are of interest to me—especially if there is evidence to support them."

"I'll be happy to show it to you after lunch" Michael replied. "You'll need to wear a pressurized suit, though."

"I'll do that" Walter replied, before he sat down again. He then resumed eating his meal alone.

"I'd like to go too" said David. "Warren was driving the boring machine that uncovered that orange rock, so I have not seen it yet."

"I'll make it a foursome" Warren said loudly. He spoke as if they were going to play golf or tennis. "I want to hear whatever conclusions you three scientists and an engineer come to about that orange rock layer."

"It sounds like Phobos really rocks!" Sophia remarked humorously, as she glanced at her newly acquired husband.

"Well it certainly did when it was coming together millions of years ago!" Michael replied with a smile of amusement. He seated himself near Sophia again, then the two diners resumed eating their meal. Everyone else did the same. Their lunch was interspersed with conversations about topics that ranged from ancient meteors to the recent dust storm on Mars.

'It seems that no-one wants to think about the war up here, yet' thought Michael, '—but it will intrude on us soon enough!'

*(16) Pronounced Air-eez-ite. Early explorers in what would eventually be called 'the Lowellsville District' found a whole cliff of it at what would later become the site of Lowellsville's Main Vehicle Entrance. The big half-dome was built in front of it.

Chapter Twenty-Eight
A Pleasant Afternoon Inside Phobos

Friday Afternoon

After lunch was eaten, Michael, Warren, David and Walter went to the places where their space suits were hanging. Two of these racks were in the small, rectangular room beside the larger, freight check-in room. The other two racks were in the geology laboratory, so the four men met each other in the corridor in front of the lab and put on their space helmets. Afterward they walked together toward their destination through the maze of corridors.

Actually the four men did not really <u>walk</u>—instead they <u>bounded along</u> in Phobos' weak gravity, as if they had springs on their shoes' soles.

"We look like those long ago Apollo astronauts on Luna!" Michael remarked via his suit's radio. He had a tone of amusement in his voice, as he and his companions bounded in pairs along a series of corridors that led to what was known in the community as 'the Miners Airlock.'

"Yeah, I once told Pam that someday she'll give birth to 'a bouncing baby boy'"! Warren replied, with a good-humored smile behind his face plate.

"Are you two <u>ever</u> planning to be <u>married</u>?" asked Walter, who was carefully imitating his base commander's hops.

"I suppose I'll have no choice, now that televised weddings are in vogue down in Lowellsville" Warren replied. "I'd hate for Pam and me to ruin a good friendship, though." He spoke in a semiserious tone of voice, so his listeners did not know if he was sincere or not.

Their momentum caused the four men to bump against each other—with their arms extended like shock absorbers—as they came to a halt in front of the airlock's door.

"We'll need to go through this thing two at a time—that's all it can hold" Warren told the group. "Michael and I will go first, then when we have finished cycling through it we'll wait for you two in the tunnel beyond it."

Five minutes later the four men were together again, with the twelve feet long tunnel boring machine parked to their left in a short, dead end section of the tunnel that it had made. The group then set out to their right, hopping through a tunnel that sloped gradually downward. As it descended, the rough walled tube curved back toward its left until it had completed a 'U' turn.

"We'll soon be at the place where I found the orange rock layer" Warren told his three companions. I had no idea at the time that it would turn out to be such an important discovery . . .'"

Meanwhile, Jay Jay and Sophia had long since left the lunchroom and had walked through sections of two corridors to the door of the artist's apartment. Twenty feet beyond it was a closed door with the words 'Radio Room, no loitering 'painted on it in red letters.

Jay Jay unlocked and opened the apartment's door, then she told Sophia "You go into the bedroom and undress. My painter's equipment is already set up in there. I'll visit the radio room for a few minutes and see if there are any recorded, incoming messages to which any of our people will need to respond soon."

"All right" Sophia replied. Afterward she walked across the narrow living room to the open door-way of the bedroom beyond it. She entered the latter and closed its door behind her. Next she walked past the open doorway of the bathroom to what she correctly guessed was a closet door. She opened that door and set her purse down beside it, then she proceeded to undress. Each item of clothing that she re—moved was subsequently hung on a clothes hanger inside the walk-in closet. When she was nude, she picked up her purse and carried it to the narrow, one person bed. She set the purse on the bed and opened it, then she took out a disk player device the size of a small, paperback book. Finally she set the device on top of a night stand to the left of the bed and turned on a recording of the mid-twentieth century composer Ferde Grofe's "*Grand Canyon Suite.*"

Sophia lay down on the bed in a prone position, facing the end of the room where the connecting door to the living room was. She then stuck a pillow under her chin and waited for Jay Jay to arrive. She noticed a wooded box lying on an old Television stand near the foot of the bed and guessed that it contained some of Jay Jay's artist's equipment.

About eight minutes later the artist opened the door of the room and a few seconds later she entered it with an easel that had been standing in a corner of the living room earlier.

"Sorry I took so long" said Jay Jay. "There was a recorded message from Earth for me to print out and take to Warren. That's all done now."

Jay Jay placed her easel to the left of the bed, then she went to her wooden box and began removing some items from it. While she was selecting these items and placing them on the t.v. stand, Sophia reversed her direction on the bed and rolled onto her right side. "What do you want me to do with these two pillows?" she asked afterward.

"Just lean them against the wall behind your back for now" the artist replied. "Later when your right arm becomes tired I'll let you rest your head on them while I paint your lower half."

Sophia complied, then she assumed the posing position that she remembered seeing in a drawing that Jay Jay had shown to her before lunch. The artist approached the bed and made a few minor adjustments to Sophia's pose, then she returned to her easel. Jay Jay took a canvas that she had prepared earlier off of the top of a dresser and placed it on the easel. Afterward she used a big artist's pencil to sketch a crude preliminary drawing of Sophia onto the canvas. She used a fifteen inch, metal ruler to help her get the proportions of Sophia's head, torso, arms and legs correct.

"I like that music that you chose" said Jay Jay. "What's the name of it?"

Sophia told her, then she added "It's what's called a 'tone poem'—an image of something created by mood evocative sounds. Grof'es *Mississippi Suite* is on that disk too. He's my favorite mid-twentieth century composer."

Jay Jay halfway listened to the beautiful music as it evoked images in Sophia's mind of the far away Painted Desert during its first movement. The brown haired artist mostly concentrated on sketching a more detailed and lifelike image of a gorgeous female body around the crude collection of ovals and an egg shaped face that she had lightly drawn earlier. She spent about a half hour on the drawing, then she let Sophia visit the apartment's small, semidetached kitchen to fill a glass with fruit punch from the refrigerator. The juice had been reconstituted inside a ceramic pitcher by adding bottled water from Lowellsville to the frozen pulp.

Sophia wore only a pair of sandal-like shoes and Jay Jay admired her model's voluptuous curves briefly before the artist visited the bathroom (which adjoined the bedroom) to pee. Afterward both women returned to the bedroom, where Sophia studied the drawing of her body and sipped fruit punch.

"Sandra, I thought Pam had a beautiful body when she posed for me, but compared to you she was just plain looking!" Jay Jay exclaimed. "I've never seen a body to match yours! I'd pay a year's wages if some plastic surgeon could reshape my figure to look like yours!"

"Thank you" Sophia replied, as she held the glass containing the fruit punch with her right hand. Jay Jay had told her on their way to the apartment to help herself to whatever was in the refrigerator during her rest breaks and Sophia took her words literally. "You haven't seen my college friend, Penny Carter, yet though. She's a beautiful redhead with a figure that's at least as good as mine" ('if she has taken good care of it lately') the model added mentally.

Sophia finished drinking the beverage and went into the kitchen to rinse the glass. Afterward she wiped the juice off of her mouth with a damp wash cloth and returned to her posing in the bedroom.

'I wonder if that tabloid story about Penny eating too much recently and gaining a lot of weight is true?' thought Sophia, as she listened to *Cloud Burst* near the end of the *Grand Canyon Suite*. 'Those tabloids exaggerate so often a person never knows what to believe and what to reject.'

During that second half hour, while the little disk player played the *Mississippi Suite*, Jay Jay drew the general shape of Sophia's bluish black hair and the details of her eyes and eyelids. In the last ten minutes she added some color at last, but it was a dark gray shading color, with some purple added on top of it. This process gave to the drawing a surrealistic—even sinister—appearance.

When Jay Jay let Sophia take her second break, the model rolled over, swung her shapely legs off of the right side of the bed and sat up. Afterward she put on her shoes and left the bed.

"You're a good model, Sandra" said Jay Jay. "You're as still as a manikin most of the time and completely uninhibited. I would be nervous and self conscious if someone was observing the details of my body like this." She then began cleaning one of the brushes that she had been using recently.

"Well, as a female artist on Earth once told me: '<u>Be</u> <u>proud</u> <u>of</u> <u>your</u> <u>body</u>, Sandra. <u>Don't</u> <u>keep</u> <u>it</u> <u>to</u> <u>yourself</u>—let people see and admire it,' so I'm trying to follow her advice. It isn't as easy as it looks, though." As she spoke, Sophia walked to where the artwork was and observed it curiously. "It amazes me how an artist can build up a picture in layers like this. How do you know which colors to use for shading purposes?"

"That's what <u>art</u> <u>lessons</u> are for" Jay Jay replied humorously. "I really wish that I had had the time—and the money—for more of them though, before I left Earth. I don't know if I can do justice to a body like yours—although <u>I'll</u> <u>certainly</u> <u>try</u>!"

"What do you think will be the most difficult parts of me to depict?" her model asked curiously.

"Well, the eyes are always a challenge—no matter who the subject is" Jay Jay replied, as she set down one brush and began cleaning a smaller one, "—but arms, hands, legs and feet are difficult too because they have so many difficult curves and widths to draw.

"In your case, though, I was thinking more in terms of your breasts and aureolas. The former are a cream color, but the latter range from a rose petal pink where they touch the nipples to a barely discernable difference from your breasts' color at the circle's outer edges—in fact, in some places it is difficult to determine <u>where</u> <u>their</u> <u>edges</u> <u>are</u>!"

"I regret that I'm such a problem!" Sophia said half seriously. I've always wished that my aureoles were better defined. I used to put pink lipstick on their outer edges, but Mike said it tasted bad, so I stopped doing that. Anyway, it was <u>staining</u> <u>my</u> <u>bra's</u> <u>cups</u>!"

"Well, believe me, Sandy, if that's the only imperfection you have to complain about, you're a lucky woman!" Jay Jay assured her. "Are you ready to resume posing?"

"Yes, I'm ready" Sophia replied, as she resumed the required posing position.

Meanwhile, in tunnel niety feet below the level where the two young women were, Warren had just led his three male prospector companions to the place where he had shown the orange sandstone to Michael Edwards that morning.

"Well, I'll be a monkey's uncle!" David exclaimed. "That really does look like sandstone! How far are we below the surface of Phobos, Warren? As I remember, you were doing the tunneling here."

I figured it out as being about a hundred and twenty-five feet" Warren replied. "We were planning to put that spent nuclear reactor fuel rod depository down here, remember?"

"Yes, I remember" David remarked, "—but I think we had better put it somewhere else now. This sandstone is worth studying! It really does look like it's a normally occurring part of the rock strata se-quench here and not a meteorite."

Michael used a camera that he had borrowed from Sophia to make some digital pictures of the orange seam of rock and of the adjoining rock strata's interfaces with it.

"I'd like to have copies of these pictures for my records" said David.

"So would I" said Walter. "These pictures could cause a rewrite of everything we astronomers thought we knew about Phobos."

"Yes, good bye to the old captured asteroid theory!" David exclaimed. "I suppose that we all thought Phobos was an asteroid simply because it wasn't round. This will teach us to be more careful about making assumptions."

"Mike says that this Aresite sandstone is a good, decorative building material" Warren remarked. "When the rest of you finish studying it in situ, we will cut it into slabs and use it to decorate the walls of our new conference room-when we have enough of a chamber excavated, that is."

"It would look pretty if it were cut into slabs and polished" David commented.

"I'd better make the photo copies for you guys myself" said Michael. "There are some nude pictures of Sophia that I made during our wedding night in there with the photographs I just made of the sandstone layer."

"In that case, I'll pay you for some copies of those!" David exclaimed.

"So will I" said Walter, "—just in case Warren doesn't let us see that portrait that Jay Jay is pain-ting this afternoon."

"Oh, you'll both get a look at it when it's finished!" Warren assured them, with a brief smile of amusement.

"Well, in the meantime I still have some film in this old Pentax of mine—although it is my last roll" said Walter. "Would two of you shine your miner's lights here and here?" he requested, as he pointed to the locations he meant. "The third guy can stand to the left of the sandstone wall's center to serve as a size reference."

Michael and Warren illuminated the rock wall while David served as the size indicator. As he posed, he looked at Michael and asked "What's it like to be married to a gorgeous woman like Sandra, anyway?"

"So far it's been fun" Michael replied with a smile. "I just wonder when I'll awaken and learn that it has all been a pleasant dream."

"Well right now I'd like to be standing where Jay Jay is standing—or sitting" said Walter, as he finished photographing one rock interface and turned toward another.

"Wouldn't we all?!" Warren exclaimed wishfully.

"Well I was serious when I offered to pay for a nude photograph of Sandra" said David.

"So was I!" Walter exclaimed. "How much do you want for it, Mike?"

"Twenty dollars each" he replied reluctantly, "—but both of you must promise me that you will never sell them—or copies of them—to anyone on Earth or in Lowellsville. Sophia might bonk me on the head with my own geologist's hammer if she finds out about this!"

Both men promised, then Michael told them "I'll have the pictures ready for you in about a half hour after I return to the geology lab—but please don't let any of the women know that I've done this! If word gets back to Sandra, I might not live long enough to spend the money!"

"Mum's the word" Walter replied.

"Me too" David promised. Afterward the four men hiked back toward the inhabited levels of the underground base. Along the way they passed a freight elevator which was used to lift rock rubble to the surface of the moonlet.

"There was some greenish brown stuff in that rubble that I think was copper ore" Warren remarked. "I'll want you two rock hounds to have a look at it when we have a chance to go outside the base—<u>after your business deal is concluded</u>, of course!" The other men just glanced at him and smiled.

Chapter Twenty-Nine
Immortalized For Posterity

Still Friday Afternoon

True to his promise, Michael provided a nude picture of Sophia to both the mining engineer and the astronomer in their offices that afternoon—along with the free images of the history making orange sandstone layer inside the moonlet. He used a recently installed computer and color printer in his labor-atory's small office space to process the pictures.

Michael also told his new friends that he had decided to name the Aresite stratum the *Warren Smith Formation*, in honor of the man who had first seen it. All of them liked the idea.

The two pictures of Sophia each showed her lying nude and prone on a bed. She was smiling as she lay facing the camera, with her head propped up by her hands and forearms. Most of her well rounded bottom was visible, as were the tops of her superb breasts. Her shapely legs were bent toward the cam-era at their knees.

Both buyers had been hoping for a full frontal view, but they liked what was visible, so they paid the agreed upon price anyway. As David remarked "If there is anything that woman lacks, it isn't really necessary!"

As for the subject of these pictures, two and a half hours of patiently posing resulted in a finished nude portrait that was more revealing of her breasts than the two clandestinely marketed photographs had been. While Sophia stood naked near the easel and admired her image on the canvas, Jay Jay began putting her paints back into their box. Meanwhile, two of her brushes soaked in a jar that was half full of paint thinner.

"Well, does it look like you?" Jay Jay inquired hopefully.

"It sure does!" Sophia replied. "I'm <u>thrilled</u> with it, Jay Jay!"

"That's a relief" the artist said. "I was afraid you might sue me for defamation!"

"Not a chance!" Sophia assured her. "Now make an <u>exact</u> <u>copy</u> of it for <u>me</u> to buy."

"Would it be all right if I started it when my <u>new canvases arrive</u> aboard the *von Braun*?" Janet asked. "This was <u>the</u> <u>last</u> <u>one</u> from the old batch."

. "I suppose so" said Sophia, with a humorous little half smile. "That will give me a few days to come up with the money."

"Okay. While you go get dressed I'll call Warren and tell him his portrait has been completed" said Jay Jay. "He will just need to give it about forty-five minutes to dry before he handles it."

"Yeah, it would be a shame to have <u>permanent</u> <u>finger</u> <u>prints</u> all over it!" Sophia remarked humorously. Jay Jay grimmaced at the thought of such a disaster.

"Honestly, Sophie! If I had a body like yours I would not be short of money <u>for</u> <u>any</u> <u>reason</u>!" the artist exclaimed. "I'd be on my way <u>back</u> <u>to</u> <u>Earth</u>, where I could <u>earn a fortune</u> as a <u>super</u> <u>model</u>!"

"<u>The</u> <u>idea</u> <u>is</u> <u>tempting!</u>" Sophia admitted, as she opened the door of the closet where she had hung her clothes, "—but I really couldn't <u>afford</u> the trip back there right now."

"Do what any <u>red</u> <u>blooded</u> <u>American</u> <u>woman</u> would do" said Jay Jay. "Call all of your friends and relatives on Earth and <u>borrow</u> <u>the</u> <u>money</u>! They would probably be glad to see you <u>come</u> <u>to</u> <u>your senses</u>!" She then picked up her telephone from a bedside night stand and punched in Warren's number at his office. Meanwhile, Sophia stepped into her blue lace panties and pulled them up.

Warren was just returning to his office from Karen Ferguson's work place when his telephone rang. He went to his cluttered desk and picked up the handset.

"Hello? Warren Smith speaking" he answered.

"Hello, Warren. This is Jay Jay" said the caller's voice. "I finished the nude portrait of Sandra a few minutes ago and it's drying on my easel now. You may come get it in about a half hour."

"That's wonderful!" He replied. "I can hardly wait to see it! There will be framing material for it aboard the *von Braun*. I ordered some a year ago."

"Good" said Jay Jay. "I'm supposed to have some new canvases in one of the ship's holds. Sandra wants me to make a copy of the painting for her."

"She must like the original one then" Said Warren. "That means you did a good job! "I'll be there to see it in a little while. Good bye."

Jay Jay resumed cleaning her brushes and Sophia had just finished putting on her bra (with her friend fastening the back strap for her) when there was a knock on the door of the apartment.

"Well, I wonder who <u>that</u> is?" asked the artist, as she set down one of her brushes.

"Maybe Warren couldn't wait to see my portrait" Sophia remarked humorously, as she reached for her coverall garment.

Jay Jay left the bedroom and closed its door behind her. Then she went to the door between the living room and the outside corridor. When she opened the door, she was surprised to see Roger Harris facing her.

"Well, hello, Roger!" Jay Jay exclaimed. "I wasn't expecting you."

"May I come in?" he asked.

"Yes, please do" Jay Jay invited, as she stepped back from the doorway. Roger entered the living room and his hostess closed the door behind him. Before she could offer a seat to him the bedroom door opened and Sophia stood facing Roger. She was wearing her coveralls, but they were still open in the form of a narrow 'vee' all the way down the front. This exposed some of her blue lace underwear (which had been designed to be more decorative than concealing). Jay Jay stifled the urge to frown or to comment about Sophia's boldness.

"Sandra just finished posing for a nude portrait" Jay Jay explained nervously, while her model made no attempt to close the front of her outer garment. Roger glanced at the exposed area appreciatively, while Jay Jay winced mentally.

"Well, I was just about to ask you to help me send a maessage to a friend on Luna, Miss Johnson, "—but that can wait a few minutes" Roger replied. "May I see the portrait?"

"If it's all right with Sandra . . ." Jay Jay replied hesitantly.

"<u>Of</u> <u>course</u>!" Sophia consented. "Why would I have it made and then <u>hide</u> <u>it</u> from people?!" She stepped backward out of the doorway and Roger entered the bedroom. Jay Jay followed him a bit reluctantly, Sophia noticed. The model then casually velcroed the lowest six inches of her coveralls but left the rest of the long, narrow vee open.

"This picture is really beautiful!" Roger exclaimed, as he stood in front of the easel and the por-trait. "I've had the good fortune to see nude portraits of Sandra before" he remarked with a happy smile. "They've always been worth viewing."

'No doubt!' Jay Jay thought cynically. "Then she said aloud "I heard you had a problem with your medicine this morning."

"Yes, Miss Mason reduced my dosage slightly and provided an anti-nausea drug to me to reduce the other medicine's side effect" Roger explained. "I feel okay now."

"That's good to hear" said Jay Jay. "Let's go to the radio room now and let Mrs. Edwards finish dressing." Sophia recognized the none too subtle hint of Jay Jay's emphasis on the last two words.

"All right" Roger replied. He then followed his hostess out of the apartment. She glanced reproachfully at Sophia through the doorway before she closed the door behind them. Sophia finished dressing, then she heard the apartment's doorbell ring. She emerged from the bedroom and walked to the main door. When she opened it, she saw Warren standing in the hallway.

"Hello again, Sophia. I came to see the painting" he stated.

"It's in the bedroom, I'll show it to you" she invited. He followed her into the bedroom and she pointed to the easel. "There it is!"_she announced grandly.

Warren stepped in front of the easel and emitted a loud wolf whistle. "Whee whoo! Sophia, this is beautiful! And it really looks like you!" he exclaimed, "—that is, if you were still naked . . ."

"I'll take that as a compliment" she replied with a proud smile.

Michael soon announced his arrival in the apartment (having been notified by Warren that the painting had been completed). "We're in the bedroom, Mike" Sophia called to him. A few seconds later he was in front of her, giving his new wife a kiss.

"Have a look at this painting, mike! Isn't she gorgeous?!" Warren exclaimed.

Michael looked and exclaimed "Wow! That scene is straight from our bedroom at home! Where's the artist, Sophie? I want to congratulate her!"

"She's in the radio room with Roger. I'll go get her" Sophia replied.

Jay Jay arrived in the living room about two minutes later with Sophia, who motioned toward the bedroom. "They are in there" the model announced. Jay Jay went into the next room, while Sophia seated herself in one of the armchairs and relaxed.

Warren greeted the little artist with a kiss on her forehead and said "Jay Jay, this is your <u>best work yet</u>! I wish I had been a fly on the wall when our model was posing for it!"

"Sophia was a good subject" was all that Jay Jay could think to say in reply. "She was very still and patient."

"I'm surprised that the paint on the walls didn't <u>blister</u>!" Warren exclaimed humorously. "I'll go enter your hundred dollars in your payroll account now, while the portrait finishes drying. If you'll come with me, Mike, I want to discuss something with you in my office."

"Okay, but Sophia is <u>not for sale</u>" Michael teased.

"I couldn't be <u>that lucky</u>!" Warren replied, as the two men went into the living room. Jay Jay followed them and said to her seated model "Stay here a while, Sophie. I want to talk to you." Then the artist accompanied her male guests to the door of the apartment. As soon as they left, she closed and locked the door behind them. Afterward she turned toward Sophia with an angry expression.

"Well, <u>Mistress Edwards</u>! <u>That was a lot of skin</u> that you revealed <u>directly</u> to one of my male guests! What exactly was <u>the meaning</u> of your <u>strip tease act</u>?!"

"Oh, you mean letting Roger see me with my coveralls open" Sophia replied casually.

"<u>Yes</u>!" Jay Jay replied angrily. "That's <u>exactly what I meant</u>!"

"<u>Roger has a life threatening disease</u>!" Sophia explained, emphasizing each word (but without matching Janet's mood). He might not live long enough to see Earth again, so I let him see something interesting whenever he is with me, just to keep his morale up."

"Oh" said Jay Jay, with her anger quickly subsiding. "I forgot about his illness. Is it <u>really that serious</u>?!"

"<u>Who knows with cancer</u>?" Sophia replied. "Sometimes a person survives it when no-one expects that, while in other cases it can return after a long absence and kill its victim quickly. That was what happened to my father. He died before I completed my NASA training. I almost left the program, but the agency let me have a week's leave instead' so I could be with him at the end."

"I'm sorry to hear that" said Jay Jay, "—but <u>why</u> did you come to **Mars** anyway? You could have earned a lot more money as <u>a</u> <u>super</u> <u>model</u> or <u>an</u> <u>actress</u> on Earth."

"<u>I</u> <u>know</u>, but <u>Michael</u> <u>Edwards</u> was <u>leaving</u> <u>Earth</u> and I wanted to be <u>with</u> <u>him</u>—even though he did need a couple of years afterward to decide that I meant enough to him for him to give up his bachelor-hood and marry me!" Sophia explained.

"Oh" said Jay Jay, sounding contrite. "You must <u>really</u> <u>love</u> <u>him</u>!"

"<u>You're</u> <u>darned</u> <u>right</u> I do!" Sophia assured her friend, "—and I'll be <u>having</u> <u>Michael's</u> <u>child</u> about <u>seven</u> <u>months</u> from now."

"Well, <u>congratulations</u>!" Jay Jay exclaimed, as she hugged Sophia. "I'm sorry that I <u>misjudged</u> <u>you</u>. Please forgive me."

"You're forgiven, Jay Jay. How could I stay mad at a nice artist like you?" Sophia replied, as she hugged her friend in return. "After all, you did make that <u>beautiful</u> <u>painting</u> of me."

"Yes, I did—and I hope Pam doesn't 'accidentally' give me a medicinal overdose the next time I'm ill" Jay Jay remarked semiseriously.

Meanwhile, Michael and Pamela had entered Warren's office behind their host. As the two visitors had seated themselves side-by-side on a small couch, Warren had pulled his office chair into an open area in front of his desk. Pamela had been summoned by her boss (and lover) via a cellular telephone that had communicated with repeating devices mounted on the tunnels' walls at various key intersections. These devices had recently been installed and were not on the lower levels of the community yet.

"Pam, Mike brought a computer disk to me with a message from Daniel Morris on it" said Warren. "Dan says he needs you down there a.s.a.p. to heal those aliens who were found by Mike and Sophia. He has finally admitted to his people that the creatures exist, so you won't need a cover story. Can you be ready to travel after breakfast tomorrow?"

"Ah'll be readih" she promised. "Ah just hope that these aliens' intuhnal anatomih is somethin' llike owahs."

"So do we all" Warren remarked. "Dam added by scrambled radio message today that one of his biologists thinks the aliens might have contracted a disease organism from Earth called 'Tubiformium militaris. Has either of you distinguished scholars ever heard of it?"

"I can't say that I have" Michael replied, with a smile of amusement at Warren's witty remark.

"Weh-uhl <u>Ah</u> <u>have</u>" said Pam. It was brought back from Afghanistayun bah some NATO sol-dyuhs an' it's been makin' a nuisance of itself evah since then."

"Well, I'm glad that <u>you</u> know about it, because this is the first time I've ever heard of it" said Warren. "I radioed Daniel to tell him that I agreed with a suggestion he made about rerouting Phobos Base's communications with Earth and Luna via a new radio tower that Dan wants to build far out on the Martian desert. He's afraid that a rocket the North Koreans launched recently might be on its way <u>to</u> <u>Mars</u> <u>with</u> <u>a</u> <u>warhead</u> <u>on</u> <u>it</u> and I share his concern. He said that someone in NASA's Houston head-quarters thought that the missile might be trying <u>to</u> <u>home</u> <u>on</u> <u>our</u> <u>long</u> <u>range</u> <u>radio</u> <u>transmissions</u>. That <u>might</u> enable it to hit either Lowellsville or Phobos Base and the <u>last</u> <u>thing</u> <u>that</u> <u>either</u> <u>community</u> <u>needs</u> right now is <u>a</u> <u>nuclear</u> <u>warhead</u> aimed at it."

"A thing like that <u>could</u> <u>spoil</u> <u>your</u> <u>whole</u> <u>day</u>" Michael agreed humorously. "I think that a decoy radio station with automated equipment would be a good idea. The sooner <u>all</u> of our long distance messages go by way of it, the safer I'll feel."

"<u>I</u> <u>agree</u>" said Warren, "and I will say as much to Daniel in a message disk that I'll be sending to him via Pam."

"<u>One</u> <u>passenger</u> with a message disk is <u>an</u> <u>awfully</u> <u>light</u> <u>load</u> for the Mars shuttle's return flight" Michael commented. "Is <u>anyone—or anything—else</u> going with her?"

"That's where <u>you</u> come in" Warren replied. "I've taken the liberty of telling a couple of cargo 'bots to carry your space suit, Sophia's and mine to the partially completed new suit locker room that's about thirty feet to the right of the old one. It's near a new airlock that I just finished wiring late yes-terday afternoon. You, Walter, David and I will be testing it as soon as two of the robots finish digging a preliminary ramp from just beyond the airlock up to this moonlet's surface. It should be ready sometime late this afternoon.

"I mentioned to you during our excursion to see the sandstone stratum this morning that I found what I suspected were <u>chunks</u> <u>of</u> <u>copper</u> in some of the rock debris from that tunnel. You, David and I are going outside to have a look at it before we eat dinner. Walter will be going with us partway so he can check on one of his remote controlled telescopes that has been malfunctioning occasionally. If you and David agree with me that the stuff I found <u>is</u> <u>copper</u>, we will be sending a load of it to Lowellsville in the shuttle tomorrow. Antwan Curtis and his robots will process it for us, then our two communities will divide the resulting ingots between us."

"Good" said Michael. "That way <u>both</u> <u>colonies</u> <u>will</u> <u>benefit</u> from your discovery—that is, <u>if</u> <u>it's</u> <u>genuine</u> <u>copper</u>."

"<u>We'll</u> <u>soon</u> <u>know</u>" Warren remarked, after which he coughed to clear his throat, due to a slight allergy to Phobos' rock dust. "Phobos needs to begin repaying us for some of the tunneling we have been doing lately."

The doorbell rang and Pamela answered it. She smiled when she opened the door and saw who the visitor was.

"May a world famous model come in?" Sophia asked humorously.

"Please do" said Pam, as she glanced at the rectangular, towel-wrapped bundle that Sophia was carrying under her right arm. Pam stepped backward to let her guest walk past her, after which the pretty nurse closed the door and turned toward the new arrival.

"Ah suppose you ah fmous <u>all</u> <u>ovah</u> <u>Phobos</u> now!" Pam jested. Everihwun wants ta see that nude poatrait of yew now that it's finished."

"Well they are welcome to look at it all they want" said Sophia. "Jay Jay did <u>a</u> <u>really</u> <u>good</u> <u>job</u> <u>on</u> <u>it</u> <u>and</u> <u>I'm</u> <u>pleased</u> <u>with</u> <u>it</u>!" As she spoke, she set the bundle on the left end of the couch's seat, after which she unwrapped it. Finally she propped it up against the backrest.

"Mah wuhd, So-phia!" Pamela exclaimed. "<u>Yew</u> <u>look</u> <u>sen</u>-<u>say</u>-<u>shunal</u>!"

"The rest of us think so too!" said Warren, as the whole group viewed the portrait. "It's unfortunate that we can't hang it in some famous museum on Earth, where more people could enjoy it."

"They'll just need to <u>come</u> <u>to</u> <u>Phobos</u> then" Sophia replied with amusement. "You need some more colonists anyway."

"We may get them now!" Warren remarked half seriously. "In the meantime, though, where shall I hang this new portrait?"

The group soon decided that the two best options were to either hang it beside Pam's portrait or to hang it on the opposite wall and facing her picture. The two men favored the first option, while Pam favored the second. Sophia, however, was undecided.

"I think either idea has merits" she said. "If they are hung side-by-side, they can both be viewed at the same time, but if they are on opposite walls, there will be something of interest on both walls."

"I like having two beautiful women side-by-side" Warren remarked.

"So do I" said Michael.

"Let's ask Roger to come break the impasse" Sophia suggested.

"Good idea" said Michael. "He's probably impartial."

"We'll just ask him to state his preference without any of us telling him which of us favors what option" said Warren.

"Ah'll go find him" stated Pam, after which she left the apartment.

"Well, Warren, what sort of plan do you have for <u>protecting</u> <u>Phobos</u> <u>Base</u> during the war?" asked Michael. "We've already had a planning session in Lowellsville."

"Right now <u>there</u> <u>isn't</u> <u>much</u> <u>we</u> <u>can</u> <u>do</u>—by ourselves, anyway" Warren replied. "There just are not enough people and robots here to defend this place effectively if anyone on Earth decides it is worth capturing."

"Maybe you should plan to <u>evacuate</u> <u>this</u> <u>base</u> and <u>come</u> <u>to</u> <u>Lowellsville</u>, if it looks like hostile soldiers are on their way here" Sophia suggested.

"I've been giving that idea <u>serious</u> <u>consideration</u>" Warren admitted, "but I think I'll wait and see what sort of military potential those <u>drones</u> <u>of</u> <u>Mr. Bell's</u> have before I make any definite decision. We might be able to use one of them for <u>an</u> <u>unmanned</u> <u>fighter</u> to <u>intercept</u> <u>a</u> <u>hostile</u> <u>spacecraft</u>."

"Now <u>that</u> <u>is</u> <u>an</u> <u>interesting</u> <u>idea</u>!" Michael remarked enthusiastically. "Of course, you would need to <u>arm</u> <u>it</u> in some way."

"<u>I'm</u> <u>hoping</u> it will <u>already</u> <u>be</u> <u>armed</u>" said Warren, otherwise we will need <u>to</u> <u>improvise</u>. "That would take some <u>time</u> and <u>a</u> <u>lot</u> <u>of</u> <u>effort</u>."

The apartment's door opened and Pamela returned, followed by Roger. "Way-ull, <u>heah</u> <u>he</u> <u>is</u>!"_she exclaimed, as Roger closed the door behind himself.

"We need your input about this portrait, Roger" said Warren, as he rose to a standing position. "Do you think we should hang it <u>beside</u> <u>Pam's</u> <u>picture</u>, or <u>on</u> <u>the</u> <u>opposite</u> <u>wall</u>?"

"I think we should <u>let</u> <u>Pam</u> <u>decide</u>—after all, <u>her</u> <u>picture</u> <u>was</u> <u>here</u> <u>first</u>" Roger replied diplomatically.

"Well, <u>before</u> <u>she</u> <u>does</u>, I want her to know that I just want to <u>be</u> <u>her</u> <u>friend</u>—<u>not</u> <u>her</u> <u>rival</u>" said Sophia, as she and Michael stood up.

Pam smiled and drawled, "In that case, we'll hang them <u>side-bah-side</u>." So the decision was made and Warren went to his robotics work shop to get the necessary small eye screws, picture wire and some other items that were needed to hang the new portrait on the living room's front wall. Meanwhile, the two women stood to either side of Roger and kissed his face.

"Well, <u>some</u> <u>people</u> really get <u>preferential</u> <u>treatment</u> around here!" Michael teased.

"Some of us <u>have</u> charisma and <u>some</u> <u>others</u> <u>don't</u>!" Roger teased back. "In any case, I'm glad our space port engineer didn't have much for me to do <u>outside</u> today or I might have <u>missed</u> <u>this</u> <u>occasion</u>."

"Way-ull, Ah'm glad yew didn't" said Pam, "but Ah hope John isn't spendin' too much time out they-ah. <u>Wun</u> can-suh patient at a time <u>is</u> en-<u>uff</u>!"

"John does tend to be a perfectionist about his work" Michael remarked. "He did <u>a</u> <u>splendid</u> <u>job</u> on our space port's runway!"

"Honestly, though, with the plans he has for our little terminal building, you'd think he was building <u>some</u> <u>kind</u> <u>of</u> <u>monument</u>!" Sophia exclaimed.

"In a way, <u>he</u> <u>is</u>" Roger stated. "Since he arrived on Mars too late to help the people who built the Pyramids of Cydonia, our space port will be his <u>magnum</u> <u>opus</u>!"

Warren soon returned with a tool box and a jar full of picture fittings. He seated himself on the couch beside the portrait, carefully turned it over and began the tedious process of measuring and pencil marking its frame to determine where the mounting screws should go.

'I wonder if he and John Clewiston are related.' Michael thought with amusement.

Eventually Warren had the picture and its frame ready to hang. Next he chose a place on the living room's front wall close beside Pam's portrait and drilled a small hole in the wall's covering material for starting a mounting screw. Finally he used a long, self tapping screw to fasten a picture hook to the wall. Hanging the picture on the hook was relatively simple and the job was done.

"Well Sandra, there you are—immortalized for posterity!" Warren exclaimed. The rest of the group smiled and applauded as they admired the results of the project.

"I'm grateful to all of my admirers for making this moment possible!" Sophia exclaimed. "I really don't know what else to say!"

"Well Ah do!" said Pam, then she went into Warren's small kitchen and got five cans of soda pop from his refrigerator. She handed a can to each of the other four people and kept one for herself. "Wah-ren, Ah'll let you do the toast" she concluded.

Warren opened his can's pull tab and raised the container above shoulder level. "Here's to two beautiful ladies who have brightened our lives considerably!" he announced. His two male companions indicated their agreement and raised their cans high. Everyone sipped some of the fruit flavored beverage and the toast was completed.

After a few more minutes of conversation, Michael said to the group "I hate to eat and run, but I want to go have a closer look at the Aresite that I brought back to my lab from that deepest tunnel we men visited. I'm curious about the origin of those little black specks in it."

"So am I" said Warren. "Let me know what you learn about them."

"I'll do that" Michael promised.

"I want to find a computer that is connected to Marsnet and send some email messages" said Sophia. "I'm curious about how well my assistant biologist is coping without me in Lowellsville."

"Jay Jay will probablih let you use huh com-pew-tuh" Pam. Suggested. "It's set up foah sendin' messages easilih."

So the social gathering ended as everyone scattered on various errands. Michael went to the geology laboratory and made some specimen slides with the Aresite by using a tungsten carbide bladed rock saw. Soon he was examining the slides under a powerful microscope. He mostly used visible light, but occasionally he applied ultraviolet light to a specimen (to see if certain types of minerals would reveal their presence by fluorescing). Whenever he found an image that puzzled (or greatly interested) him, he would consult the Marsnet's Marsopedia files. There he would summon images of various Martian minerals to the monitor's screen.

Michael was losing track of the passing of time until a knock on the laboratory's door disturbed his computer assisted, mental journey to various geologic features of Mars' topography. He looked toward the door and asked loudly "Who is it?!" (since an intercom unit had not been installed beside the door's outer surface yet).

"It's Warren. May I come in?" asked a familiar sounding, male voice.

"Sure, please do!" Michael replied.

Warren opened the door and entered the room, then he closed the door behind himself. "Well? What have you learned about ou Aresite?" he asked, as he crossed the room.

"The black specks actually have a reddish tint in most cases" Michael replied, as his visitor seated himself in the other office chair beside him. "I think the majority of them are a type of Andesite—an igneous rock—that probably came from Mars' northern hemisphere. The others are more difficult to classify, though. They might have come from a Carbonaceous

Chondrite type of meteor—or something similar. I'd like to have Walter's expert opinion about that matter, though."

"The evidence so far seems to agree with your theory of a Martian origin of most of the material of Phobos" said Warren. "Congratulations!"

"Thank you" Michael replied, "—but I would still like to know <u>what</u> <u>sort</u> <u>of</u> <u>meteorite</u> blasted that material loose. We'll need Walter to identify the culprit for us."

"We must wait a while for that information" said Warren. The robots that I assigned to dig a new exit ramp for us have nearly completed their work. Let's go put on our space suits and have a look at that metal I found in our lowest tunnel."

"All right" Michael replied, as he reluctantly pushed back his chair and stood up. "Walter can examine these slide mounted specimens after dinner."

Michael turned off the little lights under the microscope's slides, then he followed Warren to the door of the geology laboratory. "Where has Sophia been spending the afternoon?" he asked his temporary boss, as the two men emerged into the corridor.

"I think she's been helping Jay Jay to do some house cleaning in the apartment near the radio room" Warren replied, as Michael closed the door behind them and locked it electronically. "Anyway, David and Walter are waiting for us near the new suit rack room, so let's be going."

"Okay," Michael replied, as he followed Warren through a series of corridors. "You know, it isn't every day you can have your apartment cleaned by a biologist" he added humorously.

"Yeah, Jay Jay said something about 'the high cost of labor' these days" Warren replied in the same manner. Soon they saw the other two men waiting for them at the junction of two corridors.

"There's our other rock hound!" Walter greeted. "Did you identify those black specks, Mike?"

"Yes, most of it is a type of Andesite found in Mars' Cydonia region" Michael replied. But the rest is some type of reddish black, meteoritic material."

"I'll have a look at it when we return from our outing" Walter promised, as Warren led the group toward their short term destination.

As the four men approached the new suit rack room, they saw that its door was open and they could hear the noisy hum of a vacuum cleaner. Michael peeked past Warren through the doorway and saw a vaguely humanlike robot using a long hosed device to suck the pink dust off of his and Sophia's space suits.

Warren looked into the room too and said (loudly enough to be heard) "I would have had Mathilda working in here sooner, but she needed some work done on her right wrist first. I finally asked Walter if he would try to fix it this morning, since I doubted that I would have the time."

"I fixed her with a spare part for one of my telescope mounts" Walter explained just as loudly. "It wasn't difficult, really."

"I just hope she doesn't get the urge to look through telescopes all night now" Warren teased.

"You're just afraid that if she spends some time with me I'll teach her how to defeat you in chess" Walter teased back.

"He wins a couple of games against me and suddenly he thinks he's Bobby Fisher" Warren remarked to Michael. The two men stepped back to allow the robot to emerge into the hallway.

"The suits are clean now, masters" said her synthesized female voice.

"Thank you, Mathilsda" said Warren. "I'd like for you to vacuum the lunchroom next, then go to your closet and recharge for a while."

"Yes, Master Warren" the robot replied. Before she rolled away on her wheeled footgear, like an awkward child.

"Why the wheels?" Michael asked curiously, as he watched her depart.

"She was having difficulty staying upright in this weak gravity when she tried to walk conventionally" Warren explained. "Her footsteps were carrying her too far and she would develop too much momentum, then fall over. So I put her on powered skates. The power unit is in her backpack and those two flexible drive shafts operate gears that turn the skate's wheels."

"A roller skating robot!" David exclaimed. "What will some robot cist think of next?"

David and Walter were already wearing their space suits, so they put on their helmets in the hallway and checked each other's seals. Meanwhile, Warren and Michael entered the unfinished suit rack room and helped each other to put on their space suits. After they donned their helmets, they waited for the other two men to cycle through the new airlock. When they had left it and closed the outer door, Warren pushed a button on the control panel beside the inner door. The air pump began making its throbbing sound.

"When we emerge from the other doorway, you will need to step cautiously" said Warren. "The robots have not smoothed the sides and bottom of the new ramp yet. I'll send them out there tomorrow morning to do that."

"Okay" Michael replied. "When they finish, we'll have a ribbon cutting ceremony to officially open the new ramp for use." Warren laughed at the intentional absurdity of having such a grandiose ceremony for such a tiny audience.

When the airlock's green, **'Ready For Use'** light glowed, Warren and Michael entered the little compartment and Michael closed the inner door. Warren pushed the **'Depressurize'** button and the pump's throbbing sound began again.

When they emerged from the airlock ninety seconds later, the two men crossed a small, smooth surfaced landing. Afterward they slowly clambered up the rough-as-gravel surface of the new exit ramp.

"I see what you meant" Michael commented. "This 'ramp' is still sort of an obstacle course!"

Warren laughed with amusement and remarked "You're in the wrong, business, Mike. You should have been a night club comedian on Earth."

"My old college geology instructor used to say that too, but I figured I'd better not waste my dad's money by dropping the course" Michael replied humorously, as they arrived at the upper end of the ramp and stepped onto the as yet unimproved surface of the moonlet.

Warren waved to the space port's engineer, John Clewiston, who was about to descend the old entrance ramp, with his two robotic laborers following him. Michael waved too and remarked, "You remind me of a mother duck with her ducklings, John."

"I sometimes think this job is 'for the birds'!" the engineer replied humorously, before he disappeared from view into the ramp's narrow notch in the rocky surface of Phobos. The two robots soon disappeared too.

"They reminded me more of the seven dwarves heading for home in that Disney movie" Warren remarked with a smile. "You know their song: "High ho, high ho! It's home from work we go!"

Michael laughed and replied "I remember." Then he whistled the rest of the dwarves' song as the two men turned toward the space port in time to see the low mounted lamps around it stop glowing.

"Don't quit your day jobs, guys!" David's voice called through their helmet 'phones.

Michael and Warren scanned the area and saw Daniel standing near Walter few yards to their right. A safety rope supported by a row of supporting posts extended further to the right behind them. Near its far end was a pile of rock rubble, with a cargo net stretched across it.

"He's just <u>jealous</u> because <u>he</u> couldn't carry a tune <u>in a bucket</u>" Walter remarked humorously.

"Well, at least <u>I</u> <u>admit</u> <u>it</u>" David replied semiseriously. "<u>You</u> <u>won't</u>!"

"Hey guys! Is this a <u>stag party</u>—or may <u>a girl</u> join it?" asked a familiar sounding alto voice in their helmets' 'phones.

The group looked toward the new exit ramp and saw a lone figure emerge from its notch in the ground. Michael and Warren quickly recognized the pink helmet with a decal of Taz the Tasmanian Devil on each side of it.

"<u>You're</u> <u>welcome</u> <u>to join</u> <u>any of our</u> <u>parties</u>, doll!" Warren exclaimed, as she approached the four men. "We were about to visit that rock pile over there." He pointed as he spoke.

"That doesn't sound like much <u>fun</u>!" Sophia replied, as she came to a stop near her husband. "<u>I do</u> <u>love</u> <u>this</u> <u>view</u> of the night sky, though!"

"Yeah, it is quite a sight after John turns the marker lights off" Warren remarked. The group looked upward and saw hundreds of stars glowing steadily in the airless sky.

"Remember to mention this scene in your tourist brochures!" Michael prompted.

"The <u>Milky</u> <u>Way</u> is the <u>brightest</u> I've ever seen it!" Sophia exclaimed happily. "It's like the phosphorescent wake behind a steamship at night."

"Yeah, or a trail of spilt milk!" David remarked.

"In that case, the name is appropriate" said Walter. "Of course, we're really seeing <u>the</u> <u>denser</u> <u>part</u> <u>of</u> <u>our</u> <u>galaxy</u> there."

The group admired the beautiful view a while longer, then Michael said "Well, boss man, let's go see that marvelous metal of yours!"

"We'll just follow David along the safety line" Warren replied. "Everybody keep one hand on it so you won't bounce too high when you walk and become a new satellite of Mars."

"Yeah, we don't want to lose Sophia especially" Michael remarked.

So the group proceeded along the safety line, with each person forming a loop around the plastic fiber rope with a thumb and two fingers. This loop was briefly opened at each of the each of the plastic encased, steel cord, sewing machine needle-like support posts. Beyond the post the loop was reformed.

'We definitely have more bounce in our steps out here!" thought Sophia. A person couod jump like a flea in this weak gravity!'

Soon they arrived at the rock pile, with David in the lead. Nearby was a circular hole in the ground, with a simple bucket hoist mounted on sturdy, plastic encased, steel posts above it.

"Well, here's our rock pile—without any convicts busting them!" David joked, as he picked up a softball size lump of rock. "These flecks of brownish metal sure look like copper to me! What do you think, Mike?" he asked, as he handed the object to the geologist.

Michael rolled the rock over on his right hand, then he pronounced: "I agree—it looks like a copper nugget peeking out of this matrix. May I keep it for a souvenir?"

"Sure" said Warren. "Analyze it all you want."

"I'll leave you guys-and girl-now" said Walter. "I have a faulty telescope mount to check." Walter was the only member of the group with a jetpack strapped to his shoulders and he used it now to make a long, graceful arc, upward to twelve feet, then downward to the place where four small, white, plastic domes stood. Soon he had one of them unfastened and set aside. Afterward he used a small tool to tinker with the mount of an exposed Schmidt-Newtonian telescope.

"Darned show off!" David complained mildly.

"Be nice and I'll let you play with the jet pack next time" Walter retorted (without looking up).

"I don't know about the rest of you, but I'm starting to feel hungry" said Warren.

"Me too" Michael remarked. "I think it's time to end this outing and go get some dinner."

"Are you coming with us, Walter?" Warren asked.

"Nah, you folks go ahead and stuff your stomachs" the astronomer replied. "I'll be there later."

So the rest of the group turned around and followed the safety line back toward the base's nearest entrance. As they bounced along effortlessly, the northern half of Mars' planetary disk loomed above the horizon of the small moon.

"Mars looks as big as a beach umbrella from here!" Sophia exclaimed.

"Yeah, that view is <u>our</u> <u>main</u> <u>tourist</u> <u>attraction!</u>" David proclaimed proudly. "Tell your friends in Lowellsville about it and our affordable room rates when you go back there."

"I'll do that!" said Sophia. She laughed as she reached the end of the safety line and released her finger loop from it. Soon the entire group (except for Walter) was standing around he admiringly.

"Thanks for joining our outing, Sandra" said David. "You made it a lot more interesting."

"I always like to go anywhere with the boys" she replied happily, "—and I really do think that Phobos has a lot of tourist potential."

"So do I" said Michael. "When that war on Earth ends you can expect a lot more visitors up here! That view of Mars is spectacular!"

The group separated then and went to the two airlocks. Michael, Warren and Sophia used the new one. As they cycled through it, Warren told his guests "About an hour after dinner this evening, Pam and I want to introduce you two to the game of low gee basketball. "We have everything ready for it in our community's new gymnasium."

"I'll try anything once" said Michel.

"So will I" said Sophia. "It sounds interesting and I need the exercise."

When the airlock finished repressurizing Warren opened its inner door they entered the under-ground base. Afterward they walked to the suit rack room and desuited. Soon they were all on their way to the lunch room to enjoy a meal and the companionship of the other Phobosians and Mars colonists.

Chapter Thirty
Follow The Bouncing Ball.

Friday evening

At six o'clock on Friday evening, Michael and Sophia accompanied Warren and Pamela to a modified cavern that contained Phobos Base's gymnasium. In it they found an unusual basketball court, with its hoops fifteen feet above the imitation wood covered floor. The free throw line at both ends of the court was about five feet farther back than it would have been on Earth.

"Where's the three point line?" asked Sandra (who was wearing a pair of Bermuda shorts and a short sleeve blouse).

"It's the same thing as the midcourt stripe" Warren explained. "You'll be surprised how far you can throw even a modified basketball here."

Warren and Pam spent about ten minutes explaining the rules and techniques of the game to their guests. The latter noticed that the walls of the court (and even the twenty-five feet high ceiling) were padded with an impact absorbing plastic like that used on the dashboards of the Mars colony's vehicles.

The ball was made of tire material and it was filled with plastic foam, rather than compressed air.

"If we used a normal ball here it would bounce so high you could not control your dribble" Warren explained with a smile of amusement. "As it is, you will need to be careful not to use too much strength when you move your arms and legs."

They began a two-against-two, mixed gender game, with the winners being the first team to reach (or pass) thirty points. The game lasted about thirty minutes and the score was lopsided. Warren and Pam won it 31 to 12 because they were more accustomed to how the thick skinned ball behaved in Phobos' weak, modified gravity. Michael and Sandra soon learned that the hoops were easily within range anywhere on the seventy feet long by thirty feet wide court! Just controlling their own bodies' momentum was difficult. Their passes tended to be over-thrown and both people acquired several bruises from bouncing off the walls (or even the ceiling in a few instances). Fortunately, anywhere in the big room was considered inbounds. Three shatter proof, plexiglas windows in one of the long walls were the only provisions made for spectators to be present.

After the game, Michael and Sandra seated themselves at one edge of the court to rest. "I can see that we'll need some practice before the next game" Michael remarked to his still standing hosts.

"Yeah, like about a <u>week</u> of it!" Sandra exclaimed humorously, as she sat down beside him sweating and sore. "I know now how a <u>football</u> <u>player</u> feels after a game!"

"I feel more like the football!" Michael replied semiseriously. Both of their hosts laughed.

About five minutes later the two couples headed for their respective apartments to rest, shower and change clothes. It was after they had bathed together that Sophia told Michael (as she brushed her hair) "When Doctor Hudson examined me recently he gave me a pregnancy test—it turned out positive."

"Do you mean you're pregnant?!" asked Michael.

"Exactly" Sophia replied (with a nervous smile). "I hope that's okay."

"Of course it's okay!" Michael exclaimed. "I'm going to be a father! This is wonderful news!" He hugged his naked spouse and carried her to the bed. He made love to her on it for about twenty minutes before the two of them stopped to rest.

They were still resting at eight forty-five when the doorbell rang.

"Just a minute!" Michael called through the half open bedroom doorway. "Let's put on our bathrobes, Sophie."

They were still buttoning their bathrobes when they headed for the apartment's door thirty seconds later. Michael opened the door and saw David standing in the corridor, with Jay Jay close behind him.

"Well, love birds! Are we interrupting something?" David asked (with a smile on his face).

"No, but ten minutes ago you would have been" Michael replied (with a smile of his own).

"Darn it! I always arrive too late!" David teased. "Well, anyway, would you two like to play a card game called 'Martian Hearts' with us, here in your apartment?"

"Give us about five minutes to dress" Michael replied through the partly open doorway. "You can wait for us in our living room." So the two guests entered it while the newlyweds went into the bedroom and closed the door.

A short time later the two hosts emerged from their bedroom. Michael wore a tee-shirt, trousers and house shoes; while Sophia wore a short sleeved blouse, a knee length skirt and house shoes. Michael brought a deck of cards from his suitcase. He and Sophia saw that their guests had already set up a folding table (from their apartment) in the living room.

"Mike and I like to play a variant of Hearts called 'Black Lady" in which the queen of spades counts thirteen points against whoever has her at the end of a hand" said Sophia, as she and Michael seated themselves in the two armchairs and faced their guests (who sat beyond the table on the couch).

"We do too" said Jay Jay. "She adds some suspense to the game." Various other rules were discussed and were either accepted or rejected by the majority of the group. Afterward, David dealt the cards (minus the Jokers, which were not used). The last two cards were set aside to be taken one at a time by the first two people who picked up the cards that were played.

Hearts was a strange game of negative points (like golf}. A simple list was kept of how many points each person had in his/her hand at the end of each round. The person who picked up the most points started the next round. That person could lay down any card of any suit that he/she chose. The highest card played of that round's suit picked up everyone else's card played for that round. Each of the other players was required to follow suit (unless that person had no cards in his/her hand of that suit). In the latter case a high ranking card (preferably a heart or the Queen of Spades) was played.

There were no partners (unlike Bridge). Everyone played for himself or herself and tried to cast off the highest ranking hearts (or spades) on someone else. When all of the cards had been played, the last person to discard in a round shuffled all of the cards and redealt them. Play proceeded through many rounds until someone exceeded an arbitrarily agreed upon score. That person then became the loser, while the person with the lowest total score became the winner. Everyone else finished in some place between them.

The game lasted until David finally went over two hundred points (after about an hour and a half). Sophia finished with a slightly lower score; Michael was in second place; and Jay Jay was the winner. Even David (who stuck Sophia with the Queen of Spades in the last round) said that he had enjoyed the evening.

David Carlisle was a moderately handsome, forty years old engineer. He had light brown hair, gray eyes and a master's degree from the Colorado School of Mining. He was about an inch shorter than Michael and he had the same love of mineralogy. Michael and Sophia both liked him and they enjoyed talking with him between hands of the card game.

As Michael gathered the cards and put them in their box, he noticed David looking admiringly at Sophia (who was sitting on the couchant conversing with Jay Jay).

"I've never seen a scientist this attractive before" David remarked. "Frankly speaking, most of them are as plain as dirt. Not that I have anything against dirt, mind you. I've spent most of my life digging in it for various ores."

"I've spent a lot of time digging in it myself" Michael replied with a smile, "—but I found my most valuable discovery on top of the ground!"

"You men are giving me a big ego!" Sophia rebuked mildly. She didn't appear annoyed, though.

David stood up and helped Michael to fold the card table.

"Thanks" said Michael. "By the way—I've been meaning to ask you—are you a chess player?"

"Yes, but I'm not quite as good as Warren is yet" David replied. We Phobosians are having a chess tournament this Sunday afternoon and evening in the dining room. Will you be joining us?"

"Now that I know about it, I certainly will!" Michael replied. "What time does it start?"

"At one o'clock in the afternoon" David replied. "Warren is putting up some posters for it this evening. We hope to have all of our men in it and perhaps a couple of the ladies."

"I'm not as good at chess as my husband is, but I'll give it a try" said Sophia. "I enjoy the complexity of it."

"I know how to move the pieces, but that's about all" said Jay Jay.

"I could teach you some tactics and strategy" Sophia offered. "Maybe we could work on it together sometime tomorrow."

"I'd like that" Jay Jay replied. "Say about ten a.m. in my apartment?"

"I'll be there" Sophia promised. "Do you have a chess set?"

"No, but I'll borrow one from one of the men" said Jay Jay.

"Maybe you and I could play some after lunch tomorrow, Mike" David suggested.

"All right" Michael replied, "I could use some practice before the tournament. Say around one p.m. in your apartment?"

"That would be okay" said David. "I'd like to practice against the Sicilian Defense."

"Good, I enjoy playing it" Michael stated. "Now, if you don't mind, it's about Sophia's and my bedtime."

"In that case, we'll be leaving now" said David. "We'll see you tomorrow morning at breakfast."

Chapter Thirty-One
Pamela's Departure

Saturday Morning, June 54th

After breakfast on Saturday morning, Warren stood up and made a short speech in the lunchroom: "Before we send our friend, Pamela Mason, down to Mars to battle an unknown illness in some unfamiliar aliens, I want to say a few words on her behalf. First of all, Pam <u>has</u> <u>volunteered</u> for this mission—<u>nobody</u> <u>coerced</u> <u>her</u>. I will, however, make certain that she receives some kind of <u>pay</u> <u>bonus</u> for the time that she spends in the aliens' community." Everyone applauded (including Miss Mason).

"Pam has been in some dangerous places before, when she was an army nurse during the Great Middle East War, but this is likely to be her <u>strangest</u>, <u>most</u> <u>challenging</u> assignment yet. "I wish her well in it and I know that the rest of you will want to do the same. Pam, do you have anything to tell us before we send you on your way?"

Pam stood up beside her table and said "Wah-ren was right—nobodih co-uhced mih ta do this mih-shun—but he did hint to mih that he would de-hi-buhn-ate some ahmih ants an' put 'em in mah bedroom if Ah refused!" Everyone laughed. Seer-ee-ous-lih, though, Ah am lookin' foah-wuhd to some va-cay-shun tahm in Low-ulls-ville when this is all o-vah!" Everone laughed again. "Thay-ut is all Ah have ta say."

"This concludes our little program for this morning" said Warren. "I'm sure all of the men will want to kiss our intrepid medical specialist and say goodbye to her now, so I'll move out of the way and let you proceed." The men happily did so, followed by the women. Last of all (and longest of all), Warren kissed her himself. Afterward he whispered to her: "Be careful down there!" Pam nodded, then she smiled bravely at her admirers.

"Ah hav-unt been smooched on this men-ih tahms since mah sixteenth buth-day pahtih!" she exclaimed humorously. Everyone smiled and laughed together happily.

Meanwhile, the strongest of the many work robots had begun loading carbon fiber cargo containers into the Mars shuttle's cargo holds. Inside of these boxy objects (which resembled car top luggage containers) were copper bearing chunks of rock. These would be the Phobosian's important contribution to the combined economies of their community and Lowellsville.

After Pamela and Linda had left the lunch room and had gone to the old suit rack room, they had put on their space suits and helmets. Next they had entered the old airlock and had cycled through it. Afterward they had gone outside and waited on the landing pad for a few minutes until the robots were almost finished working. Finally the two women had climbed the portable stairway to go aboard the shuttle themselves.

As she entered the shuttle, Pamela carried a portable computer in a container that resembled a large briefcase. She also carried a medium-size suitcase with her other hand. She seated herself (and her luggage) in the front part of the passengers' compartment. There she used a safety harness to secure her suitcase in the seat beside her. The computer's case would ride on her lap for a while.

Meanwhile Linda had left her passenger to inspect the way that the robots were arranging the cargo in the aft part of the vessel. Afterward she had gone into the luggage compartment. It was like an overgrown closet between the passengers' compartment and the main cargo hold. There she had stowed her suitcase in the regulation manner (by strapping it to the floor). A minute later, Linda had entered the passengers' compartment.

While she approached the place where Pam was sitting (in the left front part of the compartment) Linda said: "After we begin our descent from orbit I'll invite you via the pulic address system to come up front. Then you may sit beside me in the copilot's seat."

"Thank yew!" Pam replied enthusiastically. "Ah'm reallih lookin' foahwuhd to this trip! Ah've nevah been to the suhface of Mahs befoah."

"Well, I hope you enjoy the journey" said Linda, as she squeezed Pam's right shoulder reassuringly.

"Thank yew again" Pam replied. "Ah just hope Ah've spent enough tahm in the squir-rel cage to be readih foah this juh-nih. Uthah-wise Ah maht fall flat on mah face when Ah leave the shuttle."

"Don't do that!" Linda urged half seriously, as she recognized Pam's attempt at humor. "If you feel weak when we land, I'll tell one of the robots to carry you into the terminal. In the meantime, though, keep your helmet on until that green light labeled 'cabin presr.' glows on the foreword bulkhead." Afterward she went forward toward the crew's section of the ship.

Meanwhile, Pam had fastened her safety harness and had looked outside by way of a nearby window. The left half of the big disk of Mars was in darkness, but the right half was in morning light. The planet looked like it had been cut in half with a giant knife, with the left side being disposed of afterward.

"What a strange, wunduhful sight!" Pam exclaimed, but there was no one else in the passengers' compartment to hear her. "Ah feel like a child again, goin' on mah fust long jur-nih in an ayuhplane!"

Because she had the passengers' compartment to herself, she had strapped her suitcase into the aisle side seat like a second passenger, instead of stowing it in the baggage compartment. Now it sat beside her like a mute companion. Somehow its presence felf reassuring to her.

Pam turned her head frequently to look through various windows. 'Ah'm finalih goin' to Mahs!' she exclaimed mentally. Ah'll be off of this rock foah a week oah moah! How mahvel-ous!' Still, she had some misgivings about her new assignment. 'Ah just hope that whatevuh disease those ay-liens have is not too dificult to kew-uh! Ah'm not an epi-demi-olo-gist, aftuh all! Some-tahms Ah wun-duh how Ah get mahself inta these sit-yu-ay-shuns!"

Meanwhile, Linda had walked foreward through the fligh engineer's and navigator's compartment and through doorways in two bulkheads. She was presently inside the pilot's compartment. She had closed both doors behind herself, just to prevent them from swinging back and forth on their hinges when the vessel began moving.

Linda seated herself in the pilot's comfortable, thickly padded chair. She turned on the ship's radios and used the short range set to tell the service robots to close the ship's hatches and withdraw the boarding stairs. When a series of green lights (on an indicator panel to her left) assured her that her orders had been followed, she began powering up the ship's systems. The first thing that she turned on was the repressurization system for the passengers' compartment: followed by the corresponding systems for the crews' compartment behind her and finally for the pilot's compartment. Next she followed a long check list on a clip board that was kept in a pouch on the right side of her seat. She flipped what seemed like an endless series of switches and pushed an equally long series of buttons. Many hours of reading technical manuals and of practicing in flight simulators had taught her where these items were.

Eventually a gentle chime and a green light told her that the pilot's compartment had been pressurized. She loosened the seals around the base of her helmet and removed the bulky item. Now her four inches long, blonde hair could brush gently against her shoulders.

Next she stood beside the pilot's seat to reach upward and stow her space helmet on the shelf above it. An elastic net would prevent the helmet from drifting away in zero gee situations.

Unlike Pam, who had come aboard as a relatively carefree passenger, Linda had much to do before she could even think about looking through her small group of windows at the space port beyond the ship. She took her pilot's responsibilities very seriously because she knew that one mistake might bring harm to the very expensive shuttle or to its even more precious occu-pants. She was no longer an inconspicuous secretary working for two bosses in Lowellsville. Now she was a ship's captain who was responsible for the safe completion of the Prometheus' potentially hazardous journey.

Linda could have objected to the way that Pam had chosen to use a seat to hold her suitcase, but the item had appeared to be well secured, so she had decided not to enforce the regulation against large items of luggage in the passengers' area. 'I'll give her the V.I.P. treatment during this trip—hell, she is a V.I.P. right now!' the pilot decided. 'We need her to cure those aliens so they can help us to defeat that missile that the North Koreans are sending toward us.'

When all of the ship's systems were ready for use, Linda used the short ranged transmitter to say "Phobos Radio, Shuttle Prometheus is ready for departure. Do you read me?"

"Roger, Prometheus. Loud and clear! I am recalling all of the robots now. Have a pleasant journey" Janet Johnson's familiar sounding, friendly voice replied.

Linda glanced at the life support systems indicator panel and saw that the passengers' compartment was fully pressurized. She picked up a microphone and pushed the 'Talk 'button. Phobos departure in ten seconds!" she announced through the P.A. system. "If yours not still strapped in, hold on to something!"

Pam had already noticed the green light on the bulkhead and had removed her helmet. When she heard the announcement, she had unfastened her safety harness so she could place the helmet beneath the straps of the seat across the aisle, along with her computer. She quickly completed this awkward task and returned to her seat. There she gripped the armrests as she heard the hiss of the shuttle's maneuvering thrusters. This was followed by a sudden, slow upward movement as the Prometheus broke the feeble gravitational grip of Phobos.

'I'm finalih on mah way!' Pam realized, as she looked through the window beside her. The shuttle gradually rose from the surface of the moonlet and more of Mars could be seen. It was a huge, salmon pink, three-quarter disk now.

'What a view!' Pam exclaimed mentally. 'Those NASA flight sim-yu-lay-tuhs ah good, but nothin' can match the real thang!'

"Pam, we are beginning our descent from orbit now" said a sudden, calm voice from the P.A. system. "You may come foreward and join me, but be careful and use the hand grips beside the seats and doors. We have no gravity now."

"Ah'm on mah way!" Pam exclaimed (although she knew Linda could not hear her). She unstrapped herself from her seat and rose to her feet. 'Thih-us will be one thrillin' ride!' she thought as she 'floated' into the aisle. Afterward she used hand grips on the backrests of the aisle side seats to pull herself toward the crew compartment's door.

This concludes Book One of the Lowellsville Chronicles. To learn if Pamela's mission will succeed watch for the sequel "The Pact of Olympus" by E. M. Smith in book stores a year from now.

CPSIA information can be obtained at www.ICGtesting.com
Printed in the USA
BVOW042001031111

275247BV00001B/28/P